LONDON TOWN

a novel by

I K WATSON

Also by I K Watson

Fiction:
Manor
Wolves aren't White
Cops and other Robbers
A Little Bit of Previous

Non-fiction:
Quality is Excellence

First published in 2011 by MP Publishing Limited
6 Petaluma Blvd. North, Suite B6, Petaluma, CA 94952
and
12 Strathallan Crescent, Douglas, Isle of Man IM2 4NR

This is a work of fiction. All characters and events are fictitious.
Any resemblance to real persons, living or dead, is purely coincidental.

Watson, I. K., 1947-
London town : a novel / by I.K. Watson.
p. cm.
ISBN-13: 978-1-84982-135-3
ISBN-10: 1-84982-135-6

1. Gangsters--England--London--Fiction. 2. Organized
crime--England--London--Fiction. 3. Vendetta--Fiction.
4. London (England)--Fiction. 5. Suspense fiction.
I. Title.

PR6073.A8626L66 2011   823'.914
                          QBI11-600147

A CIP catalogue record for this book is also available from the British Library

ISBN: 978-1-84982-135-3

web site: www.ik-watson.com

Artwork and website designed by
Hibernian Integrated Business Solutions
www.hibernian.co.im
Contact: mike@hibernian.co.im

Book & jacket design by Maria Smith

In memory of
Thomas Alexander Baldwin
and
Uncle George
who told the stories.
Dedicated also to
Mary Baldwin and Doffy Foord
who provided the background to the thirties,
including the undergarments.

LONDON TOWN

a novel by

I K WATSON

Chapter 1

1976

A telephone rang out across the air-conditioned room. It seemed louder, like an alarm, and carried the same urgency.

In the bathroom Dave Smith heard the call but continued to look into the mirror. He placed his razor on the basin ledge and picked up a freshly laundered towel. Slowly, while the ringing persisted, he rubbed away excess shaving cream that clung to his ears and neck. For a moment longer he studied his expression and saw the first sign of annoyance as it drew a veil across his eyes. He threw the towel aside, opened the bathroom door and moved across a grey tufted Axminster into the lounge. It was a huge room dominated by glass; floor to ceiling windows comprising an entire wall looked out across the city skyline. He stood at the window and as he lifted the receiver he gazed impassively at the familiar landmarks.

"Yes?"

"David?" A woman's voice triggered a vague memory. "Hello?"

In the background he could make out Creedence Clearwater Revival and *Bad Moon Rising*.

He said, "I'm here."

"Do you recognize me?"

"I'll never forget that Connecticut heavy breathing. It's been a long time."

"Eleven years."

"That long?"

"You made a lasting impression," she said and laughed, a clotted laugh that focused his memory so that her image came flooding back.

The hairs on his arms prickled. He saw his narrowed eyes in the glass. For a second his reflection surprised him. Without his clothes he seemed taller and younger.

"Where's Tony?" he asked. "Are you still with him?"

"Unfortunately I am." A pause seemed to go on forever before she said, "We're over here for some shopping. At least, that's what he says. But you can guarantee that it's business. Nothing happens around Tony that isn't business."

Dave nodded into the handset.

"I've got to see you, Dave," she went on, breathlessly now. Edginess had crept in. "Can you make it?"

"When?"

"Right now. This minute. You know how it is? You've got to make the most of it. I can't be sure of getting another chance. He's out for the entire day. I'm supposed to be shopping."

There was silence for a moment, even the Revival had packed it in. He said, "You still there?"

Eventually she came back on, her voice strangely distant: "I've thought about you. It's never happened with anyone else."

"Where?"

"Same place, for old times' sake… He's taken everyone with him. I'm here on my own."

"It's bloody dangerous, Sharon. Can't you get out?"

"He might have someone tailing me, Dave. You know what he's like. They could be waiting in the lobby. But you could get in. Nobody would know you're coming up here."

"Give me half an hour."

Dave dropped the handset on to its cradle and for a moment remained motionless, wondering if he'd made a mistake.

The late morning August sun burst through the cloud and bounced off the distant river and as the concrete shimmered and the glass exploded the city became a different place.

Twelve years earlier Sharon Zinn had appeared naked in *Playboy*. She was seventeen. Later that year she married an American gangster, Tony Valenti. He was a member of the New York Mafioso and she married him for his power and for his money. He was a small wiry man of forty. She was a beautiful blonde, and even without stilettos she still towered over him by a good four inches. Love had not been involved but he was happy and he liked to show her off. He would not allow the resumption of her modelling career. The elevated heels he took to wearing were, in the eyes of the Long Island dons, the sign of a flawed character.

In April of 1965 Tony Valenti accompanied Angelo Bruno on a trip to London. He brought Sharon along as an accessory. He saw her as a status symbol and enjoyed the envy – perhaps even jealousy – he detected in the faces of his associates. They stayed at the Park Lane Hilton. Bruno had come over to meet the Krays to discuss some hot Canadian securities he wanted to offload in Europe. He was also keen to expand his involvement in the Mayfair clubs and, at the time, he thought that the Krays might be ideally situated to handle his interests. That was not important. What was relevant was that Sharon noticed the eighteen-year-old Dave Smith in one of the Hilton bars and she couldn't take her eyes off him.

Even though his father had told Dave to give the Krays and their nancy boys a wide berth – for some time he'd been concerned that the twins were gathering some powerful friends in Whitehall and the media, and even the Old Bill seemed to be looking the other way – Dave was drawn to the glamour and razzmatazz that surrounded them. Celebrities from both the UK and America, along with the customary photographers from the Sunday papers, were never far away. It was in the bar that Reggie Kray introduced Dave to Angelo Bruno and his entourage and, when the others retired to a quiet corner to discuss business, Valenti had no hesitation in asking Dave to keep his wife company and to escort her, when she'd had enough, to their room. "She was a *Playboy* centrefold," he boasted. "And a movie star. If you ask her real nicely, kid, she'll give you her autograph."

She was perched on a bar stool, toying with the stem of her drink. She watched his approach through the mirror behind the bar.

"Did my clothes just disappear, or did you take them off one at a time?"

Her eyes flashed in the mirror and the beginnings of a smile tugged at her lips.

He laughed out loud.

"Was it that obvious?"

"I hope no one else noticed. Tony's kind of funny about things like that."

"He doesn't strike me as funny at all."

She lifted her drink.

"You're bored?"

"You could say."

"How can anyone be bored in London?"

"It's like a strait-jacket," she said. "Being married to these guys is worse than marrying into your Royal Family. You can't make a move without them knowing!"

"That bad?"

"You can believe it."

"Tony told me about the films."

"The movies? He tells everybody about them. They were the beach movies, surf rolling in and girls busting out of bikinis in every other frame and no one over twenty on the beach, except for Frankie Avalon, that is. At a push he was old enough to be our daddy. I was the one playing volleyball. I was the one in the blue bikini. It matched my eyes. *Beach Party* and *Bikini Beach* – did you see them?"

Dave shook his head and said slowly, "I'll watch out for them. If necessary, I'll get the family to buy the local Odeon."

"Keep going. You're pushing all the right buttons."

He gave her a long studied look.

She smiled and flipped open a red pack of du Maurier. Her gold lighter flashed.

"I'm getting a taste for your English cigarettes. Do you want one?"

He caught a whiff of petrol and said, "I don't use them."

She blew him a jet of smoke and lifted her eyebrows and said matter-of-factly, "What now?"

"Was there a casting couch?"

"Hell, in Hollywood you have to screw security just to get on the lot."

Dave smiled and glanced in the bar mirror. The far table was animated. Knowing Ronnie, the meeting would last well into the small hours.

"Drink up," he said. "I'll take you home."

"Your place or mine?"

With scant regard for their safety it began in the lift, continued in the corridor and climaxed on the floor of Valenti's suite. He left her there, on the carpet, with the hem of her evening gown wrapped around her waist and the only underwear she'd been wearing hooked around one ankle. She smiled at him and said, "You English are kind of friendly. Whatever happened to that reserve we hear so much about?"

Eleven years later Dave remembered it all. As he motored across to see her again he was stirred by the memory of their first meeting.

He left the car at the service entrance and slipped a uniformed guy on the door a tenner.

The man tapped his cap and said, "It'll be in the usual place, Mr Smith."

It was check out time and the reception area was busy. It suited him. The more faces on the ground the less likely he was of being recognized. He took the lift to the twelfth then used the stairs to Valenti's suite. The corridor with its deep spotless carpet was empty.

The years had done nothing to change her. Even now she could have stepped right out of the centrefold and still wouldn't need the touch-up artist. She stood framed by the doorway, her blond hair cascading over her shoulders and flaring in the light that piled into the room behind her.

"What kept you?" she said. "You're thirty seconds late." Her eyes flashed just as he remembered and her mouth widened into a wicked smile.

"I forgot how many stairs there were."

She waved him inside. Her skimpy, ivory-coloured slip rippled and clung to every curve.

"You're looking good."

"So are you," he said.

"Come on, let's not waste time. We've only got about eight hours. They won't be back until eight."

"Don't you want to be courted?"

"Just come here and make love to me. I've been waiting eleven years for this."

He closed the door and pinned her against it. Her lips were hot. Her tongue fluttered against his.

"Jesus!" she said when he pulled away and she gulped in air.

He picked her up and carried her toward a leather sofa. Half way across the deep pile he paused to kick off his shoes. He set her down as though she weighed nothing and sank beside her. His hands worked beneath the silk. He pulled down her underwear and raised her slip, for a moment savouring her thighs. She rubbed her legs together, moving her blond hair. It was a novelty. It hid nothing. He used his mouth and heard her tiny catch of breath.

Suddenly she was pulling his hair, digging her fingernails into his shoulders. Her body coiled, her grip became almost unbearable until, slowly, she relaxed and he heard her sigh as she released a long breath. He looked up and smiled. His lips were wet and sparkling. A thread of something, spittle or her, wavered between his mouth and her crotch and glistened in the light that streamed in over Hyde Park.

"Take your gear off," she said. "I want you to abuse me. Be rough!"

"I think I can manage that," he said as he struggled out of his clothes. She caught hold of him.

"Jesus, I remember you," she said. "It's like meeting an old friend."

"How long are you over here?"

"We fly back tomorrow. We live in Miami now."

"We'll have to make the most of today, then."

"That's what I was counting on."

He nestled between her legs and brought up her slip to bare her breasts and the years were stripped away. It was all so familiar, the tiny nipples, the soft curves rising to them. That shadowy idea, perhaps the thought of domination, thrilled him. He felt the end of her and every time he slammed in he heard her gasp and every time she gasped his smile of satisfaction widened a little more.

In those quickening moments before he let go she squealed and clamped her legs tightly around him.

She laughed, "God, this is bliss. I've waited years."

He cradled her head against his shoulder. She felt damp against him.

"You know," she said, "apart from when I've been on my own that's the first time I've come since…"

He turned to her. "You're joking?"

She shook her head. "No. It's been eleven years."

"Fuck me! That's diabolical. Why don't you buy him a book?"

"It's not the technique, Dave. It's how I feel."

"Are you telling me there's been no one else in all this time?"

"Does that surprise you?"

"Yes, you could say."

"You don't know how it is. Over here he feels safe. I get some freedom. In Miami when I go downtown I get to be escorted by two of his gorillas. Sometimes I think I'm suffocating, you know what I mean?"

"Why don't you leave him?"

She snorted. "You marry these guys for life, you know that. Where would I go? Where could I hide?"

Dave nodded, understanding even more than she knew.

"So this is it, eh?"

"Till the next time," she said. She reached up and stroked his cheek. "I love you, Dave. I know it's crazy. I know we barely know each other. But thinking of you has kept me sane all these years. Now you've filled my tank again I can go on a while longer." She sighed and pressed closer. Her left breast flattened against his chest. Her right nipple brushed against him and tickled. "Did you think of me in all that time?"

"Course I did," he said honestly. "I study that *Playboy* spread every night."

"I've got older since then."

"Not so I notice. I just wish the snaps had been taken now instead of then."

"Why?"

"They'd be more explicit now. Split fig, pictures on horseback."

She nudged him. "I think I know what you mean. Is that Cockney?"

"No, Sweetheart. It's Anglo Saxon."

Her laugh was smoky, as he remembered.

"If ever he dies," she said, "and if wishing has anything to do with it, he will. I mean, Jesus, he smokes three packs a day and gets through a bottle of JD before noon. But if he did die could I look you up?" She turned to face him. "I mean would you want me to?"

He nodded meekly. "Course I would. Blimey, I can't think of anything I'd like better."

She settled down again.

"That's what I thought," she said.

It was late afternoon when he finally made a move. She watched him dress then threw on her slip and followed him to the door.

"Let's not leave it so long next time," he said.

"I'll dream about you, David Smith."

His smile was hesitant. He nodded and opened the door. She held him back and draped herself against him. Dave half turned as he heard a shuffle behind him.

Tony Valenti stood in the doorway, his wiry Italian features darkening by the moment.

"What the fuck is this?" His voice was high pitched. It filled the room like a siren. As if dazed by what he saw he took two steps backward.

Sharon dropped her hands from Dave's neck and followed Valenti into the corridor. "It's not what you think, Tony," she said feebly.

"What the fuck am I thinking? Eh?" He pulled the strap of her slip. It snapped. She held on to the front to cover her breasts. He hit her hard, in the mouth. A fine spray of blood dotted the wall. Dave watched her go down and heard the thud as she hit the carpet.

Valenti shook, his wild eyes fixed on Dave. "I know you. Don't I know you?" He pointed at Sharon. "That's my fucking wife!" he yelled. "That whore's my fucking wife!"

Dave shrugged and moved past him.

"Where the fuck are you going you motherfucking son of a bitch?"

Valenti was a tiny man; his threats toward Dave were absurd. He kicked out. His chiselled toecap landed heavily into Sharon's stomach. She rolled over and slammed into the wall.

Dave turned back to face him. "Leave her alone," he said.

Valenti let out a strangled cry and head lowered he charged at Dave. Dave hit him once. His fist caught the little man squarely in the face. His heavy signet ring caught the flesh and ripped away the side of Valenti's big nose. Valenti staggered backward, clutching at his face. Blood streamed from between his fingers. He began to scream. Doors along the corridor opened and people peered out.

Valenti rushed again. The pain had dulled his brain. His hands still covered his face as he tried to butt Dave with the top of his head. Dave caught him again, hard, in the middle of the chest, and Valenti collapsed in a heap over Sharon's feet.

At the end of the corridor two men fought their way through the crowd. Dave looked up as he heard their approach. They were both all-American boys, built like Dallas Cowboys complete with shoulder pads. They charged toward him. There were twenty yards between them as Dave made the corner to the stairs. He went down four at a time, crashing against the corners. He covered three flights before pausing to listen. Nothing. He decided they'd stayed to help the little wop. Taking his time now, dusting himself down and straightening his clothes as he went, he made his way to the lifts and five minutes later he was in the car park. He found his car under a No Parking sign and an arrow pointing the way to the 007 Night Spot, the International Restaurant and The London Tavern. Apart from The Tower, it was the only place in town.

He was woken just after one-thirty by a loud knock on his door. Jimmy Jones stood in the corridor. He was one of his father's key men. He looked worried, his bright eyes unusually severe.

"I've been ringing," he said irritably.

"Pulled the phone out."

"And banging on the door for the last ten minutes."

"I was on the lash," Dave offered.

Jimmy nodded. "Yeah, I can smell it and I can see it in your eyes. Any redder and they'll be bleeding." His dark features mellowed. "You look like shit. Your liver needs a rest and then some."

"So what's with the panic?"

"Your old man's been going spare trying to get you."

Dave shrugged and glanced at his watch. "What's happened?"

"I thought you'd tell me."

Dave knew, or thought he did, and his gut tightened. He said, "There was a bit of bother earlier, at the Hilton."

"What sort of bother?"

"You know what these wops are like. They can't control their women."

Jimmy Jones grinned, "Is that all? And there I was thinking it was serious." His face dropped again. "Anyway, your old man's phone has been red hot for the last two hours. It's got to be something pretty important to keep him out of bed at this hour. By the time he spoke to me he was close to losing it."

Dave nodded gloomily. He didn't relish the prospect of facing his father, especially since his head was still reeling from the assault of half a litre of vodka. Although Dave enjoyed a position of authority – he took care of the family's collection business, controlled the foot soldiers, and was responsible for the franchises that allowed minor gangs the privilege of using the Smiths' name – he was still kept on his father's very short leash.

"I'll throw some clothes on. You better drive me over there."

Jimmy smiled quickly, without humour, and sat down to wait.

His father was a big man. His white hair was ruffled and the collar of his pyjama top ridged above a worn dressing gown. He sat in his favourite armchair, his legs crossed, his foot tapping so that his slipper slapped against his heel. The expanse of plain blue pyjama bottoms that Dave could see seemed somehow old-fashioned. His father looked drawn, and older.

"You've caused me a lot of grief, boy. When are you going to learn? How old are you? Twenty-nine? Thirty? Then why is it you still act like an adolescent? When are you going to grow up and start acting like you're my eldest son instead of some fucking caveman?"

"Are you going to tell me what I've done, Pop? It's too early in the morning to guess."

"You've messed with the Mafia, boy, that's what. And half their fucking armed forces are on the way over here!"

Dave pulled a face as if he had tasted something nasty. Explanations were unnecessary. What worried him more than Valenti was that he didn't know how to handle his father who had little time for impropriety, even less time for indiscretion. He shrugged and filled a glass with vodka.

"Pop, it's my fault. He started slapping her about and I lost it."

"What did you expect him to do? He brings his wife over here for a little shopping to buy presents for their celebrations and some local piss artist gets his leg over. For God's sake, aren't there enough local girls? His wife! What's happened to respect and decency?"

"Blimey, Pop, if you'd have seen her. *Playboy* centrespread."

His father scowled and Dave knew at once that his excuse had simply compounded his earlier transgression.

"They're flying him home. An ambulance job for Christ's sake! Two broken ribs, and half his nose still in Park Lane!"

Dave swallowed half his drink.

"But worse than that, boy, you know what the worse thing is?"

Dave remained tight-lipped.

"You left her to face the music. You ran out on your *Girl of the Month*. How could a son of mine do that? Tell me?"

"Pop, he had two gorillas with him. There wasn't any return in me staying."

His father nodded sadly and Dave felt a sudden stab of embarrassment. The accusation of cowardice went right to the core. It would have been difficult to find a more serious indictment. The shame of it dried his throat and he finished his drink.

His father sighed and said, "Well, for your information, he's half killed her. She'll be in the hospital longer than the wop. I hope you're proud of yourself."

"I'm not. If I could do it over things would be different."

His father nodded reflectively.

"Meanwhile," Dave said. "I better get some muscle together."

"You'll do nothing!" his father snapped. "Do you hear me? Nothing! You'll make yourself scarce, and I mean scarce, like invisible, until I tell you otherwise. Your transport is outside. Get your bag packed and your shaving gear together. I want you out of the Smoke in the next hour."

"Where?"

"You'll find out. It won't be a holiday. When I've sorted things out I'll let you know."

"Pop! How long?"

"As long as it takes, boy. I don't know what I'm going to tell your mother. Pour me a whisky." Dave filled another glass and carried it to his father. "Treat it as a lesson. Learn something. Now remember, you're going to a good friend of mine. Do exactly what he tells you. Keep your mouth shut and your head down. I'll see you when it's all over."

Chapter 2

Dave Smith was driven north and arrived at his destination just as a late, overcast dawn dribbled its grey watery colours from a bank of low cloud. His mood was darkened by the prospect of enforced idleness and when he saw what was to be his home for an indefinite period it turned darker and he silently cursed every American he could think of. Dave knew the city, the lights, the smells, the incessant sounds of life itself, and already he felt isolated.

During the journey he had considered his options and he felt certain his father was making a mistake. His best bet was to fight on ground that he knew with people that he trusted. It was not his way to run. He would have handled the jewel-studded Guineas in their Brioni suits and custom-made silk shirts with his own men and given them a permanent piece of dockland. That's what they always wanted anyway. His father's decision, which was bound to lose him some credibility, came as a surprise and, to his knowledge it was the first time the Smiths had backed away. Perhaps his father was losing touch. Perhaps the last few years of relative peace had blunted his cutting edge. Respect was the key to survival, and respect came from strength and fear, not from running and hiding. The thought of cowardice stung him again. Who was it that said *Cowards die many times before their deaths?* Julius Caesar? Shakespeare?

Through the tinted rear windows he saw a small village, not much more than a single road lined with old cottages and one or two newer bungalows. It was just beginning to stir. One or two people moved to their cars and a paperboy was making his rounds. The road forked in one place into a tiny cobblestone market triangle and beyond that, before the roads joined again, grass footpaths widened to a village green. Everything dripped.

A strange mix of sensations churned his stomach; tiredness was there, burning into his eyes, but he felt as a refugee might, or a displaced person, as though everything he had known had been brought to an abrupt end.

Throughout the journey the driver, his father's personal driver, had remained curiously uncommunicative, almost as if he'd been instructed to keep his mouth shut. He'd been polite but his answers to Dave's probing had been to the point and conversation was non-existent. Dave was left in no doubt that for the time being his links with the family were well and truly broken.

From the village the road swung to the coast and ran parallel with the beach. The air drifting in from the North Sea was damp and pungent; a watery sun glared through the grey and lined the water's edge with dirty yellow froth. The narrow B road curled away inland and now the light shafted through the trees. A small miserable-looking cottage with a poorly maintained thatched roof and weathered timbers stood only twenty paces from the road and with a thick hedgerow concealing its path until the last moment the driver overshot and had to reverse. To the left of the drive, beyond a group of derelict sheds, a carpet of windfalls lay beneath the trees and a couple of longhaired pigs grunted around them.

Dave remained seated, motionless and stony-faced. The driver climbed out and took a suitcase from the boot. He carried it to the front door then returned and opened the rear door of the car.

"This is it, Dave. I suppose you'll get used to the smell."

Dave studied the man for a moment searching for a hint of emotion. There was none. Eventually he nodded, resigned to his fate, and climbed out.

"See you later. Take care." For the first time there was a kindness in the man's voice.

"Fuck you, son!" Dave said.

The driver offered him a cautious shrug, climbed quickly into the car and turned the ignition. Dave watched the car back out until it disappeared from view behind the thick hedgerow.

The rusty hinges of the paint-blistered front door squealed into the silence as he pushed it open.

Dave dropped his case at the door. It was even worse than he'd imagined. A small square parlour was musty and damp. It was all but inaccessible because of a huge oak table that left just a couple of feet of space around its sides.

He climbed some narrow, dangerously worn stairs that led from the one small room to a small bedroom with its ceiling slanting with the roof. A three-quarter sized bed was made up and a dresser had been polished. He found a bathroom and caught sight of his haggard looks in a mirror. He was still scowling as he made his way back down the creaking stairs.

The kitchen equipment was meagre: a porcelain sink with an unfinished work surface and a grease-filled crack along the wall, an antiquated gas cooker with a loose door and rings, a small refrigerator with just enough room inside for milk, bacon and butter, an old cast-iron stove with a store of logs beside it and an enamelled kettle on top. From the stove's open door wood ash had fallen from the grating on to a raised concrete bed. A larder was filled with groceries and cleaning utensils. Dave smiled cynically. He was going to lose weight. He couldn't remember the last time he'd prepared a meal.

The murky light in the room filtered in through casement windows and was just sufficient for him to find his way around. He found a tea caddy and teaspoon, and some mugs hanging on hooks in the larder. He made some tea but could manage only a mouthful before creeping back up to the bedroom. He fell asleep thinking that his exploration of the warm, secretive areas of the woman from *Bikini Beach* had not been worth it.

He was woken by noises from below. He negotiated the stairs and found a heavy-set man holding a boiling kettle above the teapot. He was red-faced with wide muddy eyes and a nose criss-crossed with map-like formations of purple lines. His hair was short and peppered with grey. Broad shoulders thrust forward, thick eyebrows raised and the face broke into a rugged smile.

"I'm Joe Daley. You look like shit!" His shoulders relaxed. His eyes remained curious. "Dave?"

Dave nodded and accepted a mug of rich tea. He noticed a .410 leaning against the wall.

"Well, remember the name, Daley. You're my nephew visiting. My place is two hundred yards up the road. I've been told to keep and eye on you, so I'll do that. I'll be down from time to time to see to the pigs. Just remember, a London accent is a dead giveaway up here so keep away from the locals."

Dave gulped at his tea. It tasted better than his earlier effort.

"You need to run the water before you use it. It tends to lie in the pipes," Daley said as if reading his mind. "Someone will come in from time to time to clean up and change the towels. If you need anything special that's the time to ask. You won't see much of me but I'll be around, watching. If you keep your head down we don't expect any trouble. We country folk like the peace and quiet."

"This is Coddy Hughes' manor. Do you work for him?"

"That isn't your business. There are books and there's the telly. If you want to walk out, get some air, that's OK. But you walk away from company, right?"

"It's your show, my son." Dave shrugged.

"I'm not your son," Daley said sternly. "I'm your uncle." He finished his tea, picked up his shotgun and moved heavily to the door. "I'll leave you to do the dishes. See you around." He had to bend slightly in order to go through.

For two days Dave barely ventured from the four whitewashed cottage walls. He worked his way through two tattered thrillers and watched television until he was so bored he could stand it no longer. The small parlour became claustrophobic and his gloom deepened by the hour. By lunchtime on the third day he could stand it no longer and was ready to take on Daley or anyone else who tried to stop him. It took him the best part of ninety minutes to walk to the tiny village and find the Royal Oak, a red-bricked building he'd noticed on his way through.

The bar itself was typical of the country pub: panelled walls covered in watery prints of the hunt, treated ceiling joists and a spitting log fire that threatened the clothes of anyone standing within two yards of it. The fire was absurd. It was August and the temperature even outside was in the mid-seventies.

A balding publican wearing a RAF moustache and tie stood behind his bar next to a heavily made-up woman in her fifties who might have been his wife. There were a few others in the room, a cross section of rural life: some elderly couples sitting around the edge, some men playing dominoes, and a group of youngsters standing at the bar. Quite naturally most of them glanced his way; it was that sort of place, off the beaten track, seldom visited by strangers; a corner of England still entrenched in the first half of the century. Dave ordered a bitter and carried the drink to the far end of the bar, away from the youngsters.

A screech of brakes and the slamming of car doors heralded the arrival of a tall youth who led in a woman wearing spectacles. Before the other youngsters gathered around, her glance skated across the room and fell momentarily on Dave. In that instant he felt that he knew her. She was in her mid-thirties, a straw-blonde, attractive without being beautiful. Her mood was fickle as though she was unsure of herself; smiling to share a joke perhaps, smiling out of politeness, composed for an introduction then deliberate to cover a stifled yawn. She was older than the others and uncomfortable. There was something puzzling about her apprehension. Her movements were uncomplicated and confident, but her expression, more particularly in her brown eyes, gave a clue to her restlessness: she was bored.

With every opening of the street door more people arrived in small groups until the room became crowded and noisy. Smoke, curling in layers about the yellowing lampshades was whipped into spirals by the draught. Most of the youngsters were of similar stock to those found in any country public house but there were exceptions: the pedigreed, the bloodstock, parading.

Dave decided it was time to leave. He'd been warned away from gatherings. In any case he was sick of the spoon-fed crap he was hearing. He finished his drink and noticed that the bright eyes slightly enlarged by the spectacles had fastened on to him again. Her face, framed by her curling blond hair, held a trace of amusement. Her wide mouth broke into a faint smile. It wasn't friendly, or even a greeting. Dave felt momentarily flustered. He was amazed at the feeling. He wondered whether he'd been staring, for it was that knowing sort of look she gave him. Her escort, one of those exceptions, diverted her attention.

Dave made his way from the bar and found a small grocery store that doubled as the off-licence. He purchased a copy of *The Telegraph*, a copy of Frederick Forsyth's *The Day of the Jackal* – he'd seen the film starring Edward Fox a couple of years previously and thoroughly enjoyed it – some fresh bread and milk, and two bottles of Famous Grouse – the vodka they carried was a cheap make he'd never heard of – and began the long walk home. He'd covered a hundred yards or so when he caught sight of his minder, the shotgun held loosely in his arms. Dave chuckled to himself. His father had been right. It was not going to be a holiday. Even so, under the afternoon sun the beech trees around the village church were still and the hedgerows sparkled and by the time he reached the cottage there was some country colour to his city skin.

He dreamt of the Smoke, the picture-post-card city: Tower Bridge, the river, Oxford Street, Covent Garden, the stations, the complex road systems cutting through the grand buildings and the superstores with their vast windows of glistening goods, from the sleek opulence of Knightsbridge to the East End traps, from the King's Road to Berwick Street, from Piccadilly decorated in superficial neon to St James', from the abortion clinics around Oxford Circus marked for the overnight visitors who carried their unwanted lumps by the Post Office Tower, to St Paul's Cathedral, where perhaps those visitors could stop to pray for the souls they left behind.

Thunder crashed and Dave sat up sweating. The strong North Sea wind gusted, trees swayed and creaked and rain beat the cottage walls, and above the clamour of nature came the sounds of a slamming door.

Armed with a torch he'd discovered earlier and wearing a huge canvas raincoat that he found hanging on the kitchen door, he went out to the sheds. The loose door was swinging on the last of the four sheds used as storage space for gardening equipment and an assortment of rusty tools. He wasn't surprised to find a series of wet footprints on the dusty surface of the shed floor. His minder, Joe Daley, had been doing his rounds and no doubt stopped for shelter. He heard the pigs grunting in the next shed. The wind strengthened and rushed through the trees. Dave secured the door, pulled up the wide lapel and splashed back to the cottage.

It was late morning when Joe Daley pulled up in a battered green Austin. Dave was leaning on the orchard fence watching the pigs wallow in the spongy ground. The sun glared from a clear sky into air purified by the night rain. The subtle gradations of light and shade were lost. Daley's huge shoulders bunched over the wheel as he pulled on the hand brake. Driving had taken all his concentration. His eyes were curiously threatening.

"Getting around a bit?" He spoke slowly and Dave got the impression that Daley was unsettled.

"Just getting rid of the cobwebs."

The eyes narrowed.

"You've been getting rid of a few these last few days."

Dave shrugged and turned back to the pigs.

Daley pulled a sour face. He grunted his resignation. "The boss wants to see you. Dinner. I'll pick you up at eight. Be ready."

Dave smiled. So that was it. The invitation had annoyed the big man. Special treatment for the man from the Smoke was playing on Daley's nerves. Wet-nursing him was probably irritating enough, checking the grounds in the middle of the night in the middle of a thunderstorm was damned uncomfortable, but actually picking him up and acting as chauffeur was an absolute shit.

That evening in a sprawling manor house situated beyond a series of low-slung, red-bricked buildings that housed stables and a swimming pool, Dave met Coddy Hughes for the first time.

19

His father had once told him about Coddy and a friendship that had developed over the years. His high regard for the man was clear from the outset. He'd described Coddy as a thick-bodied man almost bald even at that young age, with a circular scar right between the eyes. Coddy said it was a bullet that had bounced off his thick skull but his father had discovered later that it had been from a wooden arrow fired from a bow by Coddy himself. The arrow had snapped and whipped back at Coddy's face. He had been nine years old at the time and fortunate to escape with his sight intact. Not many people knew the truth. The bullet sounded better.

Dave met a sixty-two-year-old bald man who wore a neck brace and needed a walking-frame to get about. He was thin and weak and the only hint of his past came from his eyes, fearless and faintly mocking. Time had been unkind; a car accident in his fifties, a whiplash, had left him crippled and all but housebound.

It proved to be a homely affair with Coddy heading the table, eating one-handed while his other rested permanently on a silver-topped walking stick, his wife, Mavis, to his left and Dave opposite her. Three others, girls aged six, ten and twelve, sat at the bottom end of the gleaming table. They were involved in other things, whispers and chatter and girlish giggles. They were the daughters of Coddy's daughter who was out for the evening, Coddy told him and added, "Such a handful they need a minder a piece!"

Dave felt uncomfortable, conscious that they were all watching him.

Once dinner was over Mavis took the girls through to an adjoining room to play Scrabble and left Dave and Coddy together. It was time for business.

"The girls have taken to you," he said in quiet, clipped tones. He waved his free hand. "It's the accent. They're all mad about David Essex. All I've been hearing for three years is *Rock On*, and posters for *That'll Be the Day* cover their bedroom walls." His eyes narrowed and Dave guessed it was time for the real business. "You went to the Oak. It's not a good idea. Your father has asked me to look after you until he can sort out the trouble. How can I look after you if you don't take advice?"

Coddy leant forward in his chair and filled two glasses with whisky. He pushed one across the table then settled back in his chair again.

"The village is a small place with few secrets; the stranger stands out like a nigger in the Royal Family. If you need for something you let Joe know what you want and he'll get it for you." He raised his head slightly from the pink neck brace and emphasized coldly, "This is not a request. You understand?"

Dave nodded. A mix of embarrassment and admiration ran through him. He understood immediately what his father had been getting at. Coddy's authority was clear-cut, without the need of a raised voice or the lesser man's posturing. It remained beneath the surface, and was all the more marked because of it.

"All I want to do is get back to civilization," he said quietly, and added defensively, "No one is going to look for me up here."

"Dave, it's where I've chosen to live, and as small and as peaceful as it seems, it's on the map. It's my HQ. And that makes it important." He raised his glass and emptied it before continuing. "You can guarantee that our friends across the pond have at least one contact up here because of me. Sure, it's off the beaten track and it might seem safe, but don't drop your guard. These people have a network bigger than the CIA. I don't expect trouble, especially if you keep your head down, but you've got to understand, there's no such thing as a certainty. Not in our business." He mellowed and his eyes lost their edge. "It's not so bad. Your father tells me he hopes to have it sorted in two or three weeks."

Dave's heart sank. Three more weeks in the country would drive him crazy. He'd already seen enough trees to last him a lifetime and as for the damp air that came in off the North Sea, it was simply not healthy. Coddy nodded as he recognized Dave's despair.

"I'll send the girls around to keep you company. That will get them from under my feet for a while. They love the pigs. They go out collecting the acorns." He sighed and went on, "The summer holidays are too long. All I'm hearing all day is noise, pop music. Poofters leaping about the stages – and some of them even wear make-up. Can you believe that? It's difficult to tell if they're men or women. That Bowie guy started it all, I'm sure of it. You wouldn't know whether to shake their hands or fuck them. I don't know what the world's coming to. It isn't the one I remember. God help us if there's ever another war. They'd be carrying a compact in their kitbags." He shook his head in despair and pointed to the bottle of malt on the table.

Dave took his cue and poured out more drinks.

"I prefer this to brandy," Coddy said and swallowed two measures. "I shouldn't drink at all with all the pills." He pulled a dry face. "I've gone through life doing things I shouldn't, so what the hell!"

Dave settled back, feeling more comfortable in the old man's company. It might have been the booze, he considered, but he had a feeling it was more than that. He said, "I know you met my father during the war but he's never discussed it. As far as he's concerned the war never happened."

Coddy nodded reflectively, "That's not a bad thing. Some men never stop talking about it."

"It was only recently that we discovered he'd caught one in the shoulder. He didn't tell us. It was an old-timer who used to box for Peter Woodhead told my brother Tommy all about it. When we asked Dad about it all we got was a shake of the head and something about a scratch on the shoulder."

Coddy gave a wry smile and shook his head, an awkward movement against the neck brace. He said, "That's a bloody gem. A scratch on the shoulder, you say?" He laughed out loud.

It was the first time Dave had seen any humour in the man. He toyed with the crystal, turning the glass, waiting for an explanation.

Coddy swallowed half his drink. At length he said, "You ever heard of Scratch Fox?"

Dave shook his head.

"Scratch Fox was a sergeant in your old man's outfit. It was just before the war started. They were on manoeuvres on Salisbury Plain when one of the squaddies got himself injured and needed stitching up. Fox had your father drive him and the squaddie back to the hospital but it meant kipping overnight at Fox's married quarters. During that night your father crept out of the house and drove into town to take care of a couple of small-time villains who'd put your granddaddy out of action."

"Took care of them?"

Coddy nodded and explained, "Years earlier they'd cut up your granddaddy for not coughing up protection. Your granddaddy was left bedridden. It led to him topping himself."

Dave knew that his grandfather had drowned in the Thames; he hadn't known that it had been suicide.

"What happened?"

"Your dad took care of it. He waited ten years for the right moment."

"He topped them?"

"Wouldn't you?" Coddy paused then went on, "Unfortunately, in the early morning the sergeant heard him get back. But when the filth eventually arrived Fox gave your dad an alibi. He never did understand why the sergeant lied to the police but as it turned out, Fox was the lucky one. Back home everyone knew what had happened. They treated your father differently. The thing unspoken remained between them; not respect, exactly, unless it was the respect you have for dangerous things. When war broke out they ended up in France. Sergeant Fox got half his head blown away in Dunkirk, the town. The same volley caught your dad in the shoulder. They were left behind. That's the way it was. The stretcher-bearers would pick them up later. Trouble was, the stretchers had enough to do on the beaches. Your dad carried the sergeant down to the beach on his good shoulder and found what was left of the squad, which wasn't much. He was pretty busted up himself by then. Between the two of them they looked like something out of a butcher's window."

He paused to fill his glass then went to top up Dave's and saw that it was still full.

"You want a beer?" The question was clipped and disapproving.

Dave lifted his glass and said, "This is fine."

"Listen, son, a conversation that stops you drinking isn't worth holding."

Dave finished his drink in one and offered the glass for a refill. He said, "You're telling me things I've never heard."

Coddy smiled briefly in acceptance.

"It's a funny business, Dave: that as you get older and the war gets further away, you dwell on it more and more. In the end your memory turns it from being some kind of fucking horror story into something you enjoyed. I suppose that's why so many of the old guys go back to the battlefields. They're getting off on what their memories made of it. They've started to believe their own stories." Coddy grunted dismissively and went on, "The glory! The few! All the heroic stuff! We were running backwards like no one ever ran before. And as for all those little boats! The navy must get really pissed off hearing about them. It was chaos. Carnage is the word. There were bodies all over the shop, gutted, blown to bits, stinking. The stink was unbelievable. It took weeks to wash it off. There were legs and arms and heads lying all over the place. You could have played a game of bowls with the number of heads you saw in the street. The planes never stopped. Getting on a boat during those first few days was impossible. At one stage they stopped taking stretcher cases. Your dad and the sergeant got a change of clothes from a couple of bodies. Not that Fox could do much. He was unconscious for most of the time. No one thought he'd make it. The rest of the squad had to hide both of them to get them on board, made out they were pissed on red wine. They were only taking able-bodied by then. Anyway, they made it.

"Outside Dover all the old people's homes, schools and the like, had been converted into casualty clearing stations. It was in a place called Cheriton that I first met your old man. I caught one in the neck so I must have looked a bit like Scratch Fox." Coddy touched a red scar that ran below his left ear. "Mine was fucking stupid; not even a Jerry bullet. One of our own guys was fucking about. You'd be surprised how many of our guys got shot by our own side. Anyway, these places were only holding units until you were well enough to transfer to a proper hospital and that could have been anywhere in the country. Everyone in the ward was pretty poorly. The guy who ended up in the next bed to mine had a bullet through his shoulder and was down with pneumonia and God knows what else. He was unconscious for two days and more dead than alive. That was your dad. We spent a week together in that shit-house."

The time approached eleven; the war was spent and so was Dave's description of the family and London in general. They'd opened a second bottle of malt when the sounds of a car halting on gravel marked the arrival of the tall youth from the pub, and close on his heels, in tight trousers and open-necked shirt, the woman.

She asked Coddy, "Hello Daddy, are we interrupting?"

"No, we've just about finished it. Come in and have a drink. This is Dave Smith. You've heard me mention his father. This is Pat, my daughter, and her boyfriend, James Osbourne."

"Hello," Dave said but the word got caught in his throat.

Coddy Hughes splashed whisky as he poured more drinks. The couple carried them to the bar stools at the far end of the room. Dave forced himself from the sneaked glance; he found her incredibly attractive; had it not been for similar feelings during their previous encounter he would have put it down to the malt. He heard them talking while he talked to Coddy, her low voice polished of its accent with only hints of Lincolnshire. They discussed everything and nothing in particular. She was there, on the periphery of everything, even when he faced the other way, easing off her seat to reach over the bar, stretching material across her wide hips, scratching her knee, raising her glass, beating a silent rhythm with her loose foot; a continuous movement to attract the eye.

Coddy leant forward.

"James is a bit of a wanker," he said quietly, with a knowing glint in his eye. Whether the statement was rhetorical or an indication of Coddy's true feelings toward his daughter's boyfriend or just to make Dave feel less impassioned was hard to tell.

Chapter 3

The following morning Dave decided to call London. He was itching for news of what was happening. He left his breakfast dishes on the table and began the walk to a kiosk he'd noticed on the seafront. The sky was clear overhead but streaked with cloud in front. A helicopter hovered over the sea, a speck; the constant hum of its rotor sounding like a distant lawnmower. The lane ran to a slow bend. The trees, thickly grouped closer to the cottage, thinned out until there were bare clearings of shortly cropped grass on either side. The land flattened and he caught sight of the distant red box standing incongruously before the sand dunes. It was a fairly warm morning; the breeze had dropped to a whisper and the air was charged. Before long, perspiration trickled under his shirt like some fast little insect.

The helicopter swept overhead, a startling roaring blur, close enough to look threatening and fanning the wind his way. It plunged with surprising speed and swooped back to hover before him, keeping pace. He could make out the detail of its belly and the two men through its open sides who were taking more than a casual interest in him. For a moment he considered that they were Coddy's men. He hoped they were. It hovered for about thirty seconds – it seemed longer – then soared away inland, across Coddy Hughes' manor, cutting a grey smear across the blue until it became a speck again and then disappeared altogether. The hum refused to fade, a constant intimidation, as though the machine had cut through nature itself and left its mark.

The lane narrowed over a humpback bridge across a slow-moving stream. On the other side the grass was coarser and tufted, the earth coloured with stretches of light sand. Pools of black water dotted the area, shrunken so that the rings of dark mud at their edges dried out in stages, the outer layers cracked and lifted in a mosaic pattern of brownish hues.

Dave reached the telephone when the sun was at its peak; it was unbearably hot inside and he kept the door wedged open. A minute later he was through to Jimmy Jones.

"You OK, Dave?"

"No, I'm not."

"Where are you?"

"I'm down on the farm, my son, knee deep in pig shit. The smell's so bad it makes the eyes water."

"That's what comes of playing about, Dave. Women are dangerous. You should have learned. Where's the farm?"

"It doesn't matter where. Just tell me what's happening?"

"It's too quiet for comfort. Something's going down but everyone's being cagey. There's people asking about you, and it ain't a birthday present they've got in mind!"

"Who's asking?"

"No names, just blank faces and a lot of whispers. But there's no doubt about it. It's you they want. What's going on?"

Dave ignored the question and asked, "Yanks?"

"Rock Hudson look-alikes, I'd say. Clean cut, shiny suits, cowboy boots, flashing white teeth from here to Southend, know what I mean? They couldn't be more obvious if they were wearing Stetsons, riding horses and shooting everything that moved."

"Does the old man know?"

"Are you kidding? Tell me something going down in the Smoke that he doesn't know about?"

"Has he said anything?"

"Only that you're on holiday. He's sent you away to dry out your liver, on doctor's orders. It's official. But everyone that counts knows it's a load of bollocks."

"Let's keep it that way. It'll blow over. Don't worry. I'm keeping my head down for a while. Tell the boys to do the same. If you've got problems that can't wait, then get in touch with Barry and he'll let the old man know."

"We could get hold of these geezers, Dave. Find out who's asking the questions?"

"Blimey, don't do that! I already know who it is. Just stay loose. I'll be in touch."

"Take care, Dave. I don't like the sound of this."

"I'll make out. Just tell everyone to watch their backs."

"I'll do that."

"Yeah."

"See you."

It was a relief to leave the kiosk and feel a breath of air. The sounds of the gentle waves washing in and the soulful cries from white birds that glided overhead enticed him over the bank of fine sand. He saw the horse first, about twenty yards from him, its thin reins hanging loosely, chestnut coat gleaming across its bare back. It stood head bowed, snorting. Behind the horse a trail of pits in the dry sand created a path to the damp firmer stuff at the water's edge where the prints became more defined and trailed off across the beach.

The girls stood in the sea facing the horizon, calf deep until a swell and then the water lifted to the shoulders of the shortest and to the waist of Patricia Hughes. Dave was to discover later that since her divorce she'd reverted to her maiden name. They skipped and splashed. Their girlish yelps and laughter carried across to him. They seemed totally unaware of being watched. The four of them were naked, their clothes scattered across the beach. Dave's breath was swept away as he watched, captivated, barely able to move. The bodies spanned perhaps thirty years but he would never have guessed it; the curves were as firm as they had ever been. He was looking at a bunch of golden nymphs, semi-divine guardians of nature itself. He could have enjoyed watching them play indefinitely but reserve, maybe a fear that they might discover him, turned him round.

On the road he emptied sand from his shoes and started back. He searched above the distant line of trees for signs of the helicopter but couldn't find it and guessed that it was retreating from the quickly approaching clouds. The sky had become dark and threatening with tufts of cloud breaking free and racing in from thicker stuff off the coast, casting moving shadows on the road ahead. He increased his pace. There was rain in the heavy air and beating it to the cottage would take some doing. The sound of hooves clattered behind him and he turned to see the woman. Her straw-coloured hair was wet and flattened even more by spectacles used as a headband. She'd dressed in a short thigh-length towelling robe. Looking directly ahead she manoeuvred the horse beside him. Her eyes sparkled in amusement. Or was it provocation? She seemed to know exactly how much he was unsettled and was intent on stringing it out. Her loose leg dangled freely beside him, perhaps a yard away, brushing the chestnut coat. Her robe, buttoned at the midriff, fell away either side exposing a blue wedge of bikini bottom against her pale skin. Dave pulled his gaze away and glanced up. There was a terrible glint in her eye. Without warning she kicked and moved ahead and the horse broke into a canter. He watched her round the bend, grateful that she had gone.

The first rumblings of thunder rippled ominously, forcing his pace, and when it died it left a hum of singing voices carried, presumably, from a wedding at the village church. He reached the cottage just as the first heavy splashes of rain dotted the ground.

The horse was tethered beneath the awning along the cottage wall. It backed around, stamping, unsettled by the approaching storm. Dave felt heady, adrenalin reached out to every nerve end. He was amazed by his own nervousness. He sensed the danger, a familiar feeling, and one that he normally enjoyed, and yet the warning signs tightened his chest, as if serious injury – even life itself – was on the line. Perhaps the knowledge that it was Coddy Hughes' daughter made the difference. He pushed open the door and lifted the dimness inside. She faced him, framed in a brighter square of light, perched on the edge of the wooden table with her toes barely touching the stone floor, her hands gripping the top to hold her balance. Her spectacles lay on the table next to the pile of breakfast dishes. She was smiling at his expression or at the chorus of *'All Things Bright and Beautiful'* that the increasing breeze carried through the open door. Her bright eyes flickered. Her lips parted and her smile fluttered, first in apprehension and then to something else, perhaps a dare. The robe was undone exposing her long neck, the valley between her swollen breasts, her midriff with its faint gleam of down and the blue material beneath. With her back arched over the table, she threw out the final challenge, and the gap between her legs increased.

Her wet, salty mouth locked on to his. His hand moved instinctively between her legs, bringing a gasp from her mouth that sent hot air into his. Her legs clamped around his waist parting his way, dampening the material more than the sea. He tasted the seawater that trickled from her hair, eyes, nose and mouth, convinced that she would suffocate beneath him.

Lightning cracked out of the darkening sky and it thundered again with an almighty crash that shook every window in the cottage. Even the breakfast dishes rattled together and the milk bottle jumped. The tempest was on them, inside and out.

There was no tenderness in this coming together. He tore down her bikini bottom and she tore open his flies. She cried out and he grunted. It was brutish and they ended it on the floor, their chests heaving and their mouths open as they gulped for breath. The tablecloth had come down on top of them, splattering them with milk and cold coffee and preserve. For a while they lay, raw, unable to move, against the thick table legs on the cold stone tiles.

She whispered thickly, "That wasn't making love. That was war."

Across half a mile of countryside, getting fainter all the time, down the lane, across the garden and through the open door, fading to a murmur before it reached their ears, the vicar said, "In the name of the Father, the Son and the Holy Ghost," and the congregation, "Amen."

She stirred and stood, straddling him, gazing down at him through the strands of blond hair that fell over her face. Lumps of preserve became unstuck from her stomach and splattered on to him, spilt coffee and milk found its path southward through the dark curls and down her thighs. He looked up at her, at the display between her legs.

"They're going to need a spaceship to get my bollocks back-" he began but was cut short.

She raised her finger and hushed him. He watched her move, still feeding on her movement, as she stepped across him and slipped on her robe. She picked up her bikini briefs and spectacles and without a backward glance went out of the cottage. He waited for the sounds of the horse on the tarmac, visualizing her nakedness on its back, thinking of the wet patch that would shortly stain the chestnut hair as she drained all that he'd put there.

While the bath filled Dave checked himself in the cracked mirror above the basin. His eyes were still red and fierce, still flushed by the victory. Her scent was trapped in the dried white flakes she'd left behind but this was going to go the way of the preserve and cold coffee. He drank a quarter of one of the bottles of scotch he'd purchased in the village and carried the remainder to the bath where he climbed gingerly into the hot water. Gradually the stinging disappeared leaving a positive glow and a feeling of drowsiness so heavy that it was difficult to move an arm.

The door opened and cut through the steam.

She stood in the doorway and leant against the frame. An expression of mild annoyance did not match the sparkle in her eye.

"I reached the corner and decided there was no way I could present myself like this. I thought of falling off the horse but that wouldn't be convincing, would it? I mean, what on earth did I fall in to cover myself with marmalade and milk and for God's sake, love bites? Look!" She swept back the robe to show a mark just below the elastic at the back of her briefs. "Not that I need an excuse, but it might raise Daddy's eyebrows. He's very old-fashioned and I'm not sure he approves of you to begin with. Anyway, I didn't expect any of that. I look as though I've been through a war zone!" Her top lip was swollen and there was a red patch on her chin caused by his stubble. "Anyway, it's peeing down out there."

She didn't have to tell him. The rain was beating hard against the window.

She moved into the room and gave it the once over. "Oh my God, it's even worse than downstairs. Are you sure we won't catch something?" She dropped the robe and wriggled out of her bikini. "Move up," she said and climbed in, tap end. The water flushed over the side before it settled below the overflow. He noticed the skin beginning to redden around her dark nipples.

"Here." She handed him the flannel. "You do it. You caused it." There was a look in her eye that might have been affection. He hadn't noticed it before.

"You caused it Patricia. It was all down to you."

"Did I?" she countered. "You took my clothes off in the Royal Oak, and then again at the manor. James can get very jealous, you know, and you did make it pretty obvious. Even Daddy noticed it."

Dave shook his head. He'd have to watch these country folk. He grinned and said, "That was just wishful thinking. I never thought it would come to anything. What did you expect me to do?"

Even though the rain still pelted against the glass the cloud must have parted for sunlight tumbled in from the small square window high in the wall, shafting through the steam.

She said, "The storm is almost over."

"It could easily start again."

Her eyes narrowed.

"I saw you on the beach earlier, with the girls."

"We noticed. We saw you arrive."

He tried to hide his surprise and said, "They're all yours? You're in good nick for three kids."

"I'm in good nick period, if you don't mind."

He nodded agreement. "What happened to their dad?"

"We fell out."

"Does he see the kids?"

She shook her head and said, "He's never seen Tracy. She's six. We haven't seen him since then. Daddy says we'll never see him again. He probably paid him off."

Dave nodded, hiding his thoughts. He wanted more but it wasn't going to come.

Her glance flashed over the small room then settled back on him. "This room has a certain primitive charm but there's a definite smell of mould."

"That's the laundry basket under the basin. Someone must have been keeping old socks in it."

"Now you've ruined the picture. What's wrong with the smell of the thatched roof after the rain?"

"What am I, a poet?"

"No, you're a gangster." A smile lit her face. She crossed her arms around her knees and leant back with her head between the taps. Beads of perspiration collected on her forehead. "In the pub you were staring at me. Apart from taking off my clothes what else were you thinking?"

"You looked out of place," he said. His feelings were intense, sharpened by knowledge yet tempered by guilt. Or rather, he felt he should have felt guilty. He felt that he'd abused Coddy Hughes' hospitality.

She touched her breast and flinched, then examined the small nipple and the bruising. "You did that," she said thickly.

"Yes."

She laughed and reached for the bottle. The scotch burned and she coughed. She said, "God, I hate this stuff." She eased her legs down between his and pressed him with her toes, her knees lowered sufficiently to reveal her hair broken by refraction. He grew against her foot. "Tell me about you?"

"I'm not married," he said.

"I know that much."

"I'm in the family business."

"I know that too. What else?"

"I've got a flat in London, above one of the clubs. You might have heard of it – The Tower."

She nodded. "Who hasn't? What about girls?"

"There's nothing about girls."

"I've heard differently."

"Who told you that?"

She smiled. Her front tooth was slightly crooked.

"What happened to the kids?" he asked.

"They took the short cut home. I had to bring Juliet, the horse, the long way. Tracy, Jackie and Jessica – Jessica's the eldest. She's twelve.

33

Tracy is the apple in her granddad's eye. She always has been. He makes up for absent fathers."

Dave nodded reflectively. "I can't picture Coddy Hughes with kids on his knee."

"You'd be surprised how domesticated my dad is. I took them all to London once, to see the shows, about two years ago. Tracy was too young really. We stayed at the Hilton overlooking Hyde Park. We had the penthouse suite."

Dave studied her thoughtfully, wondering whether it was her way of telling him that she knew all about the American girl and the trouble that he was in. She hadn't once asked what he was doing up here and it was the obvious question.

"Daddy takes us away twice a year," she continued. "But he can't get around like he used to so we're a bit restricted with locations. Long hauls are a bit out of the question."

"You've not thought of moving away? Getting a place of your own?"

"I've got as much freedom as I need. I'm thirty-four. Daddy accepts that. No questions. No restrictions. Discussions centre on the girls, their schooling and so on. He likes me to get out. He'd like me to meet someone."

"He doesn't like James."

"Oh, I know that." She raised her eyebrows. "James is all right."

Dave threw her a quizzical look.

"He's safe. He's very rich, legitimately so, or at least his parents are, and he's not likely to end up in prison or in some gutter with a knife in his back."

"Sweetheart, you're shooting in the dark. I'm not going to end up that way either."

"Huh! You're about as safe as safe sex the Catholic way! Have you ever seen the size of Irish families? That's how Tracy arrived!"

She shivered. Perhaps the conversation had cooled her. The water was still hot.

Dave pulled the plug and led her to the bedroom to hunt out softer towels. She stood head bowed and let him dry her. He was gentle, particularly around the cuts on her knees. He knelt behind her, wiping her legs before drawing open the towel like a pair of curtains to reveal her trim behind. He felt an urge to bury his face between her as if devouring her would be the final satisfaction.

"You leave my bum alone," she said. She turned around inside the towel. She held her legs closely together. Her slender hand did not entirely cover the extremities or the parting beneath. He let the towel fall. She moved her hand.

"You're looking from a purely aesthetic point of view, of course?"

"I think so. What's it mean?"

"It means that I'm going to fall over if you keep doing that."

He picked her up easily and carried her to the bed.

He felt her tremble.

"Be tender with me this time," she said.

They spent the following few days together. Even in that short time she seemed to have changed. She radiated; her complexion and her character smouldered as though fired by some inner furnace. It was impossible not to recognize the sparkle, the confidence, and the added spring to her step.

On Thursday she couldn't make it; she was taking the children into Lincoln. Dave found himself in the bar of the Royal Oak again. He knew that it was a mistake and that he was going against the express wishes of Coddy Hughes but things had moved on from there. It was lunchtime and the bar was surprisingly empty. The balding man served him and then went out to his cellars. He stood at the bar and considered finishing his drink quickly and getting out before any harm was done. The door opened. It was too late. And as soon as he recognized James Osbourne he knew it meant trouble.

Backed up by two friends, Osbourne walked directly up to Dave and said, "I want a word with you."

Dave turned to face him and said, "What can I do for you?"

"I want to make it clear to you that Patricia and I have been seeing one another for quite some time and that we have an understanding."

"Fine," Dave said. "That's quite clear. Is that it?"

"I want you to keep away from her. You have nothing in common;

you do not fit in. Is all that absolutely plain enough for you?"

Dave shifted his glance to Osbourne's friends who stood just behind. He gave them his best effort at a conciliatory smile. He didn't need this. Coddy had warned him. He was supposed to be lying low, keeping out of trouble. Backing down went against the grain. That upset him more than anything else. In normal circumstances Osbourne would already be chewing on the floorboards.

"There's no need for any of this," he said.

"I want your word that you'll leave her alone."

Dave sighed and said, "I'm sorry, my son, but you're talking to the wrong person. If you have a future with Pat you should be discussing it with her, and not in public."

"I'm not your son, Dave. And the discussion is with you. If you don't mind we'll leave Patricia out of it."

Dave shrugged and turned back to the bar. He lifted his pint mug. James Osbourne prodded Dave's arm and some of the drink splashed on to the bar surface. A dark veil drew across Dave's eyes and he said, "Don't do that."

Osbourne prodded again.

"I'm talking to you," he said loudly. "Do we have an understanding?"

Dave's beer mug exploded on the side of James Osbourne's face and sent him sprawling across table and chairs. Before he'd landed firmly on the floor and before his friends had moved, Dave's shoe sank into his groin. It was over in seconds. Osbourne lay paralysed on his back as frothy blood poured from his mouth and nose.

Dave placed the handle of his pint mug on the bar and turned to the others. "I told him not to do it again."

Open mouthed, they nodded in agreement, their shocked eyes fixed on Osbourne's shattered face.

The barman appeared from the back and made suitable threats. As Dave left the bar the others rushed to aid their friend.

Dave anticipated the next move. He knew that the police wouldn't get involved and he guessed that James Osbourne would cause no further trouble – Coddy wouldn't allow it – but he knew also that Coddy wouldn't let it rest there.

He was in the orchard when the car pulled up. The sun had just cleared the treetops to begin its dissipation of the early morning mist. Two men armed with shotguns left the black Rolls and called him over. The rear door was pushed open and Dave found Coddy Hughes sitting stiffly in the seat, his cane held upright between his knees.

"Morning," Dave said apprehensively while trying to gauge the man's mood. It wasn't good; he could tell that much from the tight lips and burning eyes. He wondered who would be mentioned first, Coddy's daughter or James Osbourne. He was more nervous at the prospect of hearing Patricia's name than that of Osbourne's. Even though he hadn't seen Pat since the fight her scent was still about him; he drew it in with every breath, the musky scent of female sex, unmistakable and yet personalized, unique. It was in his nose and throat, in his hair. Coddy couldn't fail to recognize it.

"David, get in a while," Coddy said calmly.

The armed men spread out either side of the car, guns no longer broken, and he wasn't convinced it was just a show of muscle. He climbed in and sat beside the diminutive figure.

"What's happened?"

"You've happened. You've arrived in my village like World War Three!"

Dave studied his new adversary. "I'm sorry about what happened. Let's cut straight to it, shall we?"

"I'm sorry too, Dave. You let me down. You let your father down. You seem to have some kind of death wish about you. You carry it around like a sign, neon lit. My feelings for your father are holding back what I'd like to say to you, but I'm surprised he hasn't taught you self-control."

"Is he all right?"

"James? All right? Well now, apart from his bollocks being somewhere in the next county and his front teeth chewing on his arsehole, I'd say he wasn't too fucking tickled."

Dave held on to a smile. Eventually he said, "I know about you, Mr Hughes. And I know that it's only these last few years that have slowed you down. If someone came in and started pushing you around, you'd have killed the guy. There'd have been no second chances. I gave this guy every chance to back off. I was almost grovelling, for Christ sakes."

"We've got nothing else to discuss," Coddy said coldly.

"Yes we have and it's more important than James Osbourne or any other public school shit, no matter who his father is. These bastards only think they're in charge."

Coddy threw up a hand and sighed. "I know what's been going on. I'm not stupid. Even Patricia's mother thinks she's sniffing glue or swallowing pills by the handful."

Dave's mouth was dry. Without realizing it he was digging his fingernails into his palms.

"I know that Patricia has obviously found some qualities in you that are attractive. Frankly, I have not. You don't actually inspire confidence, Dave. You came here with a heavy reputation, and your actions since then have given me no reason to doubt it. The reason you were sent here in the first place is because you think with your dick. Down south, so I'm told, there's a joke that Dave Smith would fuck anything in a skirt, including the odd Scot! You heard it? It's not very funny. I'm not laughing." He paused for a moment and then said, "If you're only good for one tenth of your reputation then you're not to be trusted within a mile of any woman. And by God, that includes my daughter!"

"These things are always exaggerated. It would take some kind of superman to do some of the things I've been accused of."

"Maybe," Coddy said. "But when all this is over I'd like you to go back to London, put some space between you. If in three months you still have feelings for one another we can take it from there."

"I can't do that. Patricia isn't a girl anymore. She knows what she wants. And if she wants me it's going to take an army to keep me from her. If she doesn't want to see me I'll never bother her again. But she's going to tell me. Not you, Sir."

Coddy raised an eyebrow in surprise. Suddenly he smiled and there was something approaching affection in his eyes.

"I'm going to leave it there for now, young man. There'll be no more visits to the village. Is that understood?"

Dave nodded.

The affection vanished. Coddy grimaced and said, "I'll speak to my daughter."

Dave climbed out of the car and watched Coddy's men get in and moments later the car roared off.

It rained through the afternoon and the weak light barely found its way into the cottage. Dave bathed early and towelled himself down while watching from the bedroom window for Patricia's arrival.

He was nervous at the prospect of meeting her again. It came down to violence and whether she thought his treatment of James Osbourne was justified. It came down to her attitude over the use of violence to settle an argument. He wondered how much she knew about her father's line of work and whether she accepted that it hadn't been his refined manners and his persuasive abilities over the conference table that had led him to the top. He wondered whether she accepted also that some men could never be pushed around, no matter what the consequences.

He heard the car before he saw it, a metallic BMW. It flashed past the short expanse of lane that he could see. A moment later came a screech of brakes. Two men in dark suits appeared at the entrance to the drive. The drizzle didn't seem to bother them as they looked around before walking almost nonchalantly toward the cottage. The black automatics they held seemed to cut holes through the dripping grey.

Dave was stunned. The implications were still sinking in as he saw the men duck for cover behind a low hedgerow, their attention directed toward the orchard.

Two flat explosions rattled the window. Dave leant closer to the glass to bring the orchard into view. Joe Daley stood under the trees, his raised shotgun smoking. He had already broken it and was bringing fresh cartridges from his pocket. He was standing there as if taking part in a pheasant shoot. Dave mouthed the words, "Get down for God's sake!" But even as the last word silently emerged he heard the clatter of automatic fire and watched Daley sink to the spongy ground. Bullets smacked into the mud around him. Tree bark ripped open. Daley lay still. His gun stuck in the earth and pointed at the low sky. Behind him a sow had her belly torn out. She squealed and slipped then slowly hauled herself from the mud and lumbered away, dragging guts behind her, barely concerned.

Dave moved. He put his weight against the old dressing table and pushed it against the door. He pulled his case from under the bed and tore into it, throwing his clothes aside until he found his .38, a black Smith & Wesson.

The front door crashed open. Glass smashed. He moved back to the window. A dozen coats of paint held it firm. The thump of footsteps sounded on the narrow stairs. He put his shoulder against the frame. The window cracked, the wood splintered, and it opened. The bedroom door thudded into the back of the dressing table. The opening in the window was barely wide enough to take him but he made it, and landed on the awning that ran along the side of the cottage.

The dressing table slid back and the door crashed open. A gun roared. The window smashed and showered him in glass. Dave fired one shot into the room before he lost his footing and skidded on the tin roof. Timber cracked as the awning caved in. He rolled over the lip and landed flat on his back on a freshly turned border. For a moment he lay winded, unable to move.

One of the men had remained at the cottage door and now he came charging around the corner. He was blond, about six-three. Jimmy's description flashed into Dave's mind. He was still lying on his back as he pulled the trigger. The man's blue eyes widened as he realized his mistake. The bullet caught him in the knee. He yelped, spun round and fell backwards, away from Dave. His 12-bore Spatz flew into the air. Dave fired again and saw a neat hole appear in the sole of the man's shoe.

A clatter of fire came from above. Bullets smacked the earth just a foot from Dave's head.

He struggled to his feet, shouting out loud as slivers of glass cut into him. The rain spread ragged tributaries of blood across his pale body. Keeping close to the side of the cottage he ran to the back.

An old fence extended from the side of the cottage across to the outhouses. It was rotten in parts but just about adequate to keep the pigs from wandering. Moving in a crouched position he splashed his way to the sheds. The goon who could still stand was going to have to make the same crossing to get to Dave and that wasn't going to be easy for him.

He crawled into the end shed and wedged open the door. It gave him a perfect view of the cottage.

The rain grew heavier. He began to shiver. Ten minutes went by.

"You'll hear from me mother fucker!" The voice came from the cottage. "There'll be another time, you can be sure of that!"

Minutes later he heard the car doors slam and then the engine. He stayed put for half an hour, until dusk began to fall, then he left the shed and keeping to the line of trees he circled the cottage to the road.

It was the better part of another hour before he chanced the cottage and in that time he examined it from every angle. Eventually he crawled in. He'd just finished checking the place over and was still naked when he heard another car draw to a halt. His heart sank. He pressed himself against the larder wall and held the gun to his chest.

"Dave! Dave!" Patricia's shout carried through the open door. She'd seen the smashed glass, perhaps even sniffed the cordite that still soured the heavy air. She threw on the light. As she saw him her face drained of colour.

He winked. "Hello, sweetheart," he said and dropped the gun to his side.

"Are you shot? There's so much blood."

He glanced down. He was covered in mud, head to toe, but in a number of places the mud had turned red.

"I don't think so. It's just a few cuts from the glass. But I'm hurting all over so it's a bit hard to tell." He moved forward. She stayed motionless by the door. He switched off the light and pulled her away from the doorway before peering out into the darkness.

"What happened?"

"I don't know. I think Daley's had it. He's under the trees. Go and tell your dad what you've seen, will you? He'll know what to do. Stay here till I get to the road then I'll cover you." He started toward the door.

"You're coming with me," she said sternly. "If you think I'm leaving you like this you must be joking."

He nodded, too shattered to argue. "Give me a minute," he said. "I'll put on some clothes."

"You better. Daddy's very particular about that sort of thing." She turned up her nose. "You could use a good deodorant, while you're at it."

Dave moved into the manor house. A doctor came out to check him over and sew some stitches. Once he'd gone Coddy admitted sheepishly, "There's a squealer. North or south I don't know. I'll check my end. I imagine your father will do the same in London. It must be someone pretty damned close. Apparently they had a fucking helicopter out." He glanced up to see the surprise in Patricia's eyes. He rarely swore in front of the women. "Sorry, baby, but you can't trust anybody nowadays!"

Patricia filled Dave's glass with malt. She ignored her father's.

"You were lucky," Coddy told him, obviously upset that security on his manor had been breached. "I told you to stay low, didn't I?" It was the closest Coddy could get to an apology. And it wasn't even necessary.

The attack spurred Dave's father into overdrive. He gave the Americans a foothold in the London casinos where they could clean up their dollar bills – something they'd been hankering after for years. Two days later Coddy came down to say, "I've heard from your father. He's had to make concessions to get you off the hook, but it's done. The contracts are cancelled. He wants you home." He finished. That was it. He walked past the two of them into his study and closed the two large doors behind him.

Patricia turned to him. "Before I came to the cottage that night I went to see James at the hospital. His jaw is wired up. He looks dreadful. I decided then that I didn't want to see you again. I was coming to tell you."

Dave nodded. "What changed your mind?"

"Daddy spoke to me while you were with the doctor."

Dave couldn't hide his surprise.

"He told me that James got what he deserved, that there were three of them, that he wouldn't have been pushed around either. He told me that in our family, as it is in yours, there's always going to be people who might have a go, that to be safe we need to be around people who are stronger than they are."

She carried her glass across to him and sat on his lap. She stroked his hair back and kissed him. The drink she held up threatened to spill. "I must be mad getting mixed up with you," she said lightly. "Daddy told me what you said to him. About it being my decision and not his. And if I made the right one it would take an army to stop you coming for me. Not many people stand up to my father."

"Well, is it down to you, or not?"

"Of course I make my own decisions."

"Well, I'm running out of time up here so you've got another one to make."

"I wondered about that. It would be like the marriage of two Royal Families – two manors."

"Who said anything about getting married?"

"I did," she said. "You don't think I'd live with you without a ring, do you? Daddy's very particular about things like that."

He reached forward to touch her glass with his and said, "Well then, in that case, I'm not going to argue."

She tasted the malt. "I hate this stuff," she said.

Three months later, before a vast reception with Patricia's three daughters acting as bridesmaids, Dave and Pat were married under the cold Saxon stone of St Mary's, the village church, by the Reverend Peter Ricketts, a close friend of Coddy Hughes. His prayers were for David and Patricia and for every member of the united congregation. The union was blessed.

Chapter 4

1986

The Americans had lived in England long enough to have been forgotten by the society they left behind but barely long enough to feel accepted by the new. Their absence was no longer conspicuous; Sharon's parents were dead and Tony had lost any claim to the rung of the ladder he might have been on. Cocaine had been his downfall; that and booze, and it had led to him being sent to England to work under O'Connell, even though O'Connell was old enough to drop at any moment. Tony considered it a punishment, a kind of exile. If he was remembered at all then it was as an example to young upstarts: 'You don't let personal matters jeopardize business,' and, 'If you don't control your temper you'll end up like Tony Valenti!'

In the UK, the capital of the Old World, he was still an outsider. He paid the taxes and the rates and was generous to strange charities. He attended the local church and the small community fêtes. In some ways the quieter pace of life suited him. The feeling of safety was in itself a rare pleasure. But he was still an outsider. There was an unspoken complicity between the British – the English in particular – that other races were inferior. Their ancestry had left them with a patronizing attitude, a discipline and a restraint that you had to see to believe; even the down-and-outs in Central London had more style, certainly more manners, than their New World contemporaries. Even the down-and-outs queued for Christ sakes! The English had a magnificent capacity to ignore anything remotely disagreeable – and to them foreigners were just that. The English were…insular, of an island. And the whole goddamned island could fit inside Iowa or North Carolina!

Approaching the UK at the rate of one mile every two and a half seconds, O'Connell raised his voice to counter Concorde's continuous roar.

"We've lived here five years, Tony, and you still don't know what the place is famous for?"

Tony Valenti's sharp features remained blank. "Well, it ain't their teeth, and that's for sure." He shrugged and offered, "Rhododendrons?"

O'Connell sighed and said disappointedly, "Magna Carta. Runnymede! The Magna Carta!"

"Oh yeah, remind me what that is again?"

"It's serious shit, Tony, trial by jury and all that political crap."

"Yeah, I remember now."

"Let me tell you something. We've got a lot to thank the barony for. You can't get to judges like you can get to juries." The old man chuckled. "King fucking John didn't know he was signing us into power!" He paused before adding, "The grandchildren were telling me all about it. They're doing it at school." He sighed reflectively and nodded. "They've got pages of the stuff, kings and queens, castles and knights and all that crap, and stickers you've got to stick on them. Those kids give me a lot of pleasure in my old age." He turned to the scarred leathery features of Tony Valenti. "It's a shame you never had kids, Tony. Everyone should have kids."

The old man knew only too well why Tony and Sharon had remained childless. After Sharon had been caught cheating Tony had knocked her about. The finest doctors in the world agreed that she could never have children, that the damage was too severe. O'Connell himself had tried to talk Tony into a divorce but he wouldn't have it. Valanti was besotted with his wife, children or no children. Just so long as she didn't do it again.

"It was good to see the old faces again," O'Connell said reflectively.

Tony Valenti didn't agree. He'd been acutely embarrassed by the looks of contempt that they thought were hidden from him, and the way in which his old friends had pointedly ignored him. They'd treated him like so much shit on the sidewalk and had given him the widest possible berth. He'd been hugely relieved to get back on to the plane.

O'Connell went on, "I wish I could have stayed longer. When you get to my age whenever you leave the Big Apple you wonder if you'll ever see the place again. That's something you can promise me, Tony. If I die in the rain over there..." He indicated forward. "...I want my body freighted back to Manhattan."

"You got it," Tony muttered but his thoughts were racing back to the meeting they'd attended earlier in the day.

As it was with the majority of families, relationships were occasionally strained. In this respect the Americans and their relatives in Sicily and Naples and Calabresia were no different. And as with most families the patriarchs – in this case they were out of the Cosa Nostra and Camorra – showed their issue tolerance and understanding. In return they expected loyalty and respect. They received both in large measure.

The Europeans had reached an agreement with the Colombian cocaine cartels by threatening to kill all their couriers. When the body count reached double figures, El Papa had agreed to talk. The link gave the Mafia exclusive rights to the two billion annual trade and their American relatives were given the job of handling it. With the increased supplies and vast fortunes tied up it was imperative that new markets were found. Mainland Europe was the obvious target, especially with the opening up of the Common Market frontiers already on the drawing board. Eventually their attention turned to the UK.

The Americans were already established in England. They'd been drawn like flies to horse shit by the wide-open gambling laws. They owned houses on the banks of the river at Runnymede. Their business in the UK still centred on gaming and its associated money laundering that cleaned enormous amounts of US and Canadian dollars. Heading up the UK end was O'Connell and he was summoned to meet the heads of the families in New York. He took Tony Valenti along for the ride, and to carry his bag.

Concluding his report to the leaders, O'Connell had said, "Under a thousand kilos were seized last year, mostly by Customs, mostly from the assholes on the Continent. They're not even scraping the surface. The imports are basically split into four: through Liverpool, mostly from the Crescent, and that's handled by a local gang, the Scousers, run by Vic Hannington; through the main airports, Heathrow and Gatwick, by John Bracey. A guy named Stafford Carr runs Hull. That's another port on the other side to Liverpool. He imports through Holland, and then the freelance, mostly dropped off the top of Scotland around the islands and then picked up by the trawlers. That's the import picture as near as you'll get. As far as distribution is concerned the place is split between southern England run by the Chinese, and Mick McGovern who runs Scotland. Between the two is a buffer zone controlled by various smaller gangs. The Chinks deal under the protection of the main London gang, the Smiths. There's an agreement between them that goes way back. My feeling is that in ten years or so, when the heavies move out of Hong Kong, the Chinks will want to expand. That's the picture but it isn't the whole story. Things are pretty unstable over there at the moment. Mick McGovern who runs Scotland is keen to expand southward. One of the guys he wants to move in on, Coddy Hughes, is related to the Smiths. His daughter married the eldest son. The Scousers from Liverpool are making noises and threatening to join McGovern. The whole situation is likely to blow, maybe turn into a full-scale war. If it does then someone is going to have to pick up the pieces."

From the shadows a voice of authority spoke quietly.

"The Smith's organization is best suited for what we've got in mind: a nationwide distribution. We need to pressure them into ending their agreement with the Chinese. Stafford Carr can be closed down easily. His shipments from Holland will be cut immediately. The Liverpool end is more difficult. We'll work on it. It might be that Vic Hannington takes a long vacation. For the moment we'll live with the airports and Bracey. At the end of the day he'll fall in line. If we open up negotiations with McGovern and make the Smiths aware of it, then they'll come around to our way of thinking. Is that a problem?"

"No problem," O'Connell said.

"What about you, Tony? I know it's a long time ago but these things don't go away."

Tony Valenti nodded sullenly and said, "I had a run-in with the Smith's eldest son. It was ten years ago. You all know what happened. He screwed about with my wife. I don't hold any grievances. Business is business. I put my wife in the picture and she ain't likely to do it again!"

Around the table the men nodded their approval.

"Business is business," Valenti repeated. "And if you consider that the Smiths are good for us then that's good enough for me." He lied, of course, but he was totally convincing.

"That's a wrap then," the leader said softly. "Let's get to work."

Roaring towards Heathrow at over twice the speed of sound, Tony Valenti thought about the meeting. His expression didn't alter as he considered the irony that after all this time his family wanted to embrace the people he hated more than anything in the world. And yet behind the insult lay a flicker of hope. It was just possible that in the ensuing struggle for control of the UK underworld – World War Three, Goddamnit – he would find his chance for retribution.

He glanced at the old man beside him.

"What is it?" O'Connell growled sleepily.

"Nothing," Valenti murmured, "nothing at all."

Chapter 5

Some three hundred and fifty miles north of Heathrow where the Americans had landed a fortnight before, men waited at another airport. They wandered down queues made ragged by a jumble of luggage to scrutinize the features of unsuspecting men, yet in their search they remained anonymous, hardly noticeable. Anonymity was the mark of their profession. They heard the roar of planes dropping from the low bank of dense cloud and they heard the distorted voices heavy with Glaswegian accent resounding from the speakers, unclear in the vast ringing hall. The various sounds of engines and vehicles and nervous chatter did not distract them.

Since mid-morning they had waited. They'd watched the queues shorten and lengthen, seen the small family dramas played out, seen a man argue with his wife, seen a dozen children thumped for getting in the way, seen a lost child consoled by a couple of WPCs, seen porters making their tips and plastic cups fill every available surface, and now, under the stark fluorescent strip they watched the cleaners mopping between the groups of night-time travellers, the holiday-makers doing it on the cheap. Bedraggled, fatigued people dossed down in makeshift beds, small children lay limply in the sagging arms of their parents or lolled in their pushchairs and eyes became sore and vacant and less excited. The planes kept arriving and departing, the automatic board kept flicking and the public-address voice kept ringing.

Men waited and watched, drank coffee out of plastic cups and smoked endless cigarettes. Eventually they made a telephone call. They heard that he hadn't been found in any of the stations or depots or car-hire firms and they guessed that he'd found a lift south. All was not lost, however, for men were now watching the motorway and waiting at service stations as far south as the Midlands.

All morning a great mass of cloud had moved in off the Atlantic, drawing a darker colour across the land and, by mid-afternoon, the ceiling was low and dense, bringing forward the dusk. At first the rain was heavy, blurring the dark shadows and the arcs of light thrown from the street lamps; now it was gentle and constant, filtering into the spongy earth.

The weather suited Tommy Smith; no one was going to notice a man with his lapels pulled up to hide his face. People became anonymous in wet weather, heads down, collars up, hugging shop doorways for shelter, even the colour of clothes and hair darkened to a likeness by saturation. His problem was the scarcity of other faces. Now that the pubs and clubs were closing the weather was forcing the stragglers indoors. It wouldn't be long before he was a lonely figure on the road, easily seen and just as easily picked up. The police stopping him would be bad enough for Mick's influence had reached the northern cities, but if Mick's people got to him first then he was finished. His options were disappearing. In the next half hour or so he had to get a lift or he had to steal a car. And stealing a car to drive the length of the country all in one go was going to be pretty chancy even on such a night.

Tommy glanced again at his watch. The articulated lorry that had roared down the M6 cutting through the surface water had dropped him ten minutes earlier. Since then he'd smoked two cigarettes while studying the bright entrance of a service station from between the comparative shelter of two tightly parked container lorries. Beyond the lorry park where the two giants stood in isolation, bathed in a veil of rain and darkness so that only their massive silhouettes were visible, a row of cars were parked neatly in the white painted rectangles, shiny skins glinting in reflected light as the water droplets collected together and zigzagged in crazy patterns across them. Four powerful bikes decked in superfluous chrome, angled on their parking rests, were parked haphazardly next to the cars and immediately outside the entrance, parked in the no-parking area, an empty motorway patrol car stood with its doors unlocked.

The wind increased and swept water from the top of the containers. For a few moments Tommy was pelted with heavy drops and he was conscious of the rain seeping through to his shirt. He started from the darkness between the massive trucks just as the overnight coach from Glasgow pulled in, and he was glad to mix with the stream of passengers as they filed from the coach, stepping between the deeper pools of spitting water, to the welcome of the unflattering lights of the cafeteria.

Tommy moved along a ragged queue towards a cluttered stainless steel counter. In front of him a line of people shuffled forward to order their teas and coffees, stretching their stiff and weary bodies. The queues to the toilets grew around the edge of the room; people danced from one foot to the other. He reached the counter.

"An all-night breakfast please, and coffee."

A woman serving half smiled, perhaps at his accent: London, born and bred. She said, "It's an all-day breakfast, Love, but we serve it all night as well. Can you wait a minute?" She nodded toward the queue from the coach. "I'll do your coffee."

She was tasty, something to take the mind off the journey and the depression outside. Her spotless wraparound parted occasionally hinting that she wore no skirt beneath. There was a promise there, one that would never be kept.

He nodded silently and took his drink to a stand-up counter. The tables were full.

The queues for the toilets dwindled and those people who needed to use them again lined up again, hoping to make it before the coach driver got to his feet. In a few minutes more the vast room had all but emptied. Chairs blocked the gangways between tables full of empty crisp packets and brimming ashtrays and spills of tea and coffee. A couple of youngsters appeared and began to clear away. Coach parties: twenty quid spent between them and the place left looking like the Liverpool football supporters had held a stag night.

Tommy noticed two uniformed policemen as they moved from their corner table. For just an instant one of them looked his way and he felt certain that he'd been recognized. As their eyes locked the policeman looked away and called to the woman behind the counter, "See you, Liz." She waved an acknowledgement at the swinging door. Tommy watched the policemen run through the rain to their car. In a moment a plume of smoke phut-phutted from the exhaust and the headlamps produced two explosions of light in the dark. The rain fizzed in the beams.

On the speakers the Bangles faded out and the Pet Shop Boys took over.

Tommy turned back from the window to check who was left in the cafeteria: half-a-dozen leather-clad bikers, three couples, one with a sleeping baby, an old man, two lorry drivers and a skinny girl who looked like she was on the game.

The waitress weaved toward him carrying his breakfast. She wiped over the surface of a table and laid down the plate.

"OK," she asked as he sat down.

"Looks good," he said quietly.

She paused by his table and unconsciously patted the back of her hair that was neatly clipped under a white cap. Her breasts rose against her smock. He smiled at her, almost knowingly, and she hesitated. For a moment she wondered if the term Cockney came from the word cocky.

"Cheeky sod," she said, "Sauce?"

"No, this is fine."

"That's good. You've got enough of that already."

He watched her make her way back to the counter. She'd coloured slightly, conscious that his eyes were on her. He concentrated on his breakfast. He hadn't eaten anything for over twelve hours. Lunchtime seemed a lifetime ago.

A tall young man who'd arrived on his own picked up his cup and turned to find a table. He chose one close to Tommy away from the Hell's Angels, and carefully set down his drink before pulling back a chair and easing into it.

He was gaunt and pale and his eyes were sunken under a mop of limp, brown hair. Tommy noticed the frayed cuffs and the scuffed and holed shoes. He saw the cup lifting unsteadily and the man's glazed eyes on the fried bread that Tommy had left at the side of his plate.

"You finished with that?"

Tommy's blue eyes narrowed before losing their steel.

"You want it?"

He nodded, "If it's all the same to you. I ain't eaten a thing since breakfast, kind of shaky."

"It's bad for you. Full of cholesterol."

"So's starving." He wiped egg yoke and grease from the plate. "But people still starve." He wiped his lips on his sleeve and gulped at his tea.

"Saw you drive in. It's a bad night for travelling."

"I ain't doing it for pleasure."

"Going south?"

"No choice."

"Birmingham?"

"Further, maybe, if the petrol holds out."

"Out of dough?"

The man pulled a face. "That's right, out of luck, out of fags, and out of dough."

"Times are hard." Tommy tossed over a cigarette and stretched across to light it. The thin man drew smoke deeply and coughed.

"Ta," he said and sniffed. "You're from the south, right, London, right?"

"Maybe."

"That's where I'm going, if the petrol'll get me there."

"Car might not make it. What is it, seventy, seventy-one?"

"Two point three, seventy-three, goes like a pissing bomb. Trouble is she eats the juice."

"You still hungry?"

"No, I'm all right now." He drew on the cigarette again and coughed again.

"Could you use some dough?"

"What's your game?"

"I'm looking for a lift. I'll pay you."

53

The man frowned. "What, you break down or something?"

"Yeah, something like that."

"Well, what about the petrol?"

"I'll get that."

"That'll do me then, no questions asked."

"There's something else."

The thin man scratched his forehead with dirty nails, waiting for the catch.

"People are looking for me. They're not the best. And I might have been recognised in here. I wouldn't want you to get hurt."

"Cops?"

"No, just competition, but it could turn nasty. If you went to your car, made to pull out then stop at the entrance, I'll hop in and off we go. It's got to be worth a ton if you get us to London."

The man frowned, "One hundred pound?"

Tommy remained expressionless. He lit another cigarette.

"A hundred quid," the other repeated, this time as a statement. "I don't need trouble but I can't turn that away. All right, I'll get you there." He looked up suspiciously. "Half now, so I know you ain't going to leg it. What's your name, anyway?"

"Tommy Smith."

"The footballer," he nodded, "Liverpool, right?"

"Leave it out. I'm not that bleedin' old!"

"Give us another fag then, and tell me what to do."

"How much petrol have you got in the tank?"

"About two and a half gallons, maybe three."

"Stone the crows! That won't get us half way to Brum never mind the Smoke." He reached for his wallet. "Here, here's a score. Fill her up. What about oil and water?"

"She's all right. I checked her this morning."

"OK. You know what to do?"

The other nodded. "Right, my name's Roy Alexander."

"I'll buy some more fags and a couple of rolls for you. When I see you outside the door I'll make a move."

He counted out five tens and added them to the twenty.

"I'll give you the rest when we reach the Smoke."

"Right," Roy said. He took the money and stood up. "Be ready then," he said excitedly. He reached the door before he stopped and called back, "Cheese and tomato."

The others in the room looked his way.

"The rolls," he grinned, "make them cheese and tomato."

"Right," Tommy nodded anxiously. He could have done without the advertising. He watched the car splutter into life and the wipers arcing across the glistening windshield. The headlamps, one dimmed, glared as the car moved off toward the garage. Tommy moved to the counter and paid for his meal. He bought the rolls and cigarettes and stuffed them into his leather pocket. He left the shrapnel out of a tenner on the counter.

"Come again," Liz said and gave him a smile she usually reserved for her drivers.

"I'd like to," he said and returned the knowing glance that meant nothing at all.

"Cheeky sod," she said.

Chapter 6

Starting at Carlisle the M6 cut a deep concrete groove through the Lake District and Forest of Bowland and snaked its way through the counties of Cumbria, Lancashire and Cheshire, slicing through the buffer zone of the divide and, on it, the dipped headlamps flashed in both directions boring through the incessant wall of rain. Bonnets and exhausts steamed, engines rattled and tyres whined as they sent up curtains of spray.

Roy Alexander was a good driver, alert, steady and fast. He unwrapped one of the rolls from its cellophane cover while his other hand remained firmly on the wheel. He kept to a steady sixty and cruised twenty yards behind a BOC tanker so that the spray fell before he was on it. The windshield-wipers worked overtime against the flood. Tomato juice full of seed trickled down his chin and he wiped it on his sleeve.

"Don't know if anyone's following or not," he said with his mouth full. He studied the flashing lights in the mirror.

"Just concentrate on the road," Tommy muttered.

"Been up here long?"

"Just a couple of days."

"Come by train then, eh?"

"No, I motored up on Sunday. I had to leave it." The answer came with the flare of a cigarette lighter. "You want one of these?"

Roy finished his roll and took the cigarette. He kept his eyes on the road as he bent to receive a light.

"Accident or busted down?"

"Neither."

Roy's disappointment was obvious even in the dark. After a moment he said, "Well, it's none of my business. If you don't want to talk about it, fair enough. Should know what we're up against, though. If we're being followed, I should know about it, that's all."

Tommy sighed and relented, "My old man's got business interests up north. I've been up there to sort things. He got ill earlier in the week and yesterday they got wind of it, that he was rushed into hospital. With him out of action they're trying to opt out of the deal."

"Business troubles! When you said about getting hurt I thought you meant like, really hurt."

Tommy chuckled but there was little humour about it. He said, "These Scottish bleeders have been known to cut up rough. They take their business seriously."

"What kind of business you in?"

"Entertainments mostly, consumer goods and entertainment."

"Luxuries! Ain't much call for luxuries up this way, not any more. That's why I'm going south. Got to. No choice."

"How long have you been out of work?"

"Three years now. Got a wife and kids, two kids. Never thought anyone would go hungry in this country. Didn't think they allowed it. This month we've been hungry. The kids are starting to get ill 'cos of it. They get school meals on the social but they're cutting them back and, anyway, they don't help during the school hols. I've already cut everything out till there ain't no more to cut. And you have to choose between hot water and food. What we had before and what we had to sell kept us going along with the handouts. But it's been over a year and what we had before is all gone now so I got nothing else to sell. And things are wearing out, all together it seems. I know you don't have to have a washing machine or a fridge, but Christ, things ain't geared up to not having them. Not today. Now the heating in the house is buggered and I need a new tank. The bastards ain't going to give me one either. They say the insurance should cover it and the insurance people say it don't. Who the hell do you fight? To be honest with you, I'm all out of fight."

"You could sell up."

"You're joking, right? There's millions in the same boat as me. Don't tell me you believe these bleeding figures on *out of work?* They talked us into buying, right? And then they took away our jobs."

"Never given it much thought. Never did believe anything the politicians said."

"House prices have hit rock bottom up here. If I sold out now I'd owe more on it than I'd get. And where the hell am I going to put the family? Council don't want to know. They got people camping on their doorsteps. Not only that, they'd have the bleeding kids off you soon as look at you. We've got no rights today, nothing. The right to starve, that's all. I've got to get a job. That's why I'm travelling. There's work down south. Anyway, you've got your own problems. Your old man's in hospital."

He sensed Tommy's nod.

"Hope it's not serious. I remember losing my old man about five years ago. Heart attack. Went over in the middle of Sainsbury's. We all said it was the bloody cost of food that caused it, the bloody government taking us into the Common Market. What a bleeding con job that was. Never went shopping, my old man. Mum always did all that. But she was a bugger. Moaned and groaned after him non-stop to give her more housekeeping, said he hadn't got a clue how much she spent on the weekly shop. So this day, Saturday it was, 'cos he was going on from there to see Carlisle play Oldham, she went off to buy some cheese – he liked his old cheese on toast in an evening – and left him looking at the meat counter. When she came back there was a crowd there and he was on the floor. Went over just like that. One minute himself, the next gone. I'm glad he ain't alive today to see us like this, though. He would have gone spare thinking of my girl going out with great holes in her shoes. I think that would have killed him anyway!"

The next few minutes were coated in silence. The rain was easing a little and through it the orange glow of village streetlights cut through the darkness.

"People in work ain't got a clue how we're living. That's the trouble. The highlight of the week is the *TV Times* coming out on a Wednesday. Our TV's busted now and I think that's what broke the back of it. My old girl's been pretty good. She's been cleaning and taking in washing and she ain't moaned but when that TV busted she just sat there and cried. She put up with the shit 'cos I can't afford the decorating, and she put up with the hand-me-downs and not going no place but when that screen went dead she folded up. It was then I decided to get on my bike. I left her with a few quid, enough for a week, put a tenner in the tank and took off. I'll send this hundred quid to her all right, and that'll cheer her up. By Christ it will! I'll send it first post tomorrow. I'd like to see her face, mind. Got a good mind to drop you off then turn around and hand it to her personally, so I can see her."

"Put it in the post, my son. You'll be all right."

Roy felt warmed by the conversation, lifted from his isolation. "I hope you're right, mister, 'cos I'm running out of ideas and I never had many to start with."

The road ahead began its sweep between the cities of Manchester and Liverpool. The tanker blinked and moved across to the slip road and Roy edged the Victor slowly up to the back of a container lorry. Spray splattered the windshield, fanning off the giant square of rippling canvas in front. He eased back slightly and considered overtaking, instinctively glancing in his mirror. Two pools of light, full beam, exploded in the glass and slid to the right as the car behind accelerated to overtake. Roy pulled back into his own lane and glanced sideways as the dark sinister shape of a Jaguar slipped by. From the passenger seat a blurred face turned their way.

Roy grunted, "That him?"

"Could be. Something's caught his eye, or maybe he just fancies you."

Roy tightened his grip on the wheel and eased into the fast lane again and watched the tail-lights of the Jaguar growing dimmer until they vanished into the curtain of rain. He slipped back behind the shelter of the lorry.

"Maybe we're just getting paranoid."

Tommy wasn't so sure. He sat forward, suddenly alert. He muttered, "It was better to have him behind. While he's up front he could lay something on."

"Glad I'm not in the entertainment business," Roy said. Without understanding it he sensed the danger. "There's another exit coming up. Shall I take it?"

"No. If we tuck up behind him he'll have less chance."

"They cut up rough in the boardrooms then?"

Tommy grinned.

"Course, I always knew there was no difference between the big businessman and the criminal. Come to think of it, the politicians too. That much stands to reason. They're the criminals because they have the power to do something about it and they don't. But what can you do? When the kids are starving you got to do something, right? Don't let the bastards get you down, right? But there are too many bastards in this country now; everyone's looking after number one. How do you fight that?"

"Listen," Tommy began quietly. "Forget the propaganda; virtue never was a step up to heaven's door and suffering in silence never did anyone any good." More forcefully he went on, "I'll tell you how you do it, my son. You make a noise and you keep making it till someone listens. It's the only thing anyone understands. My kids aren't starving. I haven't got any kids. But if I did and they were because some official bastard wanted it that way, then I'd climb over their counters and tear their heads off!"

"I believe you. But some of us ain't strong enough to do that."

"When you get mad enough you'll do it."

"Maybe you're right, maybe not."

"Listen, there's trouble all over. There's always going to be someone who wants your share and there's only one thing to do. You fight back. You hurt the bastard so much that he'll never come back again. You make him realize that if he even thinks about upsetting you he's never going to look the same again. And if you can make him really believe that, you'd be surprised at how accommodating he suddenly gets."

"Does that include the police?"

"The filth? Yeah, kozzers included, even the Queen of England if she comes round to threaten my family. I don't condone anyone getting hurt that doesn't deserve it. But some people are born different, they want to make trouble, they want what's yours."

"I hear it but I don't like it. I ain't into violence and I don't want my kids to be. I'd sooner walk away from trouble. There's got to be some other way."

"Let me know when you find it."

The night grew darker and the air in the car became hot and dry. Altrincham, Crewe, Stoke, Stafford, came and went, the great sprawling metropolis of the Midlands, Birmingham, was negotiated and that was the M6. They skirted Coventry and Rugby and joined the M1 and the new signs flashed Northampton and London.

The small hours crept by, the unreal time when noises seemed duller and moves made in slow motion. The traffic had dwindled and most of it consisted of lorries and coaches. The speed limits became irrelevant and plumes of spray hung behind the roaring wheels. Out of the eastern sky a pale ghost of iron-grey cloud touched the darkness.

"Maybe he's packed it in," Roy said as he fought for concentration and accelerated past another flapping canvas. His passenger stirred. The farther south they had come the safer Tommy felt. He'd considered the possibilities a dozen times.

If Mad Mick had been going to hit them then he would do so on the M6 and when that hadn't happened it would be before Northampton, and then Newport Pagnall, and now it had to be before Luton. Even Mad Mick wouldn't venture to the steps of London. That meant that at some stage in the next few minutes the move would be made. He lit two cigarettes and passed one over. Roy sensed the sudden alertness in his passenger and gripped the wheel tighter. His body coiled slightly, expectantly.

"OK, I'm ready!"

Tommy nodded.

They passed the slips to Bedford and then Dunstable, examining every vehicle they overtook. The sky was fingered with grey and without them realizing it the surroundings had picked up a monotone form. The pale light intensified and things found their drab colour. The low cloud stretched in every direction. Luton went by and for the first time in over twelve hours, since the moment he had watched the news on the television in his hotel bedroom, Tommy allowed himself a moment's relaxation. For some reason Mad Mick had called off his men. The exits for St Albans and Watford were quiet.

"I'd like to get to see the studios," Roy said. "See them making the films, eh? Maybe get some work there. That would be something." He'd seen the Elstree sign. He glanced at Tommy and winked. "We made it. You're home. Told you she'd make it. Goes like a pissing rocket, don't she?" He rubbed his neck and swallowed sorely. "I could murder a cuppa."

"You're right, my son. You've done well. Take the next slip. There's a place we can get a drink and a brush-up just off Apex."

"I never had any doubt that she'd make it. She might rattle a bit, some of the body falls off sometimes, but she's a fighter. She'll give you everything she's got. She's one of the greatest cars ever made." A large sign approached indicating Mill Hill and Edgware. Roy sat up straighter. "I get quiet excited at seeing London, like a kid."

"You've been before?"

"Came down for a weekend when I was twelve. We came by coach. Saw the Palace and the Planetarium."

Tommy grunted his disapproval. "They say the world's getting smaller but for some people it isn't. You can fly to New York in the time it's taken to drive from Manchester and you've never even seen the Smoke."

"Did the Tower, saw the jewels."

"Well, that's all right then." Tommy shook his head. "I mean, even I haven't seen the jewels!"

Something hit the windshield. Crystals of glass sprayed in with a sudden rush of cold air and water. The remaining screen milked in a crazy jigsaw and then broke into a thousand pieces that thudded into the car. Wind and rain lashed in and almost lifted the car. Instinctively Roy's foot was on the brake; the wheels screamed, the car slewed sideways and moved inexorably toward the cavernous underside and monstrous wheels of a huge articulated lorry. The nearside rear window shattered and Roy heard something crashing about his head. He watched horrified as the bonnet ripped open and sparks flew towards him. A burning sensation swept down his side and his gasp for breath left him doubled in agony. His left arm, limp and useless, dropped from the wheel, and the car lurched closer to the truck. The rear end touched and the kickback sent the Victor spinning. It turned full circle behind the lorry and rumbled and tore at the metal barrier dividing north and south. Lorries and coaches swerved to miss them, sparks flew and tyres screeched. Tommy released his belt and grabbed hold of the wheel. He screamed above the roar of noise.

"Get her over! Don't stop!"

Roy understood and ran the car on to the hard shoulder. He kept his head low to keep the rain from blinding him.

"Keep her going," Tommy shouted. "There's a turn about a hundred yards ahead."

The Victor didn't make it. The rear wheel buckled and they ran on the rim. The shaking bonnet bent upward at a crazy angle and threatened to fly off altogether. They ground to a halt twenty yards short of the slip road. Vehicles thudded past.

"We've got to get out of here," Tommy shouted. "Are you all right?" He saw the red stain spreading out on Roy's shirt and realised it was a stupid question.

"I don't know. I'm shaking like a leaf. I think I'm going to throw up."

"Save it till later. That wasn't a stone that hit us back there. We've got to leg it."

He opened the door, stepped out on to the wet surface and peered up the road between the oncoming vehicles with their pale orange headlamps bearing down, at the deep ridges cut into the barrier. He ran around the front of the car and caught hold of Roy as he staggered from his seat. A streak of blood trickled from Roy's hairline and thinned with the rain to run quickly down the side of his face. Tommy pulled Roy's jacket together and buttoned it over the deep red flood at his waist.

"I can't stand up. I can't!" Roy's face contorted and his legs buckled. Tommy helped him back to the seat. Roy gasped again and let out a long groan.

"Roy, I've got to go. The filth will be here any second. I'll look you up. You haven't seen me. You haven't seen a thing, understand?"

Roy looked up helplessly. He trembled. His eyes began to slip.

"I'll make it up to you. I'll find you and you'll be all right."

In the distance a siren wailed above the general clatter of traffic, and blue light flashed through the spray.

Tommy glanced down again and saw that unconsciousness had relaxed Roy's features. He pulled up his coat collar and began to run, splashing through the dancing puddles, across the oil stains that had created their own palettes, then he was turning his back on the rush of traffic and he was racing along the darker surface of the slip road toward a built-up area where cars were parked end to end on either side, where milk floats clinked and postmen wandered.

He found the narrow alley he was looking for and walked between the walls of brick and concrete. He sidestepped an overflowing gutter and fiddled with the rusty latch on a battered green gate. Beyond, across a tiny square of cracked concrete, he recognized a red back door and banged it until his fist hurt. He smacked on the mottled glass until lights were switched on and the sound of muffled voices came from within. Bolts were thrown back and the door opened and he looked into the astonished face of a heavy set man dressed in blue-striped pyjama bottoms and a white string vest who said, "Jesus!"

The man reached out quickly and helped Tommy into the kitchen. The door slammed shut. The wind increased in strength and drew more rain from the low cloud and sent it forcefully up the alley, pelting and rattling the green gate, lifting it over the fencing in a curved spray to collect and run down the glass of the back door, collecting the light from within as it zigzagged its way southward.

Chapter 7

The post-war three-bedroom terrace was built to a similar format across
the length of the country. The back door led to the kitchen that in turn
led to the hallway and the stairs to the bathroom and bedrooms. When
Tommy awoke it was in the curtained back bedroom. His clothes were
piled neatly on a single chair and his watch faced him from a small MFI
bedside locker. It was ten o'clock. He could hear the hum of Simply
Red on Radio One and the playful chattering of sparrows on the outside
guttering. He swept back the duvet and examined a dark bruising that
began on his ribs and swept down beneath the elastic of his shorts. He
left open the bathroom door while he used the pan and sluiced his head
in a basin of cold water. He borrowed one of three toothbrushes upended
in a plastic beaker and cleaned his teeth then considered using the razor
but decided against it. There were some things you didn't borrow.
Not today in the age of AIDS and Aquarius. He walked back into the
bedroom and sat on the bed while he fastened his watch. Shadow filled
the doorway and he glanced up. A woman stood framed in the light
from the landing, arms folded, shoulder leant against the doorframe, the
questions on her face wanting some answers.

"You've been on the radio. Least, I'm guessing it was you. A shoot-
out on the M1, some guy full of holes, coppers all over the shop."

"Don't know what you're on about, girl."

"You bleedin' well do!"

She was in her mid-twenties, darkly tanned, half-Middle-Eastern with large black eyes and shiny-cropped hair. There was a touch of rouge on her cheeks. Or was it anger?

"Where's Pete?"

"He's gone to bleedin' work, where do you think?"

It was anger, he decided.

"And the boy?"

"Round next door. I made out I wasn't feeling well. And that wasn't a lie, seeing you here!" She moved into the room and drew back a pair of thin blue curtains. "I'll go and make a drink. I want you out of here by lunchtime." He watched her walk back across the room and noticed the trim figure working beneath her pencil-line black skirt. Suddenly she stopped and turned and looked back from the landing through the open door.

"Don't you get any ideas, Tommy Smith! You're getting coffee and naff all else!"

Tommy raised his hands in mock surrender and grinned. He lay back on the bed and tried to recall what had happened. He remembered the strong arms of Peter Hough helping him to the couch and then a phone call, but that was all.

A few moments later she returned with a mug of sweet coffee. He sipped it and watched her move back to the window to gaze out at the wet tiled rooftops and the chimney-stacks throwing up white strands of smoke from the smokeless fuel.

Against the light her blouse became transparent and through it he could see the curve of her breast.

"Who did he phone last night?"

"Last night? It wasn't bleedin' last night. It was five o'clock this morning. He was going to call your brother but he couldn't get through. I don't know what the neighbours are going to think with you banging on the door at that time."

"Sod the neighbours. Come and sit over here."

"Piss off Tommy," she said and continued to gaze from the window.

"That's nice."

She half turned toward him and her eyes narrowed fractionally. "You're trouble, Tommy. You always were. You're like a magnet and bother is drawn to you. You can handle it most of the time, but other people can't and they get hurt. Now you might care or you might not care about other people but it makes no difference 'cos they still get hurt whether you do or not. Pete wanted to stay and help and get involved like a few years ago but I don't want you near him. That's why he's gone to work. And when he comes home tonight he won't even ask what happened, 'cos nothing happened. You were never here." She hesitated and drew a deep breath. "Do you understand what I'm saying, Tommy? The past is gone. It never happened. You shouldn't have come. I wish you hadn't. Pete's trying to make a go of it, and he's trying hard for the sake of the kid. He ain't got your brains and if he follows you he'll end up inside again. That's all I've got to say to you, Tommy Smith. Next time you get hurt and you walk past this house, I want you to keep walking. For you and your family it doesn't exist!"

He nodded and gulped at his coffee. His eyes had dulled at the rebuke. He leant across to the chair and fished in his jacket pocket for his cigarettes. He lit one and settled back and watched a jet of smoke stream up to the artex ceiling. She noticed the sudden flicker of his eyes, the sudden steely dullness that came down like an inner lid as the sparkle went out, and she shrank back immediately. Her recoil could not have been more noticeable had she stepped on something evil and repulsive. The fear drained her face of colour and her hand half hid her features as she pinched her quivering lower lip. She knew that she'd overstepped the mark. One word from him and she'd be back on the meat rack at King's Cross. One word from him and her efforts over the past few years would count for nothing, her plans for the family totally irrelevant. She owed Tommy and his family and she knew that the debt could never be repaid. You gave them whatever they asked for; offer them anything less and you offended them. They were not the sort of people to take for granted or threaten or voice an opinion about and now, after all this time, she'd allowed her temper to get the better of her self-preservation. The thought and her fear showed on her face.

Tommy turned his head on the pillow and looked at her, still mildly embarrassed.

"I didn't mean all that, Tommy," she said sheepishly, turning toward him. She looked at the floor, refusing to meet his gaze, knowing the cruelty she would find there.

"Leave it out, girl. You meant it all right. Forget it."

She glanced up, surprised.

"You won't tell Pete what I said?"

He smiled. "Not a word."

She nodded briefly while the relief softened her features.

"Well, shall I get in with you?"

"No, you do what you want to do."

"I want to, Tommy, but if I got the choice then I won't."

He grinned. "Once upon a time you were a slag, you know that? Now you're a lady. If you and the kid ever need for anything, just let me know."

"Is Pete included?"

"Can't be, can he? He left the firm. Once you leave, if you're allowed to, then you lose all fringe benefits."

"I left."

"No you didn't. You're just on a temporary leave of absence. Call it extended maternity leave."

She looked at him thoughtfully, considering the implications, and they didn't worry her.

"You're not like the others."

"A lot of people say that. You can't blame me for what other people think."

"I don't want the kid hurt, that's all. I want everything for him."

"Is he Pete's?"

A moment's hesitation destroyed the possibility of a lie. "He looks like your older brother but Pete thinks he's the spitting image of his dad."

"We might as well go along with that then."

"I think so," she said softly.

He finished his cigarette and reached for his clothes.

"It's time I was on my way."

"I hope you old man's all right."

"It's got around then?"

"It's been in the paper. An emergency operation, it said. They called him a property tycoon with links to the underworld."

"Stone the crows! It sounds like we've been advertising."

"Does it mean a lot of trouble?"

"We could do without it." He shrugged and added, "A bit of bother, that's all."

She walked across to him and straightened his collar and looked into his bloodshot eyes. She said quietly, "If it had been you I wouldn't have left."

"If it had been me I wouldn't have let you."

She followed him from the room, across the landing and down the stairs.

"I want to make a quick call," he said.

She pointed into the living room.

He found a small neatly furnished room: a leather three-piece, a wall unit housing a shelf of books, another of photographs of a young child, a drinks unit, a television and video, a stacked music centre, pale grey wall-to-wall and Dralon curtains over uPVC double glazing, the smell of lemon-scented polish and a gas fire. It was a hideaway and he felt like a trespasser. He punched six digits into the phone and listened to three rings before he heard a familiar voice. While he spoke he looked across at the girl and although his thoughts were on the call his eyes lingered on every curve.

"Dave? It's me. I'm home. Be about thirty minutes. How is he?"

For a few seconds he listened and then he replaced the handset.

She asked, "Is he all right?"

He shrugged. "They're seeing the consultant later."

She nodded. At the door he brushed her painted lips. They were surprisingly cold. It was a platonic kiss that reminded him of a thousand broken promises.

"Bye, Denise," he said, still tasting her, and moved into the yard. She'd closed the back door before he'd even stepped across the puddles to the gate.

The day was brighter. The rain had stopped and the cloud had become feathery and broken. He stepped into the alley and closed the

69

gate behind him, conscious of the dripping surroundings, the overflow snout still trickling and the ground beneath washed clean and glistening. The air was chilled and fresh and tinged with the smell of wet grass and the fumes of the city. He was home. The thought added a spring to his youthful step.

To the left of the darkened alley entrance a navy-blue Lada stood idling on freshly painted, double yellow lines. It idled on the fast side and it rattled as Ladas do, phut-phutting gently from its nervous exhaust. Its square shape reminded passers-by of a fifties style. The driver they saw, with his collar pulled up, the roll-up suspended from his lips, his face a mask of concentration, was instantly forgettable, nondescript, and the passenger in the back seat was hardly noticeable either, perhaps because anonymity was his trademark and, as with the driver, a necessary part of his profession.

Chapter 8

Theca, the Star of the Veldt, glanced up expectantly as her elder brother walked in from the entrance hall. Her features were classically English, her pale skin emphasized by her dark hair. Even though she was tired and drawn, her loveliness was still evident.

"It was Tommy," he said quietly and saw the relief in her brown-flecked eyes.

Every time the telephone rang it was a heart-stopping moment. The door was purposefully closed on it, so that the conversation was private. When the door opened again the same troubled questions were written in the strained eyes.

"He's back. He'll be here in half-an-hour."

At Theca's side at the dining table his mother said, "Thank God for that, at least." She lifted her china cup from its saucer and fought to control its shake. Her eyes were raw and beneath them the darkness spread out like deep bruises. "Where is he?"

"Over in Mill Hill. He's taking a cab."

"What's he doing over there?" Worry made her voice quiver. She shook her head. "Did he sound upset?"

Dave said gently, "I said we'd explain everything when he got here." He was a big man of thirty-nine, balding prematurely, fighting a weight problem, but losing. His eyes, brown and large, were dulled and sore through lack of sleep. As he sat down heavily at the table he glanced across at his sister as if to share some secret message. Theca saw it and looked at her mother. Sally was stunned like the rest of them, her face fraught and pale. In the last two days she seemed to have aged ten years. She was too wise not to appreciate what was going on – the knowing glances, the lowered voices and the door closing on the telephone calls – but she was too tired to argue.

She finished her tea and moved from the table.

"I'll go and get ready. When Tommy comes in I'll make some lunch and then we'll go. What time is it now?"

"It's ten to twelve. We've still got two hours!" Theca shrugged, irritated by her mother's fussing.

Sally turned to her son. "David, I want to call in at the shops on the way. I need some things for your father."

"Can't you send someone? Where's Lucia?"

"She's gone home for the holidays."

Dave shook his head at his own forgetfulness. Lucia always took her holidays to coincide with those of the family. Eventually he said, "I've got people sitting outside doing nothing."

"No, that won't do at all."

"I'll go and get the shopping now," Theca said, jumping at the opportunity to get away for a while. "Write a list." She turned to Dave. "When Tommy gets here you can tell him what's happening."

"Sounds OK," Dave said, hiding his unease. He left the two women busily making a list and went back into the hall. He dialled a number and spoke quietly into the handset.

"Tommy's due back. Look out for him. Theca's going to do some shopping. She'll use the Mini. Stay with her." He hung up as Theca appeared and opened the cupboard for her jacket. As she reached up he noticed her willowy figure. She'd always been on the slim side but just lately the weight had fallen off her.

"I'll call in and see Ted on the way back," she said and then quietly added, "I think we should have someone in to help out, just for the time being, particularly since Lucia's away for the next two weeks." Lucia was the live-in housekeeper, a young woman from St Michelle in northern France. She'd been looking after the family for five years and during that time had become more than an employee. She was the granddaughter of one of her father's old friends, a woman named Nathalie Mazeau he'd met during the war. Lucia had arrived in order to improve her English and she had stayed, simple as that, taken over the running of the house and become part of the family. Their parents also employed a daily cleaner and a gardener but Theca was suggesting something else, perhaps even more than a temporary replacement for Lucia.

"I don't know, Sis. It keeps her occupied. I don't think we should change things at the moment. In any case, once Lucia gets wind of what has happened she'll probably catch the next flight back."

Theca saw his point and shrugged. She opened the front door.

"There'll be two guys behind you."

"Why?" She turned sharply.

"Because they do what I tell them to do. Until we know what's happening out there we've got to play it safe."

"I don't want anything to do with it."

"That's beside the point. You're a Smith. Start acting like one. Until things are sorted we've got to watch ourselves."

"I don't like it, Dave. I don't like to be followed. I don't trust them and they make me nervous."

"You won't even know they're there. Now go on, get the shopping."

She slammed the door. Dave shook his head and smiled. In the kitchen Sally asked, "What was that about?"

"You know the Star, Ma. She's got a temper at the best of times but at the moment she's a bit emotional, like the rest of us. She flared up at the thought of a couple of minders."

Sally nodded, understanding more than Dave knew about her daughter's dilemma. The women in the family were not involved in the business and when it threatened their freedom, they felt hostility towards it.

"She thinks you ought to have someone in to help out, until Lucia gets back."

Sally tried a smile but it wasn't convincing. "No, that wouldn't do and I can manage perfectly well."

"I know, Mum." Dave reached out and put his arm around her

shoulders. "Go and get ready. I'll put the kettle on. Tommy will want a drink when he gets in."

As he filled the kettle he watched his mother walk stiffly from the kitchen past a calendar hanging by the door. It showed the month of May 1986 and the date of Friday 23rd was circled in black ink, marked because his parents were supposed to be flying out to their villa in Portugal for a couple of weeks in the sun. They generally managed a couple of weeks in May as well as the whole of August when they took the grandchildren and Lucia with them. Dave sighed at the irony. The pressure of business, particularly the noises of hostility emanating from the north, had weighed heavily on his father and he'd needed some heavy persuading not to postpone the trip.

Dave heard the door open and saw Tommy sneaking through the lobby. His clothes looked as though he'd slept in them and a watermark on his blue collar had dried to a white ring. Stubble on his chin darkened his tanned features and his bloodshot eyes lent a sparkle to the steely blue. He had the same colouring and characteristics as his mother. Both Dave and the Star of the Veldt took after their father.

Tommy's grin was reflex, a sigh of relief at being home and seeing a face that he could trust.

"Where's Ma?" he whispered.

"Upstairs," Dave said quietly. "Christ, you look rough."

He moved to pour some tea. Tommy sat down.

"I could've done without the advertising. I had some bother getting back."

Dave nodded over the steaming teapot. He replaced the china lid.

"I guessed as much. I saw the news and put two and two together. I thought about sending you an escort but you'd already left the hotel."

"I couldn't hang around," Tommy said seriously. "They knew where I was staying. As soon as I heard it on the one o'clock I was out of there. I had to leave the motor. Mick had his soldiers on the street and I wasn't waiting to see if they were taking prisoners. They were coming in the front door as I left through the back. I couldn't ring you from the hotel!"

Hotel billing systems automatically logged outgoing calls and there was no way Tommy wanted his whereabouts recorded.

"You sure they were Mick's people?"

"Who else knew I was up there?"

Dave pulled a face. His brother had a point but he was also inexperienced. Dave was wise enough to know that few people could be trusted. The family had a lot of enemies that smiled like the best of friends. A whisper in the right ear could prove more deadly than a frontal assault.

"What happened?"

"I thought we'd made it." He sipped his tea gratefully then pulled a face and reached for the sugar bowl. "Just relaxing when they hit us coming off the A41. I thought the bleedin' Chernobyl had gone off again. The geezer giving me a ride took one in the side. It looked bad."

"How the hell did they find you?" He didn't spell it out but a veiled criticism that Tommy had been followed from the hotel was left hanging.

Tommy shook his head. "Just a guess but there was a kozzer at the service station where I picked up the lift – on the M6. I think he recognized me."

"Bastards! That's as good as a direct line to Mick. He's got the motorway coppers up there totally buttoned up. They give his shipments from Liverpool a fucking escort!"

"That's what I thought. Anyway, I ended up at Hough's gaff overnight."

Dave frowned, "Pete Hough?"

Tommy nodded.

"He's not one of us, Tommy."

"I had no choice. Anyway, I got away with it."

"Was Denise there?"

"Yes." Tommy laughed in order to cover his thoughts but eye contact that went on a moment too long gave the game away. He added, "She kicked me out this morning. But I still got a right earache."

Dave shrugged his suspicion aside and said, "It was still dangerous. You should have come home."

"At the time I could hardly stand up and the filth was all over the shop."

"What happened?"

"Shotguns. They hit us four or five times. Messed up the paint work good and proper."

"Christ! It sounds like you were lucky. But so far south! It's a bit fucking naughty."

"It doesn't make a lot of sense, though."

"Go on?"

"Think about it. Mick wouldn't have made a mistake. It's not his style at all. And with a set-up like that he couldn't have been certain."

"What then?"

"I don't know. It just doesn't add up." Tommy lit a cigarette and blew smoke out with the question, "How's Pop. Is he safe?"

Dave's grunt was almost contemptuous. "You know he was bad at the wedding?"

Tommy nodded, remembering it well. His father had looked ill and both he and his mother had left the reception early, immediately after the firework display.

"He went to The Tower on Monday still moaning about his gut. His foot was playing up too. He wouldn't see Noddy and spent Tuesday morning in bed with Mum fussing around him." Dave paused while his younger brother put out his barely touched cigarette. "Tuesday afternoon he started throwing up. Theca came round, took one look and called Noddy. From the smell of it she guessed it came from the lower gut. Noddy took a look and said hospital. Teddy was over at the Castle so Theca drove Pop to the hospital herself. Panic isn't the word. She rang Barry and he got hold of me. It was theatre that same night, no messing. The girls were in one hell of a state. It was questionable whether he was going to pull through the operation. They didn't think they'd see him again." Dave waved a dismissive hand. "Anyway, some bastard over there squealed to the press and the next thing we knew the BBC had set up camp. That's when your trouble started. By the time I phoned, you'd already legged it. We went up last night but he was still shaky. I don't know whether he recognized us. He's got tubes coming out of his arms and a catheter or something stuck in him but they've eased the blockage. That's all they'd tell us. We're seeing the consultant at two."

"How's Ma taking it?"

"Hard, as you'd expect. Theca stayed here last night."

"What about the hospital? Is he safe?"

"Don't talk to me about that. It's a bloody madhouse. They've got him in an open ward. He wouldn't hear of going private. You know him and the NHS. He wouldn't even let me get him a private room. I'll have another go today but I know the answer before I start."

"You've got people in there?"

"Christ yes. Mind you, it's probably not necessary. Half the Yard is camped out over there." Dave grinned. "Still, you should see our guys. They're going to kill some poor sod with a trolley before long."

For a few moments Tommy considered all that he'd heard then he glanced up and said, "They're supposed to be flying out today. It's a shame this didn't wait until next month."

"I know what you mean, but just think if it had happened next week with him in the middle of Portugal."

They heard the sound of a light step and turned to see Sally. Tommy was on his feet immediately and went into the kitchen to hug her. She seemed small and fragile against him.

"Oh, Tommy," she sighed and pressed the side of her face against his chest. She shook away her emotion and said, "Some of your clothes are upstairs. You'd better go and change. And shave. You can't turn up at the hospital looking like that. You should have let us know where you were."

Tommy released her.

"David has told you everything? I'll make some sandwiches. You go and change now. We haven't got long. Isn't the Star back yet?"

Dave called in from the dining room, "She's calling in to see Ted."

"Oh yes," Sally's thoughts were elsewhere: in the hospital, in the past, in the fearsome future. She turned to the worktop and began on the sandwiches.

They were almost ready and Sally was just adding garnish when the door opened and Theca led Ted into the kitchen. She lifted a bulging Marks and Spencer bag on to the side.

"Hello love; hello Teddy." Even as she spoke Sally barely glanced up. "Did you get everything?"

Theca nodded and began to unpack. Ted kissed Sally's cheek and hugged her quickly, silently, before joining the brothers in the dining room.

"All right, Teddy," Dave said. It was a greeting, not a question.

Ted nodded and turned to Tommy, "How did you make out?"

Tommy said quietly, "I'm in one piece, but lucky. Explain later."

Ted glanced through the open door at the women busily unpacking the shopping. His curiosity would have to wait. He was shorter than the brothers and carried much less weight. He was forty, greying, and had about him a studious look accentuated by silver-rimmed spectacles positioned slightly low on his nose. He wore a dark-blue pinstripe with a strip of yellow handkerchief above his top pocket.

Sally carried in the sandwiches and fresh tea.

"Did the children get to school all right?" She asked.

"No problem," Ted said. "Jean came in early to look after them."

"Will they let us see Dad this afternoon?" Tommy asked.

Dave frowned for a moment and then smiled at his younger brother. He said, "They'll let us do anything we like."

Ted chuckled.

Sally's glance was sharp. She'd heard it before, from her husband, but always in jest. He didn't really believe it. Yet there was an intrinsic truth in what her eldest son had said. They did get their way and people fell over themselves to accommodate them. She knew enough about the business to know that it wasn't out of love or kindness. It was more out of fear and respect. Perhaps the two were related. Now that her husband lay seriously ill some of that respect would disappear and in its place would grow hostility and revenge. Keeping her family safe until the crisis was over was not going to be easy and the responsibility rested on David's shoulders. She was not sure whether he was ready for it. She looked at her eldest son and saw her husband and when he spoke she heard her husband.

"Are we ready then?" she heard and watched Dave lead the way. "Theca, you better take your motor. Ma and Tommy can come with me."

Sally brushed a hair from her suit jacket and followed the others into the kitchen.

Although the house would be empty, they didn't lock the doors or windows. They never did. There wasn't a villain in London who would step foot on the road without an invitation, and for good reason. In Briar Court where the two-storey house surrounded by high brick walls – the Lodge – was situated, security was tighter than at Buckingham Palace.

As the two cars pulled out, the Star's red Mini and Dave's black Rover, another car with darkened windows pulled out in front of them. Before they'd travelled fifty yards yet another car with similar windows had pulled up behind them. From the upstairs windows in various houses men watched the convoy move slowly to the corner and then sat back to continue their watch, feeling some relief that the family had left their patch without incident.

The great concrete and glass office buildings had emptied and the lunchtime crowds filled the pavements and burst into the roads. The cafés and restaurants and pubs were full. The convoy joined a stream of traffic and slid on to the North Circular. The four-storey red-bricked hospital loomed, the entrance canopy fanned out before them. Scruffy men carrying cameras and microphones leapt from their places and made for the slowing cars. As the family left to push their way through the press of reporters, two men appeared and slipped quietly into the driving seats of the cars and drove them to the park. Dave led the family to the glass doors of the lobby entrance, searching Fleet Street's faces for one that he recognized. Passers-by turned to watch the commotion, trying to put a name to the face. People inside looked stern and annoyed, upset by the intrusion, and wondered in turn who was getting the media attention. One or two officials shook their heads in dismay and muttered about the hospital being turned into a circus.

The wide starkly-lit entrance hall, smelling faintly of disinfectant, housed a shop, a café where the seats were uncomfortable and the fixed tables cluttered with empty cups and saucers, various receptions, clearly marked and signposted corridors radiating from both sides and, at the far end, a bank of lifts. The family went swiftly across the tiled floor, passing the busy receptionists. Their footsteps seemed loud and urgent. Tommy put his arm around Sally's shoulders and Theca flashed a secret message to Ted. They reached the lifts and stood aside as a couple of name-tagged specialists in white coats came out laughing. In the enclosure of the lift Tommy asked, "Was it like this last night?"

"Worse," Dave said flatly. "The TV people had a van outside but we had that moved. The BBC weren't keen on the medical programmes we had in mind. We promised them something starring their own cameramen."

The lift halted abruptly and the doors slid open. They moved out to the third floor reception and stood by an area of seats and a drink machine while Dave went across to the desk. Moments later he returned and told them, "He'll be with us in two minutes. Let's sit down. Dad's comfortable." They sat tensely, straight-backed, aware of every tiny movement. Tommy lit a cigarette. A group of passing nurses gave him disapproving glances.

"You shouldn't smoke in here," Sally admonished, thinking perhaps that was the reason for the dark looks.

"Look, there's an ashtray," he said in defence.

She saw it and nodded.

"You shouldn't smoke anyway."

They watched a tall, slim man, dressed in a dark blazer and flannels lean over the reception desk, glance their way after talking to the girl sitting there, and then approach. Under his rich tan his gaunt looks indicated something in the region of forty-five. He smiled briskly, put a folder under his arm and rubbed his spotless hands together. There was honesty in his square features. He looked carefully at the five of them and chose Sally.

"Mrs Smith?" His voice was touched with a French accent.

He sat down opposite and shuffled some papers from his file. His knowledgeable, almost sad eyes met Sally's and moved to Theca, and then addressed the others.

"It's not very good, I'm afraid. It doesn't look good. As you know we operated to remove a blockage but..." He shook his head. "It's not very good at all."

"Is it cancer?" Sally blurted out the question, fighting for control.

"There is a growth that is widespread and we've taken a section for examination. I'm unable to identify it and it will be a few days before we know whether it is malignant."

"What are you saying?" Sally asked.

The others looked grim-faced and resigned.

He raised his hands and offered, "A few weeks, a month."

Sally blurted, "A month!" She looked horrified. The thought grooved its way across her forehead.

"Maybe longer," the Frenchman added quickly, gently.

Sally was numbed, unable to speak, unwilling to comprehend.

Theca asked: "If you don't know what it is how can you tell it's a month?" Her voice was slightly hostile.

"You've always got to remember," the consultant went on, "that while I speak to you in medical terms there is someone up there who has the last say. And He might decide He doesn't want him, maybe, for a year, maybe two…"

Dave asked, "Have you spoken to him?"

The consultant nodded. "Yes, we talked this morning."

"How is he taking it?"

"He is a very strong man. We managed to ease the immediate blockage and obviously he's a lot more comfortable. We won't do much more until we get the results."

"If he'd come in earlier would it have made a difference?"

The consultant shrugged. He'd heard that question so many times. At length he said, "Even a year ago would not have made a difference."

Tommy remained motionless, gazing at the floor.

Ted said, "When can we take him home?"

The consultant seemed taken by surprise and his guard slipped momentarily. "Oh. Oh, well…" He shook his head to give himself time. Eventually he said, "Not for ten days at least. We must wait for the results then we can talk of that."

"It's important for us to get him home," Ted insisted.

"I can understand that." The sympathy hushed his voice to a whisper. "Let's wait for the results."

Sally asked quietly: "Can I go in and see him? I've brought some things."

The consultant smiled sadly, "Of course."

"I'll come with you," Theca said.

"No!" Sally said firmly. "I'll see him on my own." She stood and picked up her bag and walked, a lonely figure, toward the ward entrance.

The consultant got to his feet. "You must watch out for her," he said and collected his notes. "I'll see you again." He moved off toward the reception. Dave caught up with him and the others watched although they couldn't hear what was said.

"You know who you've got in there, Doc. What can we do to give him a better chance?"

The consultant hesitated before he said, "This is something that cannot be fixed." His voice, so gentle and sympathetic when speaking to Sally, was now edged with contempt. "There is not a thing in the world that you can buy, or a surgeon or a hospital that will give your father a moment in the world longer that he will get here. And that is not very long."

Dave's expression hardened. "Out of respect for my old man we're seeing you here; we've come to you. He's a great believer in the Health Service. Don't get carried away with the idea."

The consultant studied Dave out of narrowed eyes. Tight-lipped, he said, "It was mentioned to me that your family has, how was it put? A certain influence? Let me make one thing quite clear to you. Your family will receive the same response from me and from my staff as any other family in similar circumstances. Do I make myself clear? No more and no less."

"Did I ask you for any favours?"

"If you didn't ask, then you haven't been turned down. Is that not so?"

"That sounds like a good place to leave it."

The consultant nodded briskly, turned on his heels and left Dave looking thoughtfully after him. Dave wasn't angry or even annoyed but he thought that one day, after the event, he might hurt the man, just a little, just to make a point.

From the starkly lit waiting-room where they sat and waited for Sally, where Tommy fed a coin into the drinks machine to obtain coffee for the

Star of the Veldt, a corridor led from the lifts past the reception desk, past the ward sister's office on the left-hand side, past the sterilization room and the toilets, to an open-planned ward that housed two rows of neatly made beds. All but two beds were occupied and an attendant and a nurse were busily making ready for visiting hours. Two of the beds were screened and, from the others, patients read quietly or watched, curious that a woman had been let in early to see the patient in the left-hand bed at the far end of the ward. They saw her bending over the patient, saw their lips move as they spoke, saw her clutch his hand in hers, his face tug into a huge grin and then her tears sparkling in the fluorescent wash.

Chapter 9

Shortly after getting married, Dave had moved into a seven-bedroom detached house on the Ridgeway. Since he had inherited three children from his wife's first marriage and later added two of his own, he needed all the space he could get. Things would get easier now that Patricia's eldest daughter, Jessica, was married. The weekend just gone, the marriage and her flying off to honeymoon in North Africa, seemed an age ago.

The house stood back from the main road, guarded on all sides by a high brick wall. Tall sweet chestnuts and thick evergreen shrubs surrounded the front garden. A gravel drive reached its end around a knot of camellias. At the rear of the house was a modest indoor swimming pool with a sauna enclosure built into one end and a gym next to that.

Soon after leaving the hospital Dave's Rover crunched on the gravel. A couple of minders closed the wrought-iron gate behind him. He checked the time and knew exactly where to find his wife. Patricia was on a health kick; the necessary worry that mothers experience during the run-up to a daughter's wedding had left her out of sorts and, according to her, desperately in need of the old routine. Dave found her in the pool. She'd completed thirty lengths but her breath was barely raised. She saw him, gave a little wave and used the metal rungs to climb out. She reached for a towel.

"You really don't need all this. You look in good shape to me."

"Ugh! Look at this." She pinched an inch or so of flesh around her middle. She slipped a robe over her swimsuit. "What happened?"

Dave repeated what the consultant had said and watched her face fall. She reached for her spectacles. They slightly enlarged her eyes and seemed to increase the compassion in them.

"Sweetheart, I'm so sorry."

"Theca is staying with Mum for a few nights. We're going to see him tonight. Mum wanted to be alone with him this afternoon."

"That's understandable. God, she must be feeling wretched. You all must be. I'll get across to see her."

"I'm not stopping," Dave said. "But I wanted to let you know."

She nodded gratefully but in her eyes there remained a hint of disappointment.

Another car rolled over the gravel and moments later Jimmy Jones peered through the pool window, acknowledged Pat's wave and Dave's nod and walked nonchalantly to the open door. Jimmy Jones had been one of his father's most trusted employees and two years previously had become Dave's right-hand man. It was not uncommon to find him at the house. He was considered a part of the family. His dark visage and sharp looks were trusted and totally accepted by the children. He was a stocky, good-looking man of part Indian or Pakistan extraction. He had never been sure for his Welsh mother had never bothered to ask.

"How did it go, Boss?"

For a second time but without some of the detail, Dave recounted what the consultant had said. They said goodbye to Pat and made their way back to the cars.

"Find out about that consultant," Dave said. "He sounded French, Levy or something. He's got an attitude problem. Wait till it's all over then sort him out."

That was enough. Jimmy Jones knew exactly what was required. On occasion it was necessary to remind people who was in charge. Perhaps not this week, or this month, but at some time in the future the Frenchman would meet with a little misfortune. If he had children it might be that they disappeared for an hour or two. They would turn up totally unharmed and none the worse for the experience, but in the horror of those two hours a parent can learn a lot of respect.

Dave continued, "Better send someone to Tunisia to keep an eye on Jessica and John. And make sure someone keeps an eye on Theca's kids as well. A discreet eye! She'll go spare if she finds out."

"What now, Boss?"

"The hotel first," Dave said without changing his expression. "I'll be about an hour. Keep an eye on the foyer for me. I've got to make the hospital about seven. I'll see you in the club after that."

Jimmy Jones followed Dave across London to Park Lane and took up his station in the hotel reception. If any unwelcome face showed up and that included any press photographer who wanted faces for the Sunday supplements, he had plenty of time to warn Dave.

For Dave Smith the last couple of years had been coated in lethargy. He'd gone through the motions, hiding his sense of increasing languor from all but his wife. His feeling of detachment was fed by a growing suspicion that the old days were finished. The period of enforced idleness, the security that had existed for over a decade, had dulled the essence of his motivation. He needed an enemy, someone to fight. But just lately things were stirring again and Dave recognized the old feeling; something deep within him was beginning to spark. The trouble was one thing, the threat from Scotland sharpened his senses and pushed anger back into his eyes, hooded them so that his look was vaguely contemptuous, but Sharon Valenti played a part in it too. After all this time she remained a challenge. When her eyes flickered his way they seemed to question his masculinity – appreciating, certainly, but querying also. In a peculiar sense he felt that he had to prove something. That it was reckless made it all the more exciting. The feeling was extraordinary and mixed now with the danger, the threat to the family, it was inseparable. He was suddenly alive, heady with old sensations, and his instincts were being recharged by the moment.

Before Dave had properly closed the door on the seventh floor room – no penthouse suite this time; no suite for the wicked – Sharon Valenti had flown into his arms. Her negligee parted on the way and flashed him a nipple and a quick peep at genuine blond curls.

"Oh my darling! I thought you weren't coming. You're so late!" The words, fired in her staccato New England delivery, came breathlessly, between kisses. Her accent remained untainted by the years she'd spent in Runnymede.

She didn't stop to hear his excuse or to find out about his father. Those things would keep. She was all that he could have wished for. Being unable to bear children had kept her vagina duck-arse tight and she held him inside her and rippled against him, and he was drawn out, stretched, and the sensation was almost unbearable.

And yet there was something mildly detached and adrift about it all, a sensation of familiarity, that he felt at once comfortable and yet faintly disappointed. As he lay against her he experienced a sense of panic, an unreasonable fear that gripped his thoughts, mocking him. In that moment of introspection he felt that his time was running out, that something was creeping up on him and that sooner or later he would have to turn and face it. But there was no holding back. His release was urgent, vital, and when, through clenched lips she murmured, "Oh God! Oh my God!" a little smile played with his expression. It was not out of satisfaction, or even wantonness, simply the exquisite combination of power and self-destruction.

The guilt that Dave felt – that he should be indulging while his father lay close to death – lent an edge to his violence, and he hurt her.

While they made up afterwards she said, "Tony's got something going down. He's been making quite a few trips lately."

"Oh," he said.

"A couple back home. Thank God he didn't take me. It would have stopped me seeing you." She squeezed his hand against her breast.

"He's back now?"

"Oh yes, unfortunately. But he's buzzing. He's up to something."

"Like what?"

"If I get anything you'll be the first to know."

"Any visitors?"

"Just the usual crowd, no one I don't recognize."

"Heard anything about South America maybe?"

"No."

"What about the word 'distribution'? Heard that in passing?"

She shook her head.

"What then?"

"He sings. He gets up earlier."

"Fuck me. That does sound serious."

She punched his arm and said, "Don't make fun of me."

"Sweetheart, would I do that?"

"On the other hand, I love it when you talk dirty."

She moved her behind gently against him and snuggled in closer. He kissed the back of her neck. There were striking similarities between Sharon and his wife that had not gone unnoticed. He often toyed with the notion that the likeness gave him a certain security.

She sighed, "Christ, I'm exhausted. I could sleep."

He smiled grimly.

"Every time with you it's the same. I feel stretched to a pulp. It hurts, but in a nice kind of way. It shouldn't, but it does. Every time is like the first time over again."

"What's that supposed to mean?"

"Well, I don't know. I mean I love you, you know that, but it's something else too. I need to feel some pain. I like it. Not in any weird sense, but in the sort of submission, the laying waste, the feeling like a tom, almost, whose trick has just been a part of the rent, it's an act of vengeance, pure and simple."

"Vengeance?"

"Yes. Can you understand that?"

"I think so."

"I hate him more than anything in the world. But I'm not stupid. I know I'm tied to him for life. There's no way he'd let me go. He'd kill me before he'd do that. So taking in his sworn enemy is a small consolation. Got it?"

"That sounds like serious shit. How long have you felt this way?"

"I'm not using you, Dave. This is just an extra, the icing on the cake. I've loved you forever. You must have known that."

"It can't do any good to hate someone so much, not all the time. Anyway, if he doesn't know about it, you aren't doing him any harm."

"I know that. But the feeling is for me, not him. Let me tell you something." She lowered her voice. "I shouldn't, but what the hell. After leaving you I don't bathe or take a shower. I'll go back and tell him that I'm kind of horny. He used to be a regular little rabbit. I'm talking three or four times a day. Not that he was any good, but he's lost it altogether now. I know he's seen doctors, the lot, and they put it down to narcotics. He was in and out of hospital dozens of times. I think the episode with you started it all. He got rid of all the mirrors in the house. We're talking serious psycho shit here, a regular Norman Bates. But that was ten years ago."

Dave gulped.

"Anyway, his addiction was one of the reasons they sent him over here. If he couldn't sort himself out, then he couldn't go home. The old man O'Connell took him in hand, got him off the junk and gave him back some kind of self-respect. But it was too late for his dick."

"What's it got to do with you not taking a shower?"

"Whoah! Don't rush me. I'm coming to that. Even though he can't get it up himself he still feels he has to look after me. He doesn't, of course. He hasn't got a clue. But I let him think he does the trick. He uses his fingers and his tongue. While I'm still tingling from your touch the old fool thinks he sucking out my own release. He doesn't realize he's getting his mouth full of you! His nose – what's left of it – has been shot to hell by the coke; he can't smell the difference!"

Dave smiled.

"You don't mind?" she asked. Her back was still to him.

"No, I don't think so. I'm pleased he's not fucking you. It's selfish, I know, but I never said I was perfect." He reached to the side table for his Rolex and said, "It's time I made a move."

As he headed for the door he said, "Sweetheart, I'll have to bell you, and let you know when and where. I need to stay close to home for a while; at least until I know what's happening to the old man."

Before he closed the door she nodded her understanding and blew him a kiss over the palm of her hand.

Dave found Jimmy Jones near the lobby telephone in a position that gave him a good view of the entrance. No mention was made of Dave's diversion or the fact that he'd kept Jimmy waiting. It was accepted, a part of the job; it was questionable whether Jimmy Jones had even thought about it.

As they walked through the lobby Dave glanced through the glass wall partition into the bar and his step faltered. The years were peeled away and for a moment he was flat on his back and looking up into the lifeless eyes of a blond man.

He caught Jimmy's arm.

"Clock the fair-haired geezer chatting up the barmaid. Have you seen him before?"

Jimmy Jones peered through the glass. The tall middle-aged man was perched on a bar stool, his elbows resting on the bar surface as he leant forward to talk to a woman behind the bar.

"Yeah, I've seen him around," Jimmy said. "He came in about twenty minutes ago. Do you know him?"

"We met before; a long time ago. He had more hair in those days."

Jimmy muttered, "Didn't we all."

They reached the entrance when Dave paused. "Look, I don't believe in coincidence. Get a make on that guy, will you? How long has he been in town? Where's he staying? What his name is for fuck's sake."

"OK Boss."

"Make sure Sharon gets out of here OK. Make sure he doesn't follow her. If he does, get a couple of guys together and get in his way. It shouldn't be difficult. One of his legs is shorter than the other."

Jimmy nodded. If he was surprised by the request it didn't show.

"I'll catch you at The Tower later," Dave said and left him to it.

Dave cut across Hyde Park Corner and Belgrave Square and made a left into Sloane Street. A few minutes later he pulled up on the Embankment opposite Battersea Park. The East End seemed a long way off, much farther than two pages on the A-Z. The city was changing by the day – and he didn't like it one bit. Great chunks of it had been turned into ghettos. London had always had its foreign quarters but this was different. They had been allowed to take over. One day he would take them on. He sighed and took a steadying breath, drawing in the smell of the river. Father Thames never changed as it twisted through the decaying capital, and even when the grim sky lent its depression to the water it remained constant and somehow comforting. There was something belittling about the river and its glorious history that drew him back time and again. The ebb and flow, its heartbeat, contained his ancestral blood; it whispered to him and turned his thoughts to the past. His grandfather had died in the thick water and more than that, for the same water had washed across his father and flowed into his father's heart.

Chapter 10
1926

Memory dulls both the good times and the bad and yet enhances the thing so that buildings become taller and ditches deeper, and the in-between times cease to exist. It takes something special – a sound, a smell, a certain look – to stir a recollection. The concrete and brick and smoke and grime of the city were real enough. And so were the slums that soured the hearts of the people who lived in them.

Youngsters squatted precariously on a slate roof, held there by the worn leather of their boots. They played between slats of rusted tin and corrugated iron used to cover places of missing lead, and they hung to chimneys and flues and pipes, pointing at the great plumes of steam and the belching black smoke and the occasional tongue of flame. They squatted on their haunches and laughed and joked and smoked the dog-ends that they'd found, and they kept glancing at their lookout stationed on a higher ledge as he watched for adults and in particular the adult who used his truncheon on truants. This was their den, hidden away, and the noises and smells of the narrow soot-coated streets and dark, dangerous alleys, the canals and markets, the maze of warehouses and small businesses, the tiny yards full of black mud piles and pools of stagnant water and small piles of glistening slack, filled their playground.

"It must be time to be getting back," one of the youngsters said. His name was Tom Smith. "My old man is off down south tonight and I'd like to get to go with him."

"I like your old man," another said. His name was Simon Carter. He was heavier than Tom, but slower. He picked at tiny lumps of moss and lichen that grew on the slate and absently flicked bits of it over the edge. "He's all right. Where's he going then?"

"Don't know, really. South, somewhere, by the sea."

"I wouldn't mind seeing the sea. That would be something. One day we could take off and see it. Us lot."

"Takes a long time to get there, even in a van. If you couldn't get a lift it would take maybe a week."

"You ain't been so how do you know?"

"Southend is sixty miles. If you did ten miles a day, walking, that would be six days."

"We could do more than ten miles a day."

"Maybe we could, but it's a long walk and what would we eat?"

"Take some fruit. We could nick some fruit. What does he do in Southend, then?"

"He ain't going there. He's going south. He's going to the ports. Does every year. He said one year he'd take me."

"When?"

"When I was nine."

"You're nine now."

"Maybe he meant ten."

"He'll never take you. They all say things they never do."

"He will. If he said it, he will. Trouble is me ma. She might not want us off school!"

They broke into laughter.

A mangy black cat skirted their roof, sprang silently on to their level and approached. The boys watched its circumspection. They saw the bald patches and the fur hanging in clumps and the swollen ticks hanging from its head. The black tail flicked. Its purr turned into a shriek as the corner of a slate glanced off its side and it flashed away over the roof.

"What did you do that for?"

"They are full of fleas. Did you see him jump?"

"There was no need for that."

"Bleedin' hell, Tommy, what's the matter with you all of a sudden? It was only a soddin' tom. Is that it, because it's got your name?"

Tom turned to face the other boy. Simon grew at once concerned and even in his crouched position he eased himself away.

"I'm going home now," Tom said and moved down the sloping roof.

"See you later, after dinner," Simon shouted.

Tom eased himself over the lip of the roof, lowered his feet to a brick wall then jumped to the ground. He dusted grime from the seat of his short trousers and walked swiftly from the alley into the bustle and noise and smell of the High Street.

Lorries and vans rattled by on their balloon tyres, carts went with the clatter of hooves, bicycles hissed past, pedestrians pushed and dodged. Ahead of him the market spread out in a maze of flapping stalls. He weaved his way through the pitches piled high with clothes and junk, silver-scaled fish and freshly cut flowers, oranges in their crumpled tissues, apples polished until they shone, glinting pots and pans, and everywhere merchants shouted louder for attention. He paused by his favourite stall where the sinister ranks of second-hand furniture with its dusty smell of old wood and upholstery filled him with a reverence he could not understand; its pull remained a mystery. He flicked at a couple of boxes of tattered books marked down to a penny then noticed the Jew watching him. The owner in his navy-blue greatcoat nodded and grinned knowingly, toothlessly, and gave him a wave. Tom moved on without acknowledgement for it wasn't wise to be recognized, even less wise to be seen talking to a Yiddish bookseller. Everyone hated the Jewboys, except the Jewish girls. They were the bogeymen and always had been. Most of them lived in the slums of Whitechapel where they hid from the Watney Street gangs that controlled that part of town.

At the corner he stopped to watch tinkers go by; the wanderers, trundling past with their broken prams full of their belongings, selling their pot-scrubbers and pegs and sprigs of lavender as they went. The horse passed him and he saw the dark superior eyes of two women who sat on the cart, and they flashed him worldly smiles. A couple of mangy dogs kept close to the wheels. He watched the little parade until it was out of sight then he crossed the road and began to climb a long hill that would take him home. A coal merchant's dray drawn by a weary Clydesdale rumbled slowly toward him. It came to a standstill while a blackened coalman emptied sacks through a coal hole in the pavement. The old man saw him and dusted down his sackcloth and gave him a wide grin.

"All right, Tommy boy?"

"All right, Jack. Got to get on, can't stop. Going down south."

"That's a good place to go."

Tom hurried on and turned up the alley that led to his back gate. A tiny high-walled yard led to the back door. Limp washing barely stirred on the line. A tarpaulin covered a pile of timber. A tin bath rested against the steamed kitchen window. Three small outhouses contained coal, the WC and a mangle and washboards.

In the matriarchal tradition his mother carried the family and like most women in the district she had grown old before middle-aged. She said, "Your teacher was here earlier."

Her words caught him as he closed the back door and stopped him in his tracks. She stood at the stove stirring a dark stew. Tom worked furiously for an excuse but it was hopeless. Even though his mother's back was to him he could imagine her stern expression.

"What's your dad going to say? I know what he'll say and you won't like it one bit." She turned and looked across at him and stabbed the air with a wooden spoon. "Why didn't you go to school?"

He shrugged. "It's boring, Mum, and Mr Simpson is always having a go. You don't learn nothing."

"A lot of things in life is boring, Tommy, but you still got to do them."

"It's all history and dates, and countries I've never heard of and rivers I'll never see."

"You're right. You will never see them unless you get some learning. And history is important. It tells you who you are."

"Yeah, like Henry the Eighth. Who cares?"

"I care."

"He picks on me and Simon, says we're lousy, says Sim's got scabies."

"Most of your mates have got scabies and if they're going to do a runner every time the medical officer visits they'll never get shot of it."

"How would you like to be painted purple so everyone knows?"

She folded her arms. "It catches and so does lice. You pick it up from your mates and you'll bring it home."

"It's not their fault."

"I didn't say it was, did I? And I don't think you should change your mates either, but you could tell them the wisdom of seeing the medical officer. And so what if other people know? Half the school is down with it."

"That's all right for you to say."

She smiled gently. Already stooped in her mid-thirties, Rose's eyes were clear and brown. She said, "You're just like your old man."

"I don't look like him much. People say I look like you."

She put down the spoon, wiped her hands on her apron and began to peel potatoes. The grey in her thick hair caught the light from the window.

"What did you tell Mr Simpson?"

"I told him your dad needed your help on the van and that you'd be back next week."

"I thought Dad was going down south?"

"So he is," she said quietly.

Tom's eyes widened. "I'm going?"

"Isn't that what I just said?"

"You're a lady, you know that?"

She glanced up and for an instant he saw joy in her eyes.

"And you're a gentleman," she said. "Now go and find your dad and tell him dinner's on the table."

He was gone. The back door slammed behind him. Rose watched him race across the yard to the gate, flicking at the washing as he went. He was tanned, like his father, with a touch of Gypsy in his looks and yet she knew of no traveller in either family. He was lithe and muscular and for a lad of his age, when gawkiness was the thing, he was solid and well built. Rose watched the gate swing slowly shut then dropped a potato into the stew.

The Eagle Public House was a red brick building on the corner of two cobblestone roads. A stone statue of a golden eagle, its wings spread ready for flight, perched above the heavy front doors. Inside, the dark green walls kept the bar dim even when light poured in through the toughened windows. It was smoky and cluttered and run by Peter Woodhead whose fierce visage beneath a severely cropped head kept even the most dubious members of his clientele in order. His imposing frame capped by a familiar bowler hat helped, as did his reputation that no one would take lightly. The Eagle was a landmark, its upper floors towering over the terraced businesses and rows of houses surrounding it. It was also a well-known meeting place for those who lived on their wits. The burglars sneaked in from Hackney, the conmen and fixers from Stepney, the thieves and pickpockets from King's Cross, and the more dangerous villains from Whitechapel and the Green. They came to drink and idle and set up their deals, they came to pay their dues or receive them, and they talked in low voices and sold information. They were seldom interrupted. Good citizens knew of the place and stayed away and the police knew of the place and stayed away for most of the time. And if the police were forced to look in by their superiors, then the word was the thing and when they looked they found it empty.

Tommy Smith's place at the bar was as established as his place at his own kitchen table. From that place, with his foot on the bronze-coloured rest, with one elbow planted firmly on the bar surface to guard his pint of mild, he could observe the saloon with its tables and chairs beneath wall prints of boxing promotions and photographs of old, never forgotten fighters. Fighting was a business and Peter Woodhead had financial ties with the gym adjoining his public house. He owned it. His boys, the best fighters in town, were another reason the Eagle remained trouble free when all about them violence tumbled from the bar rooms into the streets. The talk was about boxing and dogs and the nine-day general strike and how it had stopped the trams and brought docklands to a standstill, and sometimes the proposals for the new Tilbury Docks and the way it would turn docklands, general strike aside, into a ghost town. Just lately the Zeppelin and Vesuvius had also been mentioned.

Tommy Smith was certainly interested in dogs and boxing and the strike and perhaps even the Tilbury Docks, in that order, but he couldn't have cared less about the Zeppelin and he'd never heard of Vesuvius. Like most men in the bar and, come to that, most men in the whole of the East End, he blamed Stanley Baldwin for everything.

"Be back on Sunday," he said, his voice hissing over broken front teeth. He rolled a cigarette and lit it.

"In time for church," Peter Woodhouse muttered. "Hello, here's your nipper."

Tommy turned to see his boy pushing by a group of men. One of them grabbed at the youngster and hoisted him shoulder high. "What have we got here?" he shouted. "You're training him right, Tommy. A good little middleweight, I should say." Others in the bar chuckled. There was a good-humoured affinity and the boy was perfectly safe.

Tommy grinned at his son hanging in the air and shouted, "Go on, sock him in the mouth, my son!"

The man holding the boy aloft stuck out his jutting jaw for him to hit. The boy's fist, with surprising speed, landed squarely on the man's nose.

"Gawd! Stone the crows!"

A hoot of laugher erupted as the boy was dropped.

"Gawd, he's got a bleedin' sting."

The boy looked back and grinned, swelling in self-esteem. He reached his father's side.

"All right, Tom boy?"

"Yeah."

Peter Woodhouse held a glass to the light and while inspecting it said, "You ought to send him around to the gym."

"Plenty of time for that," Tommy said. "What you after, boy? You're a bit too light for a pint."

"Mum says dinner's ready."

"We better be off then. Wouldn't want to upset her, would we? And I've got to get to the ports tonight."

"She said I'm coming."

Tommy frowned. "Did she? I wonder what gave her that idea."

"Come on, Dad. I can help."

"Could you indeed?" Tommy finished his beer and wiped froth from his mouth. "Let's shake a leg then. See you on Sunday, Peter."

"Yes, see you Tommy. And you little Tom." Peter Woodhouse paused then raised his pale blue eyes from the boy. His expression hardened. "Mind what I was telling you."

Tommy nodded and said, "I will. Thanks for the tip."

As they made their way from the bar and started up the hill he held the boy's shoulder.

The youngster looked up and asked, "What was he saying?"

"It's nothing for you to worry about."

"Go on, tell me, Dad."

"Some bleeder is playing up rough. Says we ain't paying our rent proper. Stopping people at the market and hurting them."

"We pay our rent."

"It's not for the house, boy. We don't pay rent on the house. It's all ours, handed down. It used to be your granddaddy's house and before that your great granddaddy's. And one day it will be yours." He paused to relight the stub of his roll-up before continuing. "This is business. They want a cut of the business and some of us won't give it to them. Lousy bleeders want something for nothing."

"Who is it?"

"Some nasty geezers from the Cross. Don't you take no mind to it, and don't you mention it to your ma."

"I won't, but what's the name? What's the gang?"

His father glanced down, surprised. "The KC Boys," he said. "What do you know?"

"Nothing. Simon was telling us his old man has the same bother."

"Who? Simon Carter? His old man works the docks, don't he?"

"When he can get it. He's been put off lately, and his back's been playing up. But they're on strike at the moment, or something, so it makes no difference."

"Strike a light! If they're on the make from hardship cases like that then it's worse than I thought. His mother's dead ain't she?"

"Yeah, she died when he was a kid, six or something."

His father grunted and said grimly, "Things won't get any easier for them, not now, not in the short term."

"Blood poisoning, or something. He told me. She caught it after his sister was born. Something was left behind, I think. It didn't make much sense. They cut her arms off and then her legs off and then she died. He can't remember too much about it. But it was a bit frightening."

His father nodded thoughtfully, his expression distant. He said, "Some people don't have much luck." He shook away the thought. "You tell me if you get any more whispers, boy. Sounds like you're hearing more than me. And remember, not a word to your ma."

"I know."

He grabbed his father's hand and they strolled slowly up the hill. Tommy's look suddenly engaged and he was back to his old self. He looked down at his son and grinned. "That was one hellofa shot, boy. You done well there."

Meals in the Smith's house were taken at the kitchen table. In the district the kitchen was regarded as the centre of the house and the sitting room was rarely used.

"I'll need some money off you," Rose said. "We're nearly out of everything."

"I've got some that will keep you going till I get back. I need a good trip. Funds are getting low. That bleedin' clutch is costing a fortune."

"Give my love to Elizabeth."

"You should come with us."

"Oh yes? And who would look after all of this? Just look at what happened to Molly when their place was empty for a fortnight, all the windows broken and everything gone. Even the tiles on the roof went."

"We'll only be gone a couple of days. It ain't a week, is it? We'd be back before you know it, before the word got around."

"It's not worth the chance. In any case, going all that way, being bumped this way and that, just for a couple of days. A horse and cart don't shake you around so much."

Tommy sighed. "It's the suspension. The springs ain't what they were. I'll fix them sometime and then we'll all go out, maybe, to Epping Forest or Southend for the day."

"I'd like that. I'd like to go back to Southend." She looked at the youngster. "That's where we spent our honeymoon. Mixed with the nobs in a proper hotel, we did."

"Bed and Breakfast," Tommy put in.

"Hotel," she insisted. "They just didn't serve dinner, that's all, dinner and tea. You had to come back after tea so's they had time to clean the room. Anyway, nobs go out to dinner." She chuckled. "You know that." She paused then said, "I've put some apples in the bag, and some sandwiches." She turned to her son. "If you've finished you can go and get your other shirt on, and change your socks. Your other pair is on the bed. Don't want you stinking Elizabeth's house out, do we?"

Unable to speak with his mouth full, Tom rushed from the room.

"He's excited," Rose said. She filled two cups with tea and pushed one across to Tommy. "Don't let him come to any bother."

"He'll be all right," Tommy assured her. "He's older than you think."

"He ain't growed up enough yet."

"He's a good lad, Rose. He's turning out fine."

"Make sure he keeps warm at night. It's always cold by the sea."

Tommy reached across and stroked his wife's pale cheek.

"I'll bring you something back," he said.

Rose nodded and her lips smiled, but deep in her brown eyes was a look of sadness.

Under a darkening sky the white Morris van picked up the colour of gold as it weaved its way through the crumbling terraces of the city back streets, pinking and lurching in low gears. It crawled on through the tree-lined outskirts, past the buildings with their scrubbed porches and bay windows sucking light from the silent street lamps. As the dusk crept over the city and the spiralling starlings wheeled toward the flying buttresses of the Royal Courts, a low mist lifted from the river and spread through the streets. They drove into that time when the colours dissolved into powdery opaqueness and the landscape lost all form, when the mist overtook them and snaked its way along the estuaries and spread across the hedgerows and glistening fields, when tentacles of red smeared the western sky and blackness crept from the east. In the cabin Tom snuggled closer to his father's sinewy arm and rested his head against the vaguely sinister tattoo of snake and dagger. He caught the faint whiff of perspiration and tobacco, a good clean comforting smell, and he snuggled closer still.

"You all right, my son?"

"Yeah."

"Sleepy huh?"

"A bit."

"It's the fumes from the engine, see, and the lights flashing by. Puts you to sleep."

"How long will it take?"

"Three, four hours. You get some kip if you like."

"Maybe later."

"Excited eh? Surprised your ma let you come after finding out about skipping school. Mind you, I couldn't get on with it. Never did. Sooner be out. Still, you been doing your reading and that's the main thing. Know what I mean? What you reading now?"

"Don't know, really, Two Cities, or something. Only done the first page. Had to give it up."

"How come? Your ma told me you was a good little bleeder – oops, I mean reader!"

Tom shrugged. "It said it was the best time and the worst time both together. That's stupid."

"It sounds stupid. Who wrote that?"

"A geezer."

"Well I know that much, don't I? What geezer?"

"Arthur Dickens."

"Never heard of him. I like the cowboys. I was a sucker for the westerns. I used to drive my old man hopping mad reading them all the while. Said I'd go blind."

"So what does it mean then? The best and worst at the same time?"

"It's a long time since I done any learning but let me explain it this way. It ain't easy being a father, is it? Never was. When a kid is born it needs you all the time, never lets you get near the missus or get a decent night's kip; and when it gets a bit older it wrecks your home, puts mud on the carpet, breaks everything in sight, and all you want to do is wring its bleedin' neck; and when it gets older still, it starts to answer you back and, blow me down, it starts to believe in anyone else rather than you. So all the time you got a situation, sometimes you're mad as hell and angry and hateful, all those things. But at the same time, no matter what the kid does, even when you're telling him off or thumping hell out of him, you love him all the time. You can't help it. It's inside you. He means more to you than anything else. So maybe you could say that you love him and hate him at the same time. See? Now, when that geezer wrote that it was the best time and the worst time both together, maybe he was getting at something like that. Maybe it was his way of saying you could have two feelings at the same time."

"I thought he was saying that for the rich people it was a good time and for the poor people it was a bad time."

"Naw, my son. That's always the case. Always has been. Always will be. He wouldn't have to write that down, would he? Naw, the geezer was saying something but meaning something else. These clever bleeders are like that. That's why they use big words; it's to stop a fellow understanding what's going on, see? Anyway, you read too much. It ain't a good thing. It gives you headaches and bloodshot eyes. You'll end up with glasses. If you read the talking stuff and skip all the rest you still get the story and it don't take so long, see? A good little trick, that is."

Headlights came like great flashes, blinding them, deepening the night.

"Back in the old days, before your old ma pulled you out of the hat, even when we were courting, we used to come down here, along this stretch of road. Whole families would come, the kids, parents, grandparents, even the bleedin' great grandparents. Used to load up their carts and climb into trucks and come down here to pick the hops. Stay sometimes for a fortnight or more. The men who held other jobs, like my old man, your granddaddy who worked the markets, used to come down here for the weekends. On a good summer the fields of hops used to spread right the way to Dover. Gawd, the summers were hot in them days, hardly saw a drop of rain. Kids would be running around bare foot and bare shouldered. They'd be scrumpin' the apples from the orchards over the road while the rest of us used to be picking from morning till night. I can still smell them now. A good smell; what life's all about. Your old ma used to be a sprightly little thing in those days, leaping up them wigwams to reach the top, pretty little thing full of smiles and laughter. Gawd knows what went wrong."

"What do they use them for?"

"Brewing the beer."

"What else?"

"Ain't that enough? Gawd, boy, I can't think of anything more important than that. Who needs anything else?"

"What do they look like?"

"Hops? Like fluffy sprouts, fluffy green sprouts. Rows and rows of them climbing up the wigwams and what's more, all the plants are female. That's something for you to know, ain't it? They only grow one male plant at the start of each row."

"How can they tell the difference?"

"Gawd, boy, if you don't ask the most diabolical questions. I don't know. Don't think anyone knows. Maybe they got a tadger. Maybe the seeds come in a different packet, probably. But the bees know, and that's the thing, and they do the trick, see? Go and visit an old male plant first, that's why they're put first in the row, then they go and stick their bleedin' stings in all the females and what do you know? That's it. Nature."

"What would happen then, if they didn't plant any of the male plants?"

"Well, for a start you wouldn't have any honey, would you? And if you didn't have the honey you wouldn't have any bees and without them to do the business you wouldn't have any flowers would you? Stands to reason, see? Then you wouldn't have any beer. That's a thought."

The thought produced a frown and sent him into a worrying silence.

"I never knew that honey came only from the male flowers," Tom said. His father didn't answer.

Chapter 11

The white van steamed on to a concrete forecourt of a three-storey house on the outskirts of Folkestone and parked between two cars. The engine spluttered out and the two pools of light faded slowly. A sign in the window read 'Boarding House'. The upper floors had been turned into guest rooms and during the summer months the house was filled with strangers. Before Tommy Smith had stepped out of the van, the front door of the house opened and Reginald Hurst, his wife, his mother-in-law and his two sons, Ian and Richard, had crowded around.

Reginald said warmly, "Tommy, how nice to see you. You made good time." It was an affection he reserved for few people. Elizabeth, his wife, went forward to embrace him and kiss his cheek and her perfume triggered a memory.

Greased hair speckled with grey and brushed to cover a thinning crown, a ruddy complexion and spectacles sitting half way down his nose gave Reginald the look of a Thespian. But he wouldn't have made much of an actor for Yellow Cross gas in the trenches had destroyed much of his lung tissue and left him permanently breathless and scarred his eyes so that they would weep in all weather. If he was not the perfect host, for most of his time was spent in the garden, it mattered little to the business for Elizabeth and her mother, Maud, a quiet widow who had a room on the first floor, looked after the house and the guests.

Tommy relaxed and looked at the two boys. "Well now, ain't you two grown up?" He turned to Reginald. "I got my boy in the cab. I hope you don't mind?"

"Mind? I'm delighted. Come on, bring him in, we haven't got long."

"Fancy leaving him in the van," Elizabeth admonished. She opened the door and saw the smile. "Dear me, aren't you like your mother?"

The boy clambered down and dusted himself.

Reginald told his sons, "You look after him," then added for Tom's benefit, "Mind you, he looks as if he can look after himself."

Tommy grinned and watched the boys move off to the side of the house. Elizabeth asked, "How's Rose?"

"She sends her love, Elizabeth. I'd love you to get together again. Maybe next year…" He turned to her mother, a tiny lady who shivered inside her shawl. "And how are you Maud?"

"I'm cold," she said.

Reginald laughed, "It is a bit parky. Let's go in and get a drink inside you."

"You said we haven't got long?"

"Remember Len, my brother? His wife Joyce is just about to pop. They've been trying for years and just when they'd given up, it happened. Maybe that's the secret. We were going up there to lend a hand. Well, Lizzy's lending the hand. We can give Len a spiritual hand if you see what I mean."

The door closed and cut the light from the forecourt.

The boys led Tom through a side entrance and across a lawn to a line of swings.

Richard, the taller of the brothers, explained, "Aunty Joyce is having a baby. It'll be our first cousin."

"I ain't got any cousins," Tom said. He looked up at the house that blocked out half the night sky, at the glow from the top windows. "It's a big house." He glanced back at Richard. "How long have you known my dad?"

"He's been coming every year, sometimes twice a year. Dad gets quite excited when he's coming. They must have known each other all their lives."

Ian cut in, "No. They met during the war. I heard them talking."

"Maybe. Our mums know each other. They were girls together, or something. Cousins, maybe." He pushed one of the swings and asked, "How old are you. I'm eleven. Ian's nine."

"Nearly ten," Ian said. He was a good three inches shorter than the other two and covered in freckles.

"Me too," Tom said. "I'm ten in January."

"That isn't nearly ten," Ian laughed. "I'm ten next month."

"Who cares?" Tom said.

Richard nodded and said, "Yes, you're right. Who cares? We better get back."

"You ain't expecting to see it born, are you?"

"No, I hope not. But we'll get to know if it's a boy or a girl and we'll get to hear it cry after it falls out."

The back door of the house opened and Elizabeth called, "Richard, does Tom want a drink?"

They moved along a path between flower borders to a patio. Glasses of orange squash were passed out and in the stark light from the kitchen the boys stood and listened to Reginald's laughter.

Richard said, "He doesn't normally laugh so much."

Ian said, "He doesn't normally laugh at all."

Len and Joyce Mannings' house at the top of Marsh Row was much smaller, the centre of a small terraced row. Although it was well past midnight the boys were allowed to stay up and they sat quietly in the living room and peered through the open door into the kitchen where the adults sat around the table. Elizabeth and Maud were up and down the stairs with towels and trays and the midwife joined them later and took command and then boiling water was produced in pots and pans on the stove. Len Mannings was much older than Tom thought a man ought to be when starting a family, over fifty, and his father and Reginald Hurst had to restrain him at the kitchen table or his nerves might have got the better of him. Sweat poured from his forehead and his hands shook so much that it was difficult for him to get a glass of beer near his lips.

"I was just the same," they heard Reginald telling his father. "When Richard was born I couldn't keep still for a minute. My heart was thumping till it hurt."

"The girls have got it all in hand. It's all natural for them," the voice of his father came through. "That's what they're here for. Best you stay out of the way and let them get on with it. It ain't right to see your missus like that anyway, it ain't dignified, and she wouldn't want you fussing and falling over under their feet. Best leave them alone."

"That's right, Tommy. That's what I've been telling him for the last month. They'll call us when it's all over."

The back door opened and caught them all by surprise and Bill, Reginald's next-door neighbour, looked around and waved two bottles in the air. He said, "Thought you might need some support." His wide, toothless grin was a black gash across white whiskers.

"Come on in, Bill, and set yourself down," Reginald said. "That medicine is more than welcome. Pour it out quickly before Len here has a heart attack."

The old man was half way across the kitchen when a woman's painful shout cut in from the room above. Bill hesitated and Len whispered, "Gawd save us all."

"It's all happening then," Bill said. "It wasn't just a rumour." He filled the glasses and passed one to Len. "Get that down you. It's full of iron and you need iron when you're having a baby."

Len grabbed it and finished it in one. His eyes bulged and his hands lifted to his throat. "Sweet Jesus!" he gasped. "Now I've been poisoned."

"Pretty good, eh? I've been saving it for the occasion."

In the corner of the darkened living room the boys were wide-eyed and excited, watching the doorway from where a shaft of yellow light framed a patch of carpet.

Richard whispered, "I didn't know there'd be so much shouting and screaming."

Ian said gravely, "Maybe there's something wrong."

"No, it's normal," Tom put in, "my mate Simon was telling me when his sister was born. If there's a lot of screaming then it's a girl. They come out sideways and it hurts a bit."

"It is a bit frightening though," Ian said.

"No, it's just nature. It goes on for ages sometimes, sometimes all night, sometimes a week. But it always happens at night. If she ain't had it by morning then it won't be till the next night. Simon told me. He's good at them things."

They waited for the next cry. The men talked and laughed and drank and the boys listened and the women hurried upstairs and down and stopped only long enough to tell them that everything was well and that nothing had happened save for the odd false alarm and that the waters, whatever they were, had broken.

"That sounds right dodgy," Len said and grabbed at his drink.

"No problem, mate," Tommy said. "It's the contractions or something. They squeeze the bladder, see?"

The bottles emptied and lined the table and bread and cheese was brought out to soak up the home-brew.

"The first miracle I ever came across myself personally," Bill told them, probably to get Len's mind off the situation. "Was way back when I worked the docks. It was casual then and you had to be there bloody early. To be there at the crack of dawn this particular Monday I decided to sleep out and I took my blanket and slept under the cliffs, right near the harbour. You know the place? Near the big overhanging bastard? It did get bleedin' cold. Stone me, I woke up a dozen times shivering like there was no tomorrow. The night was clear, not a cloud, and the stars were as bright as I'd ever seen them, and the wash from the waves coming in seemed louder than normal. Ships went by like fireflies and blew their hooters. I lit a fire out of driftwood. Like I say it was freezing cold. Even the bleedin' seagulls were shittin' hailstones. Anyway, every time I woke up I heard this thumping noise, like heavy footsteps. It frightened me half to death. Thump, thump, thump, all night long. When I woke up in the morning it was the crack of dawn itself when nothing seems real. The sea was black and the froth was dirty yellow. It was like I'd woken on another planet. Everything seemed different, even the colours. I've never seen the cliffs so white or so big. Then I noticed what all the thumping had been. All around me, and scattered everywhere, every foot or so, were great pieces of white chalk that had fallen down during the night. They were everywhere. And not one of them had landed on me. But down by my feet, not more than a yard away from my blanket, there was a pile of these rocks built up like a little pyramid." He nodded. "That's a true story."

Reginald threw him a doubtful look. "It's a bit of a tall story if ever I heard one."

"But true as I'm standing here," he said from his seat.

"Well that is amazing."

Tommy looked out of narrowed eyes. "Huh," he grunted and finished his drink. "You sure you didn't notice them before you turned in?"

Bill shook his head. "I'd swear they weren't there till the morning and I sure as hell didn't collect them in my sleep."

"That is a miracle," Len nodded. "There are some things you can't explain."

Another shriek pierced the room and Len filled his glass again.

"Life is a curious business," Reginald said, "Very peculiar, but there's nowt as queer as folk. Remember old Albert Ferguson?"

Bill nodded. "We'll never forget old Albert. They took him away in the end. He pegged it in the funny farm."

"What happened?" Tommy asked as he helped himself to another drink.

Another shriek, a long drawn-out wail, interrupted the conversation for a moment. When it was evident that nothing was to follow, Reginald continued: "A very odd fellow. He moved here from Ashford shortly after the war, him and his wife and son. Had plenty of money, or so it seemed, but his wife and boy walked around in second-hand clothes. Never did find out where he got his money, probably a legacy. They were a very quiet family, hardly knew they were here, but came the time when he would wander down and try to join in the conversation with Bill and me and Eddie. Used to push between us and try to join in. He was the sort who had done everything and been everywhere. We never took to him and as for his family, hardly ever saw them. But then came the day that Eddie was looking for some slates for his roof. He'd been to the local merchants who wanted a tanner each. Well, old Albert must have heard us talking and said he'd get them for half the price. We humoured him, frankly thought it was a load of bollocks. But sure enough, the following day, he turned up with forty slates. Well, of course, Eddie jumped at it. Who wouldn't?

Bill here gave him an order for some, and I wanted fifty from him. OK, he said, give him a week. A week later, sure enough, the tiles arrived. We all said what a bloody good bloke he was and for a while he was drinking with us. Then one day Eddie was over Ford's in Dover, talking to a guy in there, and discovered that this Albert Ferguson had bought the tiles there, at a penny more than we could have got them for locally. Well, what do you make of that? Obviously the guy was out to make an impression but all that happened was that he was treated like an idiot. After that he stayed indoors; went to pieces. Suppose it was our fault, really, but people must realize that it takes a long time to be accepted and trying to con your way in will work against you in the end."

"That's pretty sad," Tommy said and pulled a face. "What happened to the wife and kid?"

"They moved away. Never saw them again."

"Very peculiar, but sad," Reginald agreed. "There are lessons to be learned all over." He shook his head and finished his drink and smacked his lips. "Shall we open the other bottle then?"

Into the night the women ran up and down the stairs and the men got steadily drunk and the cries became more frequent. The boys stood it for as long as they could and then they slept. They woke much later to join the bleary-eyed excitement and celebration. "It's a girl," they were told as they were invited to share a glass of beer.

"I told you it would be," Tom said to the brothers.

"Sally she's called," Len Mannings shouted through, and from his clotted voice it sounded as if he was in tears. "And she's the most beautiful thing I've ever seen."

The brothers were led up the narrow stairs to meet their cousin and Tom tagged along. His heart fluttered when he saw the baby, and leaning over the crib he whispered her name: "Sally."

It sounded just right.

The morning whispered; a slight breeze blew in through the open window and lifted the curtains. It was fresh and full of the sea. The brothers climbed up to his top bunk and lay next to him and pulled aside the curtains. They watched two couples wander slowly through the patterns of sunshine that angled in through the branches of the tall trees at the bottom of the garden.

"Who are they?" Tom asked.

Ian said, "They're in the guest rooms. This is a hotel. Well, not really, a bed and breakfast."

Richard said, "You should stay here for the holidays."

"My ma wouldn't let me. Maybe I could ask."

Ian said, "Get up to see Sally again later. Maybe take her some sweets."

Richard said, "We'll show you around today. Show you the cliffs."

"See what my dad's doing first. He might want my help on the van."

At the breakfast table Elizabeth explained that his father had left early to do his business and had left a few coppers for the boys to enjoy themselves. He had taken the van on his rounds to buy up the second hand clothing and more importantly, the jewellery and gold from the widows along his way. He would be back in the evening. Tom felt a little apprehensive at being left in the strange surroundings of the dining room with the other guests, mostly old couples, chatting quietly, and he worked at his manners. His anxiety increased as a full English breakfast was placed before him and he fell into silence. He had never seen six different foodstuffs together on a plate before and the bacon didn't taste like bacon at all – half of it was fat – and God only knew what the circle of black stuff was. Elizabeth noticed his shyness and hid her smile.

Armed with packed lunches the boys set out to climb the hills along the coast between Folkestone and Dover.

Richard told him, "This place is supposed to be haunted with ghosts of the dead sailors who were washed up when their ships went down. But we've never seen them."

Tom kept a watchful eye on the many caves and the other dark places. They checked the snares on the rabbit runs and explored the beach and the woods and it was there they came upon a circular round tower of grey brick and concrete standing in a deep hollow that might once have been a moat. Iron steps were set in the moat wall and another set reached from the ground to a small entrance set high in the tower wall.

Tom stood wide-eyed.

"It's a Martello tower," Richard said.

They raced around the wall and clambered down the steps, crossed the twenty yards to the foot of the tower and began to climb to the tower entrance.

"It's like the Tower of London," Tom said in amazement.

A shaft of light from the entrance fell on to a rotting timber floor. Tom pointed through one of the dangerous holes. "They might be the dungeons," he said. The rising round wall of the tower sloped inward toward the roof some eighteen feet above, itself supported by a thick central column of concrete. A stairway was cut into the wall up to a small square of light in the roof. Careful on the crumbling steps the boys climbed to the top and looked out on to a round concrete disc surrounded by a thick wall. They stepped out on to the roof.

Richard pointed over the trees to the shafts of light ducking into the sea and to a smudge of shadow beyond them. He said, "That's France over there."

"Not really?"

"It is," Ian said. "That's why these towers were built, to keep the Frenchies out. We done it at school."

"It's like a castle," Tom said quietly. "One day I'm going to have one of these."

Richard grunted, "They'd cost more than you're ever going to have."

Tom detected hostility and turned to face the older boy. "You think what you like, mate, but one day I'll have one, and it won't be full of shit either."

They started back to London in the evening when the dusk was spreading purple shadows across the fields. His father was happy with the way his business had worked out for the van was fully loaded and struggled on the gentle hills.

"It was good to see them all again," he told the boy. "How did you make out with Ian and Richard?"

"All right."

"Nice lads, ain't they?"

"They're all right. They spoke a bit funny, that's all."

"That's cos they're foreigners, or as good as. Country folk all speak different, especially on the coast. It comes from them being closer to the other countries, if you see what I mean, countries like Germany and France and the Isle of Wight. Blimey, if you was to go north instead of south you wouldn't even understand them. I've been to places up north – they call it the Black Country – where you only catch one word in three."

"The Black Country?"

"That's where the coal mines are, boy, and the men up there, they walk around covered in coal-dust, black as night all day long. It's the dust that gets in their throats, it gives them an accent, see? Normal people can't understand them. But tell me what you got up to with Richard and Ian?"

"They showed me a castle they built to keep the Frenchies out."

"The Frenchies! Blimey! You've got to be careful of the Frenchies. They eat frogs, frogs and onions, for breakfast and dinner. That's why they're always so jumpy. But Dover Castle! You must have walked a fair way then?"

"We did. Went to the top of it and you could see France."

"That's a thing to tell your ma, visiting Dover Castle, seeing France."

"It didn't have no flags, though, but there was this bleedin' big moat they used to put the crocodiles in. I might try and get a book about it."

"Good idea. I'd like to see that. I never knew they put crocs in the moat."

"They did. We dug up some old bones. They might have been the Frenchies who were trying to get across."

"Blimey!"

The night closed in and they sat in silence for a while. Tom noticed that his father seemed strangely uneasy, constantly checking his mirror and even turning in his seat to check the road behind. Headlamps flared some two hundred yards or so behind them.

His father muttered, "He's keeping his distance."

Tom turned and checked the car out for himself.

"Are they following us?" he asked.

"Following us, boy? I didn't say that. Why would anyone want to follow us? Anyway, how could anyone have known where we've been?"

Even as he reassured his son, Tommy knew very well the answer to his own question. He'd told a number of people in the Eagle just where they were going, the route they intended to take and, more importantly, the time they could be expected home. And after a few drinks he hadn't been too concerned about who might have been listening. He also knew that just lately he'd been making a few enemies by deriding the Cross Gang and encouraging people to take a hard line.

Slowly the car behind crept closer and the headlights became a blaze in the rear window. It pulled out and overtook, and his father sighed a silent relief as the red tail-lights grew fainter and then disappeared altogether.

"Not a problem," his father said and winked at him.

Tom relaxed and watched the dark shapes of overhanging trees fly by.

"It ain't been as hot as it is at home but my face feels really tight."

"That's the salt in the air, boy, burns you up quicker down here. We're in the east, see, and the sun comes up in the east, so we're closer to the sun. That's why."

Tom yawned.

"Have a kip. You was up all night. Better not tell your ma or she'll have a proper go at me."

He curled up against his father's arm.

"It's been a great trip, Dad."

"You done well, boy. I was proud of you."

"I love you, Dad."

"Well then, everything's fine, ain't it? Everything's fair and fine. You get some kip if you like."

They travelled into the night and as they neared the capital the air grew heavy and it began to spit. There had been one or two sharp showers along the way.

"Another half an hour or so and we'll be home. It's straight to bed for you."

The boy stirred and looked up.

His father continued: "This rain has held us up a bit."

Wipers smudged the windscreen.

"Hello, what's all this?" His father brought the van to a halt.

Tom peered through the mottled glass at the dark form of a man caught in the beams of light. He noticed the flickering lantern first, waving to and fro, then the cape and helmet. Beyond the constable a car had slewed across the road and three men stood beside it.

"An accident," his father muttered, "Nothing to worry about."

The policeman strolled forward. Tom saw the puffy features and small round eyes. His father wound down the window.

"Bit of an accident, Sir," the constable said. "No one hurt but we need to bounce her to the side of the road. Could you lend us a hand?"

"No problem." His father reached behind for his coat. He turned to the boy and said, "Sit tight." He winked, opened the door and climbed out.

Tom struggled to see what was happening through the windscreen. The rain blurred everything. His father was sauntering toward the men at the car while the policeman carrying the swinging lamp followed behind. In that instant Tom felt his stomach tighten into a terrible knot and his features froze. His father had stopped ten feet or so short of the men and it was as they spread out before him that he appeared to recognize them. He took a step back to the van but with the policeman so close behind his way was blocked. The three men were on him instantly and without warning. The scuffle was over in seconds as blades glinted in the headlamps. His father staggered back from the group toward the van, three or four paces, before sagging to his knees.

Tom leapt out of the van and charged toward the men, his feet slapping on the wet surface. One of the men grabbed Tom's arm and swung him in the air. He was lifted five or six feet and landed on the grass verge where he rolled into a ditch brimming with dripping nettles and bramble. The men laughed as they watched the youngster disappear beneath the foliage. Tom struggled through the tearing briars to see a heavy-bodied bald man kneeling over his father just as two shotguns fired simultaneously. The explosions thudded down the wet road and the windscreen and one of the lights on the van disintegrated. The men reloaded and more explosions cracked open the darkness with orange flame. The four men ran back to their car and climbed in. Doors slammed and the engine revved and the car skidded backward on to the road, then moved forward and gathered pace. Tom watched until the tail-lights went out then he crept out of the ditch and ran to his father. The acrid smell of cordite lay on the heavy air.

"Dad! Dad!"

He struggled to lift his father's head from the muddy surface.

"Don't move me, boy," his father said gently. "They've cut my arms and legs so don't move me. Just stand by me and stop the next motor. Wave up and down. Be careful it don't hit you."

"You'll be all right, Dad. There's something coming now."

"Go on then, wave them down."

A car approached and flooded the road with light. Tom waved frantically and stood his ground until the car stopped before him. An elderly, white-haired man in the car leaned apprehensively from the window.

"Help me, mister. It's my dad. He's been hurt bad."

Before the police and an ambulance arrived, his father told the boy to lean closer and when his lips almost touched his ear, he whispered, "They'll ask you what happened. Tell them nothing. You saw nothing, you recognized no one. When you get back you tell Peter Woodhead and only him. Tell your ma you were thrown in the ditch and didn't see a thing. Understand me, boy?"

Tom nodded but his father made him say it. He said, "I understand, Dad, really I do."

And with that his father rested his head back on the wet road and closed his eyes.

Chapter 12

It was not a time from which fond memories sprang. The weeks and months that his father spent in hospital were marked by his mother's despair. There were gifts and there was charity and when the doctors explained that his father was crippled and would never walk again the van was sold and for a while the financial burden was lightened. One day, after a visit, Rose took the boy aside and explained in a severe voice in order to conceal her own anguish that his father had not only lost the use of his limbs but that tuberculosis had set into his hip. The surgeons operated and removed bone, and flesh that had turned white, and after weeks of treatment and two further operations decided they could do no more and sent him home.

Throughout that time Peter Woodhead was there. In his brown suit and red braces and leather belt, an inch of yellow handkerchief showing above his top pocket, his brown shoes shining like mirrors, he would doff his bowler and open the car door for Rose and wait until she was settled and he would drive her to the hospital and wait for her in the car, sometimes for the full hour of visiting time. Rose would never let Tom skip school but at the weekends he went with them. Perhaps because of the police involvement, Peter was the only one of his father's friends who visited the hospital. He made certain that Rose had food in the house and a little money beside and he paid the coalman. He made little of it and said that her husband would sort him out once he was back on his feet. Rose smiled at his gaffe and embarrassment had coloured his face and on that day he had driven off quickly without seeing them to the door. He sold the van on her behalf and paid her more than it was worth. It was no reflection on Peter Woodhouse that Rose considered that one day she might have to repay the kindness. The years had stripped away her dreams and taught her the cunning ways of men and until that time she had never known an exception to that rule. But in all that time, a period that lasted four months, Peter never once set foot in the house, and when Tom asked his mother about it she answered awkwardly, "He's a good bloke and he doesn't want to compromise me."

"What's that mean?"

"It means," his mother hesitated, "...that he's a nice man and you can trust him."

"I don't trust nobody," Tom murmured, "except for you and me dad."

Once he was home a few people turned up to see him. They slipped in the back way, after dark, and they spoke in whispers and while they were there Rose kept Tom out of the way. Peter Woodhouse visited two or three times a week and always he would smuggle in a bottle and keep his eyes from Rose's withering gaze. When he left his father was in better moods, propped up on his pillows, his face slightly flushed, the sour smell of drink on his breath neither here nor there. And he would say to Rose, "It's good to see Peter. Mind you, seeing him makes me realize how much I miss a drink!" And Rose would say nothing but she would lean across and kiss his bitter lips.

"Rose!"

The call came one evening just after dark. She came in from the kitchen wiping her flour-coated hands on a linen tea towel.

"I've got to get out a while, you know that. Blimey, I've forgot what fresh air is like!"

She sat on the bed and gripped the towel tightly so that he would not see her hands trembling. Her knuckles turned as white as the baking powder that still speckled her forearms. Her eyes clouded.

"Roll me a fag, Lady, and I'll tell you what I've got in mind."

Rose rubbed her hands together and concentrated on the roll-up. There was a knowing glint in his eyes as he accepted it between his lips. She lit it but the quivering flame gave her away.

"Cool down, Lady," he said, and from then on spoke while he smoked. "You know Jim the cabbie? He's going to drive me out, get me out a while. I think the morning will do nicely. I've been watching the sun slip down over the rooftop opposite and it's left a red glow in the sky, like a sign, almost. You know what they say? The morning will be fine. It will give you a chance…" His voice trailed off. Whether it was the smoke that made his eyes water she couldn't tell.

"A chance of what?" she asked. It came out coldly and not the way she'd intended.

He grunted, "A chance to clean up in here, what else? Can't do it proper while I'm lying here, can you?"

She nodded and attempted a smile. "I manage," she said.

"You manage great."

Ash from his cigarette dropped on to his vest and she brushed it off but left a grey smudge.

"I think I'll go," he said quietly. "It's killing me lying here. I can handle the pain, you know that, but what's going on in my head is doing me in. I'm lying here in a prison knowing it's a life sentence. I can't even look at you in the eye, Darling, not any more. I'm going crazy, and there ain't a way back, not this time. I don't want you to see me like this. It ain't me, is it? When someone's got to wipe your arse, then that's it, isn't it?"

"I know," she whispered. She took the cigarette and crushed it in a heavy glass ashtray at the foot of the bed. She moved across to the door, wringing her hands as she went.

"Here a minute, I ain't finished," he said and she turned back to him and he saw her glistening tears. "I love you," he said. "Always did. Always thought we'd grow old together. Always wanted to give you everything you wanted. That's all I ever wanted to do since the first day I met you." He waited for that to sink in then said, "Send the boy in. I want a word in his shell-like."

She nodded and sucked in her trembling lip.

Flames flickered and spat into the hearth from the small black-leaded grate, and sent shadows dancing across the washed out walls of the cluttered, smoky room. On the mantelpiece was a faded brown photograph of his grandparents and one of his father in uniform taken in 1915 and another, in black and white, of his parents on their wedding day. With greased hair and sporting a moustache his father looked like a spiv. He could hear his mother moving around in the kitchen, rattling dishes. The lisp in his father's voice was still evident but it was weak. In the gloom Tom was freshly amazed at how ill his father looked; the weight had fallen off him leaving sunken cheeks and hollow eyes. His skin was pale and grey and covered in a film of sweat. His shoulder blades protruded through his vest and his once hard and corded arms were thin and wasted. The furniture in the small sitting room had been rearranged to make way for his single bed but it was still crammed to overflowing. Tom sat on the bed, in the place his mother had occupied, and he clung to his father's words, sensing and yet not understanding how long they would have to last. Nothing would be the same again. He felt the great weight of his heart pressing down.

"I want you to know that I've always been proud of you, my son, and that I always will be. What I've missed you're going to have to pick up the hard way. I'm poorly now. By golly, you can see that." The last word was stretched out in the London way.

Tom blinked away a growing tear.

"You know what happened and, when you're bigger, you can sort it out. I know you will, and I know there's nothing I can say that will stop you. But when you do, you do it cold, not hot. You need to be cold when you sort out things that need sorting."

His father nodded and smiled softly and then said, "There are a couple of rules you got to remember, important rules that will get you to wherever you're going. Listen to me now, this is important. Never split on no one, not even your enemy. There ain't nothing more contemptible in the world than a snitch. Never trust a rich man. No one ever got rich by spending his own money. He got rich by spending someone else's. Never trust the law 'cause they're lying, thieving bastards, and never trust a businessman or a politician neither because they're lying, thieving bastards too. Never give them nothing. Never say nothing to them, no matter what they say or promise. Never back down from no one, even if it means you'll get hurt. Never walk away from nothing because sooner or later it'll always catch you up. Always remember that the man who gets the first good shot in is usually the one who ends up winning. If you've got troubles then there are two friends you'll always have. First is Reggie in Folkestone. You can write to him. He'd like that. The second is Peter Woodhead. He knows a lot of tricks. Listen to him and learn. Never slag him off and always back him up. There's one other thing, the most important thing, and you'll likely learn it the hard way like most of us do. There's nothing in life more dangerous than a woman's smile. If she smiles at you, you're in trouble. If you smile back you're hooked well and truly. And the worse thing is there's nothing you can do about it. You'll be helpless. The devil himself lives in a woman's smile. But even so, my son, one day you'll have a girlfriend, maybe a wife, and she's the most important thing you're ever going to have to choose. You must choose one with a nice voice because, believe me, you'll be listening to it till it hurts for the rest of your life. Never, ever, tell her about your business. Women talk. They can't help it. It's part of being a woman. Always honour the woman you choose to be your wife and have your children. Sometimes you might want to try things out that are different to what is normal. Things that are a bit racy or smutty, if you know what I mean. Well, you've got to try them out on other women, see, and never the wife. You've always got to treasure your wife and protect her from that sort of fancy, even more so when you've had a drink and those things are more likely to creep into your head. You've got to back her up, even when she's wrong, see? And that's the difficult bit that you've got to learn, and you never, ever, let anyone insult her. You treat that like a capital offence, no quarter given. These are the rules that men have got to live by, and by golly, you have no truck at all with them that don't. That's it. I can't tell you nothing else."

Jim was a cabbie and he turned up the following morning as arranged. He was a tall man in a creased navy-blue suit. A white celluloid collar cut into his soft double chin. A tie around his middle and a pair of red braces kept up his trousers. His clean features and honest eyes were different to most of the men who'd visited Tommy and Rose felt a little easier.

"You ready for the off, then?" he said to Tommy. "The cab's been polished and she's waiting just for you." Jim was round-shouldered as a lot of tall men are, caused by the constant stooping to talk to shorter men. He lifted Tommy from the bed easily, as though he was carrying a child, and manoeuvred him to the front door.

Tommy muttered, "Gawd, it's been a long time since I used the front door."

Rose said quietly, "Take care." She'd spent an age getting him ready. She'd bathed him and shaved and dressed him and she'd combed his hair and brushed his teeth. And she'd insisted he wore his Sunday best.

"Bye now," she said and closed the door quickly to cover her distress and didn't see Jim carry him down the step and across the path to the cab. Jim set him on the back seat and secured a belt that fitted under his arms.

"I rigged it up last night, my son. Stop you rolling about."

A few children stopped their game of hopscotch to watch and a few neighbours came out or peered from behind their curtains. Jim climbed into the cab, slid back the interior window and said, "Right, then, my son, ready?"

Tommy nodded and glanced up at the house for the last time and saw the wisp of smoke curling up into the bank of solid cloud.

"Ready," he said.

The cab nosed slowly through the maze of criss-cross back streets and left Bethnal Green and Stepney and the poorer parts of Whitechapel behind and swung into an area where the houses were finer with pillars supporting the porches and iron railings guarding the basements. Ahead of them, at the top of the Strand, the towers and turrets of the Royal Courts rose from the soot-coated surroundings. In front the traffic stood still, blocked solid by a stream of omnibuses and taxicabs that spilled from Charing Cross, and Jim turned the cab on to the Embankment, left again before Waterloo Bridge and headed back toward the Tower. It was high tide and under the slate-grey sky the galvanized surface of the river mirrored the buildings and the line of cranes and jibs slanting over the bursting cargo holds on the opposite bank. A low mist clung on and seeped into the cab. Jim pulled in and cut the motor.

"Used to come down here as a nipper," Tommy muttered, "watched the boats, fished a bit. Never caught sod all. It's a dirty bastard river, full of shit. Never did warrant its greatness. Ain't got no waterfalls or rapids."

Jim stood by the open door and put a Woodbine between Tommy's lips. He'd parked near a row of steps that led down to the walk at the water's edge where on a warm day couples would slowly stroll and office workers would bring their lunch boxes. It was silent now. A tug moved sluggishly through the thick waters, barges stirred restlessly, and on the wharf opposite a few men worked in slow-motion stacking boxes in front of a massive warehouse.

"I'd like to go down there and sit a while. Can you get me down them steps?"

"We'll have a go, my son."

Jim reached in and unbuckled the belt support then lifted Tommy out and carried him down the flight of concrete steps to a bench that faced the river. He set him down and the two men sat in silence and finished their cigarettes. After a while Jim stood and stretched as though the chill had stiffened his back.

"I'll go and check the cab," he said.

Tommy nodded slowly and murmured, "You do that."

Jim climbed the steps slowly, as though his legs were suddenly weighed down. He didn't look back. He sat in the cab, quite still. A minute went by, and another, and then he said in a broken voice, "Silly sod," and he reached forward and switched on the ignition and drove slowly up to the Embankment.

Chapter 13

The day was grey and overcast but in places shafts of sunlight ducked out of the dead-man's cloud.

People came out to watch the procession. They stood in the gardens and leant out of windows, they watched through open doors and shop windows. They saw the vanguard first, a solitary old man dressed in heavy black and a scuffed top hat, then the black plumed horses pulling the shining hearse. Their hooves clattered on the cobbles, their graceful heads held high, muscles rippling under the great curves of their glossy backs. Behind the hearse came the mourners. They went from the front of the house, down the hill and past the empty Eagle where the men stood silently on the pavement. They skirted the market where some of the stallholders stopped their business and bowed their heads, past the plate-glass fronted shops where the owners stood behind their windows and on past the bakery and the rubber factory. Boys lay on the overhanging slates to watch the column pass, ragged boys with grimy faces. They pointed at the people they recognized and whispered their names. This was their warren.

Tom saw them and turned his back in despair and held on to his mother's hand for some support.

After it was over, people drank and laughed and joked and stuffed themselves with cakes and sandwiches, and talked about his father as though he'd been gone a long time. The sadness of the ceremony had vanished and Tom was angry because of it. He wanted to scream out to mark his father's passing and he wanted them to cry real tears. He hid in his room and put his hands over his ears to cut out the laughter. He cried until his throat became painful.

The massive frame of Peter Woodhouse blocked his doorway. He wore a black suit and tie but his bowler hat was missing. He stretched out his braces and let them twang, and took a deep breath, waiting for Tom to gather himself.

Tom swallowed hard and sat up.

The publican said softly, "Now, now, boy." He sat on the bed next to Tom and produced a large white handkerchief. "Blow your nose. I want to talk to you." He pressed the handkerchief into Tom's hands. "I know it don't seem right when people have a good time at a wake but you got to think of it as a celebration. I won't tell you your old man has gone to a finer place and left all his pain behind, because that's not what it's about. I'll leave all that to the clergy. Downstairs they're remembering him and remembering the good times, and trying to forget the bad. They laugh and joke but that's because they're sad inside and if they didn't they'd cry. And that wouldn't do anyone any good. It's how it is. People have got to hide their sadness today and save it for another day. It's difficult, I know, and there are times when you think you're dying inside and your heart has shrivelled to nothing and the world has ended and you don't want to go on. That's how I felt when my wife died. It takes a long time for it to get easier and even then you'll never forget. But there are things you got to do, and one of them, the main thing, is to look after your ma. That's what your old man would have wanted. That's the one thing you can give him now, and believe me he'll know it, and he'll expect it. You come and see me after school, when you're ready and there's no hurry, because I need someone to help me down the gym and tidy up the bar for which I'll pay a fair wage. No more and no less. This is not a favour. I'm going back down now. I've said my piece. I want you to dry your face and blow your nose, and come down and give your ma some support. Right then, I'll expect you in two minutes."

Tom was too overwhelmed with emotion to speak and all he could feel was the unending throb of grief.

Peter Woodhead stood and went from the room and closed the door gently behind him.

Tom wiped his eyes and ran his fingers through his hair. He looked around the tiny box-room as if seeing it for the first time. In a moment he would go downstairs again and help his mother but first, he wanted to stretch out his last moments of childhood.

"Dad," he whispered, "Oh, Dad."

Things gradually moved out of the darkness and the unthinking routine that had kept them going in the few weeks following the funeral began to ease their loss. Peter Woodhead kept his word and employed Tom in the gym and in the backroom of his bar. In the bar he washed glasses and emptied ashtrays and stacked crates of empty bottles and in the gym he swept floors and tidied lockers and changed towels. It was in the gym that he learned about boxing. To begin with he watched the young boxers being put through their paces – the youngsters came from the Green and Stepney and Whitechapel, some from as far away as Swiss Cottage and Kilburn. The club had a growing reputation. It wasn't long before Peter Woodhead and his trainer introduced him to the heavy bag and the speed bag and the skipping rope and shortly after that he was sparring for a round or two. He learned how to stand and move and throw a punch and parry, how to block and counter and jab. But school and his homework always came first; Peter Woodhead was uncompromising about that. While Tom was at school Rose washed the laundry and cleaned the bars. Because of his work Tom saw less of his friends but his weekends were kept free. Peter had said from the start that Tom should not work the weekends and nothing that Tom could say would change his mind. And so the weekends were spent in the warren with Simon and his mates but the rooftops had lost their appeal.

On his way to the warren Tom would stop at the market with its stalls spread out before the Eagle and he would sneak a glance at the statue of the massive bird of prey readying for take-off. There was always something faintly sinister about it – its beak, its talons, the way its eyes fixed on him, perhaps even the cold, colourless stone – that sent a shiver along his spine, and he was glad to pass by, beyond the range of its piercing gaze. He would linger at the furniture stall and if the old Yid was not about, and if there was no sign of his mates, he would flick through the battered volumes in the tea chests. So it was on the day that sealed his future and set in his young mind the concept that violence – calculated, swift and merciless – was the only way to settle the past.

Engrossed in the titles and turning the yellowed pages slowly, he didn't see the old man creep out from behind the high wardrobes.

"You like to read?" he asked in a thickly coated voice.

Tom jumped. His eyes widened.

The old man held back, aware of the boy's fear. He wrapped his arms around his greatcoat and waited for an answer. His watery red eyes glinted.

"Maybe," Tom answered and stood his ground, "So what?"

"Books are good. You'll find everything you'll ever want to know in a book."

To make himself less of a threat the old man eased himself down into a scuffed leather armchair and rested his arms on the split rests. Tom relaxed a little. He checked the crowd again to make certain he wasn't recognized.

"What do you like to read, my son?"

"I ain't your son!"

The old man shrugged his weak shoulders. "You're not. You're right. It's a figure of speech, probably a bad one. It means nothing. If you tell me your name I will call you by that. Mine is Wiseman. Albert Wiseman."

"I know your name. Everybody does."

"Yes, you are not wrong. I have been here a long time. Some people would say too long."

"Where do you come from?"

Wiseman chuckled and raised a limp hand to indicate it didn't matter. "I am here now and that is all that matters. Yesterday and tomorrow..." His hand waved again.

"My name is Tom Smith."

"Ah, yes." He nodded. "I have heard of you, too. Your father was well known on the market, as was your grandfather before him. So then, how do you do, Tom Smith? Tell me, what sort of books do you like to read?"

"I like cowboys."

"Yes, I like those, the penny dreadfuls. But what are you reading now?"

"At school we're still doing Two Cities."

"A Tale of Two Cities?"

"Yeah, that's it."

"Charles Dickens." The old man pulled a face.

"What's wrong with that?"

The hands rose again and the old man said quickly, "Nothing, nothing at all. It is a spiteful book, that's all. Understanding is better than prejudice."

Tom shrugged and checked the crowd again. It was busy with the last minute rush before the market closed. The search was on for the bargains, the overripe fruit, the meat dressed with blood that wouldn't stand another day, the fish filleted so that the dead eyes and dull skin were not on show.

"I will lend you a book," the old man continued. "If you will read it and look after it and not turn down the pages to keep your place."

Guarding his eagerness Tom returned his attention to Albert Wiseman.

"It was written by someone who lived not far from here. He was the son of a butcher. It's called Robinson Crusoe." The old eyes narrowed fractionally. "You haven't read it?"

Tom shook his head.

A smile of relief spread over the gaunt features. "That's good. We can discuss its merits when you have finished it. It's an adventure about shipwreck and a man who finds himself on a desert island full of cannibals and cut-throat pirates, but more than that, it's about a friendship between two people from different places." From his sitting position the old man leant forward and pulled open the drawers of a battered desk. "It's here somewhere," he muttered as he rummaged through, piling magazines on to his lap.

Tom recognized a face and he was filled with instant panic. The man had appeared from the crowd and was almost on him before he turned. He found his way blocked by another man who was ready to tackle. They were within two yards of him, one either side, when he made his move and darted across the narrow walkway, shoving between the legs of startled shoppers and diving under a stall selling fresh chickens and eggs. The two men rushed after him, pushing aside the protesting onlookers. They ducked under the table but Tom had gone. The bald-headed man picked up a chicken and flung it across the stall. The rage in his eyes made the people close by back away. Some of the eggs splattered on to the floor.

"There! There he goes!" the other yelled and they raced between the stalls, pushing people from their path.

Albert Wiseman stood holding the battered book against his chest. He slipped the book into his pocket and called to the next stallholder: "Eileen, will you spell me for a few minutes?"

A plump woman wearing a heavy cardigan tucked into a moneybag said, "I'll be here Albert." She nodded sullenly, then added her concern: "Don't get involved, Albert. You're not a young man any more and it's four o'clock already!"

"We are involved, Eileen, and if it's four o'clock already then in one hour it will be five."

Albert Wiseman hurried as fast as he could after the boy.

Tom moved swiftly across the market, dodging the throng of shoppers and weaving his way through the maze of narrow walkways. Behind him trestle tables were overturned and bystanders knocked aside. This was Tom's playground and the two men should not have bothered. They were never going to catch him. They searched the market for a while longer then wandered north into the criss-cross of back alleys. It was here that Peter Woodhead found them. The publican was backed up by two of his more promising boxers.

The bald man's head cracked against a rough concrete wall. His companion had taken one blow to the gut and lay in a crumpled heap nearby.

"Jimmy Vale," Peter Woodhouse said. Beneath his bowler his usual calm expression was flushed and angry, his pale blue eyes carrying a deadly threat. "I don't want a war with the KC mob, but if that's what it takes we'll start with the first two casualties right now."

The side of Vale's face was pressed tightly against the wall. Blood trickled from his nose and mouth.

He spoke from the corner of his mouth: "Who's talking about war? We ain't come near you."

"It's the kid, Jimmy. The kid! He's under my protection, see, and I can't have big bastards like you chasing him all over town. It's not doing his schoolwork any good at all."

"His old man would have kept him in order, but now..." A muscle near the corner of Vale's visible eye began to twitch.

Peter Woodhead grunted, "The lad won't snitch. I'll be looking out for him. Tell me you understand?"

"OK, but you have a word in his ear and make sure he understands."

The pressure was relaxed and Vale turned to face Peter's towering frame. He rubbed the graze on the side of his face and mopped up the blood on his sleeve.

"You're scum, Vale, and it upsets me to have to talk to scum."

Vale walked stiffly across to where his friend lay and kicked his leg. The other rose slowly and together and without looking back they went from the alley.

Albert Wiseman emerged from the shadows clutching the book against his chest.

"I'm obliged to you," Peter said to him.

The old man nodded. "Will you do me one more service?" he said and pressed the book into the publican's hand. "The boy, he forgot his book."

Peter glanced down at the faded book and then into the old man's watery eyes.

"What's this?"

"It's a good story."

"I'll lay you half a crown he doesn't read it."

"You have a wager." The old man rubbed his hands together and chuckled loudly before moving off.

"Right then," Peter said to his two boxers. "You should be training. What are you standing around for?"

Tom Smith clung to the smouldering chimney pot and looked out over the darkening rooftops. Evening closed in and a whisper of breeze blew away the pale smoke and across the way a metal notice advertising Lyons Bakery swayed and creaked on its rusty chains. Beneath it the shadows closed in on the weather-beaten posters for Bovril and Perrier and the images of the healthy scrubbed faces of the people enjoying them. Simon clambered up beside him and squatted on his haunches.

"All right Tom?"

"All right, Sim."

"What you doing?"

"Nothing. Just thinking."

"Thinking about what?"

"Everything. Getting even."

Simon tossed some small chippings into the alley. He said, "Heard the shouting. Saw Jimmy Vale looking for you."

"Yeah, he was. That's what I meant."

"What can you do? Stay away from him, keep running, that's all you can do."

"For now, maybe, but not forever."

Simon shrugged and wiped snot on to the sleeve of his jumper.

"What shall we do then?"

Tom turned to him and said, "First we've got to get a gang together."

"I mean now. What shall we do now?"

"Wait," Tom said matter-of-factly. "We'll wait till our turn comes around and then…"

"Then what?" Simon asked and glanced across at his friend. He saw that Tom's eyes had dulled, as if an inner lid had been drawn across them. He'd never noticed it before.

"Then we'll kill them all."

Later, when the air carried the first frosts of winter and the smog hung until midday, Peter Woodhead paid his half crown to Albert Wiseman and watched as the old man's features cracked in pleasure. On his way back to the Eagle, Peter met up with Tom and said, "It has crossed my mind to invite your mother out for dinner but I was wondering whether you think it is a good idea? She needs brightening up a bit." While he waited for Tom's response he examined his bowler and dusted it before returning it to his head.

"You'll have to ask her then."

"I know that but what do you think?"

"I think she would probably need a new dress if she was to go out with you to a fancy restaurant."

Peter stopped in his tracks. Tom turned in time to see his curious expression.

"I think I know what you mean, Tom," he said.

Winter gripped the capital and dampness crept inside cracked trusses and crumbling brick. The Eagle remained a sanctuary. At Christmas, warmed by a massive log fire, the laughter and singing spilled out into the streets. Tom saw his mother in the crowd, standing by the solid, dependable figure of Peter Woodhead. The landlord was singing, his voice carrying above the rest. Beside him, his mother looked tiny and fragile, weeping silently as she attempted to mouth the song. Tom pushed his way through the busy bar and slipped his arm around her waist. She looked down at him and he saw the wetness beneath her eyes. She sniffed and smiled.

He shouted above the din: "You're a lady, do you know that?"

She held a small handkerchief to her nose and leant down closer to whisper in his ear: "And you're a gentleman, my son."

Tom saw that Peter was holding his mother's tiny hand and that she didn't mind, and saw the strange look of contentment in Peter's eyes. Tom smiled and drew in a deep breath.

"Tell you what," Peter said and rummaged in his pocket. "I noticed the hot chestnut man outside. I could just eat a hot chestnut or two. How about you?" He handed Tom some coins and watched him head for the door and felt Rose squeeze his hand.

Tom found the chestnut seller standing next to his simple brazier, his coke glowing red and turning white around the edges while his smoke sweetened the air. A few snowflakes drifted from the dark sky into the glare of the street lamps. A small crowd gathered around the hurdy-gurdy man who was belting out I Could Care For You/If You Could Only Care For Me, and a few people joined in.

He noticed the old Jew pottering around his gloomy furniture stall even though the market had been shut up for hours. He threw him a tentative wave before snatching back his hand as he caught sight of Simon Carter searching through a discarded pile of spoiled vegetables. Simon's dad sent him out to find anything that might still be usable.

"All right, Tom?" Simon called, his face brightening at the chance encounter.

Tom paid for his brown bag full of chestnuts and after a moment's hesitation wandered over to the furniture stall. Albert Wiseman regarded him. His eyes were the colours of split coal and sparkled in the gaslight.

"What can I do for you, young Master Tom?"

"Thought you might like a chestnut, that's all."

The old man wavered and frowned and gave Tom a curious look before dusting his hand on his greatcoat and poking into the bag. "That's very kind of you," he said, "Very kind indeed."

Simon called, "You all right there, Tommy?"

Tom turned and smiled and shouted back, "Yeah, everything's all right now. Everything's fair and fine."

Chapter 14
1939

To the Cockney the annual fair held in Victoria Park had become an institution, as important as any of the major festivals, but Billy Smart moved his fair around the northern districts and in the second week of April when the temperatures were hitting an unusually warm twenty-two degrees it arrived at Bruce Castle, a short walk from the enemy headquarters at White Hart Lane. Here it was that the medley of sound and colour and movement came together beneath the ancient oaks and the crowds poured in from Tottenham and Wood Green and Enfield to gather between the stalls and the pleasure rides. Here it was that the hissing naphtha flares, great globes of shimmering light, turned the smiling faces into white masks, and shouts and screams came from the riders on the flying horses and the chairoplanes and the barrel of love, and the massive spotless traction engines ticked over and belched clouds of steam.

A boxing booth, a large green canvas close to the Castle itself, was at the heart of the fair, for the northern districts, like the East End, was brimming with retired boxers only too willing to describe past glories. They lived in a vacuum of boozy memories but stayed on the lookout for any promising youngster who might make them a bob or two. In such places the youngsters could be found taking on the booth professionals for the promise of a fiver if they managed to stay the distance.

In the car park a battered black Chrysler eased next to a sleek racy

Mercedes Benz. Two couples emerged from the Chrysler and stood for a moment to admire the sports car.

"Supercharged," said Simon Carter. He was heavier than Tom Smith and wore a mop of bright ginger hair beneath his flat cap. The front button on his jacket strained against his swollen waistband. The small slip of a girl he was with held on to his hand and attempted to pull him toward the fair. Her slight weight made no impression and she gave up. She wore thick spectacles that magnified her green eyes. Her elfin face was dotted by a few freckles over her nose and cheeks and framed by shoulder-length dark hair topped by a small black hat. He went on, "Eight cylinder, independent suspension, it'll do a ton without bother."

Tom nodded and said, "We'll have some of it one day."

A woman leaning on Tom's arm scoffed at the idea and said, "And pigs might fly." She reached up and clipped some loose straw-coloured hair beneath her red bonnet. He turned to face her and she saw his stony look. She stretched up and quickly planted a kiss on his mouth. "Didn't mean it," she said and rubbed a smear of lipstick from his lips. He grinned at her quick thinking and his brown eyes sparkled in the burning light. She smiled back and adjusted a white silk stock so that it all but concealed a faint scar that ran down from his jaw. She brushed a thread from the front of his jacket.

"Right then Sim," Tom said. "If Slasher's fighting you should get three to one. Ten nicker." He pushed the note into Simon's top pocket.

"All of it? He's no bleedin' novice, Tommy."

"Nor am I, my son."

The girl at Simon's side adjusted her glasses and said, "Come on, Sim. He's the butter and egg man." Still in that awkward limbo between adolescence and womanhood her slang sounded put-on, as if she was trying hard to win points. She swung around in a haughty movement and started toward the fair, her loose dress billowing and offering a sudden glimpse of petticoat. She was miffed. Simon had promised to take her to see Deanna Durbin in *One Hundred Men and a Girl* and the fair was second best.

Tom watched her go and shook a disapproving head. "She's just a school kid. What are you playing at?"

"High school," Simon countered, "And she wears a uniform." He grinned, waiting for a nod of approval, but it didn't come. Eventually he shrugged and followed the girl between the rows of cars into the park.

Once they had gone Tom checked his reflection in the window of the Chrysler and ran a comb through his greased dark hair. He leant against the door and the girl stepped between his legs.

"Afterwards," she said and fluttered long, artificial lashes. "What shall we do afterwards?" She reached down and stroked his groin.

"Well, that depends."

She followed his gaze over the cars and pulled a sour face. "I don't know what she's doing here. I'm surprised she didn't bring her satchel with her."

"He met her last week, in the queue for the pictures."

"She's trouble, jail-bait, and he ain't actually a man about town, is he? You should have a word."

"Maybe I will." He checked that Simon was far enough ahead and nodded. "Right, let's go and earn some pocket-money."

Smoke swirled under the heavy canvas and curled up to the black ceiling above a bank of lights. Boxers from the past gazed down from advertisements stuck to the limp walls. Kid Lewis and Mendoza stood against a backdrop of the Albert Hall and Wembley Town Hall but the curtain of smoke was so thick that those at the top were barely visible. Around the central ring the tent was seething with spectators cheering each attack and booing every retreat. The smoke mixed with the perspiration and heat and the air hung heavy and full and increased the intoxication.

The professional contests, spaced between the 'have-a-go' bouts, were fought out between the booth boxers and they knew how to involve the crowd. Flailing punches, the odd splatter of blood and knock-downs in most fights, had more to do with theatre than boxing but occasionally there was a needle match where it turned out for real. Between these matches the proprietor stood up and pleaded with the foolish, the likely youngster who was out to impress his girlfriend or perhaps one who had drunk one too many. "Step up and win a fiver," he told them. "You can buy her flowers and a meal with a fiver and she might even give you a kiss! C'mon gentlemen, it's charity night. Stand up for three rounds and it's all yours. What about you, Sir? You look like you can handle yourself?" The majority of volunteers were hit just once, and then carried from the ring in an ungainly heap, yet still they came, the foolhardy and the show-offs.

On the circuit Slasher Lee was also known as Jack the Ripper because of the way he sliced open opponent's faces. There was little finesse about his boxing and he was never going to climb the professional ladder but he was rough and ideally suited to the booth. He was a solid fourteen stone, pockmarked and scarred, only the white specks in his stubble betraying his age. He was forty-one. He never stood a chance against Tom Smith. For all his hacking and wild swings he landed less than half-a-dozen shots. Stripped to his waist, light on his feet, Tom was in control from the first ring of the bell. Slasher Lee was left staggering, bleeding from mouth and nose. The crowd shouted 'easy' and the referee stopped it at the end of the first round.

The proprietor paid him the five pounds and whispered, "If you want a job, my son, see me after the show. If you don't then I don't want to see you in here again."

As he buttoned his shirt and carefully straightened his silk stock Tom threw the old man a raffish grin and said, "Lucky shot, that's all."

"You think I'm blind? That sort of luck comes from punch-bags and roadwork. Who you been working with?"

"I'm out of the Eagle."

"Well then, you piss off back down there and tell Peter Woodhead he's well out of order. Understand? So take it on the heel and toe!"

"He doesn't know about it."

"He's bleedin' well going to."

"I'm going."

The old proprietor scratched his chiselled forehead. "If you want to fight, young man, then stand up and be counted. Don't worm your way in against these old guys trying to make a crust. Slasher's been entertaining people for twenty years. He didn't deserve that. So take your fiver and piss off back to the East End. I'm surprised with Peter for not teaching you some respect. This is a gentleman's sport, or didn't you know?"

"Leave it out. If you think I'm after your poxy fiver you can stick it up your arse. We're interested in the side bets."

The old man nodded and smiled disdainfully. He turned to follow the trail of Slasher's blood, muttering as he went, "The world is changing, and not for the good."

Tom pushed his way through the excited backslapping crowd and headed toward the car park. The others caught up with him.

Simon asked, "What's his problem?"

"He thinks we were out of order."

"He don't like paying out, that's all. Cheeky bleeder! He needs a smack in the mouth."

"He's an old man. Old men don't live in the present. They live in a past that was never as tasty as they let on. They haven't got a clue about today."

They looked back and saw the old guy talking to a bunch of locals and raising a crooked finger to point their way. The men turned to look in their direction and were suddenly running toward them, eating up the ground.

Tom said, "I think it's time to scarper." He yanked open the car door and climbed into the driving seat. The blond girl got in beside him and the others piled in the back. Doors slammed shut, the engine spluttered and tyres churned up the soft earth. They moved forward just as the first man reached them and hammered his fist on the boot. A second man booted the rear bumper. They sped between two lines of cars and turned into the road. Simon peered through the rear window. "Clear," he confirmed and Tom slowed to a reasonable speed.

"You're bleeding," the blonde said and dabbed a handkerchief at his mouth.

"He caught me one. I know why they call him Slasher now. It ain't his fists at all. The leather on his gloves is all cut and rough, stuck with glue that's gone rock hard. That's what does the damage. What did you get?"

Simon reached forward with the cash. "Fours," he said. The thin girl at his side leant forward. Tom glanced into the rear view and their eyes met. Her spectacles became twin pools of light as they reflected headlamps from a passing car. She was attractive but in a tomboyish way. He guessed she was more in tune with napkins and a slice of sponge cake than where they came from. He also knew that her attempt to fit in with them was as false as her Cockney rhyme.

She said, "You frightened me tonight. You enjoyed hitting that man."

"That's what it's about."

The blonde turned and glanced over her shoulder. "So why shouldn't he? Do you think Slasher don't enjoy knocking people over?"

"No!" She shook her head, "It's more than that. He enjoyed hurting him."

Simon interrupted, "Leave it alone, Jane."

"He knows what I'm talking about."

"I told you to leave it alone," Simon said sharply. "Forget it."

She sat back and impulsively folded her arms.

"How old are you, anyway?" Simon asked her. "When do you finish school?"

"Fourteen, if you must know." She tightened her lips. "They say they're raising the leaving age to fifteen this year, which is just my luck."

The other girl snaked her hand over to Tom and undid some buttons.

Tom said, "I'm taking the old girl down to Folkestone tomorrow, early. Be back on Tuesday."

Tom adjusted his mirror to reflect Simon's features and saw his knowing wink. The blonde had disappeared from Simon's view and was bending across Tom.

Simon asked, "Is Peter going?"

"No chance. I'm keeping well clear of him till this little lot blows over. He'll go spare if he gets to hear about it. He might be an old man but he's still got plenty of clout."

Peter Woodhead's temper was the stuff of legend. His fuse was slow, and his sixties had slowed the burning process further, but when he blew he was still formidable.

The dark-haired girl said from the back, "If he's an old man, like you say, what are you worried about? What's it got to do with him, anyway?" She leant forward again and peered into the front and her mouth dropped open. "You twist! That's absolutely disgusting!"

The blonde looked up and smiled. The girl sat back, shocked rigid, her eyes wide, her spectacles slightly askew.

The blonde said, "Ain't there somewhere we can go?"

"I was hoping your place," Tom said.

"Mum's back. It's impossible."

Tom took a right along the Green and turned into the allotments. He pulled in the long grass and briars at the bottom of Hogg's Hill, a place for courting couples and, during the daylight hours, the well-heeled dog-walkers from the detached properties that lined the rented plots.

The girl in the back said, "Why are we stopping? I need to get home."

"We won't be long," Tom said and turned off the engine.

The night sky was clear and threw a pale glow through the windows and turned their faces white.

"You're still frightened of an old man!" she said defiantly.

Simon turned to her. "Listen, Jane," his voice held a threat and immediately the girl sat lower in her seat. "Some of the biggest villains in the Smoke are frightened of Peter Woodhead. Don't go by looks alone. He's the guv'nor!" He pulled her toward him and ignoring her struggles managed to get his hand inside the top of her dress. Some of the buttons fell apart. Her spectacles slipped down her nose. He tried to kiss her but she pushed against him.

"No!" she said sharply, "Simon, no!"

He attempted to shield himself from her flailing arms but one got through and hit him in the mouth.

"Fuck it! Only wanted a touch of your tits and there ain't much to touch, let's face it."

"For God's sake!" the blonde said and sat up. Her top was undone and they could make out a generous breast. Simon's gaze locked on to a crown-sized nipple.

The girl said, "Please, Maureen, I don't do this!"

"Giving him a feel isn't actually a big deal, is it?"

"No!"

"Yes, Jane! I'm sure Daddy won't mind."

"Please, Maureen, I don't want to be touched."

Maureen smiled at Simon and said, "She's just playing hard to get. We all do that."

The girl shouted, "No!" She tried to open the door but Simon held her back and in the struggle her spectacles followed her black hat into the foot well.

Maureen said coldly, "See? Shouting will get you nowhere. Something you got to learn, right? In our part of the world, men are in charge. It's always been that way and it always will be. And I'm talking about real men, not the schoolboys that you mix with. When they say drop 'em, you drop 'em, and the only time you don't is when you got your excuse, and even then some of 'em don't care." Her face broke into a grin and she added quickly, "Only kidding; just trying to frighten you. You should be someplace else, doing your homework – not here with us."

The girl twisted in her seat, struggling frantically to free herself. Simon dragged her skinny legs toward him and her back was forced against the car door, her head bent awkwardly. He lifted her dress and pushed her petticoat aside. She screamed at him.

Maureen's eyes widened in concern and she said, "Simon, she's only a kid!"

If he heard it made no difference. He struggled to kneel on the seat and bent her legs either side of him. One of her shoes kicked off into the front and Tom yelped. Simon's head hit the roof and his cap went flying. He managed to yank her knickers free of her behind and up on to her thighs. He caught hold of the neckline of her top and tore open the remaining buttons and her breasts with their tiny nipples popped out. She made a desperate effort to hold on to the hem of her dress but he brushed her hands aside and pushed both her dress and the petticoat to her waist.

"Wowee!" Maureen said but her expression had grown fearful.

The girl squirmed and her face flushed in shame. She tried to twist away and cried out. Tears ran and dribbled from her chin. For the moment the fight had been knocked out of her and apart from her sudden cry she seemed almost trancelike. Her chest heaved as she fought for breath.

Simon unbuttoned himself.

Maureen shouted, "She's a bleedin' schoolgirl, Simon!"

Again, he took no notice. The girl renewed her struggle and sobbed in quick little breaths, shaking uncontrollably, her chin forced forward on to her chest, her wide bloodshot eyes on Maureen.

Maureen turned to Tom. "He's doing her."

"Well you started it!"

"Well you can bleedin' stop it, can't you?"

Tom grunted and turned to the back. "Simon, she's had enough."

"I ain't in there yet! I think she's a virgin!"

"She can stay one. She's had enough."

They all recognized a sudden chill in Tom's voice and Simon pulled back. Trying to make light of it, he said, "What's the problem? She got in the car, didn't she? No one forced her to get in."

"She's a kid and she acts like one. We don't need trouble, and that's what she is."

Simon gave up and pushed the girl's legs aside.

Tom turned to Maureen. "Satisfied?" he asked.

She nodded thoughtfully and said, "See, all it took was a word from you."

They turned to see the girl covering herself and rooting beneath the seat. When she put on the spectacles she seemed strangely detached.

She looked at Tom and said calmly, "Now please take me home."

Simon buttoned himself and saw Tom looking at him curiously.

"What?"

"He's talking about retiring," Tom said.

"Who is?"

"Peter Woodhead. He's getting shot of the Eagle."

"That'll never happen."

"I'm not so sure. He might keep the gym."

"No, I don't believe it. Peter Woodhead is the Eagle. Always has been. It'll never happen, not unless your old girl talks him into it. Strange that is. How a little woman like your mum can control a bleeder like that. I'm surprised they never got married, really."

Tom's glance was dark and questioning. A veil had drawn over his eyes.

Rose Smith was a slender woman. At forty-eight her brown eyes were still clear but her once dark hair was mostly grey. Rounded shoulders had developed from her stoop and she looked frail but those who knew her appreciated that beneath that apparent frailty was a stubborn streak that could leave the hardest man exasperated and desperate for a stiff drink. She was up by habit with the dawn, dusting and cleaning the small terrace. Breakfast was ready by the time Tom had shaved. Shep Fields was on the Bakelite wireless set with *South of the Border*, but it spluttered. "The accumulator needs a charge," Rose said. "He hasn't been lately. We'll have to walk to the shop."

"I'll sort it when we get back."

She filled a pan with milk and set it on the stove. She collected a scoop from the milkman every third morning. Boiling made it last the extra day. She said, "It's getting serious then, this Maureen Devine?"

"What makes you say that, Ma?"

"It's been almost every night these last three weeks."

He spread some Echo on a slice of bread and said, "It's not serious."

"Good." She nodded over her pans.

"Why good? You don't know her."

"I wash your clothes, Tommy, so I know her more than you think. I've got a nose. Nice girls don't wear cheap perfume. They wash instead."

He'd paid a small fortune for the perfume but thought better of telling his mother. Instead, he said meekly, "They all wear perfume, Ma."

"It's the amount they wear that matters, Tommy. That's how you can tell if they're nice girls or not. You be careful. Girls twist men around their little fingers. That's where the word comes from."

Twist! That's what the girl had mentioned in the car. He doubted his mother knew the real meaning: the girl of the night, the little trick that always came up trumps.

They left early to miss the traffic. The gasman's pole still lanced through the low fog, the costermongers trundled their barrows to fetch the early fruit and vegetables, and the city stirred.

"I remember the first time I came down here with Dad," Tommy told her and slowed the car so that he could take a closer look at the sprouting hops. "He told me about when you used to come down here picking them. The summers were always hot, he said."

"I remember," she whispered. "I'll never forget."

He recognized the glazed look that came over her whenever her thoughts were filled with nothing but yesterday.

She shook the moment away and said, "Every September we'd come, the whole street, the whole of the East End more like. It was like home from home. We'd stay in the hopper huts." She smiled wistfully. "They say they were good times and so they were, but they were hard times. When you were born your cot was the top drawer of the dresser. The war was still raging and we thought it would go on forever and your dad had been away for most of it. If it hadn't been for the few weeks he was sent home with a busted disc in his back you wouldn't be here now. It took more than a bad back to stop your dad's...you know... enthusiasm."

"He never talked about it, the war, I mean."

"He wouldn't, would he? He was in the trenches like every other man his age. But things weren't easy. By golly, we were scraping for a lump of coal. Even a handful of slack was like gold dust. Your old man used to be the first down in Billingsgate to collect the fish heads. Fish heads, I ask you! We couldn't even afford the bleedin' fish to go with them." Her eyes filled in reverie and she dabbed them with a small handkerchief. "He did the best he could for us, and that's all any man can ever do. He was my man and I chose him, and I wouldn't change a thing. Life was never easy, like I said, but your dad had a way of brightening the day. When he died, he took me with him. If it hadn't been for bringing you up I don't think I'd be here now." She sighed. "But life goes on. Peter's asked me to marry him."

Simon's comment came back.

"He wanted to speak to you about it, to find out how you felt, but then decided it was none of your business. I told him no."

"Not to speak to me?"

"That I wasn't getting married again."

"That had nothing to do with me, did it?"

"No."

"That's a relief."

"But I'd like to know what you think?"

"I think you're a lady."

She smiled and bucked up. "And I think you're a gentleman, my son."

"I think you should do whatever you want to do, Ma. If you want to be with Peter, be with him, and if you want to marry him, then that's OK too. Sod other people and what they think."

"I'll never think of anyone like your dad. After him anyone else is going to be second best. I can't marry Peter thinking that. It's not fair on him."

"Did you tell him that?"

"It's not easy to tell a man that."

"You don't need to tell him. He understands. And you don't need to turn it into a competition either."

"I thought you'd hate the idea."

"I want anything that makes you happy. If the old man could come back and tell you one thing that he'd want more than anything else, it would be for you to have some happiness and security. If Peter makes you happy even if it is in a different way, then that's good enough. Where would you live?"

"That's the other thing that made up my mind. It would mean moving into the Eagle. I'm not giving up our home. Number sixty-four is filled with memories. Nothing is taking that from me. And Peter doesn't think it right that he should move into your dad's house."

He didn't tell her about the rumour that Peter was thinking of giving up the Eagle. Instead he said, "It's your house now."

"So I said no, not at the moment thank you very much."

Elizabeth Hurst and her sons, Richard and Ian, came out to greet them as they unloaded their bags from the car. Rose and Elizabeth embraced happily, their voices high in excitement. It had been two years since their last meeting when they had travelled down for Elizabeth's mother's funeral. That had been different. For one thing it had sharpened Rose's own loss.

Rose peered around and asked, "Where's Reg?"

"He's not been well." Elizabeth ushered them inside and said, "Come and see him."

Reginald Hurst's hairline had disappeared and left just a few dark strands trained to lie flat across the top of his head. The continuous weeping of his eyes had left painful tracks through the deep purple that spread across his cheeks.

"He doesn't do a lot now," Ian Hurst told Tom, "Potters about in the garden, that's all. It's his breathing that's done him, breathing in the gas. Young Sally's been his saving grace, kept him going. Watching her grow up has given him a new lease." Ian, freckled, a mop of curly ginger hair, had grown heavier than Richard, and sharper. Although a year younger he now seemed to be the dominant force.

"Old Bill next door died last year," Ian went on. "And that didn't help at all. That hit him harder than we know. I think he enjoyed the company of the old bugger, or his fantastic schemes. They found him in the greenhouse, bottle of his nettle wine in one hand, bottle of weed killer in the other. We figured he'd taken a sup out of the wrong bottle. Silly old sod! The weeds liked his poxy wine, though. Within a fortnight of his funeral they covered his greenhouse. But the old man's never been the same since. Except for Sal, that is. She calls in on her way home from school every day and that brightens him up a treat. No matter what he's doing he'll get ready for that. Funny what a young girl can do. Funny how they can turn the clock back, even for an old man."

The women were in their element. They talked non-stop throughout lunch, oblivious to the others. While they spoke, tied up in the old days, Reginald Hurst told the boys, "It's a funny business. When I considered retirement I always thought that I'd want nothing more than the garden. And while Bill was alive so it seemed to be. The garden was a sanctuary, a study, and a place to lose oneself, a men-only club where we could shout over the fence and make bets on who had grown the longest runner bean, where we could have a crafty fag and sample the latest home-brew vintage without getting earache. It was where we discussed tactics in our battle against the whitefly. But some very odd buggers have moved in next door. Now the Spanish war has ended all they seem to want to talk about is Hitler and Europe and getting involved. Go out and say good morning and all you get back is 'I see he's done this or that'. They're too young to remember the Somme or they wouldn't be talking that way. Funny thing is, I can't be bothered with the garden any more. Apart from the runners I've turned it over to flowerbeds. Least, Elizabeth likes them. And it keeps the church happy where she does the flowers." He gazed into space for a moment, then shook his head and filled up his wine glass. "So tell me, what have you been doing? You got a job?"

"I'm still with Peter Woodhead," Tom said. "Boxing is still business, then there's the pub. I look after it more and more now. I think he might even retire." He shot his mother a knowing look.

Reginald's sigh sounded critical. He nodded toward his sons and said, "I wish this pair would get a trade under their belts."

Ian stood from the table. "C'mon Tommy, I'll show you around."

Tom followed Richard into the hall and caught up with Ian.

"Where are we going?"

"A bit of business," Ian said and winked.

Leather-skinned men in oilskins and thigh-high boots and heavy polo-necked sweaters and sou'westers unloaded their open-topped boxes of fish and stacked the empty crab and lobster pots, while above them and farther out to sea, the white birds wheeled and dipped over the marble swell, their shrieks and soulless squawks carrying across the docks. A warm southerly breeze carried salty air past the slow moving cranes and the vast stores of pallets and drums and the unfinished hulls half submerged in oily water, rusty in parts, red-primed in others; it held the smell of pitch and fish, and smoke from the welding rods as they sprayed great globules of cascading sparks; it carried the staccato clatter of pop-riveters and the clanking and whining of steel wheels on slackened rails.

Ian and Richard led the way to the Harbour Inn, a two-storey black and olive-green building with cracked trusses and blistered boarding. It creaked and reeked of age, an age of tall masts and one-eyed and one-legged men. It reminded Tom of a tall faintly sinister Jewish man in a worn greatcoat in a crowded market place, and of Daniel Defoe's classic. They entered beneath a green painted sign advertising Burton's Mild Ale that swung silently from a rust-red bracket. As they moved through a gloomy bar grizzled faces looked up from pint mugs and dark eyes glinted from the shadows. They ordered drinks and carried their glasses to a table. As soon as they were settled the men shuffled into a line and, one by one, left an envelope on the table. There was little eye contact. The business was concluded in minutes. The men returned to their various groups or headed for the door. Without checking the contents of the envelopes, Richard stuffed them into his jacket pocket.

"What's going on?" Tom asked when it became evident they weren't going to explain.

"We collect a bit for this guy named Bryant," Ian said and wrinkled his nose. "It's like an unofficial union, without the messy rules."

"There are rules," Richard said coldly.

Ian grinned, "Yeah, but they're not written down."

Tom said, "It's a racket."

"Naw, it's not that. It's work, and if they want the work they got to ante up. It's being looked after when you're sick or in trouble. Call it insurance, if you like."

"Call it what you like, it's a racket," Tom insisted. "And I bet half the gear off those boats ain't ending up where it should."

"We don't ask questions."

"If we did we wouldn't get any answers," Richard said, not sharing his brother's enthusiasm.

"Bryant looks after us," Ian insisted. "We do our bit and the rest don't concern us."

They stayed an hour and in that time thirty or more envelopes were passed to the brothers. From the docks they visited two more pubs close by and the procedure was the same.

Tom was intrigued and asked, "How do you know if someone's short changed you?"

"Goodwill," Ian explained. "We've been collecting for six months and we've never been short. No one will upset Bryant. It doesn't bear thinking of."

They dropped Tom at the house before moving on to see Bryant with the collection. Reginald Hurst let him in and explained that his mother and Elizabeth had gone for a walk along the shore. He was waiting for Sally.

She came in and dropped her satchel on the table. She gave him an odd thoughtful look; her blue eyes a mix of mischief and mild curiosity. There was an ease about her movements.

"You remember Tommy?" Reginald said as he stooped painfully to place a tray of tea and biscuits on to the coffee table.

She smiled unaffectedly and nodded. "I remember you Tommy Smith. It's been two years."

"Yeah, you've changed a bit."

She swept back her long black hair. "You haven't. Apart from the scar, that is."

He grinned. "You wouldn't believe the traffic in London. I got hit by a tram."

She laughed out loud. "I'm supposed to believe that?"

He felt slightly awkward in her presence and it surprised him. He wondered what it was about her that made him feel uncomfortable. He decided it was her innocence.

He said, "Would I lie to you?"

Her shrug was barely noticeable; her slight shoulders rose and her eyebrows rose, and then she turned and knelt beside the table to pour the tea.

"So…?" Reginald said.

"School was fine," she answered. "And it's warm for April but the summer holidays still seem a long way off."

"That is not what I meant."

"I know what you meant."

"Well then?"

"English was um, arithmetic was um, history was ugh and geography was…" She cocked her head toward Tom, "Sugar and milk?"

"Yes, two sugars."

The old man moved across to the upright, eased himself on to a stool and began banging out some notes. Sally glanced across at Tom and coloured slightly.

Reginald's voice rasped: "Sally, Sally, pride of our alley…"

Tom felt a strange sense of delight and yet mildly embarrassed. He felt like an unwelcome guest, an interloper. Finally, when she was ready to go, she said quietly, "If you want to walk me up the road and say hello to Mum and Dad, he should be home by now?"

"That's a good idea," Reginald said. "Joyce is always asking after you. I'll knock off these cups before the girls come back."

As they started up Marsh Row toward the terraced housing, Tom asked, "What does your old man do?"

"He's a porter at the Grand," she said. "He fixed up jobs for Ian and Richard but they turned them down."

"I wouldn't fancy that either."

"It's better than nothing," she said matter-of-factly, "And that's what they've got at the moment. Reggie doesn't like what they're doing now."

"Does he know what they're doing?"

"He knows they've always got a few bob, more that they could get in a proper job. My dad thinks they're turning into villains."

Tom grinned. "He probably says the same about me."

She nodded. "He does."

A black Morris slowed by their side and Richard leant from the window and called, "Hop in Tommy."

He turned to Sally and shrugged. He said, "Another time, maybe."

She swung her bag and walked on and didn't look back, but he heard her voice: "Maybe."

He climbed into the back and slammed the door, surprised that neither of the brothers had acknowledged Sally.

"What now?"

"Little bit of bother. We thought you might be interested." Ian glanced up into the mirror. "What's with Sal?"

"I was going to say hello to Len."

"Why bother? He's a bloody nuisance. The old bugger keeps sticking his nose in and upsets the old man. And she's taking after him."

"You said earlier that she was doing him good."

"She is, but she ain't doing us any fucking favours."

Tom sniffed the air. "You've got a leak in here."

"No," Ian grinned. "It's been like this for ages."

Tom shrugged. He hadn't noticed it earlier.

In the front Richard exchanged a glance with his brother and laughed.

Ian parked half way up Dover Road and seemed satisfied to sit watching a pair of large wooden gates opposite.

"You going to tell me what's going on?" Tom asked, irritation creeping into his voice.

Ian glanced at his watch. "Patience ain't a virtue anymore, is it?"

The gates led to an old brick stable block that had been converted to garages. A green sign pinned to a brick wall to the left of the gates read: Bulk Earthmoving.

Richard reached forward to a bag at his feet and Tom heard the clink of glass. He watched silently, knowing now what they were about and angry at the way they were implicating him. He wondered whether it was bravado, showing the guy from the Smoke a thing or two. Even as the question entered his head the gates swung back and a white-haired man of about sixty stooped awkwardly to fasten the bolts.

A tarpaulin-covered truck shuddered and smoke plumed from its exhaust as it began to back out through the gates. The old man led the way to check that the road was clear. For a moment he gazed directly at the car then, with the rear of the lorry already moving into the road, he raised his hand and beckoned to the driver to carry on.

Without a word the brothers swung open the car doors and climbed out. Ian crouched beside the car and began striking matches. By the time he stood again, Richard had thrown four bottles. Two of them had smashed on the tarpaulin and two had fallen from the canvas and smashed on the road beneath the rear wheels. The old man heard the bottles smash and spun round to face the car. His expression turned to panic and he backed away toward the gates, realizing too late that his way was still blocked by the lorry. The driver remained unaware of the danger. Ian's bottle seemed to travel in slow motion, the burning rag in its stopper barely noticeable in the stark afternoon light. It landed and smashed and a sheet of orange flame enveloped the back of the truck.

Black smoke all but hid the entrance. There was madness in Ian's laugh as he threw another bottle.

Tom's gaze was fixed on the roaring flames. He heard shouts coming from the yard. He saw the old man stagger from the inferno, his arms waving frantically as his clothes blazed. He barely noticed the brothers climbing back into the car or the doors slamming shut and it was only the sudden acceleration that pulled him back.

A few cars coming down the hill skidded to a halt and the drivers along with a few passing pedestrians ran to help. The fuel tank on the lorry exploded and blew parts of the wall across the road. One of the drivers was flattened against his own car. A great cloud of dust and smoke obscured any view save for the red glint of licking flames.

They took a right out of Dover Road and slowed down. They bells from a distant fire engine caught them up. Ian drove in silence. They left the car on a garage forecourt. A scruffy attendant wiping his hands on an oily rag approached them. He chewed on a matchstick.

"You're late!" He waved a set of keys. "Who wants these?"

Ian stepped forward and exchanged them for his own then led the way to another car. For the first time Tom began to appreciate the extent of Bryant's organization. They weaved a trail back down the hill through a series of shabby back streets and approached the docks again. A few minutes later the brothers led him through an archway set in a terraced row. They moved into a small courtyard surrounded by double garages. Just inside the entrance two men leant across the bonnet of a car. They seemed to be busy stripping down the engine but apart from their clumsy wielding of the wrenches there was something else about them that gave their game away, perhaps the hardness of their expressions and the soulless eyes.

They moved through three more doors and a short corridor before Tom was led into a dimly lit drinking club occupied by a dozen or so men grouped mostly around a small bar. Three men at the far end of the room played snooker. The game along with the conversation in the room halted as they walked in. Ian left them just inside the door and approached the main group at the bar. In the centre of the group a short, heavy-set man perched on a tall bar stool with his feet dangling six inches off the floor. One manicured hand rested on the bar, toying with a drink, his other held a fat cigar. His well-cut brown-checked suit hid to some extent a barrel chest and an expanding waistline but could do nothing with his monkish hairstyle swept back to conceal a bald crown. Beneath thick-rimmed spectacles his eyes were steady and bright as he watched Ian's approach. After a short exchange Ian beckoned the others forward.

"Hello, young man," the man said to Tom. His voice was unexpectedly rich. "Ian tells me that you're down from the Smoke?"

Tom nodded, his expression giving nothing away.

Ian said, "This is Mr Bryant."

"I understand you helped the lads out this afternoon," Bryant said.

Tom shook his head, "No, not me."

Bryant frowned. "You were there?"

"Where's that, Mr Bryant?"

Bryant smiled quickly and lifted his cigar. Without taking his eyes from Tom he blew a stream of smoke towards him. Eventually he said, "Good. I like that."

From outside came the noises of cars breaking hard and doors slamming, of shouts and whistles. Most of the men in the room started for the doors but Bryant raised his hands and they stood back. He turned to Ian and his voice held an icy threat.

"I do hope you weren't followed."

Ian shook his head, his eyes wide, "No way, Mr Bryant."

As the sounds of shouting and heavy footsteps grew closer Bryant turned back to Tom and said, "I don't care for coincidence, young man. It's strange that you should be turning up with the police right on your heels. I do hope your shoes are spotlessly clean."

Tom remained impassive; he returned Bryant's searching look until the older man looked away and the doors burst open and half the Kent constabulary filed into the room.

Chapter 15

Tom Smith was not conscripted into military service, but it was hardly a free choice that landed him in an area south of Bulford in the late summer of that year.

It had become quickly evident that someone in Tony Bryant's organization was an informer. The police held a huge dossier of overwhelming evidence. The book was thrown and a number of people faced charges of corruption, fraud and conspiracy to commit. Both Ian and Richard Hurst were charged with GBH and sent down for six years. Tom Smith got away with it by the skin of his teeth and by the good fortune of knowing Peter Woodhead.

Over the years Peter had spread his own brand of goodwill and many people owed him favours. By the time he met Tom in a small private room in the police station some of his friends in London had already been to work. Although Tom would almost certainly end up before the local bench charged with being an accessory after the fact it was a foregone conclusion that he would get away with a stern warning about the company he kept. Peter also knew that had Tom's involvement been any greater then the sort of favours owed to him would not have helped. Goodwill only spread so far. His connections were based on friendship and in some circumstances only threats would do.

"I'm hugely disappointed in you, boy," he scolded. He took off his hat and flicked away a fleck of dust. "You let us all down, me, your mother, and the memory of your father. It's not just this latest business. Something like this was bound to happen. It's been on the cards for a long time. Family honour means nothing to you. Your priorities have been flushed away while you've been pissing around and I'm ashamed for your mother's sake. Things that needed doing are left undone." He paced the room. He replaced his bowler and pulled it low, throwing his face into dark shadow. His angry eyes glistened and fastened on to Tom. "Your brief is outside. He would like to tell the bench that you brought your mother down to Folkestone before going off to join the army. He has already reached an agreement on this."

Tom shook his head and said, "No way!"

"Think seriously about it, boy. Any day now you could be called up. This is the only guarantee we've got. This is not a choice. You understand me?"

Effectively, Tom Smith's immediate future was sealed.

Lightning ripped open the darkness and projected an eerie green depth to a ragged sky. Rain swept in great arcs and drummed a constant beat on the acres of canvas, seeping through seams to saturate anything inside, including the air itself. Between the tents the ground was churned into black muddy piles.

Situated on the flat south eastern sector of Salisbury Plain, rows of double-berth tents spaced in regimental order at four feet apart, radiated out from a large central headquarters and mess tent. Pale lights glowed, dissolving into the dark curtain of mist and rain. The larger tents at the centre of the camp were silent, and the only movement came from a sentry making his occasional checks. As the evening had worn on and the likelihood of the rain abating had receded, his patrols had become less frequent. Under his cape few people would have recognized the sentry as he stepped gingerly over the sodden ground, lingering under the cover of tent awnings. Yet there was the gypsy about his dark visage and youth in his step. It was after midnight when lights were turned up in the orderly tent and the brighter light poured from the flaps and the sounds of commotion filtered through the deluge to the closer tents and from his cover the sentry watched and listened and a rueful smile flickered across his face.

Captain James Harold Roskilly sat behind a rough collapsible dining table, his polished brown leather boots firmly embedded in thick mud so that moving a foot required effort. His grease-flattened straw-coloured hair caught the light from a lamp hanging above him.

He spoke in slow clipped tones: "I will not t-t-tolerate t-t-this kind of behaviour. What have you got t-t-to say for yourself?"

A young private, standing at attention before the CO's table, kept his wide eyes locked on to the lamp above the officer's head. Perspiration oiled his flabby features and collected in black rings around his neck.

A sergeant, standing easy by a blackboard and easel, watched the scene unfold. His lips were tight but a spark of mild amusement played in his eyes.

Eventually the private said, "Nothing to say, Sir!"

Captain Roskilly nodded slowly, his critical gaze moving to the other men in the tent. It lingered on three men near the entrance. Of these, only two corporals were standing. The third man, another private, was being held up between them. Blood trickled from his mouth. His face was white and sweat collected on his forehead.

"Where is t-t-the instrument?"

The sergeant stepped forward and placed a pair of long-nosed pliers on the table. The officer studied the tool and tentatively prodded it with his cane. He shook his head disbelievingly.

"You pulled out his t-t-tooth with t-t-these?"

"Sir!"

"With his consent?"

"Sir!"

One of the two corporals holding up the wounded man coughed for attention.

"What is it Corporal?"

"Sir, Pinchera here has been complaining about the toothache for a week now. Wouldn't see the dentist or the MO. It's been driving him potty, Sir. Driving the men in his billet potty too, Sir."

The CO shook his head and wondered what he was doing in the middle of nowhere with a bunch of utter dimwits while his boots were being ruined.

"Why wouldn't he see t-t-the dentist?"

"Fright, Sir! Had a bad experience as a kid and swore he'd never go back." The corporal was on a roll and continued, "Macloud, here, Sir, trained as a dental technician, and it was the men who cajoled him into pulling Pinchera's tooth so they could get some sleep."

"Dental t-t-technician?" The captain narrowed his eyes as he regarded the dim-witted soldier. "I see. Well, you might have left his gum behind. I'm t-t-taking a dim view of t-t-this episode. It's damned irresponsible."

"Yes Sir!" The soldier stood even taller. "Large roots, Sir! Very sorry, Sir!"

The captain searched the private's face for a hint of mockery. He said, "You've put t-t-the entire exercise in jeopardy. We were rather counting on Pinchera. He's one of our t-t-top marksmen."

Hearing his own name spoken, the wounded private regained some consciousness and released a long groan.

"T-t-that's enough, Pinchera!" the CO snapped. He turned to the sergeant and shook his head. "I've heard enough of t-t-this. Sergeant, get t-t-them out of here!"

The private saluted, wheeled and smacked the mud as he tried to march from the tent. In his haste he knocked a hanging lamp and left shadows sliding across the canvas. The two corporals, with Pinchera hanging heavily between them, followed Macloud from the tent, expressions held firm as they tried to hold on to their laughter.

From the shadows and through the swirl of rain the sentry watched the four men stagger across to the mess tent and heard their sudden burst of raucous laughter.

In the tent the lamp stopped swinging and the shadows hardened again. Captain Roskilly said, "T-t-the boy's a fool. Sort him out Scratch."

"Macloud's a bit slow on the uptake. Fact is, Sir, if he went any slower he'd be going backwards. Meningitis as a baby, I heard."

"God help us all if ever t-t-the balloon goes up!" The officer lifted a curious eyebrow. "I'm rather surprised t-t-to find he's a dental t-t-technician, however, and I shall now brush my t-t-teeth more vigorously."

He glanced at his pocket-watch. "Look at t-t-the t-t-time!" He rubbed his eyes. "I'll leave it in your hands, Scratch. Get Pinchera over t-t-to t-t-the MO. He'll need stitching up. If you can get him back by eleven hundred and if he's in any shape t-t-to perform, then we'll put t-t-the entire matter behind us."

"Right, Sir."

Captain Roskilly stood stiffly from the chair, slapped his leg sharply with the cane and reached for his heavy coat. The sergeant left him buttoning up and found the others in the mess tent. Macloud fussed over Pinchera, trying to clean his tunic. The corporals stood aside by the coal burning ranges and Soyer stoves, drinking tea from tin mugs while they watched. The sergeant moved to the steaming dixie and poured himself a drink. He said, "Dental technician?"

The corporal who'd spoken in Macloud's defence laughed. "He was a cleaner at Bart's, Guv, cleaned up the orthodontics department."

The sergeant grinned. "If we can get Pinchera back to the range in time it'll go no further."

Relief evident in his eyes, Macloud said, "It was an accident, Sarg, you know that."

"Go and get some kip," the sergeant told him.

Macloud took a last look at Pinchera whose groans were muffled by a towel held firmly to his mouth.

The sergeant turned back to the others. "Go and find some transport. Expect us back by eleven."

Corporal Woods pulled a face. "He keeps passing out, Sarg. Someone better go with you. He might be in shock."

They turned to look at Pinchera who had slipped from his seat and sat head-bowed on the floor. The towel he held was more red than white.

"Where's Smith?"

"He's pulled SD."

"He'll do. He'll be glad to get out of the rain." He adjusted his cap and fastened his cape. "Transport," he said. "On the double, and give me a hand with Pinchera."

Sergeant Adam Fox was also known as Scatch Fox, a nickname bestowed thirty-one years earlier by his older brother. It resulted from a bout of chicken pox and the pockmarks it left behind. Scratch Fox was not envious of any man, and certainly not his brother's lofty position in the navy. The sea held not the slightest interest for him. The thought of it brought back memories of Devonport and Exmouth and Portsmouth and of a father who was rarely at home. His brother had followed his father's footsteps into the senior service but at an early age Scatch Fox left home and joined the ranks of the old enemy. His ambition stretched no further. When the stripes arrived they had little meaning other than the pay increases and a slightly better standard of mess. He was unlike the others who found their places in the ranks and were content to hide away so that where stronger men were lost, they survived; he survived through luck and cynicism and experience, but never by ducking. He kept out of trouble, something not easily achieved in the ranks, found a certain security, a few friends, a willing wife and twin, seven-year-old daughters of whom he was immensely proud.

Apart from Pinchera's continued moaning they drove silently to the hospital. Smith was noted for being uncommunicative and his spell of duty in the storm had done nothing for his mood. It was one of the reasons Fox had chosen him. At the hospital they learned that a splinter of root was left behind in Pinchera's gum and they were going to gas him in order to dig it out. Fox was told to pick him up at nine the following morning. He explained the situation to his driver before adding, "We might as well get some kip. You'll have to bunk down on the couch."

It was only now, on the short drive across to the married quarters in Queen's Avenue, that Scratch relented and asked, "Where did you get the scar?"

"Someone didn't like me."

"You were lucky. It could have hit something."

"If you say so, Sarg."

"What happened to the other guy?"

"He wasn't so lucky."

Fox shrugged his massive shoulders. "Think you're a hard man, do you?"

"I don't think about it. Just keep my head down, that's all. Do my time then get out of it."

"You'll be here for some time yet."

"I don't think so."

"You obviously don't listen to the news, boy. There's a war on the way. We're going to need every fighting man we can get."

"I'm not getting my arse shot at for King and Country. If there's no money in it I ain't interested."

Scratch smiled wisely. "Oh, there'll be plenty of spoils all right, but not for the likes of us."

They drove across to the avenue and a three-bedroom terrace just outside Aldershot. It was still raining heavily as they went along the path between the perfunctory ranks of dripping pansies. There were few hardy annuals in a soldier's garden. The porch shielded them from the rain while Scratch searched for his key. Within minutes he had thrown Tom Smith some blankets and pointed the way to the couch. In no time at all he was in bed and closing in on his sleeping wife. At about six in the morning something woke him and it was some moments before he realized it was the front door opening and movements downstairs. Before he slept again Fox wondered what the young squaddie had been up to.

The morning brought clear skies. Light from a late August sun shone through the thin curtains.

Vicky Fox was not a beautiful woman in the conventional sense; beneath her brown cropped hair her nose was too sharp, her chin too prominent and her green eyes in her long face too close together. And yet, at thirty, she still drew the eye of many men. Her long body, five-ten of it, was thin, but her hips were wide and her legs shapely. She was not a particularly good wife or mother. She was not house-proud – few army wives ever were, except when they were overseas and then they became highly critical of their amahs – and she had never been consistent enough with the twins.

Scratch Fox loved her more now than when they had first met.

"You really are a dunce!"

"What?" He lay back against the headrest.

"I've just paraded in my drawers for a complete stranger."

Fox grinned. "I bet he enjoyed it." He took a mug of strong tea from her. "Have the kids gone yet?"

"They've just left. They wanted to wake you. What time did you get in?"

"About two. There was an accident and we ferried one of the lads to the hospital." He gulped his drink and placed the mug on the bedside table. "I better make a move."

Vicky kicked off her slippers, sat on the edge of the bed and threw him a knowing look. He reached forward and grabbed her.

While they ate a hurried breakfast, Vicky said, "There's talk of evacuation. The Wilcox's are off to Hitchen or somewhere, north."

"Wives too?"

She nodded, "So long as the kids are under twelve." She shot a glance at Tom but his gaze was on his breakfast plate and he seemed unaware or not interested in the conversation.

Scratch spoke with his mouth full: "There's time enough for that."

"Dolly's boy caught the measles," she said. "Ours are bound to get it."

"I expect it'll be the week after next. They generally get something to coincide with leave."

"Dolly's had a bad time of late. She's trying to catch up on her clubs. Doug isn't helping much."

"Doug should have put his foot down years ago!" he said sharply enough to make Tom look up in surprise. "You've only got to check her wardrobe to see where their cash goes."

Vicky took away the empty dishes. From the sink she said, "There's a letter from Alex."

Fox grunted his customary lack of interest in his brother's affairs. He'd never got on with his brother's wife.

"She doesn't say much. They're both well. Ralph is due back from Dartmouth this week. Julie has left home and gone to live in Oxford."

He raised his eyebrows and chuckled. Tom smiled as if sharing the joke.

"I suppose she's old enough. I keep thinking of her as a little girl." Fox grinned. "I expect Ralph was struck dumb by the idea."

"With all this talk Alex wanted the family together. She's convinced it will start very soon."

"People are jumping the gun, getting a bit hysterical."

Tom nodded his agreement.

Fox went on, "I suppose it's understandable. The newspapers don't help." He pointed to the headlines. "Look at them: Henderson in Berlin, Last Chance Negotiations! See what I mean?"

Vicky shrugged, "I'll see you on Saturday."

"Lunchtime," Scratch agreed.

The men moved across to the kitchen door. Tom paused and said, "Thanks for the breakfast and...everything."

Scratch shot him a warning glance.

Tom tightened his lips and stepped out onto the doorstep.

"You're welcome," Vicky called after him and threw him a worldly smile.

Before following Tom Smith out, Scratch glanced back at the room, the worn army-issue furniture, the wall cupboards that were never deep enough, the well-used kitchen table, the chipped Belfast sink, the matt cream walls faded in places by the scrubbing brushes of families moving on and cleaning away the finger marks.

Vicky lingered over a kiss.

"See you," she whispered.

"Love to the girls," he said.

She watched him walk down the path to catch up with his young squaddie and smiled inwardly, curiously relieved.

They had travelled a couple of miles when Scratch Fox turned to Tom and said, "Where the hell did you get to last night?"

Tom's eyes stayed firmly on the road. "Not me, Sarg. Slept like a baby till your good lady showed me how friendly the locals are around these parts."

"Mark this well, son," the sergeant warned. "Not a word about that in the camp. And don't take the piss out of me. I heard you come in at six,"

"Well, if you heard something it must have been the wind. I heard a noise at about that time myself."

Scratch Fox grunted and concentrated on the road ahead.

Chapter 16

The squaddies in B Company were warned upon arrival that their platoon sergeant did not have a Christian name. Sergeant Eunice Dovey's parents had lived in an isolated village in Devon and had been blissfully ignorant for a number of years until their son had arrived home from his first day at school and asked them why they had given him a girl's name. Before accepting their mistake they checked it out in a book of Christian names borrowed from the local vicar and thereafter took to calling their son Ice. The nickname stuck, but in the forces where official documents were a necessary way of life, secrets in the lower ranks were seldom kept for long.

Sergeant Ice Dovey would start their square bashing with: "We're not teaching you to march out here, soldiers, we're teaching you to obey orders so that you snap to it without thinking. We're teaching you to become machines so you don't think for yourselves. We do this so that when we tell you to go over the top to get your fucking heads blown off, you fucking well go! Let's talk about a soldier, shall we? Military life is about boneheaded discipline and discomfort, it's about shitting and shaving and eating to order, laying out your kit just like we showed you and getting your brasses gleaming and your boots shining like mirrors, it's about you and them, and them is not only the enemy. Them also includes our own good civilians with whom we no longer mix. You have nothing in common with them anymore and you'll never be allowed to fit in with them again. Your past lives are over. We're going to play you God Save the fucking King until you're sick of him and we're going to turn you all into fucking killing machines so that Jerry will be shaking in his boots just at the thought of you being shipped over there! Any questions?"

That was how it started but that was some weeks earlier and now his twenty run-everywhere recruits were labouring on heavy ground.

Sergeant Dovey turned his back in disgust and said to Scatch Fox, "You'd think that by now they would have learned to use a shovel."

The trench digging had been in progress for over an hour and yet parts of it were only two spits deep, the bindweed barely disturbed.

"I wouldn't let them loose in my garden," the sergeant muttered beneath his breath. He marched out to the rank of men, a short stocky figure made even fuller by the heavy khaki uniform, and shouted, "If the bleedin' Boche could see you now he wouldn't have any hesitation about waging war on us. You're like a bunch of bleedin' ballet-dancing, arse-sniffing homos. You should all be in the navy searching for the golden rivet. Squaddies who can't dig trenches in double quick time gets their arses shot off, and squaddies without arses ain't any good in this man's army. I've heard it whispered they ain't much called for in the navy either. We're going to get this right even if it means staying here till Sunday morning!"

A chorus of 'Yes, Sarg' blasted back.

Dovey turned back to Scratch Fox in despair.

At the far end of the row, out of the way of the sergeants, Private Macloud gave Private Pinchera personal tuition. He did this by digging Pinchera's trench for him and Pinchera was a very slow learner. Since his return from the hospital Macloud had mothered him and Pinchera had made the most of it. He moaned continually about his mouth wound and exaggerated the number of stitches with every telling.

Corporal Woods jogged up the slight incline, wheezing and holding on to his overhanging belly to stop it from bouncing.

"O.C. Sarg," he gasped at Scratch Fox.

Scratch nodded and turned to Dovey. "Back to barracks, what's the betting?"

He followed the overweight corporal down the slope. A vehicle was parked outside in the visitor's area but it wasn't until he saw a uniformed policeman inside the HQ that he realized it was a police car. The constable stood just inside the entrance. His officer, in plain clothes, sat at the table beside Captain Roskilly. All three men turned towards the sergeant as he stood to attention.

"Scratch, at ease. Sit down." The captain indicated a vacant chair at the table. "This is Inspector Childs from Scotland Yard."

The policeman's smile was cold and sour. His dead eyes gave nothing away. He looked at Scratch and said, "How well do you know Private Tom Smith?" His voice was surprisingly polished.

Scratch addressed the captain. "Not well, Sir. He's been with the Company for three months."

The inspector rubbed his chin, hiding his mouth. "Last Tuesday night he accompanied you to the hospital?"

"Yes Sir." Scratch frowned, mildly surprised that the civvy police were involved in Pinchera's accident.

"We're concerned with Smith's movements from the moment he left camp to the time he arrived back at..." The policeman glanced down at his notepad, "Ten-fifty the following morning."

Scratch turned to Captain Roskilly. "What's this about, Sir?"

Captain Roskilly said abruptly, "Just answer t-t-the questions, Sergeant Fox. Can you vouch for Smith's whereabouts during t-t-that t-t-time?"

Scratch nodded, "Yes, Sir. We drove back to my place and got our heads down for a couple of hours before picking Pinchera up."

The inspector asked, "Where exactly was that?"

"Queen's Avenue."

"What time did you arrive there?"

"Gone three."

"How long was Smith left alone?"

"A couple of hours or so."

"So in that time he could have left the house without your knowledge?"

"If you can tell me what it's all about, Sir, I'll tell you what I think."

166

"I'm not interested in what you think, Sergeant. It's the facts we're after." Before continuing Inspector Childs took his time lighting a cigarette he took from a silver case. "However, I will tell you this much. During that Tuesday night two men were stabbed to death. Both attacks were related. The word on the street is that Tommy Smith, Private Smith, is involved. In order to eliminate him from our inquiries I would like him to have an alibi."

Sergeant Scratch Fox nodded and then, perhaps because of the inspector's attitude, he lied. "Apart from a few minutes here and there when I dozed, Smith kept me awake for most of that time with his snoring."

The inspector finished writing in his notebook. "It was a long shot, anyway. It would have been an hour's drive either way. Even if he took off as soon as you got there he wouldn't have got back much before six. I'll need a statement from you, just to tie up the loose ends."

"As a matter of interest, Sir, who were the victims?"

"An old villain," Inspector Childs said, "Name of Jimmy Vale. He was housebound, crippled by arthritis, but a right tearaway in his time. His throat was cut from ear to ear, damned well nearly decapitated. And just a mile away, a cousin of his, an ex-copper would you believe, met with the same knife. He was gutted like a fish. Neighbours heard the screaming but they saw nothing or they're keeping stumm. It's got all the hallmarks of a gangland killing but the word is that both of these jokers were in some way responsible for the suicide of Tom Smith's father." The inspector stood from the table and buttoned his jacket. "Thanks for your help, Sergeant." He offered his hand.

Scratch stood up and shook it.

Once the policemen had left, Captain Roskilly said, "Scratch, one other t-t-thing. We've been put on stand-by. Let's be ready t-t-to leave at..." he glanced at his pocket watch, "Eleven hundred."

"Stand-by?" Ice Dovey looked hard at Fox. "Can we read anything into it?"

"Shouldn't think so," Scratch shook his head. "Lay you odds we're stood down by three."

He looked across at the group of men still digging and still making little impression on the land. At the end of the row, beyond Pinchera and Macloud, he caught sight of Tom Smith. Their gazes met and in that instant Sergeant Scratch Fox knew the truth.

The stand-down and back to barracks call stimulated the men and by ten-thirty, three ten-tonners were rolling between the thick hedgerows of Salisbury Plain, the canvas flaps billowing open to reveal the faces, delighted at being off the spade-work and looking forward to the fried delights of the NAAFI rather than the insipid stews and rank sausage-and-mash turned out by the field kitchen.

The unit was stood down at five minutes to three.

Scratch Fox, his wife and neighbours, Doug and Dolly Winter, drove to the sergeant's mess in a dark green Morris 8. Getting ready in the gloom of reduced electricity supplies and rooms that hadn't yet been successfully blacked out had not yet been mastered and they had to wait ten minutes for Dolly to emerge. The car lights were muffled so that only a narrow strip of the road showed up. The blackout had been in force since 8.22 the previous evening and with the sun setting well before eight it was already causing chaos, markedly so on the roads. No one had anticipated the difficulties or how seriously the authorities were taking it. The freshly called-up ARPs with their badges, whistles and respirators were swaggering along the streets in their armbands, flexing their pint-sized muscles. While the men parked the car, the women, as was their custom, went ahead to use the cloakroom. The car park was full. There was no moon but the stars were bright enough for them to find their way around.

"Something on tonight," Doug muttered cheerlessly.

"It's in the air," Scratch agreed.

War was imminent; everybody knew it. The buzz on camp was palpable. Some delighted in the prospect, particularly at the barracks.

"How's the boy?" Scratch asked, changing the subject.

"Spotty. Your two are bound to get it." Doug Winter was a handsome, well-groomed man of forty. They had first met during a posting to India and had known each other for twelve years.

By the time the women appeared they had bought drinks at the bar and moved to a table at the rear of the mess. It was their usual table, a position unchanged over the past year. But things had changed. The windows were lined and thick curtains were drawn. All rooms seemed smaller, even at home, and a strange sense of claustrophobia added to the foreboding. There was excitement and anticipation along with fear and gloom. They watched the women approach, Vicky in her blouse and black wraparound skirt that would occasionally split at the thigh, and Dolly in a well-cut flower-patterned dress that to some extent concealed her weight problem. Dolly reached the table first and gulped at her gin and tonic. "I want a lot of these tonight," she said.

"Celebrations are supposed to be after the battle," Doug muttered dryly. His wife gave him a curious look. She was a Cockney and proud of it. Doug had recently been made staff and she was proud of that too. War or the threat of it had always been a time for regulars to increase their number of stripes or, as in this case, the fixing of a crown.

A red-coated band, the Ron Fairburn Five, struck up 'There'll Always be an England', a song that had come out in the summer and at the moment seemed particularly appropriate, and the crowd nearby raised their glasses and cheered. Some couples on the floor stopped dancing and joined in. The atmosphere was charged, the expectancy heavy. The boisterous humour, the laughter, the hum of loud voices – it was a party and it was convincing. No one could deny them a war.

Scratch glanced at his wife and saw her lips moving.

"Sorry, I was miles away."

"On another planet, I should say. We are toasting Doug's promotion." Her voice held a gentle reproof.

"Sorry, mate," he said to Doug. "I must be tired." He raised his glass.

The false smile and the abruptness of his tone left Vicky looking at him inquisitively. He saw her look and wanted to explain that he found the gleeful anticipation of his colleagues unsettling. He made an effort, swallowed his drink and tried to amuse them with a description of Pinchera's tooth-pulling affair.

"I know him," Doug put in. "The wop, right?"

"His granddad was an Italian, I think."

Ice Dovey joined them along with a young woman he introduced as Mary Reynolds clinging to his arm. Mary was a bright, cheerful girl he had met in the NAAFI just a week earlier and they had already become engaged.

Vicky told them how the twins had become hysterical when trying on their gasmasks. The smell of rubber had made Sarah ill.

"This silly sod," Dolly punched her husband's arm, "came in through the back door wearing one of them; gave me a bleedin' heart attack!"

"I thought you liked rubber," Doug put in.

The others laughed.

A boisterous group of Canadian non-coms pulled their attention to the bar. One of them was staring at their table and only glanced away when he saw them looking.

"On attachment, manoeuvres," Dovey told them.

Vicky noticed that her skirt had fallen open to reveal a long expanse of thigh that had been in the man's line of sight, and she self-consciously pulled it together.

One of the numerous attendants approached with a bottle of champagne in a silver bucket and addressed Scratch Fox: "With the compliments of Major Harris, Staff?"

Scratch pointed to Doug Winter. "He's the culprit."

"The toast is to a bloody war…" the waiter began. The others joined in, "…And quick promotion!"

Dovey offered his glass for filling. "Stone the flippin' crows. I never thought I'd see the day when this happened. I suppose it means we'll have to take more notice of the old bugger now."

"You take notice of the rank, not the man," Scratch said.

"A company man, eh?" Doug said and exchanged glances with his wife as if the comment confirmed an earlier concurrence.

Vicky tugged at Scratch's arm. "Come on and dance," she said softly, concerned at his reticence. It wasn't like him at all. She led him to the floor and embraced him. The band had struck up a Glen Miller number, Tuxedo Junction. "What is it?" she asked. He felt her warm breath on his neck.

"It's all so bloody stupid. They don't remember the last one. Memories are short."

Over his shoulder she saw the young Canadian looking at her again and was glad her husband hadn't noticed.

"It's excitement," she said. "They don't mean it."

"Is that what you think?" He directed her towards the exit. "Come on. I need some air."

She shot a backward glance at the soldier again and saw his look of disappointment. She felt her stomach flutter. A sense of elation she hadn't known in some years coloured her face and she was grateful for the dimmed lights.

He led her along a corridor that had all the lights removed in order to comply with the blackout regulations, and out of double doors to the narrow lawns. The evening air was cool on her arms. They walked slowly in silence. A sentry near the unlit guardroom peered their way, his torch barely raised. He recognized the sergeant, and then moved back inside. The stars were as bright as they'd ever seen them and a shooting star died as they watched.

"The civvy police turned up during the week asking questions about Tommy Smith, the young lad who stayed the night."

"Oh, what about?"

"Those two old guys murdered in the city. It was in the papers, made the headlines in the Mercury. He's mixed up with it somehow. His father used to know them. It all happened on Tuesday night."

"They suspected him? How horrible. One of them was crippled, in a wheelchair."

"He went out, you know, on Tuesday night. I heard him get back about six in the morning."

"What did he say?"

"He said he never went out."

"Did you tell the police?"

"No. Maybe I should."

"Well I don't think he had anything to do with it."

"A woman's intuition?"

"He thanked me for the trouble and for his breakfast and he folded his blankets."

"That's all right then, isn't it?"

She smiled and threw her arms around his neck.

A few miles north of them the darkened city was clothed in her battledress. Barrage balloons swayed ominously above her, dark shapes, darker than the midnight sky, snuffing out the stars.

Some hours earlier Tom Smith had been recognized at the Palais. He was in uniform; without the CO's express permission uniforms had to be worn during any leave of less than seven days. He was making use of a rare forty-eight hour pass and that meant time spent with his mother and Peter Woodhead and then a night on the town with Simon and the girls. Peter had warned him that someone had mouthed off and that people had heard that he was due home for the weekend. Some unfriendly faces, remnants from the Cross Gang or more likely the White Hart Boys who wanted payback for the Bruce Castle fiasco, were asking questions. "Can't blame 'em," the old man added. "Slasher Lee's still looking for his top teeth and you were well out of line!" It was the first time Peter had mentioned the affair and Tom had assumed he hadn't heard about it. He should have known better. There was very little that happened south of Watford that Peter Woodhead didn't hear about.

The weekend had not been a total success and he looked forward to the anonymity of the parade ground again. Attitudes had hardened in a subtle way. People, even his mother, and certainly Simon, were waiting for him to broach the subject, and the strain of silence was telling on them also. At the Eagle people were wary of him. He recognized their glances and heard their whispers. In the close-knit community the neighbours knew and in the market the store-holders knew. Of those who knew him only Maureen and Peter Woodhead acted as if nothing had changed. Even that was not strictly true of the old man. There was warmth in Peter's handshake that he'd not known before, and a mark of understanding and acceptance, even approval, lay in his knowing look.

The thing unspoken remained between him and the rest; not respect, exactly, unless it was the respect one had for dangerous things.

The pessimistic news on the BBC Home Service had done nothing to reduce the number of people waiting at the bar and it was in the mirror behind the bar that he recognized two faces that he'd last seen at Bruce Castle. He wondered whether he'd been followed. More likely someone in the Palais had recognized him and tipped the wink. A third man appeared who was obviously a part of the group, for he was looking at the others for instructions, and now all three were closing in behind him. He hit the first with a heavy glass ashtray. Its sharpened crystal-shaped edges smashed into the man's face. A flick-knife flashed in the second man's hand and slashed the side of his jacket. Tom Smith knew he was facing an amateur and grinned. An expert would have buried the blade. The man took a step back before Tom smacked him in the mouth. He went down on one knee and Tom drove a boot into his side, certain that he'd shattered at least three ribs. The third man made a speedy retreat. Around him people were diving out of the way, tables and chairs overturned and glasses smashed. A couple of security guards in blue uniforms and built like brick walls were trying to muscle their way through a crowd intent on getting away from the trouble. Tom tried to lose himself but people stepped aside, moving quickly out of his way to leave him exposed. He caught sight of Jane in the crowd. She stood watching out of wide disbelieving eyes. He shouted, "See you at the car!"

He didn't wait for her response but instead jostled his way through the crush and headed for a side exit. When he pushed his way though the double doors and hit the night air the security guards were still fighting their way through the darkness of the exit corridor. By the time they arrived in the street he'd turned a corner and was out of sight. Even in the blackout Shepherd's Bush Road was surprisingly busy even for a Saturday night. He hurried along the dark pavement, head down and collar up and turned another corner. His car was parked in the forecourt of a garage owned by a friend of Simon. Simon had fixed the lights two days previously so that only a faint glow emerged to light their way. Five minutes went by and Jane appeared, holding her coat together. She climbed in beside him.

"Where are the others?"

She brushed her coat down over her knees and turned toward him. Her spectacles glinted in the moonlight. She looked older. Make-up and false eyelashes had done the trick and got her into the club.

She said, "They must have seen us together 'cos they're still hanging around Simon and Maureen like a couple of shadows. One of them is getting medical treatment and they've called for an ambulance. There's blood all over. The police were going in as I was coming out. Simon insists he met you tonight and doesn't even know your name. He doesn't want to lead them to the car so he'll see you back at Maureen's once they've given up. He said don't forget you've got the beer in the boot."

Tom nodded and turned the key.

"Will you run us home? It's getting late for me and even with this moon I'll never find my way in the dark."

He turned the car left into Kensington Road. Green Park was just a spit away. He could be back in less than ten minutes and he did need a drink. Not the box full of beers that Simon had loaded in the car but the bottle of whisky in the dash would go down a treat. His side was beginning to sting and he could feel a dampness spreading out. The flick-knife had obviously caused more damage than he'd first thought.

She pointed out a narrow, three-story townhouse in the centre of a terraced row of six. Each house had three wide steps leading between two columns to a porch and a heavy mahogany door with brass furniture.

"Blimey!" Tom said, not hiding his surprise. He pulled in.

She turned to him and adjusted her spectacles. "Will you come in?"

"I shouldn't."

"I know you shouldn't but I've heard you often do things you shouldn't do."

"Where did you hear that?"

"Oh, you know, around, that you're a very dangerous man. Since you've been away things have been said."

"That's nonsense; people gossip, you know that. They've nothing better to do."

"Maybe, but people believe it, and I've seen the way people treat you."

"Like chase me all over town, you mean?"

"That's what comes of being famous."

He smiled.

"So who are the faces you're talking about?"

"Simon and some of the others he hangs around with, mostly from the Eagle. You're friends, I know, but at the same time they're frightened of you."

"Take no heed to it. People like to mouth off and it's causing me some grief, as you saw earlier. But it was just the White Hart Boys out to make a name for themselves. It's nothing to worry about."

"Well, are you coming in? You can have a drink or you can get back to the others."

"I should get back. Maureen will be waiting and Simon will be panicking about his booze. It's my last night and I don't want to waste it."

She shrugged and reached for the door handle.

"Jane, you shouldn't be messing around with us."

She paused and turned back.

"This is a really nice place. It's a different world. We come from different places, you and me. Your place is full of good manners and elegance and safety. Oh, I know you try and hide it, probably for our sakes, but it doesn't wash. Never has. We treat it as a bit of a joke, really, all this la-di-da stuff. Not unkindly, you understand, but you're not one of us. Our place is rough and uncouth and dangerous. You'll get yourself into trouble or worse, even hurt. I'm not telling you to go away, I like having you around, but you ought to for your own sake."

"You'll never hurt me, I know that much, Tommy Smith. If you don't want to come in, that's fine."

"I didn't say I didn't want to. I said it's a bad idea and I told you why."

"I heard what you said."

He nodded.

She turned to the door again.

He hesitated, then: "Have you got any bandages in there?"

She frowned. He pulled aside his tunic and showed her the stain on his shirt. Even in the powdery light she could make it out, glistening and black.

"Oh my God," she stammered.

"It's only a scratch, but I wouldn't mind it cleaning up a bit."

"Come with me," she said and climbed out of the car. By the time he started up the steps holding up his bottle of whisky she was at the front door searching for her key.

She held open the door and said, "You really didn't need that. Daddy has a full cabinet and I'm sure he wouldn't mind if you helped yourself. Not from the decanters, though, I believe he checks those with a ruler every time he comes home. Not on my behalf, but he thinks the cleaner might be helping herself to the odd tipple."

She led him into an entrance hall decorated to resemble white or pale stone. There were doors on both sides and in front a curved Portland stone staircase. Beside the stairs was a tall wooden sculpture that he couldn't make any sense of – it might have been of an animal or even human – and a shelf on the right was loaded with more carved figures and a vase of white roses. The place was spotless and shining in electric light.

While she took off her coat he stood motionless, taking it in. He said, "It's a like a museum."

"Not like a home, you mean?"

"No home that I've ever been in."

She hung her coat and closed a gleaming cupboard door. "This way," she said and led him past the stairs to the kitchen. It was the biggest kitchen he'd ever seen outside a restaurant, with white units and beech tops and tiles from floor to ceiling. There was even room for a table with four chairs around it and along the far wall a massive Welsh dresser full of sparkling china he could almost see through. "Take off your jacket and shirt and sit there," she directed, indicating a chair at the table. She sounded like the old nit nurse and her attempted bossiness tickled him.

There was something about her that didn't add up; she seemed too self-confident, as if walking across the threshold had changed her into someone else. She was no longer the schoolgirl, more like the mistress of her own house. She was fourteen, coming on fifteen, she had said. He found the idea perplexing and wondered about her parents, her mother in particular.

The kitchen was warm and slightly smoky. He watched her adjust her spectacles again and then open the door of a cast-iron stove to shovel in some coal. She slammed it shut and pulled a lever to activate the back boiler then turned to him. "The water is already warm but in ten minutes or so it will be hot." She carried two glasses to the table and took the bottle out of his hands.

"You look as though you've seen a ghost, Tommy Smith. I told you to take off your shirt. I can't clean you up with you wearing it." She poured out the drinks.

He shook himself to sense. "A bit taken aback, that's all. We knew you were a bit posh but I didn't expect this." He lifted a glass to his lips. "You're too young to drink."

"I know," she said, leaving her glass on the table. "And I don't even like it. One drink and I'll be on the floor."

He took off his shirt and twisted to inspect himself. "See, I told you, just a scratch."

"It's more than a scratch and it's still bleeding." She waved a bottle of Dettol antiseptic liquid in his face. "I hope it stings. You can pretend to be Robert Newton and grit your teeth. I saw Gaslight. Did I tell you?" She used a wet cloth to clean the wound then finished with a length of waterproof tape. "Not perfect, but it will have to do. Once the water's hot you better sit in the bath and clean yourself properly. It's run under your waistband. Pass them out to me and I'll see if I can clean them."

"I don't think so."

"Don't worry. I won't look."

"Where are your parents anyway?"

She led him into the drawing room, another high-ceilinged room filled with cream and green-striped fabrics and thick rugs and strange carvings, some of which looked almost human. A huge window overlooked the road. She pulled the blackout blinds and then the curtains. His mother had made do with a tin of paint and brown-paper screens. He heard a switch and the lights flickered on. On the far wall a carved chimneypiece surrounded a massive fireplace that was laid and ready for lighting. There was nothing lying around; everything was in its place; even the striped cushions were placed inch perfect on the armchairs and sofa. Tom was dazzled and shook his head in wonder. One wall was filled with books. Robinson Crusoe jumped out at him and he had a vague recollection of the old Jewboy at his market stall. "Everything you ever want to know is in a book," he heard the old man say. He grunted and shook the memory aside. The past was too dark a place for this light and airy room.

"Daddy works at the War Office," she told him matter-of-factly. "The Directorate of Supplies and Transport under the Quatermaster-General's office. Apparently there are angry words being exchanged between his office and the Minister for Co-ordination of Defence. Just who is responsible for what remains a grey area and has not been thought out. Before the balloon went up it didn't really matter, but now all hell has broken loose. So he's taken his toothbrush. Because of the flap they've bunkered up – his words, not mine – and he won't be home until tomorrow night and even then it will be a flying visit." She paused and gave him a thoughtful look. "I'm supposed to be staying with my Aunt Etty, but after about two in the afternoon she won't know if I'm there or not. That's the time she finishes her first bottle of gin."

"Where's your mother?"

She turned to face him. Under the electric light her green eyes seemed to have paled.

"I haven't got a mother."

"You never said."

"You never asked and anyway, why should I?"

She led him back to the stairs and began to climb.

"What happened to her?"

"I never knew her. It's a bit of a family secret, really, one of those skeletons. Aunt Etty's vocal chords are loosened after the second bottle. After she gave birth to me she went mad and had to be put away. There's nothing else to tell, really."

Tom nodded, his face falling.

She laughed. "It's all right. What you never had…"

He followed her up three flights.

"Your dad brought you up?"

"That's a bit strong, really. It was mostly his sisters. There's Aunt Etty and Aunt Edith – she's up north in Epping. I spent my first years running around the forest." She slid open a glass door and led him on to a roof terrace. It was a riot of colour with potted geraniums and daisies and tumbling lobelia surrounding a wrought iron table and chairs.

He gazed across the night skyline and down at the streets below where the odd car slid stealthily by. "Blimey! It's beautiful. I'd love to show my old ma this place. She wouldn't believe it. I'm looking at it and I don't believe it. You've got everything you could want here. Why do you want to mess around our part of town?"

She shrugged. The bright stars caught her spectacles again and turned her face into marble. She whispered, "I've got everything here except a life."

"That's not true, I'm sure." He put his empty glass on the table.

"A daily comes in during the week, but she's getting on a bit now. If anyone brought me up then she had more to do with it than most. Daddy is working most of the time. He always has done. And when he's home he's working in his study. That's out of bounds. It might have been different had I been a boy."

She led him back down a flight of stairs and pushed open a door. She turned on the light and said, "There you are. The water will be hot enough now. Don't forget to wash behind your ears." She manhandled him into the room and stood waiting until he passed out his uniform. He was left alone staring at another bright room full of mirrors and bathroom fittings, the biggest bath he'd ever seen and a sparkling water closet, and towels so soft and fluffy they were more like furs.

While the bath filled he checked out the shaving gear, toothbrushes, perfumes and medicines in the cabinet, enough to open a chemist shop. He climbed into the hot water and scrubbed using Lifeboy – none of that Perfection cut up into chunks that was all he'd ever known – and he used coconut oil on his hair. Blimey, he was becoming a proper dandy. He smiled at the thought and wondered what Peter Woodhead would say if he could see him now. He cast the thought aside and concentrated on another. The evening had taken a wrong turn and he knew it. Time was running out and he needed to get back to the cheer of his own surroundings, or at least Maureen's surroundings, surrounded by her legs. She wasn't the most enthusiastic lover he'd ever known and was apt to fall asleep – pass-out was the term – but she was easy and her bonny breasts with their full-crown nipples were as comfortable as he'd ever slept on. And it was his last chance to score for God knows how long. He was considering making a move and getting on his way when the door opened and steam wafted and she stood there, framed in the doorway. She carried two crystal glasses. Her spectacles steamed up and she approached the bath carefully, both drinks leaving a trail of splashes on the stone floor tiles. She pushed a shaking glass towards Tom. He took it and swallowed half. She held her own drink with both hands and sipped at it before placing the glass on the shelf above the basin.

"'Struth," he said. "You don't give a geezer much of a chance, do you?"

She wore her knickers and her spectacles and nothing else. She took off her spectacles and cleaned them with a towel. She was as blind as a bat without them and it wasn't until she replaced them that she saw that the water remained clear. He hadn't used the bath salts. Her eyes filled the lenses. Two great bowls of astonishment. She stood dithering and fixed her gaze on the floor in front of her. He was uncertain whether it was his own nakedness or hers that caused her nervousness. He looked at her small breasts with their dark pointed nipples. Her body was as milky white as her cotton knickers. Her hips jutted and her stomach was pulled flat. He wondered if she'd ever eaten a decent-sized meal in her life. He couldn't get the schoolgirl image out of his head, freckles and all.

"Are you going to stand there all day?"

Eventually she looked up at him. "No," she confirmed.

"Well, get out of here then and let me finish up."

She looked down at him and adjusted her spectacles so they perched on the end of her nose. For a moment she looked older, like a bookkeeper studying the accounts. "You're aroused," she said.

"Well, I'm not surprised with you part undressed and standing so close." He waved her away. "Well?"

"You say drop 'em and we drop 'em, isn't that how it goes?"

He grinned. "I never said that."

"You can say it now, if you like."

He shook his head, unsure of himself or the situation.

She shrugged and without hesitation took off her knickers. She followed the line of his gaze and looked down at herself and said, "What's wrong?"

"Nothing's wrong. I'm surprised, that's all."

She looked up and said earnestly, "I'll have to keep my glasses on." She clambered in and sat between his legs with her back to him. She passed the soap over her shoulder. He lathered up and began to soap her shoulders and arms and then he reached forward and covered her breasts, feeling her tiny nipples against his soapy palms. He was beginning to throb and a moment's panic yanked him back from the edge. He stood up too quickly and water splashed over the side. Before she could turn he reached for a towel and climbed out, and turned away from her.

"What's wrong now?" she asked, frowning.

"You are. This is. I was enjoying myself too much and forgot how old you are. I need another drink. You finish up and pull the plug."

He left footprints on the tiles and found her bedroom where she'd left the bottle along with her discarded clothes. He might have guessed that there would be a four-poster with a lacy canopy hanging like a curtain of secrecy over cream-coloured bedclothes, not that he'd ever seen a four-poster outside a shop or a photograph, certainly not in real life. He poured a drink and finished it in one then refilled his glass. There was no sign of his clothes so he wrapped the towel around him. A clock on her bedside showed one o'clock and a silver-framed photograph next to it showed a well-dressed gentleman in his forties. Lying beside it was a copy of Picture Post. He lay back on the bed and cradled the drink on his chest and studied the film posters stuck to the far wall. There were pictures of Bing Crosby, Gary Cooper, Deanna Durbin, and Jean Harlow in a bathing costume looking like something out of heaven. A poster of *Fire over England* hung between *Pygmalion* and *Boys' Town*. He decided she'd spent her life in the Gaumont or Rialto.

The canopy pressed down, the front of it resembled a blade of a guillotine ready to drop. He'd been sentenced in his absence, perhaps for what he was thinking. She was still playing havoc with his thoughts. He knew he should have retreated when the going was good. He knew also that it was now too late.

She walked in and stood beside the bed and after a moment said, "I'm ready."

"Where are my clothes, Jane?"

"They're hanging by the stove. They should be dry in a few minutes. Can I have some of that? I'm in need of some fortitude." She reached down and took the glass and swallowed half the drink. She pulled a face and placed the glass on the bedside table then sat beside him. "Shall I keep my glasses on? I can't see a thing without them."

"Whatever you like, Jane."

"Unless the towel has a life of its own you're getting aroused again." She saw the uncertainty and smiled and leant toward him. "Tommy Smith, there's no obligation, no promise, and no responsibility." She kissed him gently on the mouth. When she pulled back her spectacles were skew-whiffed. She reached up and straightened them. "So you can have your wicked way with me without worrying about the consequences. You can touch me, you know, I'm not going to break."

"That's just it, I think you might."

"You stopped Simon and I'm glad you did, but someone's going to and I'd like it to be you." She giggled and lay beside him.

"This is a bad idea."

"Are you trying to frighten me?"

"Yes."

She laughed. "Well, you're not succeeding and you're not getting out of here until you make love to me. I never once imagined that it would be me making the running!" She wriggled beneath him and spread her legs. "So make me a woman." She reached up and kissed him and her spectacles fell off. She said "Ouch!" and held her breath.

A siren woke him. He guessed it was another test. The room was stuffy and warm and Jane was cradled in his arm, only her face and splash of dark hair showing above the bedcovers. She lay undisturbed by the alarm, eyes closed and her face relaxed and oddly beautiful, coloured by the sunshine squeezing in from the cracks in the blackout blinds to find its way around the side of the curtains. Dust particles hung in the air above her. He checked the clock: eleven thirty-five. Gently he eased her aside and went naked on to the landing. As he climbed the stairs the wailing grew louder and more urgent. He slid open the glass door and stepped on to the roof terrace. The siren became a scream and he felt his heart beating faster. The sun was warm on his bare skin and for a ludicrous moment he thought he was still dreaming. Birds flew over, black panicky streaks in the glare, and in the distance silver-coloured barrage balloons rose above the rooftops, their loose skins changing shape even as he watched. Above the din he heard shouts of "Take cover!" and "Where's your bleedin' gas mask?" He moved to the wall and looked down. People were crowding in the street below, gazing fearfully up at the sky. More were filing out of their houses to the green where a half-finished public shelter had been fenced off. An ARP warden armed with gas mask and helmet was waving frantically for them to get back inside but no one was taking the slightest notice. A policeman on a bicycle joined in the shouting.

"What is it?"

Jane stood in the doorway, shielding her eyes from the sun. Without her spectacles she looked different, naked. In the brightness and from the explosion of light that bounced from the glass, her pale body shimmered.

"I think the war has started," he said solemnly.

"Don't be silly."

In that instant the sirens stopped and the voices in the street became clear. Someone shouted that the music halls and football matches were off, and someone else berated the policeman for using his whistle. "Against the law, that is now, or didn't you know!"

"See, I told you so," she said. "Daddy says Neville Chamberlain's a coward and all his huffing is just swagger, that he'll never go to war because he's got nothing to go to war with, that the regular army is overflowing with TAs that think a box magazine is something to read and that webbing is something found on a duck's foot."

As if to underline her point the long, even whine of the all clear sounded.

She smiled knowingly and said, "Come back to bed. I haven't finished with you yet."

Later, listening to the BBC Home Service on the wireless and after God Save the King had played out Alvar Liddell and the news, he said to her, "I've got to get home for my kit and get back to barracks."

"You don't have to go."

He noticed how delicate and defenceless she looked. He said quietly, "Yes I do."

"A lot won't go back."

"Do a runner you mean?"

"I'll come with you."

"It's a nice thought, but I don't think so."

"Damn Hitler and Chamberlain both. They've taken away the future and last night I was looking forward to it, and I never felt that way about it before."

At the door he paused. "Will you be all right?"

She nodded glumly. "Daddy will be back soon, I'm sure. He won't wait till tonight. Not now. He'll want to make sure I'm OK."

"And are you?"

She nodded.

"Thanks for last night. It was the best...you know?"

A sudden smile lit up her face. "Fuck?"

"Yeah, that's the word I'm looking for. It was the best I've ever had."

Her voice lowered to a whisper, "You're welcome, Tommy Smith, but I really don't know what all the fuss was about, I'm sure."

He nodded thoughtfully and closed the door behind him.

He left the house in Green Park wondering how on earth he would ever end up living in a place like that. Of one thing he was certain, no one was ever going to give it to him, and he knew that in Great Britain today the divide was far too great for him to ever earn enough to afford it. That left him only one option and he was going to have to take it.

Chapter 17

Movements arrived quickly. Captain Roskilly called Scratch Fox into his office and asked "Feel like a holiday by the sea, Sergeant?"

"Orders, Sir?"

"We're on our way. The gunners can get one of t-t-their customary send-offs ready."

"What part of France, Sir?"

"France? We've been given t-t-the Isle of Wight, guarding some kind of communication installations. Jolly important work, I'm sure." He glanced from the window at the watery sky and the clouds packing in above the barracks and said, "T-t-too late in t-t-the year for France, anyway." The captain produced one of his rare smiles.

They were would-be warriors and their hearts beat faster and their thoughts were full of the deeds of glorious forebears. It was an adventure. Most of the recruits had never crossed the sea and some had never seen it. Only the old-timers – the regulars – had made the trip before and knew of the horrors that lay waiting and of the incompetent old men at the back who would send them to the front. But even for them memory dulled the bad times. It was an odd experience of rising panic and excitement, of being herded and led unthinking from place to place under the growing awareness that freedom had been left well and truly behind. They were prisoners now, in uniform and as good as shackled, slaves to the overbearing noncoms and the overweening comoffs.

And so it was to the Isle of Wight and it was not until the fourteenth of October that further orders were received and sent them within hours to the European mainland. They arrived in an area of mostly flat farmland where the farmhouses and outbuildings had long ago been abandoned, and where the apples and pears in the orchards had been left to rot. During the following weeks life became drudgery, the drilling, the inspections, the guarding, the digging of gun pits and trenches and the filling of sandbags to build dugouts, the queuing with their mess tins at the RASC cookhouse wagons for tasteless stew that was cold before it was served, a total cut-off from the world they had known, and the officers battled against complacency. Men dawdled through the vacuum and other men, such as Pinchera, revelled in it. He was the platoon joker and he'd found a captive audience. The shortening days of idleness, punctuated only by the design of their superiors and the snaps of colder and wetter weather, moved on toward the winter.

A sharp northerly had swept a thick belt of cloud from the lowlands and it had rained for two days. Under cover of darkness a three-tonner spluttered and its shielded lights illuminated a few feet of churned ground in front. A sentry, rifle slung, hood and cape glistening and dripping, squelched in the mud. The dimmed beam from his torch found the driver's face.

"Fuck this for a living," he muttered. He held out his free hand. "Raffle tickets?"

From the driver's seat Tom Smith passed an envelope through the window and said, "Two white, two blue."

"I want a red."

Tom grinned, "On the next run, maybe; maybe tomorrow."

"Tell Frederick I want a fucking red BEF or you can count me out. And I want Saturday's date on it! I'm taking enough chances here, even in the rain. If I don't get it you can tell him to fuck himself!"

The sentry stepped back and opened the compound gates. Lightning cracked open the heaving clouds and a distant rumble came over the ridge. For a moment a sign on the wire fencing flashed STRICTLY NO ADMITTANCE and beneath it AUTHORIZED PERSONNEL ONLY and the trees around the perimeter glowed in powder blue before disappearing again into the darkness. The rain lashed harder and drummed on the truck's canvas. The sentry stood back and waved Tom through the gate. The lorry lurched from the mud and turned right on to a tyre-rutted road that ran through a field of farm outbuildings and prefab huts. What had been a cowshed was now their billet, its concrete floor covered in palliasses. The guns and vehicles were housed in the barns and haylofts, the cookhouse and guardroom in two smaller buildings next to them. The officers were billeted in houses in the village, cosseted both by their batmen and the owners of the properties, but part of the old milking area of the cowshed had been screened off for them to use as their temporary HQ. Only an occasional dim light glowed through the blackout. Tom drove out of the camp and through another field where the vague outlines of a squadron of De Gaulle's cavalry had set up a temporary billet. A line of tethered horses, disturbed by the thunder or the noise from the truck, stamped and snorted. Lights from oil lamps and stove fires flickered from the abandoned farmhouses. The French had never taken much notice of standing orders; they were anarchists at heart and nothing would ever change them. They were on their way in the morning, or so the rumour in camp had it, to meet up with the Chars'D'Assault some miles to the southeast. The road continued over a stone bridge and down a gentle slope through a wooded valley to the hamlet of St Michelle.

In the passenger seat Norman Dileva said, "That guard is going to give us some trouble. He's getting greedy."

Tom's eyes were narrowed in concentration. Rain sheeted the windscreen and blurred even the few feet of road that he could see. A rare light flared and died in the village below. The villagers were more observant than their military. "Just keep your eyes peeled," he said irritably. "We don't want the redcaps or the fucking prefect sniffing in the back, and the gendarmes love the rain. It's the only time they get a proper wash."

"I was just saying," Dileva said ruefully and lit a Gold Flake. He flicked the spent match from the window.

Tom relented and nodded. "You're right, Norman. He is a greedy bastard and we'll have to sort him out."

They travelled through the narrow roads of the silent village and across the glistening cobbles of the town square where the church and the hôtel de ville were dark shadows against the pressing sky, and slowed at the back of the Café Veronica. Before they'd come to a halt, two men appeared and opened the gates to a courtyard. Tom reversed in and the gates were closed again.

Their dimmed lights found a short fat man standing before the doors of a garage where a section of floor had been lifted to reveal a deep pit and the top of a large tank that sat in it. He wore an overcoat and scarf. The brim of his flat cap threw his sombre features into shadow. He called to the two men approaching from the gate, "Quickly, get it unloaded."

Tom climbed down and ducked out of the rain beneath the garage roof. He said, "Evening Frederick. Make sure your guys refill the drums to the top. When we unloaded last time we could hear the water making waves, like they were half empty."

Frederick turned on his men and said angrily, "Did you hear that?"

The two men looked at each other and shrugged their Gallic shoulders.

"The other gear is in the back, including six pairs of officer's boots, brown, sizes as requested. It wasn't easy. Your guys must have the smallest feet in Europe."

Frederick waved a loose hand at his men. "Let them unload." He turned back to Tom. "Come inside and I'll pour a *Remi*. It's not a night to be outside."

Tom nodded and said to Norman Dileva at his side, "Keep an eye on them. When you've finished up I'll see you in the front."

Dileva moved under cover and cupped his hands to light a cigarette, content to watch from the shelter of the garage.

Frederick led the way to the back door of the Inn. In the kitchen they carried drinks to a blazing log fire. Tom took off his cape and sat down and let the brandy warm his heart. He recognized a girl pottering in the back, rattling dishes. Her name was Nathalie and she had been in St Michelle less than a week.

Frederick pointed towards a large cardboard box sealed with tape. "Make sure you take the captain's dinner, with the compliments of the Cafè Veronica, a goose and fresh eggs."

"He does like his boiled eggs for breakfast."

"There is also a bottle."

"He was rather taken with the last one you sent, Chateau Veronique, vintage '17. He even made a note of the name. He's going to get his mess back in Aldershot to order a crate."

They laughed loudly.

Frederick shook his head, "The ruling class!"

"If the bleedin' war ever starts for real then God help us all."

"And it is coming, for some of us. There is no doubt about that. This funny war – drôle de guerre – will not go on forever. One day soon the fighting will start..." He left the sentence hanging and nodded reflectively.

Tom said, "I'm going to need some more red tickets. With so many runs things are getting awkward, different guards on duty, and they all want a piece of it, that's beside the squaddies on the inside. The depot doesn't run itself, and every fucking thing has got to be countersigned. There's no such thing as good will anymore. Old-fashioned values have gone out the window."

Frederick pulled an unhappy face. "The girls are not so happy with the red tickets. BEFs are bad for morale. Booze and entertainment we can live with, even the free meals, but free fucking for the entire night? It's unheard of. They are complaining. Between them they are losing maybe eight or ten gratuities in a week, and these all-night sessions give the clientele time to experiment. The girls, they don't like experimental, you understand? These girls are not from the streets."

"No red tickets, no gasoline and definitely no more officer boots."

"I know. You don't need to tell me. But just...use them carefully, discriminately, just maybe two or three in a week, more whites and blues, less reds.

More dishes rattled and Tom's gaze was drawn to the girl. Frederick noticed and said in a lowered tone, "She was at the ESC, the graduate school in Lille and, more than that, she was a…dilettante…dramatics, you know? She played minor parts at the Opêra de Lille. That's something, isn't it? An actress living under my roof! But everywhere is bad and you have to earn a living. You have to eat! The depression hit everyone. Everyone was starving. Her studies along with her theatrical aspirations have been put on hold."

"Maybe she's still got friends who could swing a couple of tickets to the opera?"

Frederick grinned, "Even if she hasn't, I have." He winked. "Even so, I am keeping her special, for a special occasion and for gentlemen only."

"They're in short supply around here, the same as your red tickets."

Frederick shrugged. "She has to be treated tenderly. Leave the others to the more boisterous." He smiled and showed some stained teeth. "Just three years ago three-quarters of Lille's population was hungry and as for the people who lived in the surrounding villages…" He shook his head and sipped his drink. "People made a living any way they could. But now…?" He grunted and waved his hands. "Things are just as bad. Three hundred and fifty thousand refugees came over the borders, mostly Jews, mostly from Germany. And down south the story is the same but with the Spanish. Two hundred and fifty thousand Spaniards walked into southern France." He gulped at his drink. "What can we do? And they are just the official figures. There are internment camps all over, and more going up every week, but they don't come close to solving the problem."

Tom sighed, "There's problems all over."

"Not like here. Here we don't have the North Sea and the Channel to halt the flow. And now, my friend, it is worse than ever. There is panic and fear…" He looked up and met Tom's stony gaze. "Do you trust me, Tommy?"

Tom considered him for a moment and slowly shook his head. "No," he said.

Frederick let out a dry laugh. "That's good. Trust no one and then you can't be disappointed. But can I trust you?"

Tom smiled and met the older man's gaze.

The door opened and Frederick's wife came in with the sounds from the bar – laughter and loud voices, some of them from French Cavalry, the chink of glasses and the scratchy music from a gramophone. Her name Veronica was on the café door.

"There's a full house," she chided. "People are sheltering from the rain and you sit in front of the fire talking, as if there's nothing to do!" She moved to some drawers, found what she was looking for and backed out.

"I won't be long," Frederick said contritely. "This is business."

She closed the door behind her. The flames trembled in the sudden draught.

Frederick pulled a face and said, "Women!" He glanced across at Nathalie and then at the closed door. "All women are good actresses, until they get married!" He edged his chair closer to Tom and said, "Let me explain what is happening."

Tom was warmed by the brandy and his eyes were drawn again to the girl as she bent across a rough wooden table to scrub the top, the outline of her underwear showing through her skirt and her breasts swinging beneath her loose top. He pulled his gaze back to Frederick.

The café owner smiled knowingly and his grey whiskers separated as if shot by static. He opened a handkerchief and pushed it towards Tom. A few tiny stones caught the flames from the fire and glittered. "Do you know what these are?"

"They might be diamonds or they might be glass. I'm not an expert."

Frederick nodded thoughtfully. "They are diamonds," he confirmed.

"I'm not in the market for either."

"You couldn't afford them even if you were."

"What then?"

"As you know, or you might not know but it makes no difference, the diamond trade throughout Europe, including Great Britain, is run more or less by the Jews. The same goes for America. It's an exclusive club. It always has been. They like to keep it in the family. My brother Ernesto owns a small second-hand shop on Vincennes in Paris. He makes a living but he's stupid. He has no business acumen, no enterprise. He will die dreaming of what it might be like to have money in his pocket."

Tom emptied his glass slowly, certain that a con was on the way. The girl moved from the table and his eyes flicked her way again.

Frederick said, "Do you want her?"

"I'm choosy, and I'm squeamish about paying for it and, in any case, not many people would mark me down as a gentleman."

She flashed him a haughty – almost worldly – look before turning back to the sink.

If she was a virgin, he decided, he was a Chinaman.

Frederick made a suitable noise. He poked at the fire, raising sparks and spilling ash. At length he said, "The thing is that many Jewish businessmen in the Low Countries, particularly Amsterdam, have already fled to Britain and America. The dealers have transferred their stocks to England to save them from the Germans. The British have thought up the wonderful title of the Correspondence Office for the Diamond Industry to set up and store – and more to the point – to register the stones for the duration of the war. Some dealers aren't happy with the register or the British fascination with record keeping. Some less scrupulous dealers have found themselves in a dilemma. That they find themselves in this situation is entirely their fault. They have not planned for the future, even though the signs have been there for a long, long time. Events have now overtaken them. And that is where men like us come in. One man's difficulty is another man's opportunity." He threw Tom a lop-sided smile. The brandy was telling, but not as much as he made out. "Savings," he went on. "Little nest eggs…treasured heirlooms!" He shrugged, as if he wasn't too bothered, as if he was talking about small change. "Put together for a rainy day, put together over generations, and now the rainy day is here."

The wind increased and sucked at the flames and the rain pelted against the shuttered windows. The girl looked up alarmed and shivered. She wrapped her arms around herself.

Frederick smiled, "Can you hear it, the rain? What a lovely sound it makes. It's the sound of money!" He filled the glasses again and returned the half-empty bottle to the hearth. "And now these foolish people find themselves in a situation where their movements and business activities are under close scrutiny. So now they panic, and who can blame them? The Jews aren't welcome anywhere. Think of the Croix-de-Feu and Action Française, and even the Popular Front wasn't good enough for the right-wing in Lille."

Tom shrugged. "We've had our own problems with the blackshirts and the BUF. You won't have heard of Cable Street."

"Oh yes, I know about that. It was when the workers on the London docks helped fight off Mosley's mob. I heard very well."

"Well, then you know it's not just here."

"Britain will never set up internment camps for the Jews, of that I'm sure. Too many of them are in charge of your country and your major industries and your less than free press. Anyway, in normal circumstances the dealers would transfer their nest eggs to Paris, for safekeeping, but even my brother Ernesto is worried. And I think he has every right to be. The Maginot does not make me sleep easier. They think, and I suspect, that the British government will, for all its posturing, line up with your Royal Family and come to an agreement with Hitler. They think that France along with all Mainland Europe will be forfeited, relinquished, that's the word. Germany will have Europe and Britain will have her empire and the two will live happily side-by-side. So now they want to hedge their bets."

Tom sat straighter in his chair, his interest picking up. He remained stony-faced but curiosity set aside his earlier misgivings. In the East End confidence tricksters were two a penny but he'd come across nothing like this before.

"So now we must take a lead from the governments and in a similar way we must protect ourselves from all eventualities. Some friends and colleagues have – how shall I put it? Some goods that they would like to put into safe keeping. These goods have a certain personal value, nothing much. They want to move some of them to London, to my cousin who owns a small shop in Bond Street."

"Bond Street?"

"Yes, it is only a small establishment and he barely makes a living. But he has a safe that is guaranteed unbreakable."

"There's no such thing, but even so, you're talking about smuggling and dodgy goods?"

Frederick sipped his drink. Eventually he said, "I suppose it is and they are. When it comes to gemstones, provenance is a simple cut or polish away, if you see the finer point. That is why the safe delivery of such goods could be a very profitable exercise."

"How big are these heirlooms?"

"There is nothing that wouldn't fit into a small package that could be carried quite easily in the bottom of a kitbag."

"Tell me what you have in mind and I'll tell you if I want a part of it?"

"Your friends are given seven-day passes to get home and Christmas is coming. I understand that there will be a lot of soldiers going home for Christmas. Their kitbags aren't checked at the ports. No one cares. The civil authorities have passed the responsibility for the military over to the Military Police but they haven't got a clue. Traffic they can direct but anything else…"

Tom nodded. Most of the MPs he'd come across couldn't even control a football crowd.

"The soldiers going on leave could carry a few packages with them and someone could deliver them to my cousin."

Tom grinned. "You're a funny man, you know that? Is your name Arthur Askey, or what?"

Frederick gave him a blank look.

"*Band Waggon!* Hello playmates! He's on the wireless." Eventually Tom gave up and said, "You Frenchies are not sophisticated."

"I don't understand."

"You must know that nine out of ten of your packages would go missing. Come to think of it, so would the bleedin' squaddies who were carrying them. With something to sell in their pockets they're not likely to come back, not if they've got any sense."

"I know that. And that is the problem."

Tom finished his drink and scratched his chin. At length he said, "Let me have a think about it."

The girl caught his eye again. Frederick saw the glance and said, "Have you changed your mind about Nathalie?"

"No, but she doesn't need to be a lip-reader to have understood what's been said here."

Frederick smiled. "She is family, and family I do trust."

"Are you Jewish, by any chance, Frederick?"

The older man shrugged, "Only on my mother's side."

Tom laughed and Frederick raised an overgrown eyebrow, surprised that the young man had understood. He asked, "And your family?"

Still laughing, Tom shook his head, "Maybe the odd pikey in the old days, but no Jews. Fuck that for a living."

Frederick nodded and said seriously, "So now you know why I'm panicking too!"

And so it began.

Over the weeks Tom and Norman Dileva had formed an unlikely rapport, not friendship exactly, for never had the collaboration been on an equal footing, but Dileva recognized that the relationship provided all kinds of fringe benefits. Special errands for the captain or the newly arrived Lieutenant Savage took up much of their time and allowed them to dodge some of the more onerous tasks dreamt up by their sergeants. Dileva found that he was increasingly committed to his colleague and what had begun as the means to an extra meal ticket developed into a useful and lucrative association. He also recognized that in sticking close to Tom other people gave him more respect than he was used to and for a man who was not particularly quick-witted and hitherto had come from the wrong end of the East End – his mother imprisoned for prostitution and his reputed father one of her customers on shore leave from a Barbadian ship docked at the Albert – this was manna. Most of his childhood had been spent in a Stepney-run orphanage for his dark visage had ruled out any chance of adoption. For the first time in his life he saw in Tom an opportunity that might just lead to better things. A man who could make a profit in the back end of nowhere like this was the one to follow.

As for Tom, with his additional activities taking up all his spare time and indeed, a large part of his working time, he used Norman Dileva more and more and to his surprise he began to find the little man not only useful – something that at first he'd found amusing and strangely suspect – but good company too.

With Dileva's help he enlisted a dozen others to the cause. There was the promise of spending money to go with their seven-day passes and that was always gladly received, and there were favours to be had at the estaminet, but more than that, the main selling point of the proposition was the preferential treatment handed out on the work details during one of the coldest winters on record when a continuous north-easterly blasted them for days on end and whipped its freezing fingers through clothes and windows and cracks that were barely visible. Digging gun pits and slit trenches and building dugouts in snow-covered, rock-hard ground was to be avoided at all costs. Influenza and pneumonia were widespread and even frostbite was not uncommon.

Sergeant Caesar Ashton was in charge of the squad leave rotas as well as the work detail rotas and he was the key.

His fondness for women was well known, and so was his vulnerability. He had been engaged six times and on each occasion had been left emotionally wounded. Most men would have conceded defeat and admitted that a steady relationship was not for them, but when the budding actress Nathalie caught his roving eye such thoughts of defeatism were set aside. Her role was well rehearsed. By the time Frederick and Tom had coaxed her, aided by the enthusiastic Dileva, she was script perfect.

As Tom watched her performance from the bar, his father's words came back to him. "The most dangerous thing in the world is a woman's smile." He remembered the lisp and the lop-sided expression. "And if you smile back, my son, you're hooked!"

And Caesar Ashton was smiling back.

Of course, Sergeant Ashton wanted to know why these men were to be given preferential treatment, and the idea that they were friends of hers cut no ice. Indeed, jealousy sparked in his eyes, and it was left to Tom to confide in Caesar Ashton that the real reason was to keep Nathalie cleaning and serving rather than joining Frederick's other girls in providing the F part of BEF. The delivery service that these men would supply – a few French cigarettes and a bottle of vino for Frederick's business associates in London – would mean that Ashton could keep Nathalie's charms all to himself – assuming, that is, that the sergeant was able to seduce her. And with regard to that final point, Tom could help him. A word from Tom in Nathalie's ear that she owed her continued chastity to Caesar Ashton should do the trick and she would be forever grateful. In reality, Tom instructed her to hold out for as long as she could and on no account should she let Caesar win her over until the end of January at the earliest, in which time most of the seven-day passes would have been issued. Sergeant Ashton was hugely indebted and Tom became his new confidant and was the first to be invited to his engagement party.

Christmas arrived and on Boxing Day Tom was granted a seven-day pass. He spent most of it with Rose and Peter Woodhead although one night he met up with some of his army buddies who'd decided to stay in the capital rather than make their way north where their families had been evacuated. They went to the Windmill where it was a lot warmer than on the pavements and ended up touring the clubs around Soho where you could get a drink, and a lot more, at any hour of the day or night. The snow that covered most of the country hadn't yet reached London but the temperatures were diving and they could sniff frost in the air. The home front had settled down. There was the devastating news of the sinking of the Royal Oak, of course, but on the western front nothing seemed to be happening. The unnecessary blackout was the cause of most complaints, particularly when it was reported that Paris was lit like a Christmas tree, and because of it the roads had become dangerous places. If Jerry waited long enough he wouldn't have an enemy to face. Four thousand people had already been killed in road accidents. Evacuees began to filter home and the initial panic had been replaced by a sense of lethargy and people were held in a trance by the strange stalemate that had taken place across the Channel. A raft of restrictions had been rushed into place and some of them already rescinded. Rationing was to begin during the second week of January and the dressings of war were more obvious but the main difference was the amount of khaki and two shades of blue, and the green of the WVS, that he saw at the stations and in the streets. The ports themselves were heaving. The country was getting ready while the general public remained perplexed. Perhaps Frederick had a point after all. Many people began to suspect that behind the scenes negotiations were taking place and dodgy deals were being struck. The major routes were clogged with military vehicles and the Home Guard was on parade with wooden guns. In the Eagle they sang *Kiss Me Goodnight Sergeant Major* and *I like a Nice Cup of Tea in the Morning* and Peter Woodhead served turkey sandwiches and mince pies left over from his Christmas specials. His mother wore a Persian lamb coat that Peter had purchased from Aquascutum in Regent Street. He'd written on a card 'Kind Regards, Peter'. Rose said to Tom: "He's such a lovely man. He took me to see *Cinderella* at the Coliseum and bought me a party dress at Marshall and Snelgroves no less – in Oxford Street! Then just the other day he turned up and whisked me off to the ABC in Kensington High Street…" She was referring to the Aerated Bread Company's bakery and restaurant. She shook her head and sadness crept into her voice. "I just don't know… He stood up to listen to the king on Christmas Day. And when he heard about the Stanholme there was a tear in his eye. He said to me he wanted to be forty years younger so he could go and give them what for! I told him not to be silly, that he was still fitter than men half his age." He gave his mother some French perfume and a kiss, and Peter a bottle of the finest wine from Frederick's cellar and a handshake.

'Mind Britain's Business', read Mosley's latest campaign and it reminded Tom of Frederick's comments and that he had business to attend to. When Simon Carter and Jane joined them in the Eagle, Tom left his final instructions for the collection and delivery of the heirlooms and left Simon with enough capital to pay the returning squaddies. "Don't let me down," he told his old chum, knowing that the money would be a huge temptation. Simon's family was one of the poorest he had ever known. His father was drinking more than ever and his sister was in hospital somewhere up north. She'd been sent to help out on a farm and been run over by a tractor. "When I come home, we'll go into business and you'll be a rich man."

Maureen, the blonde with the crown-sized nipples, had remained strangely absent but no one said a thing, and Tom didn't ask.

When he got back to St Michelle he met the winter but for comfort he held on to memories of a second night with Jane. It had been as good as the first and that hadn't been bad. She had turned fifteen, the raising of the school leaving age had been postponed, and her father had got her some secretarial work at the War Office in the neo-Baroque building on Horse Guards Avenue in Whitehall with its thousand rooms and two and a half miles of corridor. An easy place to get lost in and she did just that. After the third day she didn't bother turning up, she told him, and no one missed her, not even her father.

"Gawd Almighty, it's cold," he said to Frederick. Chilblains itched like buggery on his hands and feet. Someone said that a good soaking in piss was the cure but it hadn't helped at all.

Frederick tut-tutted the idea and drew in a deep breath of freezing air. He said, "You islanders have been softened by the Gulf Stream."

Beneath blankets stiffened by frost they slept in their clothes including their greatcoats and balaclavas. The water froze and ice needed breaking in order to wash and shave. Fires were forbidden in case the smoke gave away their positions. Another half-witted order since anyone within five miles couldn't fail to notice the camp. Vehicle engines were turned over for ten minutes every hour day and night. Icicles grew longer than a man could reach and didn't drip for weeks on end and solid grey snow clouds hung low and stretched to the horizon in every direction. When the sun did manage to break through it was just a frozen circle above the powdery fields. It was a miserable existence and once the thaw began the rain came with it and they were soon bogged down in fields of mud. Dampness invaded the buildings and crept into their clothes and over their groundsheets to their blankets. Mildew spread from their feet and turned their testicles green. The men began to smell as rank as the floors and crumbling walls of the cowshed.

The only buzz in the camp came from the news that Vera Lynn was doing the rounds and that they might get to see her. If they couldn't get Jean Harlow or, even better, Dorothy Lamour, then Vera would do just fine.

Caesar Ashton's engagement party at the estaminet provided some further relief and for the evening at least, it gave them an alcohol jacket against the chill, and half the squad turned out on special twelve-hour passes. The men, with the women in mind – not that they were ever out of it – did the best they could to make themselves presentable, and some even paid for baths and the use of private bathrooms in St Michelle's. It was a huge success and even a few of the officers made an appearance. Frederick arranged for some extra girls for the evening and Nathalie looked pretty and rather virtuous.

Captain Roskilly was not used to Frederick's Remi and his face flushed early on. He said to Sergeant Fox and Sergeant Ice Dovey at his side: "He managed t-t-to get hold of t-t-two t-t-tickets to the Opêra de Lille and t-t-they're like gold dust. Good Lord, the ent-t-tire brigade HQ was t-t-there. It was a wonderful evening. I escorted Madame Keppel. She's a widow and owns the house where I'm staying. Her husband was killed in t-t-the last lot. We had supper at t-t-the Delphi t-t-then went on t-t-to t-t-the t-t-theatre. He's a very useful man. We're fortunate t-t-to have him on t-t-the t-t-team. I don't know how he does it, I'm sure."

He glanced across the crowded bar at Tom and Norman Dileva.

Sergeant Fox rubbed his chin and shared a knowing look with Dovey. "I've got a few ideas and none of them are good."

"We shouldn't knock enterprise, Scratch. I find it rather encouraging when I see t-t-the little men using t-t-their initiative. It bodes well for t-t-the country and t-t-the future. And Caesar seems t-t-to t-t-think very highly of him."

Dovey said, "That's something else that worries me."

The captain gave his sergeants an odd look.

The girls flashed between the covers of drab khaki, becoming even more attractive as the drink took hold. Their thin dresses rippled and clung and revealed how little they wore beneath. People danced. Men waited for their turn, clutching their tickets. Booze flowed and the plates of food arriving from the steaming kitchen were quickly demolished. A woman from Lille sang in French.

"What is that song?" Tom asked one of the girls.

"Wherever, I think it is, or whenever."

"I recognize the tune. What are the words?"

"We talk like this way before, but I can't remember when it was. You dressed in the same clothes as before but I can't remember when it was. Where or when! You know it!"

Another song began and the girl said, "This one you know. Underneath the light, by the barrack gate…"

Tom smiled. "Yes, I know this one."

"Then you can dance with me, Tommy Smith, free of charge and without a ticket. Frederick tells me you don't go with girls, only boys, but dancing doesn't count."

Tom thought about explaining but instead shrugged and took her in his arms.

Frederick caught his eye and doffed his flat cap. He was happy. His till was ringing a merry tune.

Even when he was not on an errand for Tom it was not uncommon to find Dileva, along with his mates Bedstead Jackson and James Jessel, at the estaminet. They dreamt up various reasons for their visits, mostly to do with the welfare of Captain Roskilly. They were there the day peace was shattered and it was the clump of their hobnails ringing urgently on the cobblestones that broke the rural silence. Theirs were the only movements around the village save for a plume of smoke that spiralled lazily into a patch of early summer sky. They ran up the narrow road from the village and along the wheel-rutted path where a few mechanics tinkered on a line of ration vehicles.

Their rush into the granary – a building commandeered as a more suitable HQ than the screened area in the cowshed – surprised everybody there, and they gathered to hear the news. Captain Roskilly emerged from the dark, cordoned-off quarters to listen, closely followed by the thin frame and weasel looks of Sedgewick, his batman, who held the captain's freshly laundered battle-dress blouse to his chest, and then the platoon sergeants appeared from the various recesses. While his friends hovered at the entrance, Dileva saluted to no one in particular and said breathlessly, "It's started, Sir. Jerry's invaded!"

That the news came second-hand should not have surprised anyone. For the last few weeks the BEF had kept wireless silence to preserve security so the radio network was relatively untested. The batteries on the wireless trucks needed charging and the field telephones were so unreliable that the signal linesmen were treated as a joke. Communications relied almost entirely on DRLS or the public telephone system.

Lt Savage dressed in his vest and with his braces looping over his britches, appeared from the backroom. His 7.65 Webley pistol was drawn and waving.

He stammered, "Where is Jerry?"

"About one hundred and twenty miles that way," Dileva said, pointing over his shoulder.

Lt Savage looked from Dileva to the captain and said, "Oh, I see," and somewhat self-consciously he holstered his gun.

The captain raised an eyebrow and Scratch Fox shook his head and turned to see Eunice Dovey's tight-lipped look of disbelief.

Eventually Captain Roskilly slapped his swagger into the palm of his hand and said, "Cool down, and t-t-tell me precisely what you know?"

"Down at Veronica's place, Sir. They're listening to the Belgium wireless, but they can understand it – it might be in French. Jerry's invaded all right. There're reports of him coming from all directions. Frederick is really worried. He's saying that now all the men will be sent north he'll be out of business."

The Captain nodded thoughtfully, "Invaded where, exactly?"

"Holland and Belgium, Sir, about thirty minutes ago. There're no details but it's definitely started."

Captain Roskilly turned to Scratch Fox and Lt Savage who was busily buttoning his shirt. "T-t-this is quite int-t-tolerable; t-t-that we should hear t-t-the news from the local brothel. Get hold of t-t-the interpreter. Get hold of HQ. We need details."

Caesar Ashton manoeuvred across to Deliva and bent to his ear, "What I'd like to know, Deliva, is what you were doing in the café in the first place?"

Deliva thought for a moment and said, "Looking for eggs, Sarg, for the captain's breakfast."

"And did you happen to notice if that beautiful young lady Nathalie was there?"

"She was indeed, Sarg. Wearing one of them plum-coloured see-through camisoles with a lacy bit around her..." He spread his hands around his groin.

The sergeant narrowed his eyes.

"Only joking, Sarg," Deliva said quickly. "She's missing you terrible and now she's worried when she's ever going to see you again. I told her not to worry and that you'd be back before she knew it. She said she'd wait for you, just like Josèphine waited for that other geezer, whoever he was."

Caesar Ashton nodded his understanding and his face softened. "That'll be Josephine Hutchinson," he said. "She was with Paul Muni in the *Story of Louis Pasteur*. Lovely girl, she was; but not a touch on Nathalie."

Across the countryside vehicles began to rumble, messengers rode their motorcycles and polished bugles rang out the call for officers to Company HQ.

Their orders put them on the tail end of the battalion, and their battalion, the last in the brigade, began to push forward into Belgium just after lunch. Captain Roskilly led in a 15cwt driven by Deliva. Scratch Fox and Caesar Ashton sat in the back studying the maps that the captain had brought back from HQ. It quickly became apparent that they were quite useless, dated before the last war, showing roads that didn't exist and missing others that did. Lieutenant Savage had commandeered a shining Humber Snipe but the captain would have none of it, insisting that Sedgewick load the rear seat with his gear and guard it with his life. The lieutenant had enlisted Blakely the mess steward to act as his batman and he sat in the front nursing the lieutenant's small leather suitcase.

"T-t-the Second Oxfords are in front of us, so just follow t-t-them," the captain said. "But keep a close eye on t-t-those maps. Never did t-t-trust an Oxford man!"

Caesar shared a curious glance with Scratch and decided the maps must be upside down. He tried them the other way but still shook his head in dismay. He was looking for Brussels to use as a landmark but couldn't find it.

Regimental police skirted past on their spluttering bikes, moving along the column of roaring engines.

Captain Roskilly stood and shouted above the din, piercing the air with his stick. "Keep your distance, t-t-twenty yards is t-t-the spacing!"

He was wasting his time. The road was packed with vehicles, bumper to bumper. In the back of a ten-tonner, Tom Smith looked out at the lines of traffic and breathed in the heavy choking fumes. Beside him, Corporal Wallis said, "This is a bloody fiasco. If Jerry hits us now they can take out the entire brigade."

Corporal Woods agreed. "They'll never have an easier target."

They sat nervously throughout the afternoon listening to the grind of gears and the clank of engines. The exhaust fumes became all but unbearable. They peered up at the sky, searching for the expected attack and during the afternoon they spotted a few high-flying aircraft, but they remained distant specks.

"T-t-this is all rather uncomfortable," Captain Roskilly said. "T-t-the whole of t-t-the BEF moving into battle position, the light beginning to fade, and yet we've not heard a single report of Jerry t-t-trying t-t-to stop us."

Caesar Ashton said, "Maybe they're bogged down somewhere. Maybe there's been a counterattack."

Captain Roskilly turned to face Caesar. "I fancy not. Jerry's got t-t-the strength, all right. It's just possible he's keeping air cover for his major push but it doesn't make much sense."

"Whatever the reason," Caesar muttered. "It's a bloody Godsend."

Darkness crept out of the hedgerows and the convoy met with a fresh challenge. The population of Belgium blocked the roads, heading in the opposite direction. Belongings were pushed in prams or wheelbarrows, or carried in horse-drawn carts. Horns blared and people shouted and argued with the police. Into the night the column crawled along and in the trucks the men watched the flow of locals heading south. At the side of the roads an assortment of vehicles and carts had been overturned. Information came from the motorcycle police in front about broken haycarts blocking the road ahead or that the road wasn't marked or that the guide had disappeared. They heard rumours that the Belgium army were destroying their own bridges to hinder the British advance, a move to – hopefully – placate the Germans, just as the cancellation of their treaty with France had done four years earlier. It came as no surprise, for their senior officers had warned them that the Flemings were not to be trusted and were more likely than not in league with Jerry. And the available maps, the motorcycle police said, were hopeless.

It was a crowd of bleary-eyed soldiers who eventually stepped down from the trucks into an unknown terrain.

"Where are we?" came a voice out of the night.

And the reply: "In the front line, mate. That's all you need to know!"

Bedstead was dead, or dying, and Wallis was dead. Corporal Wood's legs had been blown off and so had Caesar Aston's head. Caesar's head had exploded. One moment he was talking to them, whispering, telling them to stay down, and the next his head had disintegrated. His face had torn open in every direction until there was nothing left. His body had stayed upright like a huge puppet, with the end of his windpipe wriggling, until slowly, what was left of him sank to the earth. Pinchera was hit in the chest by one of Caesar's eyes. Flecks of flesh and bone and brain had speckled the rest of them and some of the men flicked the stuff from their uniforms as if getting rid of some dangerous insect. The barrage opened up with great shattering explosions, the sheer volume of noise pitching them to the earth, hands flying instinctively to cover their ears. Each salvo whined, screamed and thundered louder than the last. Bricks and mortar crashed about them and dust hung thick to cut visibility to a few yards, billowing this way and that by the force of fresh explosions. Cordite and smoke mixed with the dust and every man was coughing and fighting for breath. It was the end of the world. Bedstead panicked and ran, thrashing through the barbed wire. When they pulled out a little later they passed him caught up on the wire, hanging, main arteries gashed and still dripping into dark glistening pools beneath his limp hands. Wallis caught it when they pulled back. Something larger than a .303 ripped through his throat and when Corporal Woods turned to help him a shell landed at his feet. They went, heads down, running and choking, to regroup in a safer place, if such a place existed. Staying put meant annihilation. Half the squad was out already and they hadn't fired a single shot. As they clattered along the cobblestone roads buildings erupted and crashed down. Behind them, between the explosions and the constant thump of artillery fire, a rattle of machine-guns and a steady whine of engines grew louder. Above them, dive bombers screamed, dropping their loads into the rising black clouds.

They grouped in some woods and listened to the distant battle, exhausted, covered in dust and stained with blood that came mostly from Caesar Ashton. They sat heads bowed, or lay, or propped themselves against the trees. They smoked in silence, bewildered, shaking their heads. Scratch Fox took stock of what was left of the squad. Eight men were grouped together. Tom Smith lay apart from them, stretched out under a canopy of branches, eyes closed and arms folded over his Lee-Enfield. Captain Roskilly also lay on his back and some way from the rest, while Macloud, the would-be dental technician, did what he could with a small first-aid kit. During their rush across the railway lines the captain had fallen down the embankment and spiked himself on his swagger stick.

"Did anyone see Blakely?" Fox asked.

Eventually Deliva nodded. "He went down the canal turn. He was with Paddy and the lieutenant and walked right into the panzer tank."

That meant that the radio, maps and compass were lost. Scratch kicked Pinchera's outstretched leg.

"What happened to the Bren?"

"Sarg, we was doing a four-minute mile down there. I never even saw the Bren. Not that the Mark Two was any bleedin' good anyway. Even on the range they was always jamming. Sooner have a Tommy gun, with a box mag, of course." The film of dust on his face cracked as he smiled. "Shall I go back for it?"

The sergeant scowled, "Be careful I don't make that an order, son."

"Where's our bleedin' RAF, that's what I'd like to know?" Pinchera asked no one in particular. "Or even the French Air Force. Have they got an air force?"

"Indeed they have," Private James Jessel said authoritatively. "But they're still flying Nieuports and Spads. They wouldn't be much good here."

A series of fresh explosions, much closer, shook the ground and leaves began to dance and fall. Some of the men struggled to their feet. Between the blasts they could hear aircraft overhead and a distant grind of tank engines.

Deliva pulled a face and said, "Don't like the sound of that. How long do we wait for them, Sarg?"

It was a good question and the sergeant glanced across to see how Macloud was getting on. The squaddie approached him, wiping his hands on a length of bandage.

"It's not good," he said quietly, out of earshot from the rest. "I've done what I can and that isn't much. It's gone through his gut and he needs an operation, like urgently. All the shit and what have you is swimming into his bloodstream and that means blood poisoning and that isn't good. The fever has already taken hold."

"Can he walk?"

"Yes, I suppose he can, if the pain lets him and if he wants to die even quicker. Sarg, we're talking about hours here, not days. He's passing out even now, in and out of it, sweat is pouring off him. He needs his guts pulling out and cleaning and patching and then sewing back in."

Scratch nodded. "Macloud, I could almost believe you know what you're talking about."

He walked over to the captain and could see immediately what the private had been getting at. Captain Roskilly was grey and sweat dribbled from his forehead to leave black lines through the dust that caked his face.

"Scratch!" the captain managed. "It's good t-t-to see t-t-that you're still in one piece. It's damned inconvenient, all t-t-this, and damned bad luck. I broke my stick. It's been with me for years."

"Yes, Sir."

"Who's with you?"

"Eight, Sir."

The captain shook his head. "Have you seen Lieutenant Savage?"

"He didn't make it, Sir. He was last seen charging a tank, on foot, shooting at it with his pistol. Pinchera reckons it ran him over."

"Good Lord. How magnificent. What magnificent men we are. How I wish I could have been t-t-there and done t-t-that." The officer sighed. "Did you see what happened t-t-to t-t-the rest of t-t-the outfit?"

Scratch frowned. The captain had been there and seen what he'd seen. "We were running like hell, Sir, don't you remember? Unfortunately we were running in the wrong direction, into Jerry lines. The rest of the lads have got a five mile head start with Jerry well and truly between us."

Captain Roskilly winced. Scratch couldn't work out whether it was from the news or the pain in his gut. He went on, "We'll have to make a detour back and try to link up."

"Bit of a fiasco all round. Still, spilt milk I suppose. You'll have t-t-to t-t-take over, Scratch. Sorry t-t-to put you on t-t-the spot."

"Yes, Sir."

The captain tried to sit up but failed and gasped, "I t-t-think I might have t-t-to stay put, sit it out, so t-t-to speak. I'm feeling rather poorly."

"I'll get the lads to rig something up. We'll manage somehow."

"Get Sedgewick over here, would you, and t-t-thank Private Macloud for looking after me."

"Sedgewick caught one in town, Sir."

"Did he? Damnit! T-t-that is bad luck. He'll be hard t-t-to replace at short notice. He made a damned fine cup of t-t-tea."

Scratch turned back to the group.

"Time's up," he said. "Smith, you come with me. The rest of you pack up. Get some branches together and tie a couple of coats around them to make a seat. We'll take it in twos but we're going to have to carry the CO. Move out in five minutes."

Tom Smith stretched away his stiff back and carried his rifle across to the sergeant. He patted his gun and muttered, "Never even got to fire it. All that small arm training in red ink was a waste of time. Still, might come in handy for shooting rabbits when we get back."

Scratch Fox grunted and said, "You'll get plenty more opportunities." He led the way to the edge of the wood and used his field glasses to scan the area below. A few miles away to the west and beneath a dipping sun, the battle still raged around the town. Stukas dived between black puffs of ack-ack fire and dropped their bombs into the rising clouds of smoke. The geometry of the place was defined by the criss-cross of railway lines and a straight narrow run of a canal. He marked the line of their retreat. They had crossed a bridge near a warehouse and industrial area and followed cobblestone back roads to the outskirts and then crossed a ploughed field to the wood. He concentrated on the town itself, the pall of dirty smoke and the buildings reduced to rubble. Two tanks appeared out of the smoke. Tom Smith tapped his sergeant's arm and pointed to their right where twenty or thirty figures trailed behind more tanks.

"It's all over, Sarg," he said, stating the obvious. "We've been running the wrong way."

The sergeant used his glasses again and concentrated on the southeast of the town where the canal ran into another thickly wooded area. The battle seemed to be shifting that way. "That's where our mob is," he muttered. "That's where we should be."

"That's the way we came in," Tom nodded. "We followed the canal into town."

"We'll head southwest from here and then cut across and try to meet up with them."

"They've got a five mile start, Sarg, with Jerry up their arses. We'll never catch up with them and if we try we'll end up in even deeper shit."

The others were waiting in the falling light. They grouped on Tom rather than the sergeant.

"What's happening down there?"

Tom told them. "Out lot are retreating west with Jerry on their tails. You better start getting a taste for sauerkraut."

Scratch pulled them together and examined the makeshift chair. "It will have to do," he said. "Get the captain on board. I'll take the lead. Keep the noise down and unless you can speak German that means fucking silence!"

They marched until night became a starless canvas and the dark became so severe they couldn't see the man in front. The blackout lasted an hour or so and they spent it in the woods, silent apart from the captain's groans, listening like frightened animals for any sound. Aircraft continued to fly across and the ground still trembled under the thump of explosives and the more distant artillery fire. Occasionally they broke from their cover to watch the lurid glow of far-off fires and an occasional stream of tracer bullets.

Dawn touched the eastern sky soon after four. It was enough and they moved out again, rubbing away the damp that had seeped through their greatcoats and uniforms. Captain Roskilly was much worse, slipping in and out of consciousness, and could no longer sit upright. Using some of their webbing as supports between longer branches and their greatcoats as a cover, they lashed up a stretcher. Not that they needed to wear their greatcoats during the daylight hours. The temperatures had been climbing steadily and uncomfortably for over a week but dropped quickly once the sun had disappeared.

They heard noises long before they saw what was happening. The thickly wooded area gave way to gently sloping farmland and cutting through it from north to south was the road that they'd motored along almost three weeks previously. It was still blocked solid by the mass exodus of the civvy population. A stream of people, livestock, cars, trucks and carts moved slowly southward for as far as they could see. They considered dropping the captain off on one of the vehicles but they were making better headway and still hoped to meet up with troops from the company, if not the remnants of their squad. Keeping half a mile between themselves and the civvies they continued south until, at mid-morning, they arrived at an intersection, a narrow road running east to west. They struck west and within minutes a ten-tonner had stopped beside them. Canvas lifted from the sides and the faces of wounded men peered out. Some looked shell-shocked, others were bandaged, and most were covered in dust and grime.

The driver, unshaven and raw-eyed, looked down at the bedraggled group and grunted contemptuously.

"Heading south, Sergeant?"

"What's Jerry doing?"

The driver shrugged, "They were held up for a while. The RTR and the Durhams put up one hellofa show trying to punch a hole south of Arras but that's fizzled out now." He indicated over his shoulder. "They're about twenty miles east, maybe less, and sixty miles south and southwest. I've just dropped off a bunch of MPs to try and clear the crossroads. There's a lot of heavy gear got to come back this way. We're going to hold them along a new line from Calais to Cambral and then north to the coast twenty miles west of Antwerp, that's what I heard. It's supposed to be hush-hush but everyone's talking about it."

Scratch waved his men aboard. "Wherever you're going," he said to the driver. "It will do us. Is there an MO on board?"

"No, but I'm trucking this lot to the Ypres canal. The First Corps have a field hospital there. As you can see, we've all been seconded to RAMC."

A few hours later they were unloading with only a gentle valley between them and the Ypres-Comines line. They could barely make sense of the activity around them. Sappers were making ready to blow the bridges and were smashing the fortifications on the eastern side. Tents, sleeping bags and tyres were piled high ready for burning, other equipment was already on fire. Charges were being set under the gun emplacements and any transport that was of no further use. They left the captain at the field hospital and went off in search of their unit. What they found was utter chaos, units in tatters, groups of bedraggled soldiers wandering aimlessly looking for food and water and, more importantly, no sign of anyone in command who was willing or able to tell them what to do.

"Dunkirk?" Pinchera said as he tucked into a mess tin of stew from one of the few field kitchens still operating. "I've never heard of it. How far is it?"

"Thirty odd miles that way," James Jessel said.

"Well, I've never heard of it," Pinchera repeated glumly as the distance sunk in. He'd already got blisters the size of half-crown pieces from their earlier march and they were all out of boracic. "It's obviously not famous for anything, is it?"

"It's a seaside resort, a bit like Southend, but without the mud and jellied eels and the London day-trippers, of course. There was a steamer from Folkestone."

"You've been there?"

"Indeed, five years ago. I remember a church in the town centre, named after St Eloi, the patron saint of goldsmiths."

"Forget the gold and make sure your canteens are full," Scratch Fox told them. Once again the sky was clear and the temperature was climbing. "It's going to be a long walk and I don't fancy our chances of picking up a taxi."

They'd been told that transportation was out of the question and they'd have to hike it. Most of the troop carriers were still farther north where the bulk of troops, including their company, were retreating directly west to the coast. The march wasn't easy. Most of them were already blistered and exhausted from their earlier retreat. The roads were jammed with what appeared to be the populations of Belgium and Northern France moving in the same direction. Lorries, cars, horse-drawn carts and prams and anything else that could be driven, pushed or pulled lined the roads, and the number of refugees grew with every passing hour. In the other direction armoured cars, half-tracks, gun carriers and a steady stream of ambulances tried to get through to hold the retreating lines. Despatch riders and MT corporals on their BSAs and Nortons weaved in and out carrying the latest orders, trying desperately to keep up with the chain of command. At the bottlenecks of bridges where Sappers were laying more charges, MPs waved frantically, fighting yet more losing battles. Abandoned vehicles built up at the side of roads. A line of Humber staff cars going their way was given priority and waved through. They heard the distant clatter of machine-gun fire and the louder thud of artillery fire and aircraft attacked them with cannon and bombs. They passed burned-out half-tracks and armoured cars and a couple of the staff cars that had sped by earlier. Engineers were busy destroying all the equipment that couldn't be carried, including heavy guns that had run out of ammo and motor transport that had run out of fuel. They were setting fire to piles of tents and tyres and boxes of uniforms and unopened mess supplies. Field kitchens and portable latrines were wrecked and torched. Smoke billowed from their fires. ME109s strafed the roads and Stukas dropped their bombs, blowing apart the cars and carts, and the mattresses and worldly goods they carried, and the men, women and children who ran blindly and terror-stricken in search of cover. In some parts the stagnant water in the ditches and dykes had turned red. Bodies were left where they had fallen. Feathers from a busted eiderdown fell like snowflakes. For a while they got off the road and travelled cross-country where the odd oak or an isolated thicket and maybe the occasional small wood of poplars and chestnuts offered some slim protection but, for the most the landscape was flat and featureless and offered no shelter at all. Most of the farmhouses and barns and lesser outbuildings were on fire or were already gutted. They met another narrow road blocked by charred vehicles. Items of clothing from broken or looted suitcases scuttled past them to lead the way, caught in a welcome breeze. They searched for water in a ruined farmhouse where a line of pegged washing stirred, untouched by the war. Beyond the broken walls they found the huddled remains of a family of five, scorched and welded together and outside they found two decaying horses, their polished saddles glinting, their tethers still attached to rings in the wall.

James Jessel said, "I'd never seen a body till we got over here. We're not human anymore. All this has dehumanised us. We'll never be normal again. Had you ever seen a body before, Sarge?"

Scratch Fox grunted.

"What about you, Tommy?"

Tom Smith nodded and said, "As good as. There wasn't much life left in them when I left, that's for sure."

The sergeant gave Tom a long studied look before striking off again and the men hurried after him.

In an orchard to the north, where the men rested before moving over the bridge, pigs were pulling at the intestines of one of two people that had fallen there. They looked like farm workers. It was there that Dileva had thrown up. It was there also where Pinchera lost it for a while, kicking wildly at a fallen gatepost and firing a string of shots at an aircraft that was at least two miles distant.

They trod through a series of craters that were still smoking and sidestepped chunks of red horseflesh and the remains of the horseriders – some of de Gaulle's finest. And as they neared the canal turn where the final rearguard action was to take place and a combination of Coldstream and Welsh Guards along with a group of stray Buffs were making ready to fight around the bridge at Bergues, the Stukas came back and a bomb landed between what appeared to be an entire class of primary schoolchildren, still in uniform, being shepherded by two nuns. A tiny head fell between them, boy or girl they couldn't make out.

"Where's the fucking RAF?" someone asked, but there never was an answer.

There were still some ten miles to the coast and they kept their heads down and well out of the way of the sharp-eyed NCOs; stray soldiers were being ordered back into the line and that wouldn't do at all. They also noticed a group of stragglers, remnants of the DLI push from Arras.

"Those boys don't take prisoners," someone said. Everyone had heard about the massacre of three hundred or more German prisoners of war.

"They're a bunch of miners," James Jessel said. "They've more than likely never heard of the Geneva Conventions."

"Bits of paper," Deliva said. "They just sounded good at the time. Once the balloon goes up, rules and the finer points are meaningless.

Look around you. War is about killing people and just because they put their fucking hands in the air doesn't make them friends. Death or slavery, they should be the only options."

"For those Jerries slavery wasn't an option. In any case, what about withdrawal or, indeed, running like scared rabbits, as we have been doing?"

"Retreating in an orderly fashion is all right," Deliva grinned.

And so, using their rifles as crutches, and with their boots filled with pebbles to cause realistic limps, their uniforms stained with Caesar Ashton's blood and brains, they would pass muster, and did.

No one was prepared for what they found in the town, and then on the beach. The town had been reduced to a smouldering ruin. Buildings were flattened and corpses littered the streets. Blackened girders and reinforcing bars stuck V-signs to the blackened sky. St Eloi had collapsed. Jessel had said, "I will build my church and the gates of hell shall not prevail against it," and left them thinking he was shell-shocked. Drunken French soldiers fired their guns into the air and drank from bottles of wine looted from the restaurants. Smoke climbed from the burning rubble to mix with the great black clouds that drifted from the burning oil tanks on the front. Power supplies and water mains were shattered. Fountains shot out of broken paving. Corsair remained untouched, sword raised in defiance. And so did some of the men as they fired wildly at the shadows of aircraft. But it was mostly bravado. They were a defeated mob and most of them hadn't fired a shot in anger. Most of them hadn't seen a glimpse of a German soldier. There were mangled bodies everywhere, limbs and heads and torsos, but mostly limbs, some of them partially eaten by scavenging dogs and rats. The RAMC were doing their best with the injured but with so many and the roads blocked by fallen masonry it was an impossible job. The makeshift ambulances were stuck and getting blown to bits and the stretcher-bearers had nowhere to go. They kept to the backstreets, away from the NCOs who were still busily rounding up likely infantrymen – sacrificial Joe Soaps – to reinforce the southern rearguard and buy some time for the rest to flee.

Some later reported that a Messerschmitt 109 came out of the smoke, a hard-lined silver streak, others that it was a 110, but in truth it might have been any make of enemy aircraft. It was on them in an instant and gone before they knew what had hit them. Tom Smith felt a blow to his shoulder, as if someone had thumped him with a sledgehammer, and he saw Scratch Fox turn away from him. There was a skid mark across the sergeant's head; no hair, just a thick red line that widened as he watched.

The cause of an explosion that followed the aircraft's burst of fire also remains unclear. Some said it was a bomb, others that the cannon fire had hit an ammunition dump and others that it was a gas explosion. Norman Dileva was caught in the blast and lost his left leg. It was the reason he couldn't outrun a south London gang in a race for his life fourteen years later. James Jessel lost some of his gut and almost died of septicaemia in a casualty clearing station in East Kent. Pinchera's right ear as well as his clothes and his genitals were blown away in the resulting shockwave. The little wop put on the bravest face of all.

Chapter 18

Nothing changed. Behind her battledress of patchwork netting and sandbags, gun emplacements and Ministry of Home Security posters, the city's nakedness exposed a comforting familiarity, its great buildings and institutions a fortress. Tom Smith felt good to be back, excited even, but this affection was tinged with sadness as though his today was perfect, his tomorrow uncertain, for while he knew that nothing changed, he also knew that nothing would ever be the same.

The unchanging river moved heavily beneath him and he breathed in the memory of the docks, the spices and the fruits, the fish and the dank, musty smell of oil. The grey water reflected the galvanized sky; the barges, moored for the night, moved sluggishly, beating a tired time to the river's heavy heart. The cranes and jibs, secured in their loop-holes, crazy patterns against the sky, strange silent statements of a commerce that went on; and the abandoned quays seemed somehow fragile, while the swelling tide lapped so slowly against the ancient stanchions.

He wanted the feeling to last, this heady mix of euphoria and apprehension; he wanted his city to wash over him and cleanse his darker thoughts. He'd made it! He was home!

A train clattered by into the station and a tram's warning bells rang out. A convoy of military trucks overtook him and he gave a half-hearted wave to the drivers. The buff and green jigsaw slipped across the plate glass rectangles of the shop fronts, the windows themselves criss-crossed with brown tape. A policeman on a noisy motorcycle escorted them, his steel helmet and gasmask strapped to his back. The station, its entrances and the square beyond were packed with people, khaki and green and two shades of blue, kitbags and packs and suitcases, luggage piled high and ribbons on summer bonnets fluttering in the breeze. There was chatter, and laughter, and brave goodbyes, and loudspeaker messages, and a steam train screaming above it all. The city was swamped in squaddies wasting their time, faraway from home, suddenly free from the soul-destroying fatigues, the square-bashing, and the polishing of brasses. In this state of enforced suspension, their forty-eight hour passes tucked safely in their tunics, they drifted through the city in a state of uncertainty, wayfarers, displaced, trying to keep out of trouble but finding the endless regulations, both military and civilian, impossible to live with. It was a disorientating time with the front lines over there, somewhere, and the home front totally bemused. Tom moved across the crowded square past the fountains and the lions and the pigeons. He kept his gaze off Nelson, boarded up in any case, and the souvenir and seed sellers, and made his way past the sandbagged National. He wandered into the other square and on down to the Circus and recalled telling Maureen Devine that any couple that held hands in front of Eros would love each other forever. He smiled when he saw that the winged archer had flown. This was no time or place for the God of Love. It was a time for other things: cruelty and hatred, perhaps, and an icy heart that could set emotion aside.

It was time to go home and say hello to his mother. He completed the loop and hopped on a crowded trolleybus and clung to the rail the rest of the way. He got off near the bustling market place. Nothing had changed. The street traders still yelled out their knock-down prices, their potential customers still flowed in long slow lines between the pitches, the baked potato carts and caravan café's still smoked and the last of the muffin men still rang their bells, the tie men still sold French letters out of the false bottoms of their suitcases and the public lavatories still reeked to high heaven. A jellied eel and pie and mash stall had set up outside the Eagle and next to it a semi-circle of Sally Annes played and sang, banging their tambourines and calling people to the war against Satan.

Rose was in the kitchen, her forearms dusted in baking powder. The wireless was on and Judy Garland singing *Over the Rainbow* filtered in from the other room. When he filled the doorway she looked up and her heart melted into her eyes.

She said, "Tommy! Oh Tommy, I expected you earlier."

"I was late getting out of hospital, Ma. You know what these doctors are like. They keep you waiting forever. The trains were full to bursting and I walked some of the way, just to calm myself. You wouldn't believe the crowds."

"You shouldn't walk so far. You're here now, in one piece. Sit down and I'll make you some tea."

"That will put everything right," he said and put his arms around her tiny frame.

"It's good to have you home, my son." She buried her face into his shoulder. Realizing it was his wounded side she pulled back.

"It's all right, Ma. You press as hard as you want. My boxing days are over and I can't lift my arm as high as I'd like, but it'll be all right. It'll get easier, they said."

"Oh, Tommy," she whispered. "I thought I'd lost you. When that policeman knocked I thought I'd lost you. And look at the weight you've lost! There ain't an ounce of flesh on you."

"You're a lady. Dry your tears."

"And you're a gentleman," she sniffed. She pushed him away and smiled. "Go on, sit down. I'll make some tea."

"That'll make everything fine, Ma. I've missed a good cup of tea, and your pies. You wouldn't believe what I've been fed on these last few months. They should take you on to teach those army cooks a thing or two."

Minutes later she placed a tray of tea and scones on the table. She sat opposite and watched him eat.

"What are you going to do?"

He shrugged. "I'm out of a job, honourably discharged so they say. I'm a bleedin' hero." He patted his shoulder. "And this is my medal. But you're right, I'll have to find something and I don't mean the bleedin' Civil Defence."

She nodded.

"I'll look Simon and the others up. They must be earning a bob or two. You never know, maybe Peter can push something my way. Whatever, I'll sort something out so don't you worry."

Weeks went by. In the second week of September three hundred German bombers unloaded on the East End before moving to the centre. Four hundred and thirty people died and sixteen hundred were badly injured. During that week Tom made a visit to the small jewellers in Bond Street. He'd met Frederick's cousin Nicholas Green during his New Year leave but it had been short and sweet for his shop had been busy. People wanted extra links in chains and necklaces they'd received for Christmas and found they didn't fit. The owner was a short fifty-year-old man in dark suit and tie. Cologne scented the air around him. Only the artful eyes gave away his family links and they held his cousin's deep-seated wariness.

He was singing: "Stick a fork into pork and give it to the Jewboy!" He looked up from his polished glass counter and offered Tom a broad smile. Maybe he was happy that the bombs had missed him for another day. "Around these streets it's the kid's favourite song. The Gentile children of the East End! How many times have I been called a Christ killer? I've lost count already. I never killed Christ, you should tell them, just the same as they didn't kill Jeanne d'Arc or Thomas Becket." He sighed. "Everyone is moaning about the rationing – at least it's something different to the blackout – petrol, bacon, butter, sugar, meat, tea, margarine. I think they're blaming me for that too. But the cost of coal – elevenpence for a hundredweight – that is daylight robbery." He shook his head in exasperation. "And if this coming winter is anything like the last then we're going to need a lot of coal. As if the bombing wasn't enough, now our own government wants us to die from hypothermia. The country is built on coal. Why should it be so expensive, my customers ask? And what can I tell them? Nothing. I can tell them nothing. And tell me, what's the point of the blackout now? All the Germans have to do is look for the fires that burn from their previous raids. They must be able to see the smoke from France."

Tom placed the package on the counter.

"What's this?" Green asked curiously and very deliberately prodded it with a stubby finger. Blood had stained the wrapping.

"It needs a wash, and so does what's inside it. It's the reason I've been delayed a few months."

The older man threw him a look of understanding and nodded slowly. "I was beginning to think this one had got away. I should have known better."

"Yes, you should have done."

"Quite so," the jeweller said and cleared his throat, for a moment unsettled by Tom's stony glare. "If this were to go on you would be in serious danger of becoming rich, Mr Smith, but unfortunately I think it is safe to say that this will be the last consignment from that particular place. We shall have to think of another way." He moved the package to a drawer beneath the counter and handed over an envelope.

Tom pocketed the envelope and headed for the door.

"I heard from Frederick at the beginning of July. He sends his regards and the girls send their love. He was in Marseille, trying to negotiate a passage to Casablanca. That's the last I heard of him." He shrugged, "So what of the future? Perhaps you would be interested in more work in the retrieval business?"

Tom paused at the door and turned back. He was curious but remained silent.

"You might not know this, but most of our boys in blue have been conscripted and temporary, innocent and extremely gullible officers have taken their places. There are a lot of people taking advantage of the blackout, particularly the draft dodgers and deserters."

Tom waited for the point, his expression cold and unchanging.

The jeweller produced a slip of paper and slipped it across the counter. He said smoothly, "This is a list of names and addresses of people I have enjoyed serving, mostly old ladies who like to sparkle in the dark. I would like to think that it is only the bomb-damaged and empty properties that would warrant your attention."

"Why me?"

Green said shrewdly, "You have already shown you can be trusted and Frederick thinks highly of you. You have come with his recommendation and that is good enough for me. And you don't mind taking risks." He made a wide, expansive gesture. "The young take risks, and the old do not." He shook his head and smiled. "You youngsters, I don't know, I'm sure. How I'd like to be young again and fit enough to run." He rubbed his side. "It's the heart, you see? It gets us all in the end. It's payback time."

Tom picked up the list and said, "In the pub they call it bomb chasing. They don't write about it in the papers, of course, but it's a dangerous game." He moved to the door before adding, "I'll think about it."

Two weeks later Tom Smith pulled at the gold bands on a woman's swollen fingers while she stared at him out of dead eyes. It was the third body he'd found in the collapsed house. No one had escaped the bomb that had fallen through the roof and blasted out the back and sidewall of the two-storey building. It was the eyes he hated most. They accused him. They didn't glisten and the sclera was whiter and the shrivelled irises seemed to be sinking into it. The explosion had ripped away her housecoat and her hair and exposed sagging white flesh cut open by great shards of glass. Her blood was still channelling through the dust. He pulled a lace tablecloth over the body and red patches immediately spread out on the fabric. He tugged at the rings again. This time they slipped over the fat fingers. He put them with the others in his jacket pocket.

The blast had taken away the front hall and most of the staircase to the upper storey but a pile of rubble created a ledge for him to climb and gain access to the front bedroom. Somewhere in there was an overflowing jewellery box, hopefully in one piece. Nicholas Green had been right. The old Jew girls, particularly the widows or the spinsters, didn't trust the banks and kept their various legacies tucked away. A broken pipe above a brass headboard hissed a deadly message and he knew that time was running out. Sirens shrieked and more distant explosions shook the floor. Bricks and roof tiles crashed into the hole where the hall had been. He turned out a chest-of-drawers and peered into the dark recesses of a wardrobe. It was then that his forearm was stung and he heard an unmistakable crack. Then the voice, loud and clear: "Stay where you are!"

Tom moved instinctively, his retreat already mapped out. A second bullet made a neat circular hole in the wardrobe but he was already clear. The bedroom window had been blown out and an eight-foot drop to the back garden gave him his escape. A small garden led to an alley. With the brown boy charging around the block to cover one end he was left with only one way to go and that led through the inferno.

Through the smoke and dust the air itself glowed orange. The flames and flashes reflected in the water and in places the water itself was on fire and blue flames darted across the swirling surface, licking the orange air. Great chunks of masonry rained down and golden froth filled the crannies. The river craft rolled and bucked and burned and sank. Cargoes spilt and floated and burst open. Banks of smashed warehouses burned ferociously; red London brick turned redder. Dense smoke belched from every opening and timber cracked and burst in cascades of sparks; goods melted and coursed from broken walls and flowed into the water where clouds of steam rose to the deepening layers of smoke. People scurried and hid and died, clothes smouldered and skin blistered. Bombs and incendiaries continued to fall and huge explosions blasted great paths through the buildings. Other bombs fizzed and detonated in the air and deadly shrapnel rained down. In the raging heat inflammable goods exploded and spluttered and oil drums cart-wheeled high into the jet-black smoke.

The heat and smoke forced him below the burning dock timbers. He soaked his jacket and covered his head. The crash of falling debris increased to a roar as another wave of bombs exploded, some in mid-air. Entire buildings collapsed and crashed down across the fire barges. People swam for the banks, others floated in the oil-stained water. He stepped out again and made his way across the coiled hoses and suction pipes that snaked across the slipways.

The brown boy chasing him was all tin hat, cape and leggings, a tall gangling figure, his .303 held chest-high as he ran, huge hobnails crunching on broken concrete and glass. He met with a choice: continue the chase or assist an old couple half-buried in their fallen shelter. He had no choice.

Tom Smith climbed across a covered coal barge and leapt through the flames of the burning wharf timbers and made his way east, ducking and weaving through the devastation, treading glass and breathing smoke and dust, sidestepping the fountains of water that spewed up from the shattered mains. He came eventually to their temporary base, a converted brick-built stable, the centre-court of which was used as a milk depot. Before he went in through paint-blistered doors he glanced back at the river. Above the rooftops the sky glowed under a black umbrella. The earth still shook and windows still rattled but the battle was distant; only a few roads, a few back-to-backs, lay in the way, but apart from a stray bomb, it might have been another world.

"Stuff this for a living," he said to the three faces that turned his way. "My retirement plans were nearly fucked well and proper today!"

Simon came to meet him. He'd taken to wearing a Homburg, a gangster's hat with a wide grosgrain band that looked faintly ridiculous. "What's happened?"

"Moorgate has been bleedin' levelled, I'd say."

Pinchera exhaled a stream of smoke from his Gold Flake. "Lambeth Walk caught an aerial torpedo, John Lewis in Oxford Street needs a new paint job, and now Moorgate – it's a bleedin' liberty. We should have taken care of that one-bollock bastard while we were over there."

"At least he's got one," Simon said.

Pinchera laughed but it was half-hearted and edged with heartache. The dry self-depreciation of the thoroughbred Londoner didn't suit him. The old sparkle might have been blown out of his dark eyes but his grandfather's Latin blood still ran hot and cold.

Tom grunted, "Yeah, yeah, like you've got a short memory. If you remember we were running backwards like no one's run before. Think of all the Jocks we met from the Fifty-First, and those geezers in the French Ninth, all annihilated to save our skins. We were bleedin' cowards mate. We never even tried to put up a fight."

"That's only 'cos we were ordered to. No one gave us the option to stand and fight. It was the officers that decided to run, not us."

"Just as well they did or we'd have been queuing up in front of the Pearly Gates!"

Simon put in: "You'd still be queuing. I've got a feeling they wouldn't let you in. Nor any of the rest of us, come to that."

Their laughter was cut short as Tom held up his arm. "That brown shirt took a pot at me. The fucker means it!" Since the army had been brought in to handle the looters they'd brought with them a shoot on sight policy.

Pinchera leant forward to examine the wound. His hair parted over the hole where his ear should have been. "Just a scratch," he said.

"Two inches lower and I'd be one arm short."

"What are you saying?" Simon asked.

"I'm saying that it's heavy enough out there without some arsehole with a .303 chasing us from here to Southend. He's starting to know our runs. And what is more, my son, one day he's going to get lucky and actually hit what he's shooting at."

"So we ought to sort him out then," the third man said and limped forward on one leg. He'd been promised a tin replacement for the missing one but there was a long waiting list and in the meantime he made do with a crutch. Norman Dileva's infectious grin carried across the room.

"Sorting him out would be easy but his replacement might be a better shot."

"What then?" Dileva asked.

Sorting out the brown boys proved easier than any of them anticipated. It was down to some Air-Raid Precautions warden uniforms that fell into their hands. Disguised as wardens they were left unhindered to search through the bomb-damaged houses and shops. Even while the bombs dropped and the smoke rose and the incendiaries clattered across the roof slates, they remained in the thick of it, until breathing became all but impossible and their hair began to singe. On occasion they carried signs reading 'Road Closed' and 'Danger – Unexploded Bomb', and actually enforced the evacuation of properties that remained undamaged. Jane joined the small group and spent her time delving through catalogues to identify some of the less obvious ornaments and relics that came their way. She'd become something of an expert on hallmarks and trademarks and all the other stamps of value and even Nicholas Green was impressed and had taken her aside and keeping it between the two of them – his request – quietly offered her a job in his shop, an offer that she had just as quietly declined. She hadn't conceived and that was a relief for she and Tom had never bothered with any precautions, but Maureen Devine had. Within days of Tom being shipped to the Isle of Wight Maureen had taken up with a bank clerk from Mill Hill East and three months later they had married. She now lived in a terraced house in Hendon, close to her husband's family. Since then her husband had received his call-up and because of a few hours he'd spent during his youth in a dinghy on a pond in Enfield he was despatched to Devonport, where he was given a navy-blue uniform, a duffle-coat and a one-way ticket to the north Atlantic.

Rose had not seen the Hursts for over a year, not since Peter Woodhead had driven her down on a day trip. Lately the channel ports were restricted and that meant the end to her trips but news that the Mannings had to journey to the capital so that Len could visit a specialist hospital put Rose in a tizzy and she wouldn't hear of them staying anywhere else. The letter contained only sketchy details of a stroke and the tests that were necessary and that Len would be admitted for at least two days. Someone had pulled some strings to get Len into a London hospital at a time when they were overflowing and couldn't even cope with the casualties of the unceasing air raids, never mind the servicemen who needed specialist treatment, and it wasn't until much later that Tom discovered that Tony Bryant's fingerprints were all over the ticket. It was payback for Richard and Ian Hurst taking a hefty slice of Bryant's rap. Not that the Mannings or, indeed, Reginald and Elizabeth Hurst knew anything about it. It was business, nothing more than the wheels of the underworld slowly turning and travelling along a familiar path. Even the walls of Maidstone prison weren't high enough to check the spread of Bryant's influence and it shouldn't have come as a surprise that his connections went beyond the borders of the Garden of

England. Rose's problem was where to sleep them all and she decided to give up her room for Joyce and Sally, and she and Tom would somehow make do in Tom's tiny bedroom. Tom smiled at his mother and told her that he would stay at the Eagle. She seemed too excited to question the fact that he rarely slept at home in any case. She spent a week cleaning what was already a spotless house. During that time her anticipation grew out of all proportion and she was like a schoolgirl again. Tom was both surprised and delighted but by the end of the week both he and Peter Woodhead were glad to get out of it.

Tom had already moved most of his gear into one of the rooms on the Eagle's first floor and he slept there more often than not. The gym itself had become redundant. The war had ended the interest in boxing. Most of the men had been called up and the youngsters evacuated. Peter's visits to see Rose at number sixty-four increased and it was impossible to date the precise moment he moved in on a permanent basis. The days that he slept at the Eagle became fewer until people realized he no longer slept there at all. He installed a husband and wife team to run the bars and left the management of the buildings entirely to Tom.

People had begun to notice their activities in the old milk depot and Simon's enthusiasm for rebuilding smashed motorcars could no longer be used as a reasonable excuse, especially during the night. It was also too close to the docks and the main target areas of the Luftwaffe. Eight terraced houses just three hundred yards distant had been flattened in the previous week. They rented a ground floor flat in a Victorian town house in Wood Green, away from the danger areas, and installed Norman Dileva as tenant, and the day was spent in moving their smaller goods from the yard into the cellar of their new premises. They had all been excused further military service but unfortunately people were being roped into fire service and the home guard. For the moment Simon Carter was also a free agent. He told people it was down to his ginger hair but he confided in Tom that it was a congenital heart defect that had been causing him some grief for some time – something he thought was indigestion. His mother had died when he was six but his father had explained – waffled on in a drunken haze – that he'd been born with a hole in the heart, whatever that was, and had needed intensive hospital treatment. That was why he was overweight, his father told him. Because he never got the exercise that normal kids would have got. He never went scrumping or chestnutting or setting fire to whatever you could set fire to, like normal kids did.

They were still left with the problem of their bulky gear and Tom thought he had the answer. He caught up with Peter Woodhead and said, "I was wondering about the Eagle and the gym?"

"What about the gym?" The old man asked. He was wearing his black suit and tie, with his bowler pulled down to his ears.

"Before all this started you had it in mind to sell up?"

"I'm still undecided. But I am thinking about retiring altogether."

"Would you sell me the gym?"

Peter pulled a face. "I won't ask about where your funding comes from, Tommy Smith, but what would you do with the gym?"

"I'll keep it until I can afford to level it and build a castle in its place."

The old man shook his head.

Tom realized his explanation wasn't good enough and added, "Well, boxing has had its day. I thought of snooker tables in the front and behind it a private drinking club for after hours."

"I'm too wise and know too many people not to know what goes on, Tommy. I'm not stupid either, so don't take the piss."

"Well, we're making a few bob on the black market, you know that much."

"I've got no problem with that. What else?"

Tom grinned. "In the back I thought we might organize a few card games or something."

"A gambling club, you mean?"

"Yeah, that's what I thought. With the racetracks and boxing rings closed down the punters are begging for some action. I've got a long line of bookies along with their touts looking for work. They ain't all that on joining the CD."

Peter woodhead made a dismissive sound but his pale blue eyes glinted. He knew exactly what Tom was getting at. The Civil Defence services were taking anyone they could get their hands on.

"And what about the baths? You'd rip 'em out just like that? They cost a fortune to put in."

"We could keep some of them and turn them into private rooms. There's always a call for rub downs and massages. These squaddies milling around with nothing to do during their two-day passes can smell crumpet at a hundred yards. And they've all got their King's Shilling tucked away."

"Prostitutes and gambling dens. What next, I ask myself?"

"We'll cater for a more exclusive clientele."

"Where are you coming from? You need to walk before you can run, boy. For a start, prostitution has gone through the roof. With all the men in training camps and away from home every housewife this side of the river is dropping her britches for a five-pound note. And what about the local nick? They'll need sorting. And have you thought about the competition beside the respectable housewives? There are a lot of hard bastards around these parts that won't like more competition. And speaking of competition, there are thousands of draft dodgers knocking around who've all got it in mind to make a few bob. The police are picking up twenty a night just in Effin Forest. You can guarantee they'll all be working the black market. Your supplies might not be as easy to come by in the future."

"I'll look after the amateurs but I was hoping you might have a few contacts you could put my way to sort out the local villains. You've got the Old Bill and the local councillors in your hand, I know that. Like you say, the priority has got to be the professionals."

The old man gave him a long studied appraisal.

Tom went on, "And Len and Joyce coming up here reminds me I've got some unfinished business in Folkestone. We're going into partnership with a transport company called Bulk Earthmoving. We need a lot of trucks and figure to get in on the ground floor. They've got the transport and the streets of London have got the rubble and we know a few geezers who are putting out the contracts."

Peter rubbed his chin. "I remember Bulk Earthmoving from the court. Same outfit is it?"

"They don't actually know about it yet."

"Tony Bryant might be inside but he's still got plenty of muscle in the Cinque Ports. And he's got a hold on most of the transport."

Tom's eyes narrowed and an inner lid drew across them. Suddenly they were as cold as Peter had ever seen them.

"A lot of the transport is being requisitioned. You could end up with nothing."

"We've got a contact in the War Office who's putting in a good word with MOS and it gives us carte blanche to move some goods around."

"You're talking about Jane's father?"

Tom raised his eyebrows in surprise.

"I told you I know everything that moves around here. When are you going to believe me? Anyway, what's with the carte blanche? You didn't pick that up down the gym, I know. Moving in exalted circles, are we? And who is we? You said we? Simon Carter?"

"Simon's a mate, you know that, but I wouldn't actually depend on him to run the books. He's a bit short on grey matter. I've got a geezer called James Jessel to look after the paperwork. He was an accountant in Civvy Street, knows what he's doing and, what's more, he knows the score."

"And who else?"

"Some old mates from the regiment, and another guy I met in the hospital. A geezer named Coddy Hughes. He's got some influence up north."

Peter Woodhead nodded slowly. Eventually he said, "Anyone who takes over the Eagle will know exactly what you're doing, Tommy. There will be no way to hide it."

Tom shrugged. "I thought about that. It's a problem."

"You take the Eagle as well. And I'll take a slice."

Tom frowned. "Come again?"

"It's non-negotiable, boy. I won't interfere but I'll be here for advice and, like you said, I've got the contacts. In this enterprise you're going to need every one of them. And I don't want your mother knowing anything about all of this." He paused and looked a little self-conscious before continuing, "That's something else I wanted to mention. We've decided to get married. We haven't put a date to it yet but I was hoping you would be my best man."

"I'll be giving her away. Am I allowed to do both?"

Peter Woodhead offered his hand and Tom hid his surprise well and shook it.

He arrived home to find a note from his mother explaining that she'd gone to the hospital with Joyce and Sally and could he pick them up. Rush hour traffic delayed him and sirens began just minutes before he reached the hospital entrance.

The bombs fell in waves, rocking the foundations, shaking the earth in great deafening eruptions, filling the air with dust and smoke. Joyce screamed at him and pulled his arm but he could barely hear her above the din.

She shrieked, "It's Sally! She's down there!" and dragged him towards an underground entrance where a crowd of people fought to get out. The weak and the old and the unlucky were trampled and crushed. Blood streamed down arms and legs. Panic had got them out and now they ran blindly into the road oblivious to the falling masonry crashing around them. He knew the danger. Marble Arch, Balham, Bank and Liverpool Street had all taken direct hits and the stories he'd heard had been horrific.

Rose shouted in his ear, "I sent her down when the sirens started! Joyce was still in the hospital. I went back for her."

Tom turned to Rose and shouted back, "I'll find her! You get to another shelter! I'll find her!"

His mother nodded. She wiped her cheeks and spread grime across her face. She pulled on Joyce's sleeve. "Tommy will find her!" she shouted. "We can't do anything here." She turned back to Tom and said, "Find her, my son. For God sake bring her home!"

Tom pushed them away and turned back to the crowd. As he fought his way through he heard more explosions smashing the buildings opposite and saw huge flames licking over the rooftops. He jostled and shoved his way through the panic. The smoke and dust grew thicker. He threw people aside to get to the wall and edged down the steps. A man in front fell and clawed at his legs. Tom lifted him to his feet.

"What's happening down there?"

"A bomb came through. The tiles came off the walls and hit us like a ton of shrapnel. There's a fire down there and there's water coming in. I think it's the river. There are bodies all over!"

Tom let go of the man who promptly fell again. He struggled on, throwing people from his path. The crowd eased a little. The able-bodied had made their escape. He made quicker progress over the others and reached the platform. The well with its track was under water and bodies floated. The wounded and the frail, mostly women and children, had gathered on the platform and some men in uniform were trying to muster them. The smoke had thinned out and he saw the gaping hole in the tunnel linings where sludge and earth had surged across the platform. He clambered across a pile of shifting black dirt and found another pocket of helpless faces, crying and moaning. A warden with his coat in tatters and covered in mud was doing his best to help them, pulling an old woman from the pile. Another man was lifting the children to comparative safety. Sally was propped against the curved wall with one leg bent beneath her. She was covered in white dust and filth and her hair was plastered to her head. Water streamed from the wall behind her. Her lower leg was gashed and bleeding. She saw him and shivered violently. She gripped his arms tightly, staring up at him out of wide unblinking eyes, unable to speak.

"It's all right," he said. "I've got you." He lifted her easily and realized her ankle was broken. She cried out and pressed her wet face into his shoulder.

"It's all right now, Sweetheart. I was always going to find you." He carried her forward and joined a group that was making its slow way to the exit.

Two separate incidents carried Tom Smith's name beyond the local neighbourhood and into the outlying districts of London and yet, in hindsight, one led seamlessly to the other. The first concerned Norman Dileva's mother. Her home had been targeted by a family of racists who took exception to Norman's dark visage and daubed her front wall with paint, broke her windows and pushed dog faeces through her letterbox. The family – father, mother and three grown-up sons – lived at the end of the same road and subjected the neighbours to a reign of bullying and persecution. The coloureds had never been welcome in the East End and trouble was always breaking out in the communal shelters. Before the war Mosley had half the East End villains on his payroll and some areas were coined as fascist manors. The main targets were the Jews and the area around Whitechapel, their old slum haunt, faced most of the violence, but any foreign face would do.

Tom went ballistic when Jane told him about it and confronted Norman.

"Why didn't you tell me?"

"It's personal. Why should I involve you?"

"You're part of the family, Norman, and that means I'm involved already!"

Tom took three of his friends as back up. It was just after blackout and they kicked in the back door and stuck shotguns into the faces of the father and the two older brothers. They held down the younger brother and lit a paraffin Bunsen burner and made it clear they were going to cook his face until it was the same colour as Norman's. It wasn't necessary. The family agreed to clean up the graffiti and to become model citizens. Norman Dileva's mother was treated like royalty, her front garden tidied, her shopping often collected from the shop.

Gossip spread. The incident was given an East End colour.

The size of his organisation increased in personnel as well as assets. The draft-dodgers were a cheap and willing workforce and from their numbers Tom found some reliable and handy faces.

Nicholas Green found him at the gym.

"Mosely might be in Holloway," he began, rolling the words around his mouth before they came out smooth and wet. "But many of his old lieutenants were not interned with him and they are still causing us trouble." He lifted his shoulders and opened his palms in a little Jewish tic that reminded Tom of his cousin. "If I may say so, the BUF might be proscribed but that's just a name. Although they have taken off their black shirts the fascists are still marching through our streets."

Tom raised his hands. "What would you have me do, Nicholas? Threaten them all with a Bunsen burner? They won't frighten as easily as that."

He shrugged again and the end of his tongue edged past the tips of his sharp front teeth. He gave the corners of the room a shifty glance to ensure their privacy. "A man with your obvious skills could give it some thought. I have a lot of friends in the East End who are still having their windows smashed, their children are still attacked by these thugs and their wives are frightened to go out. One of my very dear friends was kicked to death. And the police won't help. They have more pressing problems, no doubt. They are not on our side. They have made that quite clear. I have been asked to let you know that certain people would be willing to pay for the security of their property. There are owners of approximately fifty establishments, homes and businesses, who are interested, and once you have shown them what can be done, many more would follow."

"I'll think about it," Tom said.

On the way out they heard strange noises coming from the back of one of four vans parked in the yard. Nicholas Green frowned and said, "Chickens?"

"There's a lorry load of them, redirected from Norfolk. The driver got lost. They call it misappropriation. We've got to offload them before someone complains about the squawking. Let's face it, Nick, people are getting totally pissed off with powdered eggs so we're doing them a favour. There's also some red meat coming in – they call it venison – all the way from Sandringham. It's got the royal stamp of approval. Bit expensive, and it tastes like horse – I tried that in France and believe me it is shit – but apparently there's a meat shortage."

The jeweller scratched his chin. "Quite so, but I might be able to help you," he said. "Chicken soup is still in fashion in certain quarters."

They laughed.

It was an off-the-cuff remark, spoken in jest, and yet it led to a fruitful introduction.

From a small family-owned butchers that at the time concentrated on Kosher goods, a colleague of Nicholas Green named Jonathan Hilkowitz found himself with a steady supply of fresh meat when his competitors were found wanting, and shortly after the war ended he founded a chain of shops that forty years later became one of the largest supermarket chains in the UK. He never forgot Tom Smith and without fail a hamper containing wine and a fresh goose arrived on Tom's doorstep every Christmas Eve.

A week after meeting Nicholas Green at the gym, the main command post and administrative centre of what was left of the East End Fascist organisation was set on fire and eight men were left for dead. Three subsequently died from gunshot wounds and two from accidental injuries, falling from the roof of the building while trying to escape. There were no arrests and no press releases and no one saw or heard a thing and the attacks on Jewish shopkeepers in East London ceased almost overnight. Some people who heard about it blamed the government and their secret agencies for both the attack and the subsequent cover-up, but the people who mattered knew the score.

The protection of small shops, pubs, clubs and businesses became a profitable branch of the business and the income it generated soon exceeded that of the black market, transportation and looting put together. Protection rackets had always been rife in London, as they were in all the major cities. In return for a fixed fee a gang would protect an establishment from other gangs and persistent troublemakers. For the business owners it was the only way to stay in business and unless they affiliated to a particular gang they could end up paying to several gangs at the same time, with the additional danger of being caught in the middle of a gang war. But there were so many scams available they had to pick and choose and a lot of their time was spent on recruitment. There were the girls, of course, and they turned over at an alarming rate, and an increase in their illegal gaming activities, but there was also a steady market in ration books and coupons and 'essential trade' documents that required forgery. He tied up more and more with Coddy Hughes and brought some of the mine owners along with distribution and filling stations under control. None of it was without risk and on occasion it seemed like the front line would have been the safer option.

Chapter 19

The war was over.

People moved in a new no-man's land of readjustment and recovery. The euphoria of victory was soon replaced by the reality of the cost. Peter Woodhead married Rose and officially moved into number sixty-four. No one pointed out that he'd been there for some years. The Eagle Public House was one of the last casualties of the war. A V2 rocket landed next door and her sidewall was knocked out. The stone eagle flew from its perch above the heavy doors and smashed into the pavement. Rose said it was Hitler's final insult to us, a V-sign. The public house was rebuilt and the reception was held there in the newly furnished rooms. Behind it, the gym became Tom's headquarters. It had been extended to hold a couple of offices as well as a small living area. The business had expanded beyond all expectations. Funds from loan-sharking and the collections from the small businesses and shops were used and laundered into buying up cheap war-damaged assets, with property high on the agenda. The distribution and transport business had also taken off, particularly from the channel ports, and this was ideal for the import of tax-free goods and the recreational drugs that were becoming more fashionable as the post-war depression took hold.

Through the office window Tom watched James Jessel approach. Behind him a few of the girls were getting ready for business. Nylons and garter belts had replaced loose silk stockings and rayon.

Jessel opened the door. "There's someone downstairs says he knows you. He looks like trouble. Dressed like a tramp. I seem to recognize him from somewhere but I don't know where."

Tom sighed. The streets were full of tramps and beggars, displaced – misplaced – persons, men who'd come back from the war and found they could no longer handle what they had before. He said, "Give him the price of a pint."

"I tried that, Boss. I thought he was going to stuff it down my throat."

"Well, call Barry and Richard. They'll get rid of him."

"They're keeping an eye on him now. He isn't going anywhere till he sees you."

Tom pushed his chair back. "What's his name? Did he give you a name?"

"No name. A big chap. He's got a scar across his head from here to Southend. It looks like someone's had a go with a chopper."

Tom's eyes narrowed. He nodded thoughtfully and said, "Send him up. Be careful with him."

James Jessel was surprised and raised his eyebrows. A few minutes later a tall, heavy-bodied man walked unsteadily into the office. A worn greatcoat hid him from neck to knee. The face was drawn, the hair, almost iron-grey, swept sideways over the scar. There was no hint of recognition in the cold eyes.

"All right James. Close the door behind you."

Again James Jessel was surprised. He shrugged and backed out. He was well out of the office when the memory came flooding back and stopped him in his tracks.

The man heard the door close. He stood motionless in the centre of the room, head bowed, staring at the floor. His eyes were shot and the skin beneath them dark and sore. Patchy grey stubble covered his chin. His hands remained deep in his pockets.

"Hello Sergeant," Tom said without a hint of sarcasm.

The man looked up. His eyes flickered and narrowed as though he was trying hard to focus. For a few moments he gazed at Tom as if not recognizing him, then his sunken eyes flooded and tears glistened on his cheeks. He turned back to the door.

"Wait!" Tom moved quickly around the desk and placed a hand on the man's sleeve. "You're going nowhere," he said. "Come and sit down and have a drink at least."

The man looked up again and gazed into Tom's eyes. "Are you going to try and stop me? You and whose army?"

Tom held up both hands. "It's up to you Sergeant. No one is forcing you. I'd never even try to do that. The least you can do is to have a drink with an old army buddy."

The man nodded sullenly and Tom led him to a chair at the side of the desk. He eased himself into it as though the movement was painful. Tom filled two glasses with whisky and pushed one across. He left the open bottle on the desk.

"I've been doing some paperwork," he said and swallowed half his drink.

The man nodded and reached for his glass. His hand shook. He winced as the alcohol touched the cracks around his mouth.

"See they patched you up pretty good." He raised his arm to his shoulder and grimaced, "Me too."

The man smiled humourlessly. "Headaches!" he stammered. "I get the headaches."

"How's the family? Your wife – I'm sorry, I forget her name – and the kids, how are they?" Tom remembered the sergeant's wife; her image came flooding back. He'd been dozing. The curtains had kept the room in darkness. She'd thrown open the door and stood, open-mouthed, wearing nothing but her knickers, throwing up her arms to cover herself. All he'd got was her silhouette against the light in the hall, but it was a sight to savour and one that he would never forget.

The answer, when it came, was almost whispered, "Dead. They're all dead."

Tom pulled a face. "What happened?"

"Not really dead, just gone."

"Gone where?"

"It's the headaches, see?" The eyes narrowed again and the glazed look came back. "I can't stand them. I go crazy, smash the place up; smash my head against the wall."

"Have you been back to the hospital?"

"Four years. I was in hospital for a year, then the loony bin. Thought I was mad. Probably am. Everybody's fucking mad!"

"Where's the family now?"

The man shrugged. "Better off without me. She went off with a Canadian. Moved to Canada, see, and took my girls."

"Bloody hell, Scratch, I'm sorry." Tom felt helpless. "What about your brother, the navy man?"

"He was on the Hood in forty-one. I lost touch with his family."

"How did you find me?"

"You're getting well known. I heard your name. I remembered, see? Remembered those bastards you knifed and the cops and I helped you. Did you know I helped you?"

"I guessed you did." Tom's expression turned dark. "But let's not fuck about, Sergeant. Are you laying something on me?"

"Threatening you?" The man looked away, his expression clouded in disappointment. He finished his drink.

"What then?" Tom asked.

"I don't want your charity, never that!"

"You don't look like you've eaten anything solid in a week."

Fox laughed, "A week? It's been more like a year. I don't want help."

"You might not want it but you need it."

The eyes had filled again.

"I'm finished," he said and looked up and met Tom's steady gaze. "I've got nothing."

"Yes you have," Tom said gently and refilled the glasses. "For a start you've got an IOU from me and they don't come better than that."

Shortly after the meeting with his old sergeant he drove to Folkestone for a business meeting with his partners at Bulk Earthmoving. He met up with Sally and they walked back from Dover along the coast. They had planned it and Joyce had provided a picnic basket.

"See your leg's healed up." He remembered carrying her out of the station. She'd never been far from his thoughts.

She lifted her foot. "Not even a scar." She grinned. "I was in plaster for almost two months, though. You wouldn't have taken a shine to me then."

"What makes you think I've taken a shine to you, Sally Mannings?"

"Tommy Smith, you can't fool me. You've got a twinkle in your eye that's as bright as a beacon. And you know what a beacon is, don't you? It's a warning."

Light filtered through the thin material of her floral-patterned skirt and showed him the outline of her legs. He was acutely aware of every movement she made as she trod lightly over the rocks.

"Why do people dream," she asked suddenly, surprising him.

"I don't know. I guess it's a time when the brain does its filing to get shot of the rubbish. And you know what filing is like before it's put away, all a jumble. That's why dreams don't make any sense."

"Well, I dreamt about you, Tommy Smith, and maybe that's why, so my brain can throw you out with the rest of the rubbish."

"What was the dream about?"

"You were chasing me," she said and her eyes sparkled.

"Did I catch you?"

"You'll never do that. I'm too fast for you."

The concrete and steel scars of war that they negotiated would take decades to heal. Along the front, below the cliffs now glowing in the fiery afternoon light, the waves lapped across the strange geometry designed to hinder the expected invasion. In parts, at times, the sea washed directly on to the cliff face and created an impassable barrier, but now the tide was out and a line of froth picked up a glowing florescence and a faint breeze sent tufts of it across the pebbles.

Out of a silence broken only by the breaking water and the occasional call from a swooping gull his voice sounded deeper than usual and she frowned at him when he said, "Over the years I had a bit of a dream too."

"Well?" She turned and waited for him to catch up.

"It was about you."

"What about me? Maybe I shouldn't ask."

"All I wanted was to be with you."

A combination of surprise and amusement played across her face. Settling on amusement she smiled quickly and said, "Well, that's got it said. But Tommy, you're too old for me. In any case, I know you've got loads of girlfriends. I heard your mother telling mine. I would never share anyone. Never! Come back when you've given the rest up and you're rich and famous. Such things take years off a man." The subtlety spread to a grin. "Anyway, you're a villain. My dad says you're a hoodlum. I want more than that."

He recognized a truth behind her jibe and his eyes hooded in embarrassment. He felt the pressure behind them.

"You're a villain," she repeated. "And I've always dreamt of princes."

He reached for her hand and was surprised she didn't snatch it away. Her hand was warm and easy.

"Oh, Tommy," she sighed. "I want to do so many things and I wouldn't care to do any of them if I was with you." There was a sudden sadness in her eyes as she reached up on tiptoes to kiss his cheek. "Let's get back," she said in barely a whisper. She made to pull away but his hands on her waist stopped her.

Her eyes darkened and she said, "What?"

He leant down and kissed her mouth. She pushed against his chest. Restricting him became a struggle and she slipped back on to the sand and pebbles. He was beside her immediately, holding her down with one hand on her shoulder. The look in his eyes frightened her and she tried to scramble away but it was hopeless. He pulled her blouse aside and bared her breasts. Shyness turned her face red and she looked up the cliff face then left and right down the beach to make certain that no one could see them. For the moment the thought of being seen outweighed all else.

She stopped moving and her look was curious and questioning.

"I dreamt about your breasts," he said and stroked them. "They were always going to be beautiful, just like the rest of you. I dreamt about us being together. Sometimes, after I just woke and before things became real, I thought we had. I used to lie there disappointed, willing myself back to sleep."

She said quietly, "Please don't do this."

"I've got to. I can't stop. Not now. Then maybe I can forget you and get on with the rest of my life."

She lay there motionless, waiting for it to happen.

He sat there for an age just looking at her and stroking her breasts and then her belly and still she didn't move. Instead she watched the gulls wheeling and diving and heard their cries. In the distance a small boat moved sluggishly across the choppy water, heading for Dover.

Eventually she looked back at him but he'd turned away from her and was no longer holding her down. She frowned, unable to understand but relieved for all that.

He said thickly, "Get out of here, Sally."

She pulled her clothes together. Still perplexed and unable to understand what had stopped him, she struggled to her feet and without looking back she walked away from him, stumbling in her haste.

For hours Tom Smith lay while the dusk crept in. He was suddenly aware of his isolation and wondered what it was that moved men to destroy those things they held most precious.

The street lamps were flickering when he knocked on the Mannings' door.

Joyce Mannings opened the door and her angry eyes widened fractionally in surprise. Her hand trembled but the door remained steady. Her voice was hushed and sharp. "You're not welcome here, Tommy Smith. You never will be again. It will be better if you go now."

He sighed, "I can't do that, Mrs Mannings."

Her drawn features raised slightly

"We trusted you," she said quietly. There was nothing more to add. Behind her Len Mannings appeared in the small cluttered hallway. Reddened eyes found their mark on Tom.

"I can't fight you, Smith. But by Christ I'll find somebody to cut your filthy throat!"

Joyce backed into the hall to hold on to her sagging husband.

"The stroke did for him," she whispered. "But you've broken his heart. I can't believe it of you. Not Rose's boy."

She wrapped a protective arm around his thin shoulders and led him into the back kitchen to his rocker.

Tom followed them through the dimly lit hall. The kitchen was close and full of steam. The windows were coated in condensation. Sally looked up from the table, first at her parents as her helpless father was guided to his chair, then at Tom in the doorway. Her mouth dropped open in shock.

"I told them what you did, and what you didn't do. But what you did was unforgivable," she said.

He nodded and met her gaze. "I've not come here asking for forgiveness. I've come here to ask you to marry me. If you give me the chance I'll protect you and your family for as long as I live."

Her parents, Len sitting and Joyce bending over him, remained motionless, open-mouthed, staring in disbelief.

"I love you, girl," he said. "I always have. You'll never find anyone who loves you as much as I do. I promise you that I'll never hurt you or embarrass you again and I'll never look at another woman; not because of this promise but because I'll never want to."

In the unforgiving kitchen light her frown seemed almost painful.

"I'm not a beggar and this is as close as I'm ever going to get to it. If you send me away now I won't ever come back. If you want the world I'll die trying to get it for you."

He turned and left them and retreated down the cluttered passageway. He left the front door open and stepped on to the path. In the orange wash of the flickering gaslights and under the midnight-blue canopy of night where the stars were brighter than ever, the sense of finality was so acute that for a moment it left him with a sharp stab in his chest and he knew that the wound would never heal.

He heard a movement behind him and turned to see her, half shielded by the door.

Sally held the door wider and said clearly, "I didn't tell you to go, did I?"

They were married seven months later, and David Smith was born two months after that.

For their fruit and flowers anniversary, after leaving the growing toddler in Rose's safe hands, he took Sally on a Vickers Viking to Paris. She was terrified and her hands shook all the way. He'd booked a suite at the legendary Crystal Saint-Germain-des Pres that looked out over St Michel and the Notre Dame and had arranged for a cocktail dress and new shoes to be laid out on the bed. Using the pretext of a business meeting he left her in a taxi at the airport, telling her that he would meet her in the restaurant. The management of the hotel were waiting for her arrival and gave her an elaborate welcome. She knew very well that it was a set-up but she was still amazed by the opulence of the suite and by the style and extravagance of the clothes.

He was waiting for her at eight, dressed in his dinner jacket. When she walked into the bar area of the restaurant eyes turned her way. She looked quite stunning. The slinky dress clung to her and showed her shape to perfection. She moved easily, elegantly, and her quietly confident smile, more in her eyes than on her spreading lips, showed she knew just how much interest her entrance had provoked.

She flicked at his bowtie and said, "Looking for a date?"

"Lovely dress," he said quietly.

She glanced down before meeting his teasing gaze again and smiling demurely said, "Think you're clever, Tommy Smith?" She paused, before adding, "You look pretty good yourself."

The *maître d'* welcomed them with a flourish and made a wide, expansive gesture toward a raised platform where a five-man ensemble immediately struck up and a woman sitting on a high chair at the microphone began *Where and When*.

The *maître d'* flapped his hands and walking backwards with practised ease led them to their table, watched all the way by other diners who perhaps wondered who the celebrities were. He held back her chair before flagging a waiter. Napkins twirled and were placed on their laps, a cork popped and champagne burst into glasses.

Tom said, "Why do they make such a big deal out of a napkin when you haven't even ordered yet?"

"This is madness," she whispered. "A wonderful madness, but how can we afford it? You've already spent a fortune on this dress."

He smiled but remained silent.

"Tell me?"

"All I'll tell you is that if we couldn't afford it we wouldn't be doing it. Now stop asking questions and enjoy yourself."

It was the first time that Sally fully understood that people were treating her husband with a certain reverence and she couldn't decide whether it was simply business or something else, something darker that she didn't want to think about. She'd noticed the unlikely esteem in London, more than the usual respect a workforce might have for the boss, and she was well aware that some of his dealings were on the shady side, not that she ever asked about such things, but that it had crossed the Channel brought home just how influential her husband was becoming.

The group finished the number and the singer opened her palms toward their table. People were still curious and Tom's acknowledgement was a little self-conscious, a hint of a smile and the raising of his glass.

Sally pretended not to notice and instead busied herself with the menu.

He flashed a quizzical look and said, "I didn't know your old français was this good."

"You shouldn't be surprised. When you were busy beating up the world and everyone in it, I was going to school, remember?"

At the mike, the American singer Ella Fitzgerald was giving it *April in Paris*.

"Come and dance," she said suddenly and that did surprise him. She knew very well that he had two left feet.

"I suppose the school taught you to dance as well?"

"It was compulsory. You should have tried school, Tommy Smith. It wasn't all bad and you might have learned a few social graces."

They joined a few other couples already on the floor. Sally was a natural and she had an enthusiastic audience. Perhaps the dress and the way it clung like a second skin had something to do with it but if she was at all perturbed by the attention it didn't show. Tom, in comparison, was hopeless, his movements laboured, his sense of rhythm nonexistent. By now she was accustomed to it and watched as he mouthed the steps – one, two, three, – and looked down at his own feet, willing them to move. The spectators seemed quite bemused, covering their spreading grins with napkins and hands. Sally couldn't help herself and her shoulders shook as she laughed. "You're worse than ever."

He grinned back, sharing the joke.

"I'll teach you," she said. "In time for our golden anniversary you'll be able to lead."

Ella Fitzgerald finished her song and began *I'll Never Forget You* and it threw a more sombre mood on the room.

They moved back to their table where he told her, "I should tell you about this place. It's a meeting place for writers and painters. They come from all over the world. Some of the best jazz players come here."

"I love it," she said. "And I love the First Lady of Song too."

He frowned. She'd surprised him again.

Over her shoulder Tom saw some old friends. Nicholas Green and a few of his grateful friends had clubbed together, made the arrangements and paid for the party. Frederick and his girls threw them wide smiles and lifted their champagne glasses to toast the celebration. Frederick shouted, "Everything all right, Tommy?"

Ella Fitzgerald paused in her song and looked across at the strange Frenchman in his flat cap surrounded by six beautiful girls and wondered who he was. Sally turned to look also.

"Everything is just fine, Frederick," Tom called back, "Fair and fine."

It was 1954 and The Tower began to rise above the grey surroundings. The run-up to the year had been spent in South Africa. Sally was pregnant but agreed to join Tom on his business trip. He went to arrange a shipment of weapons and to organise the import of some hot stones on Nicholas Green's behalf. A heart attack had laid Green low and he'd come to rely on Tom's organisation for more than just security. Tom was also keen to recruit some soldiers to look after the trade in arms and to guard his expanding collection business. Other gangs were starting to make noises and interfere with business – Benny Hill and Jack Spot were competing in gaming clubs and girls, and their involvement in spielers and the club circuit was growing; the Maltese were expanding their protection rackets; a couple of young upstarts, Ronnie and Reggie Kray, were beginning to find their feet. But most of the problems were coming from south of the river. Appeasement was not an option. The white South Africans were mercenaries, but they were the best. And Tom went to hire them. In Cape Town some dodgy shellfish laid Sally low for a few days, and given her condition she ended up in hospital. She soon recovered and her seventh-month figure was a common sight around the pool. She took in Table Mountain and even bumped around on a two-day safari to shoot some of the big five. Theca was born in January, a month after their return. So the year started well but it was to take a bad turn.

Tom was in The Tower office with James Jessel and Barry Theroux. Barry was just twenty. He had joined the firm two years earlier after Simon Carter was killed in a motorcycle accident and had quietly established himself in the casino as a first class dealer. Tom had noticed him and tested him out on a few of the easier collections. He had handled them without a fuss and his move into the office was a natural progression. South of the Border was playing on the wireless, mocking them. James Jessel turned it off and grunted his dismay. They'd just received news that the South London mob had struck. Norman Dileva had been stabbed in Brick Lane and Tom had dispatched Pinchera to St Bart's to get the latest news.

"That spells it out," Jessel said. "They're coming for us. There's no longer any doubt. We can't protect ourselves, never mind our clients. Norman getting caught like that will be all over town by opening time. By the morning we won't have a customer base left. We need to pull the collectors off the streets immediately. They'll be the next targets." He shook his head. "We give them what they want or we make a run for it, which is what they want anyway."

"Running is not an option," Tom said sharply.

If it had all happened two months later when his South African recruits had arrived things might have been different but right now he didn't have the muscle to make a decent stand.

He shook his head and said, "And we're not paying up front so they get even stronger. I agree we need to look after the bagboys but I need some breathing space. I need twenty-four hours. Can we hold out that long?"

"I'll send word that we want to talk, that we're not stupid and will concede a couple of points, maybe south of Commercial Road."

"They'll want Whitechapel and Mile End."

"At least we keep Bethnal Green and Hackney."

The phone went. Jessel answered and his face told the story. He turned back to the others. "Norman's dead. He bled to death before he reached the hospital."

Tom sighed and said angrily, "So it is war, and we need an ally. I'm going to take out every last one of the bastards and afterwards I'll make sure we never find ourselves in this position again." His eyes were hooded and on fire. He said to Jessel, "Make the call. Buy me some time." He turned to Barry. "Get the car ready. We're going to Folkestone to talk to Bryant's mob." He paused and turned back to James Jessel. "Take care of Norman's mother. Anything she wants."

Tom's main concern was that enlisting Bryant's organisation to help clean up South London would undoubtedly create problems for the future. He remembered an old story about inviting the wolves into the house. Bryant would never be satisfied with a pay-off; sooner or later he would want to run the show. But that was something he would deal with when it happened, for now he needed Bryant's muscle and for the moment that was all that mattered.

It was over very quickly. Within a week South London had capitulated, their leaders had disappeared and would never be found and their forces were on the run. Tom agreed to pay Bryant a percentage of the East End take but Bryant moved in his own people south of the river.

Exactly a year later Tom sent his old sergeant to Folkestone. In one dark night Bryant and the main faces in his gang were rounded up and sent to sea. They sank immediately or swam but none of them were good enough swimmers to make it back to shore. With the help of Coddy Hughes' outfit that now controlled huge swathes of the Midlands he cleaned up what was left of Bryant's army in South London and established an alliance that would last a lifetime.

Minders watched from the bank, hidden by a wall of rhododendrons. Tom, clutching David's hand, knew they were there but Sally, pushing the pram, remained blissfully unaware. Tom stooped beside his son and pointed across the river to a barge chugging slowly toward the bend that would take it to the Isle of Dogs and the Millwall Docks. Closer to the water he felt the strange rhythmic beat that carried him back to another time, a message from the past, just a whisper from his father's lips: "Never walk away from nothing..." he heard and then, "There's nothing more dangerous than a woman's smile."

The sun was high and Sally adjusted the lacy hood to keep the glare out of Theca's eyes. She saw Tom's thoughtful expression and threw him a quizzical smile.

"What is it?"

"It's nothing, Sweetheart. Everything's just fine."

They moved on along the path, just an average family, a passer-by might think, out for a stroll along the throbbing river, making the most of the spring sunshine.

Above them, on the bank, the minders remained hidden as they checked out the passers-by, their handguns, loaded and ready, tucked securely beneath their dark jackets.

Chapter 20
1986

"Dad! Dad!"

The old man shook away his dream and glanced at the three people in the cubicle. A curtain had been drawn around his bed. A translucent tube running into his right nostril tightened and he moved his head forward to release the pressure. Another tube ran from his left arm and looped upward to a bottle of glucose. He felt tied up, totally restricted. His sleep had been too deep. Slowly the shapes that moved before him found their form.

Theca, his Star of the Veldt, sat close, leaning forward, holding on to his mottled right hand with both of hers. Her eyes were sore, yet wide, begging for his attention. Sally sat to his left, fussing in her bag, bringing out a bottle of orange juice and fresh, neatly folded pyjamas and newspapers. Ted, Theca's husband, stood close to the end of the bed. It was his first visit to see Tom and he was shocked to find just how ill he looked. Beside the apparent weight loss the skin on his neck was grey and loose and his brown eyes were dull and speckled. His thinning white hair was ruffled and his normal imposing frame seemed somehow fragile and weak.

"Hello darlings."

Tom's eyes flicked to each of them in turn and rested on his daughter. Although glazed they appeared to caress her gently.

"Hello Dad," she said bravely.

"My, you've turned out so beautiful," he said weakly.

"What have they done to you?" she whispered.

"Baby, I'm happy. They're shooting me with so much dope that I can't feel a thing. And it's all legit, paid for by the NHS. Half the town could score on the shit they're pumping into me." He chuckled.

Theca looked across at her mother.

"They said he was ill," she said, "but he looks great to me."

Tom looked from the women to his son-in-law.

"Hello Teddy boy!"

"All right, Tom?" Ted said thickly.

"Gawd! Glad to see you're wearing your best suit to come and see me." Tom grinned and turned back to Sally, "Hello, Darling, you been all right? Have they been taking care of you?"

"Everything's fine," she said and in a rush added, "I've got the photographs back."

"Did they come out? Let me see." He reached for his spectacles, careful not to knock the tubes or the glasses on the cluttered side table.

Sally handed him one photograph at a time.

"Look at little Alan, and there's Mark, and there's little Tommy. Here's one of the girls together."

Tom chuckled. "Have you heard from Jessica and John?"

"They phoned last night. It's too early for a postcard from Tunisia. Maybe it will come tomorrow."

"He'll be too busy to write postcards," Tom laughed. He finished looking at the photographs. "How many came out? I was having trouble with the camera. Ted, count them. How many are there?"

Ted took the photographs and began counting. He lost it at fifteen and began again.

"Dave and Tommy are outside," Sally said.

Tom nodded. "Well, boy, how many?"

"Twenty-six."

"Well, done them, didn't we? Twenty-four film, twenty-six shots. There's nothing wrong with that camera!" He turned back to Sally. "Frenchie saw me just before opening time. Told me he'd seen you all this afternoon. So now you know."

Sally sniffed.

"It'll be ten days before the results are through," Ted said. "We'll take it from there."

"Don't be bleedin' daft. It's all over, boy. They had a look and there's nothing they can do."

"That's not what he said, Tom. He said he didn't recognize it."

"Bullshit!"

Ted shook his head.

"Sorry about the holiday, my love." Tom squeezed Sally's hand. "We should have flown out today; would have been sunning on the Algarve by now."

"Sod the holiday," Sally said. "I just want you to get well. I just want you to come home."

Tom turned to Theca. "How's my star? Been helping your mother?"

"They all have," Sally said.

"What about the kids? They're not missing school, are they?"

Theca shook her head and grasped his hand tighter.

"Take your mother out for a cup of coffee," Tom said gently. "Send in Dave and Tommy. Ted, you stay a while. I want a few minutes with them. Then you come back and hold my hand again. I like you holding my hand, Darling. Even when I doze off you keep holding it. I've been so tired lately. It must be the stuff they're shoving in the drip. Now, go on both of you. Go and have a cup of coffee."

Sally leant across and kissed his cheek. "I'll see you in a minute."

"Go on then," he said gently.

The girls left Ted looking down into Tom's tired eyes.

"There have been other things, boy, over the last few months. I wasn't born yesterday even though you lot think I was."

Ted nodded. He looked at the floor, not wanting to meet the old man's searching gaze. Eventually he said, "You should have said something."

"Yeah, and end up emptying a bag of piss every twenty minutes for the sake of an extra couple of weeks. I don't think so." He shook his head and whispered so the people beyond the screens wouldn't hear, "I had a diabolical time back there. They didn't put me out proper, you know. I was strapped up and saw myself hanging over a bath – a white bath – while they cut me."

Even though he guessed the old man had dreamt it, Ted nodded.

Dave and Tommy walked in and took seats beside the bed. Expressions were fixed.

"All right, Pop?" Dave asked.

Tom waved Dave's concern aside and regarded his youngest son. He said, "Blimey! You look cream-crackered, boy."

Tommy flashed him a grin. "I was up most of the night."

"Gather round then," Tom said and waited for the others to lean forward.

"First things first," Dave said. "Pop, I want to move you to a private ward. We've got to make you secure."

Before he'd finished speaking Tom was shaking his head.

"You're not having me in bleedin' BUPA. How many times do we need to talk about it, eh? I told you, boy, every time someone pays for private health they accept there's a second-class service for everybody else. The poorest in this country should get the same health care as the Queen of bleedin' England. Anything else is criminal. Enough said. Let's not have any more repeats. What do you think this is, the BBC?"

"I ain't talking about the rights and wrongs, Pop," Dave insisted. "I'm talking about security. Forget the private hospital, if that's what you want, but things are warming up out there and it would be easier for us to take care of you in a private room. I can't have soldiers marching in and out here, can I?"

"What's all this then? Soldiers! You think this is World War Two? With all this lot in here no one's going to try it on. In any case, the place is crawling with Old Bill. They outnumber your guys three to one. I'm safer staying put and, what's more, I like the company." He nodded to a gap in the curtain where in the next bed an old toothless wonder was smiling stupidly their way. "Anyway, show me where it's written that I've got to make it easy for you?" He chuckled. "Now, quickly, let's get down to business. Tell me what's been happening?"

They began to whisper.

The Italian-Americans, know sometimes as the Mafia, sometimes as wiseguys, with their supplies of dope from Central and South America, wanted to organize a nationwide distribution, with their gaming clubs and other business interests fronting the operation. Because of his arrangement with the Chinese, Tom was against the deal and Coddy Hughes was against the trade altogether. Coddy's point blank refusal to deal in dope was fuelling the current situation. Mad Mick McGovern who ran most of the Scottish cities was not only prepared but was eager to expand into Coddy's Midland territory. Coddy had grown old and soft and his organization lacked its previous strength. People no longer feared him and when that had gone so had respect. It was only his connections with the Smiths that had kept him in business so long.

"Coddy won't change his mind," Dave whispered. "Not today, not next year. The bottom line, Pop, is that Mick is going to hit Coddy. In order to do that, he's going to hit us. If we're forced into an open war we'll all come out of it so weak the Yanks will move in without raising a sweat. Christ! The Godfathers already own Runnymede and it isn't the sunshine and their strolls around Windsor Castle that's keeping them here. They're sitting, waiting like a pack of hyenas. They've already got their kid's names down for public school!"

Tom nodded grimly. He opened his hand and relaxed, swallowed loudly against the tube.

There was a savage irony in what his eldest son had said. The Americans with their wop families had got their foothold in Runnymede because of Dave; concessions to get him off the hook, to have those contracts cancelled all those years ago. Of course, the injured party had argued long and loud about letting Dave get off scot-free, but he had been overruled. It was business. To the men who controlled the business that was all that mattered. Tom remembered how he'd agreed to launder a large slice of the proceeds of their narcotic business through his clubs and allowed the Americans inroads into the capital's gaming.

He sighed. "So, how did you get on, Tommy?" he asked his youngest.

Tommy shrugged and said, "I never got to see him, Pop. Went through the prelims and had a long chat to McLachlan, Mick's banker, who seemed pretty enthusiastic and was trying to set up a meet. I was waiting for the call when I heard about you on the one o'clock."

Dave interrupted: "He was waiting to talk to Mick, Pop, explain that we would negotiate with Coddy, but as soon as Mick heard about you he tooled up and moved against Tommy."

The old man examined his youngest son.

"You all right, boy?"

Tommy gave him a raffish grin.

"You be careful."

"Tried to take him out," Dave continued. "Look! It's headlines."

Tom scanned the newspaper and said "I've seen it already. It's well out of order. Who's this other guy?"

Tommy said, "He was giving me a lift."

"Find out where they took him. Look after him."

"That's all in hand, Pop," Dave said. "Ted's taking care of it."

Tom glanced at Ted for confirmation.

"I've got his wife coming down, got her and the kids booked into the Savoy. It looks like he'll be off work for a few months, and they'd got fuck-all to start with. I figured maybe a monkey up front and a ton a week plus the rent. After that we can use him. Tommy rates him as a driver."

Tom nodded. "That's good. Mind, should have used your bonce. She isn't going to feel at home in the Saveloy, is she, poor cow? Get one of the girls to take her out and buy some clothes for her and for the kids. Can't have them looking out of place. Get her hair done, the business, right? Make sure she's met at the station and lay on a car to take her to the hospital. We can't have her catching buses. Make sure you see her personally, Ted. I want her to understand she's not on her own. We owe the family and we pay our debts."

Dave was eager to move on. "Anyway, we've had out problems. Mick's a mad bastard. We haven't faced anything like this before."

"Who hasn't?" Tom laughed quietly and his eyes lit up. "Who hasn't?"

"Even our friends are getting jumpy. The coast is holding back, Liverpool who knows? They're coming to see us tomorrow. I was thinking of postponing it."

"Don't do that, boy!" Tom grunted. "These Scouse gits only come down here once a year and this year they'll be looking to see that we've got it all under control. They'll be looking for weaknesses. As far as we're concerned it's business as usual. There's no problem. Problem! What problem? A few murmurs from north of the border, call that a problem? That's what I want them to think. Confidence, boys, that's the ticket. Give them their leg over and send them home thinking we're stronger than ever. Make sure you've got it all in hand, Ted, like last year."

Ted nodded.

"Dave, I think you better go and see your father-in-law," Tom went on and sighed. "See how the land lies. I think, maybe, it's time he thought about retiring. See what he's got to say. You better get up there in the morning. After that we'll be in a position to talk to these guineas. I know they'd prefer to deal with us. They trust Mick even less than we do."

He shifted his position on the bed then glanced at his youngest son.

"Tommy, you better get some kip, boy. After that I want you to help Ted sort out Liverpool. If we can stay friendly with them it might keep Mick guessing and buy us some time." He turned back to Ted. "Teddy boy, I want you to stay close to The Tower as a link. The Castle will have to manage by itself. Get Bernard to take over the accounts for a while. He's done it before. There might be a cash-flow problem before long, especially if we have to buy some extra muscle. You better see our bankers and let them know we might need some heavy and sudden cash withdrawals. They'll sort it out. And Dave, safe houses, get them stocked up, get them ready, make some promises."

Tom leant back on his pillow. "I'm getting so tired. You better get on with it. Send the girls back in. Be careful, all of you. Take care of your families. Take no chances. Make sure there's someone with the kids. And put some extra security on all the houses. Dave, you better send someone to Tunisia to keep a discreet eye open. We wouldn't want to spoil their honeymoon, would we?"

Dave didn't tell him that he'd already sent minders to look after Jessica and John. Instead he said, "Jessica phoned earlier. She knows you're ill, that's all."

"That's good. I don't want them worrying. I don't want anyone knowing the truth. I'm here for investigation and that's all. Mind you, they'll get the papers even if they are a day late."

The boys nodded gravely.

"Send in the girls," Tom ordered.

While they waited in the waiting area to go into the ward – two at a time the rule said but the staff stretched it to three – the family had barely noticed the old man in the corner and if they had they were not sure whether he was a visitor or a patient. Dave had glanced his way but instantly dismissed him as harmless. He was old, well over retirement, his tall, heavy-set frame emphasized by a thick navy-blue overcoat reaching below his knees. In the heat of the hospital the coat was absurd and Dave disregarded the man as a dimwit.

The old man waited hours until the family left the hospital, until the sister and the nurses called for an end to visiting time, and then he made his move. His movements were purposeful and plodding, made with the stiffness and pain of arthritic joints, yet a power was still evident. Skin had folded and pulled away from his dull grey eyes, cheeks had sunken and become blotchy. A circular brown scar on his temple fed a ragged, hairless tributary across the side of his head. Age had opened his pores and mashed his nose and what might once have been a physical attribute could now have been a spongy embarrassment. But age had also diminished all feeling of vanity along with all other such profound thoughts and what was left was an automaton.

A petite Chinese nurse moved from her desk to stop him. "Excuse me, Sir," she began and put her small hand on his arm. He stopped and slowly turned to face her. Her pretty eyes widened fractionally as she recognized danger and her step back was instinctive.

"Just a few minutes then," she said and quickly walked away.

From the middle of the aisle he watched her go and remembered a conversation. Chinese women walked like men; there was no swing of the hips; flat arses and slant-eyes. All women were full of crap! The next one who even looked at him was going to get her eyes poked out. As he watched her hurry away the shadowy image of another girl ghosted into his head. She was Chinese too. There was blood everywhere. He was tearing at her clothes. She was screaming. Or was she laughing at him, laughing through the flames and smoke of hell? He shook away the memory and smiled inwardly; there was no change to his expression.

He knew that at least two men were watching him closely as he approached the corner bed. A porter and a man in the bed opposite were both on Dave's strength. Dave had paid the registrar a small fortune to get his men into the hospital. The old man saw how Tom Smith waved away their concern with the slightest movement of his hand. The porter continued stacking his trolley and the man opposite buried his face again in the *Daily Mirror*.

If the old man was surprised at how ill Tom looked it didn't show. The grey eyes softened as he settled back in an upright chair. The plastic creaked as it took his weight.

"My old friend," Tom whispered. "You're looking good."

"Crap! I look like shit. And you?"

Tom gave a faint resigned shrug that barely troubled his shoulders. He touched the translucent plaster that held the tube to his nose.

"It's been a long time, Sergeant."

"You're right, too long. I remember the old days, Tom. I dream about them."

Tom Smith nodded slowly and said, "I know what you mean."

"There's no harm in it, is there? At the end of the day that's all that counts, isn't it? Memories! That's all we've got left. We sure as fuck can't take anything else with us."

"I haven't gone yet."

"I didn't mean that."

"Tact was never your strong point." Tom smiled.

"We fought some fucking battles, though, didn't we? Remember the South Coast and Bryant, the look on his ugly boat when we told him to walk the plank? And Chinatown, now that was a bit special."

"I wasn't there."

"No, you weren't. I was." The old man's eyes glazed in reverie, getting off again.

Tom studied his worn features. He asked, "What have you been doing lately?"

The big man grunted. At length he said, "Waiting for your call."

"Well, now you're here." Tom nodded. "Are you ready to help me out for one last time?"

As he read into the words the big man's eyes betrayed him. He reached forward and put his huge hand over Tom's, careful not to knock the drip feed, and felt the cold touch.

He said respectfully, "You ask me as if there's a question. You've never had to ask yourself whether you can count on me."

"I know that, my old friend. I know that. In forty years I've counted on you more than anyone and no one ever knew it. We've hardly met a handful of times in all that time and there's been no recognition for you."

"That's the way I wanted it."

Tom looked saddened. He nodded and said quietly, "It's a waste."

"It's not!" The old man trembled in a sudden burst of anger. "It's not a waste!"

"Well, my friend, I am in desperate trouble. And I need your help again."

The grey eyes flickered enthusiastically. He seemed delighted.

Tom continued, "But what of afterwards? There will be no more calls. What can I give you?"

"Forget the future. Who cares? There is no fucking future. Look at me. I'll even have to hurry on this one or I won't make it. Tell me what you want?"

"Lean closer then. I'll whisper. This lot could be wired."

The grey eyes narrowed slyly, flicking here and there in search of the hidden devices. He nodded and moved forward so that his ear was only inches from Tom Smith's lips.

Shortly after the old man had left another man in an ill-fitting white porter's jacket that stretched at the seams across his broad shoulders, lumbered forward across the linoleum floor and manoeuvred a trolley stacked with books into the ward. He was what they called a volunteer worker but in order to get the job for just an hour it had been necessary to threaten the regular volunteer with a choice of castration or a long cup of tea at the hospital café. The charity worker had thought for quite some time before deciding on the tea.

Totally ignoring the calls from other patients, grunting an apology to a small nurse he almost flattened, he pulled up beside Tom's bed. Beads of sweat ran from his grooved forehead over his craggy tanned features. His path through the ward was marked by a trail of paperbacks on the floor. He mopped his face with a huge white handkerchief and blew out his cheeks. Mike Mountford had been with Tom, off and on, for thirty years. While Raymond Jones had been the most famous, and probably the best, cat burglar in the country, Mike Mountford had established his own reputation as the fireman, the torch, equally at home with explosives or matches.

"See you haven't passed your driving test," Tom joked.

"Hello, Boss," Mountford said in a deep breathless voice. He turned up his hearing aid. "That's better. Now I can hear you."

Something in his small green eyes offered affection. Nothing else about his looks did.

"Mike, boy, how are you?" The speckled hand raised and beckoned him forward. "Come closer. You can guarantee the filth is listening."

"This is going to be difficult then 'cos I'm having trouble with the old hearing lately. How are you with the sign language?" Mountford smiled. "How are you Boss? I've been hearing some diabolical rumours about your health."

"Tell the bastards that I haven't gone yet! What's been happening?"

"Dave's coping pretty well. Bit heavy-handed but that's to be expected. He never was a ballerina, was he?"

"I hope not, Mike. I think you'll find that ballerinas are all women."

"Huh! What about that big geezer with the long hair, Nuri something or other? Nuri Gella?"

Tom grinned.

He remembered his father sitting him on the bed and telling him that in his lifetime he would be lucky to find half a dozen men that he could trust, really trust, and that even they could not be trusted with your woman. He shook away the memory.

Mike Mountford waved at the warm air. He said, "Now Tommy's back, Dave will calm down."

"Tommy was lucky," Tom snapped. "For Gawd sake, it sounds like the Royal Family on one of their pheasant shoots. This is England! London! Not the fucking Falls Road. I mean, for Gawd's sake, shotguns!" He shook his head in dismay. "You knew Mad Mick in the old days, didn't you?"

Mountford nodded slowly. "He was a smart arse little toerag even then. Always was a curmudgeon, never any humour about him – typical bleedin' Scot. He dropped out of Edinburgh University to join the Marines before ending up in London and hitting it off with the twins." The fireman snorted. "As soon as they were banged up he pissed off north again. No one heard from him for a couple of years and then he surfaced in Glasgow…"

Tom Smith knew Mick McGovern's history by heart. He changed the subject. "The Scousers are coming down tomorrow. Will they line up with us?"

"Doubt it," the fireman said earnestly and shook his head. "Arseholes have been waiting to spread out for a long time. See this as their big chance."

Tom's eyes hooded. "Will they go it alone or will they line up with Mick?"

Mountford offered him a thoughtful look. "That's a tricky one. If Mick has made them some promises they might be tempted."

"I'd hate to see any trouble on The Barge.

"They ain't that stupid, Boss. The best they could do is Ted. He's the only family that's going to be there."

"No. I told Tommy to help out."

"Still, they ain't going to cause trouble with Dave on the loose. It's Dave they're scared shitless of. You and I know different, or at least we think we do, but the faces out there, and that includes north of the border, think Dave's a fucking psycho!"

Tom sighed. It sounded like resignation. He said, "I'd still like to have a few people in reserve."

"I know what you mean, Boss. Leave it to me."

Mike Mountford stood up to go. "Do you want one of these books? I've got the Godfather here somewhere."

"No," Tom sighed. "Saw the film. I can't be bothered with fiction." He chuckled, and then he looked up and said seriously, "Take care of my family, Mike. This thing could get out of hand. Let me know what goes on."

"OK, Boss."

The trolley rumbled on its way to the double doors and was left blocking the lift entrance.

Alone again, Tom lay back with his thoughts. His main concern was his eldest son and whether, given the present climate, Dave would keep the lid on his temper. He had always been impulsive, his fiery temperament had often got in the way of reason; violence had all too often been his first resort. This flash temper was a sign of immaturity. To an extent age had brought it under control but it was still there, just a little deeper beneath the surface. When he looked at Dave he saw a cold heart; there was about him a mark of fury. He exuded danger like some people exuded sexuality. Tom's world was full of heartless men, their cruelty legend, yet even they feared his eldest son. In the whole of the Smoke, a city filled with the violent, the uncompromising, the most dangerous of men, Dave held the position of dubious veneration. It was largely undeserved; it had grown from rumour, that he had been involved in this and that, particularly the Chinese Wars that left a dreadful scar in the hearts of many men. But it was there, nevertheless, this respect, this reverence. Tom Smith thought about these things and hoped that his eldest son would remain in control. Dave's short fuse was the one variable in his careful plan.

Chapter 21

The Eagle Public House had been partly demolished in the war but they had rebuilt it. It was here that Tom Smith had first set up in business. It was gone now for the property developers and bent councillors had destroyed the old city far more effectively than the Luftwaffe ever could. They worked from the inside, like a cancer, and just as deadly. They had destroyed a way of life, a history, and in its place they had put something else, something superficial, far removed from Old London Town. They had stolen its soul. In place of the Eagle a multi-storey office block towered over the surroundings and the locals called it The Tower. The gymnasium next to the Eagle had gone too, for boxing was a thing of the past – some people did not believe it – but the land had stayed with the family. On the site, a hotel took its neighbour's name and under quiet green neon spelling out THE TOWER a doorman welcomed the visitor. The Tower Casino with its nightclub and hotel that included six penthouse suites among its one hundred and sixty bedrooms had become a London landmark and was frequented by celebrities from the studios and the castles. Together with its sister clubs, The Arsenal, The Moat, The Fortress and The Castle in London, and The Martello on the Kent coast, it was the legitimate end of the Smith family business. The Barge on the river was their latest acquisition but The Tower remained the jewel in the Smith's crown. It had been their first to open and it remained their headquarters. In the offices behind the restaurant, away from the casino's gaming tables and the noise from the nightclub, the business was conducted. Adjacent to the offices was a four-roomed suite and it was here, in the private bar that the brothers and Ted would meet.

The Smiths had a legitimate workforce of some four hundred and sixty people and this figure did not include the part-timers and the cleaners and the vast army of small, independent businesses that relied on the Smiths for subcontract work, nor did it include the businesses that the Smiths part owned or had a vested interest in; even that was just the tip, the up-front, insurance-stamped brigade; beneath the surface at least that number again relied on the Smiths for a living. The accounts department along with HR, payroll and purchasing was stationed over at The Castle where Ted spent most of his time but it was here, in these offices and the flat next door, where the major decisions were made.

Tommy's role was still incidental. To a large extent his father had kept him on the periphery of the business. His further education had come first. It had come as a surprise to both Dave and Ted that the old man had chosen his youngest son to make the Glasgow trip. They decided it was a ploy and that by sending his least experienced emissary their father was showing Mick that he was regarded as nothing more than a minor irritation and barely worth considering. For the most, Tommy was shielded, certainly from the collections and the potential violence that they involved. He stuck closely to his father, away from the running of the business for that, on a daily basis, was passing more and more to Dave and Ted.

Dave thought it was a good thing. He recognized compassion in his younger brother and that was dangerous. If not a weakness, exactly, it was certainly a handicap. Their business was war, it was fought on the Capital's streets, and compassion meant anarchy. Criticism, differences of opinion and even voices raised loudly, were put down swiftly and clinically. Anything else would mean government by the people – and that inevitably meant no government at all.

The Tower Casino earned a handsome profit but more importantly, its laundry service was invaluable. Together with the Ritz and Casanova it made London the most successful square mile outside Las Vegas.

In the business the problem was and had always been the laundering of dirty money. Vast amounts of hard cash were generated from racketeering and drug-trafficking spin-offs and while the casino could handle a large chunk it was still necessary to use the jeweller in Park Lane as well as the Mayfair financiers. It was getting more difficult all the time. The old Marbella run that had been useful for many years was now fully committed to the South Americans and so had a lot of the 'helpful' banks now relocated in South America, Chile in particular, closer to the cocaine producers. With Tom's approval it was left to Ted to come up with an alternative and he found it on Sheddon Road in George Town, the capital of Grand Cayman, the quintessential English colony of church spires and brightly coloured wooden shops. He'd come to an agreement with a suburban chartered accountant in Hampton Wick. His business debts had been cleared and his casino marker for fifty-five grand cancelled. Under the guise of day-trippers from a cruise liner and carrying suitcases each containing 1.5 million in sterling, he and the accountant stepped off the tender on to the quayside, and joined the daily flock of like-minded guys from the US with similar missions in mind. They were there to meet the accountant's 'colleague', a fifth generation Caymanian who owned a number of businesses including Smith Cove Limited. The three million was to be invested via Smith Cove Limited into a Cayman based liquidity fund that traded on the overnight currency markets. Three companies (marine salvage and insurance were always good bets) were to be incorporated in the Isle of Man – Barrule Limited, Snaefell Limited and Meayll Limited – of which the accountant would act as a director along with an Isle of Man resident who was supplying the registered office. The money would be registered in the name of Meayll Limited and sit in the fund for three months or so before being paid out to the accounts in the Isle of Man. The resident would then arrange for the purchase of council houses in Liverpool or some other northern city where property prices were spiralling. Barrule Limited and Snaefell Limited would act as advisors to Meayll Limited and receive large commission payments through the accountant's client monies account. This in turn would find its way back to the family. Since then the trip was made on a monthly basis, not by Ted – he had other business to take care of – but by trusted employees whose National Insurance contributions were now being paid for by the debt-free accountant in Hampton Wick. The suitcases they carried were considerably heavier than the originals.

Dave made The Tower in the late evening and met Barry Theroux, his manager, in the lounge. A group of minders in dark suits sat at one end and acknowledged him in a friendly relaxed way. He knew that at least two of them were packing and that the others could lay their hands on a hidden store of shooters within seconds. Theroux was in control; quiet, unassuming, thoughtful and unruffled, he'd started working for the firm as a croupier and had remained with the family all his adult life. A handsome man, spotless and manicured, his dress was immaculate. His voice was level and dependable.

"Evening, Dave. The others are upstairs."

Dave nodded. He was hungry but decided dinner could wait. He rarely dined in The Tower's French restaurant in any case, preferring to have a tray brought up to his room. Most days he just wanted to eat without making it an event.

He asked, "Anything going down?"

Theroux shook his head. After the attack on Tommy he'd tightened security and brought in more muscle. "Pretty quiet," he said. "The trouble has kept some of the regulars away."

"We could do without it," Dave muttered. "But it was always going to be this way."

"There's one or two staying loyal. Omar has asked for the penthouse tomorrow night."

Dave insisted that gratis suites were checked out with him personally, just as his father had insisted on doing in the old days. He gave Barry Theroux discretion when it came to the standard rooms but the suites were different and kept for very special clients. Most of them were in the public eye, politicians, high court judges and other dignitaries. They often brought along their mistresses or boyfriends in the certain knowledge that their reputations would remain intact. Family values and holier-than-thou principles could still be proposed across the hallowed floors of the Houses and across the benches of the courts without interruption.

"On account that he dropped a million last time I think we can afford it, don't you?"

Theroux smiled tightly and went on, "There are a couple of footballers pissing it up, as they do, but we'll keep an eye on them."

Footballers were regular customers but they had never learned to hold their booze and often got out of hand. They were hopeless gamblers, particularly when they were showing off with their 'away' girlfriends, so they were always welcome. More to the point, their clubs would never argue about payment for damage or to cover any disruption, and it was always cash in hand. Football was another business where cash transactions kept the taxman out of the game.

They paused at the Showcase Restaurant to watch a few scantily dressed girls kicking the air. The place was quiet and a quick glance confirmed that most of the customers were tourists. Waitresses in short black skirts weaved between the tables searching for tips. *Where and When* filtered from the stage. It was his father's favourite tune. Nicole Ricaud was at the microphone and making a good fist of the number, singing half of it in French. She was taking time off from *Showboat* in the West End and was tied to four shows a week for a month in exchange for her husband's marker. Small change for the prestige she brought with her. It was as good as a royal stamp of approval. At any other time she would have filled the house.

Dave pulled a face and said, "All this fucking aggro makes you lose your appetite."

"It's the same upstairs," Theroux said. "Plenty of street punters but the heavy rollers are giving it a miss."

A short, smartly dressed woman of about sixty approached them. She was slightly overweight and breathless, her face and body showing the droop of age.

Dave said, "Hello, Jane."

"How is he, Dave? I'm hearing all kinds of rumours." Beneath her thick spectacles her green eyes filled with concern.

She was in charge of the hotel staff across the entire firm. More than that even, for she had the old man's ear and she clearly loved him to bits. Dave had often wondered whether there was more to it, and that perhaps they'd got it together in their younger days, but he would never dare ask. His father was an intensely private man who'd become more strait-laced as the years had gone by. What was very clear was that his father had always found time for her, no matter how trivial the problem. He indulged her in situations where he would have dismissed other people out of hand. On one occasion he'd heard her bossing him around and with the exception of Dave's mother that was unheard of.

He took her hand. "It's not good, Jane. Would you like to go and see him? Apart from family you're the only one he'd be glad to see."

She shook her head and her eyes brimmed.

"No," she whispered and flicked away a swelling tear. "I don't think so." She wandered off, looking older, and suddenly abandoned.

Dave and his manager watched her go and shared an equivocal glance before moving across the deep royal-blue pile to the lifts. Tom used to quip about the carpet: 'We're establishment, ain't we?' and that knowing sparkle would light his brown eyes.

"Seeing Jane reminds me," Barry Theroux said. "The old man Hilkowitz has been on the blower."

"That old market trader; what does he want?"

Theroux grunted. Hilkowitz owned a supermarket chain that kept half the farmers in the country in business.

"He didn't want to concern the family at such a time but if the worst comes to the worst he'd be honoured if you'd let him take care of the arrangements."

Dave sighed. The chain also owned a string of funeral directors and chapels of rest.

"Breaks your heart, doesn't it?" he said. "But our old man would probably prefer the Co-op." He paused to consider the request and went on, "Get back to him, Barry, and tell him you've spoken to me and that the family would be very grateful for his help. We won't forget it."

"He knows that, Dave."

A cover-girl receptionist in a blue uniform smiled brightly with promise as they passed her counter. Dave left Theroux at the lift and made his way to the office.

His brother and Ted had already raided the bar. They watched as he filled another glass and followed him as he moved across to the window to look out over the shining city.

"Well, what do we do?" Dave turned to face them. "I'm not sure we can wait any longer before making some decisions."

"Like what?" Tommy asked sharply.

"Like giving some of it back; maybe you hadn't noticed but there's an army on our doorstep. Unless we start dishing it out they're going to march in here! Having a pop at you was just the start."

"That's well out of order, Dave, and you know it. We do what he tells us, right up until the time comes that he can't tell us anymore. After that he'll leave us some instructions." Tommy was adamant. He shook his head angrily. Somehow Dave's suggestion was an insult to his father. He turned to Ted for support. "What do you think?"

"I go along with you, Tommy. I think we can afford to leave it for a while."

Dave relented. He knew he was on a loser. "Fair enough," he said, "But don't forget that the people who dealt with the old man aren't necessarily going to deal with us."

"He knows that. He won't leave us in the air. You're underestimating the business, Dave. They'll deal with us."

A knock on the door interrupted them and they turned to see Jimmy Jones.

"Sorry to barge in," he said in his Welsh accent.

"All right, Jimmy?" Tommy asked.

"Peter Hough's outside. Wants to know if he can have a word?"

Dave cut in: "What the fuck does he want?"

Tommy turned to the others. "He did me a favour last night."

Dave nodded. "Yes, that's true. You come in too, Jimmy."

Jimmy whispered into the corridor and was followed into the room by Peter Hough. Peter stood by the door shuffling his thick frame from one foot to the other.

"All right, Pete? What is it?"

"All right everybody. Dave, you know I left the firm? I left on good terms, mostly for the kid's sake. I done two years and I thought that was it. Now I hear of your troubles and I can't stay away. Take me back, Dave, you won't regret it."

"Hang on a moment, Peter," Tommy said. "What about Denise? She doesn't want you back in this game."

"I know that, Tommy. Christ! I know that. But there ain't another way. I've given it a crack but it ain't me; eight to five, fucking around, doing the same thing day in and day out, pressing this and that button. It ain't me."

"You did Tommy a favour last night and I'm grateful for that, Pete. If you want a few sovs to hold you over it's not a problem."

"No, Dave. I ain't begging. Fuck that. I want you to take me on again. I know I'll have to start at the bottom. But I ain't taking nothing I don't earn. Never have. As for last night, let's just say I was glad to help."

Dave looked from Tommy to Ted. Eventually he said, "All right, Pete. Stick with Jimmy. He'll use you."

"Cheers, Dave. You won't regret it."

"I better not." He nodded. "All right, wait outside."

Once the door closed Dave turned to Jimmy Jones. "Watch him, Jimmy. I'm not sure about him." Dave's eyes narrowed as he wondered whether he'd made the right decision. "There was a time when he was useful but he was nicked for a garage load of dodgy videos and the toerag never said a bleedin' thing to us. Free enterprise isn't encouraged, so watch him. I'm not sure he wasn't fucking around with more than a bit of puff, either. Those silver bins he used to wear always hid his minces from the day. Know what I mean?" Dave paused and made sure Jimmy caught his glance before asking, "What did you find out?"

Jimmy shrugged and said matter-of-factly, "A Yank. His name's Herman Tartt. He's been over here two months. He works for Runnymede, drives for Clough and Valenti. He had a couple of drinks and left about half-an-hour after you. You were right about the limp, Boss. He uses a stick. No problem. He wasn't interested in anyone else."

Dave understood and nodded.

"What's that all about?" Tommy asked.

"Nothing, just a face from the past. It's not important." Dave changed the subject and addressed Jimmy again. "Let's get down to business. Let's talk about The Barge and keeping the scousers happy. Is your end sorted?"

"All tied up, Dave," Jimmy confirmed.

"Teddy will sail with you like last year. It's important for us that it goes right."

"Right then, I'll see you tomorrow night Ted. I better get back. I think Barry's got more minders down there than he's got customers."

"Know all the faces?" Dave asked.

"Yes, no sweat."

"See you, Jimmy." Before Jimmy Jones closed the door, Dave added, "Keep an eye on Houghie."

Jimmy nodded and pulled the door shut behind him.

Peter Hough never stood a chance. At an early age his future was already mapped.

At a day old he became a statistic, abandoned. Foster parents took him as a baby. At the age of thirteen and because his foster parents could no longer manage, he was moved to a boarding school for delinquents. He was placed as an 'Unwanted Child' but it was the only place on offer. From there he went to St Alban's children's home and then Sparrow Herne children's home in Bushy. At seventeen he went to a working boy's hostel in Houslow. He'd been dipping all his life, sometimes wallets from coat pockets, anytime from shops. Now, at the hostel, he was introduced to burglary. Two of the lads went out every night and a strange, middle-aged man made frequent visits to collect any goods they stole. His first job, with one of the lads who showed him the ropes, was a milkman's house on a Thursday night. Milkmen are not supposed to keep their collection money at home, for insurance reasons if nothing else, but they invariably do. It proved an easy tickle, smashing the kitchen window, the key left on the inside of the back door, in and out in a minute flat, and they were out with almost three hundred pounds. It had started, and within three months it led to a six-month stay at a young offender's detention centre in Nottingham. He'd been grassed by one of the other lads. His first lesson was that there was no such thing as honour among thieves. The DC was run along military lines, uncompromising and tough, but even while he was there he was getting high on the memory of his jobs. On the outside again he progressed from breaking glass to a syrup skin of cloth and a plumber's plunger. He learned about security alarms and shaving foam – cavity wall filler was even better – and that the Old Bill rarely took notice of shop alarms, that broad daylight was the best time and that end of terrace or detached were the easy options. He was fined and put on probation; he did six months and then two years and then eighteen months.

In the Scrubs he shared a cell with two other men. He bathed once a week. His food was steamed. With the exception of his cellmates he never talked to other prisoners. He never talked to the screws. There was never any counselling.

In Pentonville there were mice and cockroaches. The place was filled with tramps and dropouts.

In Wandsworth dope was the thing. There he learned how to spill bleach on to the nonces and how to sprinkle Ajax on to their food without getting caught.

In High Point parcels were thrown in over the fences and dope was the thing again. A lot of the screws were bent.

It was shortly after his release from High Point that Jack McVitti introduced him to Dave. Dave never had a lot of time for Jack the Hat but until booze, black bombers and purple hearts got the better of him he enjoyed a reputation as an East End hard man. Peter Hough spent more and more time with Dave until eventually he began to drive for the family. This led to other things, including a spell on the collections. Things went well until he began to deal privately and he was done for receiving.

When he was released he moved in with Denise and for two years he worked in a machine room, pressing studs into metal boxes. Now he was back. He was working for Dave again, but this time he had long-term plans.

Chapter 22

Theca was named after a wild rose. Her parents were visiting South Africa when Sally was pregnant. Food poisoning put her into hospital. Tom turned up with some local flowers called Theca, the Star of the Veldt. He kept the label and when his daughter arrived he had a ready-made name. He still called her his Star.

She and Ted had started dating when she was a fourth-former and he was at university. When he left the London School with his accountancy credentials under his belt, Tom had invited him to join the firm and she saw even more of him than before. Marriage had seemed like a natural progression. It was only later that she realized that she loved him more like a brother than a lover and that her marriage was like an opera without the aria. It ate into her soul and eventually into their relationship. She still loved him, but as before, it remained a non-physical and distant feeling, more a sense of deprivation than of loss.

Knowing that Dave had put minders on her, Theca took special care to lose them in the traffic build-up around Marble Arch then used the next ten minutes to confirm it before parking her car in a cobblestone Victorian courtyard in Grosvenor Gardens. She didn't notice the pale blue Escort parked opposite on a yellow line, or the two men in the front who seemed to take not the slightest interest in her. Once she was inside the mews flat the men relaxed, finished their animated conversation and got on with the serious business of watching the street. Beneath their seats were loaded revolvers that they would use without hesitation. They were soldiers, top class, veterans of Bloody Sunday and Goose Green, selected for their pitiless qualities, and paid accordingly.

It was a quiet corner of London, a spit from the palace and the tourist hordes, a place where celebrities could live in comparative seclusion. Birdcage Walk was a few hundred yards away and the Star and her lover had spent many hours during the spring wandering with the courting couples that poured from the packed offices, as if the Walk offered them privacy or at least immunity, during their stolen lunch hours. Hand-in-hand the couples went across the greenery, enjoying the anonymity, the secretary and her boss, the junior buyer and the copy typist, the lovers, feigning affection, excited by the mystery, moving through the ritual of deceit and exaggeration. If the Walk offered Theca and her lover respite it was during the endless afternoons in his flat above the courtyard where, uninhibited, the restraints of marriage cast aside, they wrapped around each other on a joyride of passion. They made love until they were sore and shattered and until they fell into a post-coital sleep. And then it had been like a dream, until the next time.

"God, I've wanted to see you. I've thought about ringing you a thousand times. I needed to know that you were all right."

He closed the heavy door behind her and they embraced in the wide entrance hall.

"Hold me, please. I'm not all right." She dropped her brown *Chanel* handbag on to the polished floor.

He sighed, "Bad news?"

"My father's dying."

He nodded quietly. "What can I do?"

"Hold me," she whispered and began to cry. Her tears marked the wool of her grey jacket. He led her by the hand toward a sofa.

"You need a stiff drink. Come and sit down."

Theca broke free and moved into the kitchen. "I'll make some coffee. I can't face a drink." She found a tissue and wiped her eyes. Since the start of this she carried a pocket full of them. He stood aside and let her get on with it, knowing that she would tell him in her own good time.

"They operated and found… They couldn't do anything. He's got a few days, possibly a month." Her dark eyes brimmed again. He watched a tear splash on to the stone-flecked work surface.

"Well I need something stronger than coffee," he said and walked into the drawing room.

A few moments later she found him standing by the open veranda doors studying the skyline, his features drawn and worried. She watched him lift a brandy glass to his lips. She had a fleeting memory of his bed and glanced toward the bedroom door. She'd been naked on top of the quilt, on Friday because Dave's eldest was getting married on the Saturday, and she'd heard: "This city could be called igneous." He'd spoken quietly, deeply, in a voice still thick with sex. "It was raised from the Great Fire, and then again in the blitz, and now it is on fire again. Look!" He'd pointed to the window, at the dusky skyline that blazed with the dying sun. The colours tumbled through the high windows and turned her body into gold, the gold around her neck into liquid fire. She'd turned for a better view, arching her back so that her pointed breasts rose irresistibly, and he'd reached across to their tips. "As long as you remain a part of this fiery city," he'd said, "then I shall love it."

That was when she'd reached her decision. The leaking sun had helped. "I'll tell Ted next week, after the wedding," she'd said quietly. "I'll speak to Dad first."

Seeing him now, somehow smaller, it was difficult to imagine the scene.

"It's all so unreal," she said. "Noddy – our doctor – came to see Mum and he was devastated by the news, had no idea. He said that Dad must have been hiding the symptoms for a long time. It was just like him, stubborn, wouldn't let them mess him around. He is such a…dignified man!" Theca used the tissue again. "And now there's trouble. I don't know the details but I know the signs. Everyone is being so secretive."

She glanced around the tidy room and took in the dark leather upholstery, the glistening spider tables, the audio equipment and the unit holding a collection of exquisite glass ballerinas they'd picked up in a small shop in the New Forest. For a fleeting moment she thought the place was cold and masculine – even the sparkling ballerinas held an icy touch. There were no signs of family or history, no silly paintings that the children had brought home from school, no photographs – although she knew he had one of his kids next to his bed. It was like an expensive hotel room before the suitcase was opened. But it didn't matter. In due course she would change it all.

It had been almost a week since their previous meeting.

That Friday night – she'd got home late after seeing him – was spent in silence with Ted, watching the TV. He was in a pensive mood; there were problems at The Tower that he wouldn't discuss. He'd spent the day with her father and her brothers worrying the problem, making decisions. Ted went to bed early and left her fretting about the next few days. Saturday was busy and took her thoughts from such things; getting herself and the children ready, meeting up with her parents and travelling together to the church.

It was a good wedding on that 17th of May. The air was sweet and touched by blossom. In front of the church the grass was lush. Both families came together and the festivities overshadowed other business.

But her father looked ill.

"He's tired," Sally told her. "He won't take time to rest."

They watched him fussing around with his camera, taking pictures of the grandchildren and anything else that moved.

The vicar quoted Corinthians and Jessica, Pat's eldest – and Dave's by adoption – smiled coyly. She looked radiant and very much in love. St Mary's Church was full. People stood at the back and in the aisles. The grandchildren, dressed in lace and black satin, chased each other and hid behind the tails of the morning suits. Youngsters, trendy friends of Jessica and John, outnumbered the family.

"It's like the bloody King's Road," she heard Coddy Hughes mutter.

Confetti scattered in the breeze.

The wedding breakfast was held in The Tower's imposing ballroom, as were the later celebrations. Dave had led his daughter into a waltz while her husband John danced with Patricia. Coddy and Mavis sat watching from the side, loving every minute, pampered by half-a-dozen waiting staff that Dave had personally instructed. Even though her father's leg was giving him trouble he pulled Sally on to the floor. She could still hear him counting the steps – one, two, three – and looking down at his heavy feet while her mother grinned happily over his shoulder. But for all that, for all his determination and good intentions, the pain had got the better of him and her parents had left shortly after the firework display. Tom had told Sally to stay and enjoy herself but she wouldn't hear of it.

Theca shook her head. She should have realized how serious it was and how ill he had looked. Hindsight made it easy. But at the time her mind had been on other things: her lover, on her plans to tell her father that she was leaving Ted, and now she had to live with the guilt.

Was it only the following day, the Sunday, that she'd watched her father fooling with the grandchildren on the drawing-room carpet? Even though he was in pain – she'd put it down to his leg playing up again – he was letting them jump all over him.

On Tuesday Tom was too ill to get out of bed and Sally called her. She saw Ted at home much later. Her expression had collapsed and her sobs were uncontrollable.

"What is it?"

"It's Dad," she cried. "He's in hospital and I'm never going to see him again!"

History! Tom had come through the operation… Perhaps it was fate, she thought. Perhaps God was punishing her. She shook away the absurdity. Suddenly all of it was in perspective. The future would have to wait. Only her family mattered.

Theca sat straight-backed on the edge of the couch, knees together, formal, holding a saucer in one hand and lifting a cup to her lips with the other. There was no way for him to embrace her. He sat opposite in a wide armchair and placed his glass on the spider table.

"I have to tell you this," she said seriously between sips of her coffee. She looked at him earnestly, trying to gauge his reaction. "You've seen the newspapers and the television reports so you know what they're calling him. They aren't spelling it out but sooner or later one of them will, and anyway, the implication is there all the same: gangster, hoodlum!"

He nodded.

"Some of what they say is true," she went on. "Some of it is not, and some other truth is probably far worse. Some of the papers are even suggesting that the shooting in Mill Hill had something to do with him. They talk of gang war breaking out. You have never asked me about my family and I have never volunteered the information."

He held up his hands, palms outward and said, "I don't want to hear this, Theca. I'm interested in you, not your family."

"I am my family," she said timidly.

"Even so…" he began.

"Whether you like it or not I am part of their world. There is no way that they would break the tie and no way that I would want them to."

"I wouldn't ask you to do that."

"I realize what they mean to me. How much they mean. You would have to accept my family."

"Perhaps they wouldn't want me."

"I want you and they will respect that." She spoke surely, with authority.

He shrugged weakly.

"I want you, Theca. I wouldn't ask you to give up your family. That wouldn't do at all."

She stared at him in silence, wanting to tell him more but finding it impossible. For one thing she knew little about the business. It was the unknown that frightened her above all else. She heard the stories, the gossip and innuendo, but all her father had ever said was to take no notice, that some people would always find fiction to explain success in order to excuse their own failure. And when, later, she had asked her brothers, they had terrified her with tales of such terrible butchery that her father had been furious and since then neither of her brothers had ever mentioned the business again. Even Ted would not confide in her, fobbing her off with the idea that he was only on the periphery, dealt with the books, that sort of thing. Even today she had no idea whether the stories were true or not but her curiosity had turned to anger that she should be treated so differently from the boys. Shielded, that was the word. Perhaps it had been necessary to keep it from her mother, even Pat to an extent, but Theca was different, stronger; her father's blood flowed through her. Perhaps because she was younger and had come of age in an era of equality, she would never accept those places reserved exclusively for men. More than that, those places had become a challenge to her, there to be scorned, their doors battered down. She had a right to be taken into his confidence, as much right as the boys. And jealousy had nothing to do with it. Now it was even more imperative. If there was a real danger, and since her minders had been increased she guessed there was, then she ought to be told. But more than that, there were vast areas of her father's life that remained a blank and now she needed to fill in those details before it was too late. She needed a tie that was unbreakable, a bond that would reach beyond his death. Only an understanding of his life would achieve that.

"Obviously you didn't have a chance to speak to him?" he said, interrupting her thoughts.

She shook her head, her gaze on the floor in front of her. Eventually she looked up and said, "All of a sudden things look pretty impossible."

"We'll work it out," he reassured her. "Let's take one day at a time."

She attempted a smile.

She remembered their first meeting. It seemed like yesterday and yet, in another way, a lifetime ago. It was in an art gallery in Kensington. She was casually dressed in T-shirt and jeans, sunglasses perched on her head. Her friend, Margaret Caveille, had some of her work in the exhibition. Theca had sat for one of the paintings and there she was, hanging on the wall, naked and nervous, showing a vague vulnerability that only the artist had realized. And there he was in his sharp dark suit, gazing up at her likeness, until he turned and locked eyes with her. That was the start of it, she supposed, for during the next half-hour or so their gazes met a dozen more times as they followed the crazy routine and the other people in the crowded room ceased to exist.

"I want to tear your clothes off," was the first thing he said.

She had given him a long, knowing look and said, "I was beginning to think you weren't going to ask."

For her part, she remembered, if it had started out as fun, an exciting irrelevance, it had progressed quickly to become all-embracing so that he was never out of her thoughts. It took over her life with such intensity that she ceased to exist when they were not together. And she did strange things then, because love after a barren time makes all things possible. She lifted her legs in the air and displayed herself, and she smiled and felt a freedom, an almost narcissistic thrill as though she saw herself through his eyes. And she was surprised at his look of surprise because in a sexual way she did not think that she could surprise him.

But the past is just a memory, she told herself, and the memory moulds its own design; pain follows happiness as feelings are forgotten or die like star shells that burn out and fall back to the ground. Yesterday's joy becomes irrelevant and the last orgasm as meaningless as last night's dinner.

Nothing was important. Not any more. All she could feel was her shrivelled heart and she knew that nothing would ever be the same again.

Theca spent the early evening at the hospital with her mother. They sat on either side of the bed, Sally holding one hand, Theca the other. Sally spoke, or whispered, and Theca listened and clung on to every glance that her father offered. Inside she was dying and she fought to hold back her tears. Her stomach and her chest felt so heavy and yet empty and nauseous, bereavement before the robbery. If her father didn't figure in the future then she wanted no part of it either. For an absurd moment, in that chair beside the bed, she wanted to die with him, and she thought that she could.

She was staying with Sally for a few nights but could not bear the thought of the same conversation suffered these last few hours, nor could she stand a prolonged visit to her own home. She wanted to see her children although for the moment even they had become of secondary importance, but she didn't want to see Ted.

Theca pulled up at her parent's house, conscious of the car that pulled up twenty yards behind her.

Her mother made no attempt to get out. Instead she said, "The nurses, especially that little Chinese one, said he is such a kind man, always asking if it's too much trouble for them to bring something. A real gentleman, they called him. I told him, you tell them, I said. That's what they're there for, but he won't." She hadn't stopped talking since leaving the hospital. "Fancy him saying sorry about the holiday. I told him not be such a silly sod. As if I care. And did you see what he put on the form, the consent form? Under hobbies he wrote grandchildren. But he looked well, didn't he?"

Theca said, "I was there, Mum." There was a note of resignation in her clotted voice, perhaps even irritation.

Sally unbuckled her seatbelt and opened the door. She hesitated and said anxiously,

"What time will you be back?"

"I'll tuck in the kids and make sure Jean's all right. Say eleven."

"I'll still be up. I can't sleep."

"See you later."

Sally watched the Mini pull out and gave a tentative wave and noticed a dark Rover pulling out behind it.

Theca checked her mirror and as she saw the other car drawing up behind her, she swore under her breath. She drove quickly across to The Tower, hoping to catch Dave.

It was mid-evening and Dave felt physically exhausted. His day had been spent making the security rounds, tightening up his forces, the enforcers, the minders and the foot soldiers, ensuring that the safe houses were armed and stocked. Getting hold of weapons was easy enough, even a civilian with two hundred quid in his pocket could pick up a revolver in a couple of hours simply by asking around; Spatz pump-actions and self-loading Brownings were still favourite with the robbers and they were more expensive, but just as available. Having them in the right places was a major factor in an underworld war. Faces on the street were even more important. Security was everything. First priority was the safety of the family, and then the clubs and collection points. They needed watching around the clock; visitors and punters and even employees were scrutinized on their way in and out. Every face was clocked. Anyone acting remotely suspicious was pulled aside and finger-fucked. The attack on Tommy had surprised Dave, infuriated him, and made him realize just how vulnerable they were. Years of peace and, to some extent, appeasement, had led to a run down in their forces. Even when his father had got wind of Mad Mick's increased activity he'd done little to balance the scales. Dave had argued with him that it was necessary to increase their strength but the old man had remained unresponsive, not wanting to appear aggressive. His father listened but, as the weeks went by and Mick continued to strengthen his forces, he did nothing. And now it was probably too late. Mick was breathing hard on Coddy's doorstep and as a final insult – a challenge to fight or run – he'd hit Tommy. Without his father's backing there was only so much Dave could do on his own. Even his brothers wouldn't act without the old man's approval. But the time was fast approaching when Dave would have to take over and he wasn't at all certain how the others would react.

He lay on the couch in the back room drinking vodka and looking through the two-way mirror at the early punters, watching the graceful and not so graceful women moving about the bars and tables, enjoying their movement. It used to excite him to watch and although it was still a pleasure it no longer led to other things. He watched the gamblers moving beneath the soft lights of the chandeliers, their every move taped by the ceiling cameras and scrutinized by a bank of monitors. Every square inch of the casino was recorded. The cameras could pick up every digit on a slot machine and every number on the roulette wheel. They could see the shake of a nervous hand and the sweat build on a desperate forehead. They could see trouble before it even started.

Dave looked at the gamblers and wondered where all the little grey men had gone, the husbands who worked a shift and then went home to their wives and were satisfied with a meal and a warm house and the flickering monotony of the television.

Some of the richest men and women in the world passed through The Tower's grand foyer into the casino. Some of them came to hide away, and winning was not on their minds. It was a retreat from reality, from the stress of business, from wives, from mistresses, from life itself. They were as bored and as shackled to their lifestyles as anyone else. In the gaming halls where the odds levelled the playing fields and their money couldn't buy them luck, there was an element of sleaze and even danger, a touch of excitement to stir the blood, it was like visiting a brothel where you paid your money for a cold fuck. His father had told him that with them it was not about money for what they might lose was meaningless. For them it was an ego trip, trying to beat themselves up against odds that were unbeatable, but they would never experience the true gambler's rush from betting money they couldn't afford, when they could feel their nerves stretch to breaking and savour the bitter-sweet thrill of turning over a winning – life-saving – card.

"Never chase money," his father had told him. "When your luck is out you lower your stake and when it's in you raise your stake and if you find yourself slipping back to even you walk. Never play machines. They're for lowlife only. The only game that you've ever got a chance on is blackjack. And even then you need a seat close enough to force the dealer's hand. But always remember, whichever game you play, if you play it long enough, you'll lose."

His father need not have bothered. Dave had never been a gambler, not on the tables. He got his royal flushes in other ways.

There were two areas of the legitimate business that required his special attention. Recruitment was one of them. Over and above HR Dave relied on his own specialist team that reported directly to him. The employees were checked and rechecked, their backgrounds probed until there was nothing left to know. The dealers and cashiers and even the camera monitors were followed, their bins emptied and the refuse checked, their bank accounts scrutinized. If they bought a new car or drank expensive wine or splashed out on a girlfriend, Dave wanted to know about it. If they were in trouble financially then they were hauled into the office. If the business could help them before they started helping themselves then all well and good. The other area he kept on top of was the purchasing department. Although Ted remained in charge Dave kept a close eye on the buyers. The turnover of hardware was immense and that was before the figures for damaged and worn-out goods were enhanced. Staff uniforms, bedding, chinaware, silverware, slot machines and even packs of cards were purchased by the truckload. Add to that the consumables, the foodstuffs and drinks for the many acclaimed restaurants and the cleaning and laundry supplies that arrived on a daily basis then the underground loading bays were always busy. The subcontract side alone was staggering and required a dozen full-time employees to cover the paperwork for the maintenance of the equipment and building repairs.

He shook the business from his head and concentrated on the women again. There was one in particular in a glitzy, sequinned number, leaning so far over one of the roulette tables she was flashing the back of her knickers.

When Theca found him he was two-thirds into a bottle and looked tired and drawn. He might even have dozed for the woman playing roulette had gone.

"You drink too much," she said haughtily.

"You might not know this, Sis, but vodka stops the clap. You drink enough and you can't do it!"

He was honestly pleased to see her. There was warmth between them not shared by the others. Only her father was closer.

She mixed a scotch with dry at the bar, dropped in some ice and carried it over to the window. She looked down on the glowing city.

London! The Smoke!

And somewhere he was out there.

She wondered what he was doing right this moment. Was he thinking of her? She shook away the thought before it led to that horrible mouth-drying moment. She sipped her drink.

London! An island!

One hundred and fifty feet below her, bathed in the streetlights, the streets seemed unreal, the night traffic and pedestrians miniaturized, moving in slow motion. The city made her shiver.

"This royal throne of kings, this scepter'd city…" she murmured quietly, playing with *Richard II*.

"I think England comes into it somewhere," Dave said.

"I know that."

She turned back from the window and sat next to him. For a while she sat drinking and watching the customers then she turned to him.

"I'm leaving Ted," she said, her voice oddly unemotional, as if what she said was of no consequence. She felt suddenly sheepish.

Dave lifted his eyebrows and pretended to be shocked. For some years he'd watched her relationship with Ted disintegrate. He'd heard about her small circle of friends and the time she spent with them in the Kensington restaurants – on the second floors, of course – or in the bowels of Annabel's or Tramp's; a group of disillusioned women who were clinging hopelessly to youth, a time when all things were possible, letting alcohol draw its dizzy veil on reality. And six months ago he'd heard about her affair. He'd hoped that it would fizzle out, as these things often do. He believed that there was no way his sister would hurt her children. He'd been wrong but he was not surprised. Theca was as headstrong as he was; passion and physical contact were all important. It hadn't always been that way. There had been a time when she'd been as prudish as her father. Dave remembered when his sister had actually given him some grief when she suspected he was cheating on Pat. She and his wife had always been close. They'd had their youngest children within a month of one another and that was always a good starting point for building an intimate friendship. At one stage he'd considered talking to his father about her but had decided against it. There was no point in upsetting the old man if the thing had died a death anyway. It was going to blow apart now, though, for Ted was family. He knew as much about the business as any of them – more than most – and the business could not afford any falling out, especially not now. Not while the world and God knew who else were against them.

"What's happened, Star?" he asked and for a moment she saw herself in his round eyes.

She raised her hand in a throwaway gesture. "We've been bad for some time and I met someone else."

"Who is it?"

"Does it matter?"

"I suppose not."

"I love him, Dave. I love him. All I want to do is to be with him."

"What about the kids?"

"They're resilient. They'll get over it. Kids do. They won't be the first or the last."

"It'll be the first time in our family."

"If there was another way, but there isn't."

"Christ! They'll be devastated. They might get over it but they might not."

She shook her head and gulped at her drink, then said, "I've been over it a thousand times. Do you think I've arrived at this decision without thinking it through?" She seemed helpless and fragile. "I can't go on any more, Dave. Obviously I'm not going to do anything until…" She left the sentence hanging.

"Has Ted got any idea?"

"I don't think so. He should have but I honestly don't think he's noticed. Or he doesn't care. I've come in later. I've not been interested. I've treated him badly, flaring up at the slightest thing. I don't think he's noticed."

"Is there any chance at all?" He paused and filled his glass again. "What about a holiday? Couldn't you and Ted go away for a few weeks to sort things out?"

She smiled quickly, without humour. "You're not listening to me, Dave. I don't want to be with him any more. It's over. I don't love him. I don't desire him. I can't bear him touching me. I want to be with… someone else. I'm not going to change my mind. Not now. Not ever. I can't live without love."

"Love dies, Star, you know that. It fades away and dies, like people. Most people aren't in love. They just live together. In the beginning it's wonderful and exciting and you want to eat it, but it never stays that way. What happens then? Will you find someone else?"

She pulled a face. "Maybe I will, if that's what it takes. But I don't agree with you. Love only dies if you let it die. Look at Mum and Dad. Has their love died? There's more there, after forty years, than we've ever known. Anyway, this is beside the point, Dave. I'm telling you now and I'm going to tell Ted after...when Dad..." Her mask slipped and a tear glistened.

"You'll break Mum's heart, Star," he said heavily.

"I know," she nodded sadly.

For a while they sat in silence, drinking, fixed gloomy expressions watching the customers without seeing them. Brother and sister, a yard apart with a light year between them. She was thinking about her father and whether love was strong enough to keep him alive; he was thinking about her lover and whether death would save her marriage and, more importantly, save a split in the family, save an interruption to the business: love, the only thing worth living for, and death, the only certainty in life.

She glanced up, wide eyes curious, and asked, "How do you think Mum is coping?"

He shrugged. "She's stronger than you think. Grief is no stranger to her. Nothing's going to hurt her as much as when Mick died. She'll handle it." The vodka was speaking and he couldn't help himself telling her something else. "I'll tell you something now that nobody knows, not even Mum and Dad. When I was thirteen and you were six, before Tommy was born, Mick was three. They always told you that Mick died in a traffic accident, right?"

Theca's brow ridged in concentration.

"He didn't," Dave said and shook his head. His eyes glazed, not in the Smith veil of anger, but into confession. "Remember the railway track that went down the bottom of the garden? I was with a couple of mates in the back garden. Mum told us to play with Mick. We didn't. We took off over the track. We must have left the gate open because Mick followed us. It was one of those electric lines. I never told anyone I saw. They took Dad to the hospital. They wouldn't let Mum see the body."

Theca reached forward to grasp his hand but it was not enough and she knelt beside him and put her arms around him.

"Oh, David, why didn't you tell us?"

"They blamed me. Of course they blamed me."

287

"No! No!" She shook her head.

"It never goes away, not entirely."

"Well it's about time it did. You couldn't know. How could you? Kids of that age don't think. No one was to blame. You should have told us."

For the first time in her life Theca understood what had eaten her brother's soul. For a moment she felt incredibly close to him.

A vodka tear brimmed in his eye and he flicked it away angrily as though his emotion was something to be despised.

"When Dad came back from the hospital I was waiting for him in the front room. I watched the door open. I was frightened to death. I'll never forget the way he looked: his tie undone, his collar all over the place, his eyes so red they were almost bleeding. When he walked up to me I thought I was going to get the beating of my life. Suddenly his great arms came around me and he whispered, 'I love you, boy. We'll never speak of it...again.'" The last word was all but lost.

Theca buried her head into his warm lap. "Oh, Dave, what's to become of us?"

He stroked her soft hair.

"I feel so defenceless," she said.

"I know, Star. It's like being cut off, lost at sea. Perhaps it is sea-sickness we're all feeling." Gently he raised her head. "I've got to get some sleep," he said, wanting to be alone. "I'm going to see Coddy first thing in the morning."

"Just tell me one thing more. Does Pat know about this?"

He shook his head. "No one knows."

"Well I think you should tell her." Her eyes glazed reflectively.

He looked at her, looked into his own eyes, at his own features, beautiful on Theca, and he realized just how much he loved his sister and how, before long, he was going to break her heart.

Dave drove home without an escort. He drove carefully because of the booze. The conversation regarding the past, his final admission – something he had decided he would never divulge – left him dejected and self-critical. He needed the comfort and familiarity of Patricia, the security of her gentle breasts and the warmth of her breath. Only then, wrapped in her protecting embrace, could he sleep. He dropped a tear on to her breast and whispered, "Your love is the only contentment I have ever known."

She stirred and took him in her arms.

Chapter 23

Dave left the Smoke as the dawn ghosted out of the darkness. During his drive north to meet his father-in-law he recognized the places and yet he felt that strange feeling of detachment, as though he had seen them before but only in his dreams; his sense of isolation was acute. He cut a line through Spalding and Boston and across the southern edge of the Wolds. He thought of Coddy and his father, old men now, broken. The end of an era was drawing in. The men, the legends, were dying out or were shut away, effectively dead. Things were changing; today's villains were international: bankers, politicians, even presidents. The day of the odd firebombing, the leaning on an occasional shopkeeper, the messing up of a pimp's front teeth, those days had gone. Jessica's marriage was not yet a week old and he'd spent a long time with Coddy and the family at the reception but they had not discussed business. It was a rule unlikely to be broken that at such times such things would not be mentioned. No matter how pressing the problem it would keep.

Some places seemed to unlock memories; they brought them together like a treasured collection and offered a sense of familiarity and comfort, even a false security. For Dave, his father-in-law's manor some way north of Skegness was one such place. He found easiness there, an intimacy that came from the past, and an acceptance also. In a strange sense he had come to share his wife's roots and he looked upon the place as a second home.

Whenever he approached the manor his thoughts turned to the girl he'd married, as she was, the long-limbed nymph rising from the water or that fleeting view when she'd stood over him in the tiny parlour of the stone cottage. They were shadows now, nothing more than blurred images from a distant place. His thoughts turned to Sharon and the grief she had caused and the way he'd gone back to her time and again, addicted. After a long absence she had contacted him five years earlier and they'd been meeting regularly ever since. Sharon Valenti, his perfect fit.

He shook away the thoughts and concentrated on the present. He didn't give much thought to how he would approach his father-in-law. That could be played by ear. But only God knew what Coddy's reaction would be to the idea of retirement. Dave's gut feeling was that the old man would start World War Three; certainly the Coddy Hughes of old would have played it that way. He would have marched into Glasgow on his own and taken it apart. But time was the enemy of passion, of strength too; he'd seen it in his own father, this tiredness, and he'd recognized it in his father-in-law for many years.

Security had tightened. Two men came out of the brick building and gave his Rover a close examination before recognizing Dave and opening the wrought-iron gates. They waved him through and closed the gates immediately behind him. The guards had obviously telephoned the house for Coddy Hughes was on the steps to meet him. He was wearing his neck brace again; he'd left it off at the wedding. In faded jeans and blue shirt Coddy looked younger than at the weekend. The wedding and the travelling it had involved had been a strain and it was good to see that he'd recovered so quickly.

It began to rain. The stiff leaves of the vines and creepers that climbed up the walls of the house began to dance, shot by heavy drops. He parked the car and dashed up the steps to the sheltered porch where Coddy waited, ten yards perhaps, but his grey V-necked pullover had changed to a darker shade by the time he got there.

"Come on in, Dave. You had a safe journey, I hope," Coddy said in his gravel tone and put a close arm across Dave's shoulder. The unlikely physical contact and the grave expression gave Dave the feeling that Coddy had been primed about the reason for his visit.

"Do you want to brush up?"

"No. I'll have a drink first."

"Mother is out so we've got an hour."

Dave tried his best to relax in a leather armchair while Coddy poured some coffee. He carried one across the parquet and handed it to Dave then went back for his own. Eventually he sank into his own chair and raised the footrest. He sighed as the weight was taken from his back. He balanced his stick against the arm and leant back with his drink, toying with the cup while studying Dave out of – almost – mocking eyes.

"That's a relief," he said. "Simply to sit down after standing gives me considerable pleasure. When your body begins to fall to pieces it doesn't take much to please you." He lifted his cup. "I'll drink to your old man," he said.

"I get the feeling I'm here under false pretences. Which one of us has got the news, Coddy?"

Coddy smiled and touched his nose.

"Tom told me all about his gut last weekend. It was reaching crisis point then. He knew it. For some months he's spent a good deal of his time putting his house in order."

"I'm not with you."

"You will be, don't worry. Your father has known for some time how serious his condition is. You don't get so close to death with gut cancer without certain symptoms. You think you've come all this way to tell me that your father is dying? You think he sent you up here to ask me to retire and hand that Scottish son of a bitch everything I've built up?" Coddy smiled affectionately at his son-in-law. "Dave, you have a lot to learn about me, and about your father."

Dave shook his head.

Coddy sighed, "Mad Mick! He's hated the English all his life. His granddaddy was caught up in the French port of St Valery-en-Caux on the twelfth of June, nineteen-forty. He was a Highlander, one of the Fifty-First that got hung to dry when we ran to Dunkirk. The entire Highland

Division was sacrificed so that we could get home." He shrugged. "But here we are, and it doesn't help that your father and I were two of those that got away. I got away a few days before the evacuation proper but that's beside the point, and another story. We guessed that Mick would make his move as soon as your father went down. That's one of the reasons he held off the hospital so long, to give Tommy a chance to deal or at least to get back safely. As it happened, Tom couldn't hold out long enough. But it ended well. Unfortunately he didn't get the chance to talk to you and once he was hospitalised he couldn't take the chance of being overheard by your brothers. This is for your ears and not theirs. You're up here to meet Mad Mick and the Americans, O'Connell and Valenti from Runnymede. We're going to listen to what they've got to say."

Dave's stared in disbelief. His eyes became slits. "I don't believe this! Valenti! He was the guy that caused all the grief before."

Coddy waved a dismissive hand. "He's just a voice. He's so old now he's probably forgotten. But Mick wasn't open to negotiation unless we had the Guineas here. It was your father's idea."

Dave felt a flush of anger. He could handle Valenti and the injury to his pride, no matter how much it hurt, but the fact that his father had confided in Coddy rather than him left him wounded and utterly perplexed. Maybe his father didn't have confidence in him after all. He wondered what other surprises Coddy had in store. He finished his coffee but his eyes betrayed him.

"Family doesn't come into this," Coddy said as though reading his thoughts. "Once you're in the picture you'll understand what I mean. What I'm going to tell you now goes no farther than this room. It will become a burden to you. You can't even discuss it with members of your own family; and when your father is dead only you and I will know about it. And sooner or later, when I'm dead, you'll have to find someone else. Someone on the outside, someone you can trust with your life. And you've got to start looking for that person now. Grooming him and getting to know him so well that there can never be any doubt in your mind. Maybe somebody already springs to mind. Who knows? I don't want to know. No one must ever know who you choose." Coddy sighed. "So, it was not about my retirement. I'm too old to retire! It was about your coronation."

Coddy's wife arrived home earlier than expected and made a fuss of Dave then fed Coddy his medication and insisted that he took his late morning rest. Coddy had given up arguing about such things long ago.

"You'll have to wait a little longer. We'll talk later," Coddy assured Dave as he went stiffly from the room with his wife right behind him.

Dave showered and changed in time for lunch. They took up the conversation again later, in the drawing room. Coddy let Dave pour the malt and light the forbidden cigars. He looked comfortable in his slightly raised armchair with his footrest six inches from the floor – lord of his manor. His eyes were fiery and alert, watching Dave's every reaction, the scar between them paler than Dave remembered. His head held stiffly by the pink brace, bald and shining in the light that piled in through the window behind him, barely moved as he smoked his cigar or flicked the ash or lifted the crystal glass to his lips.

"Every organization needs muscle, you know that. We've all got our armies, our enforcers and soldiers. Occasionally a job comes along that is so delicate, or even dangerous, that members of the family cannot be involved. Neither must they know anything about it for if they knew, not only would it worry them, they might want to get themselves involved. Equally there are times when members of your own organization need minding and sometimes it's best for an outside agency to do this. It saves the possibility of recognition and so on. Take your sister, for instance. She has a problem handling such things. If she doesn't know she's being watched because she doesn't recognize the men watching her, then there's no problem."

Dave wondered whether Coddy and therefore his father knew about the Star's affair. Could it be possible? And what about Sharon Valenti, did they know about her? The questions kept coming.

Coddy continued: "Occasionally, and I can't remember the last time, one of our own people goes off the rails and needs putting right. If we use our own people it leads to tension on our own doorstep, it builds mistrust and insecurity. You know what I mean? At such times an outside firm is required. But the only way you can trust an outside firm is if they work exclusively for you. It is even better if they don't know they are working for you. If only one man, someone perhaps, who owes you his life, someone you can trust with yours, if this man is sent to recruit his own muscle, then you are reasonably safe. Your father has such a man who has such a firm. He uses him when it's necessary and when there is no alternative. It's your father's secret weapon, his chief enforcer who, in turn, has his own army of enforcers. We only know the one man, and that's the man who put it all together, Scratch Fox. Sergeant Scratch Fox."

"Dunkirk," he nodded. "I remember you telling me."

"When Fox got back he was in hospital for about a year. From there it was an institution, shut up with the real mad bastards. Half his brain had been blown away in France and what was left was the evil part. It turned him into the cruellest son of a bitch you're ever likely to meet. When he came back with half his head missing his wife ran off with a Canadian, took the kids with her. That might have had something to do with it. But because your father saved his life, and then later helped him at a time when he was totally helpless, when he was going through the agonies of losing the only things that mattered to him, it developed a loyalty second to none. And this was the man your father chose to run his secret army."

Dave was shocked; his mouth dropped open in amazement and yet even as Coddy spoke certain things began to fall into place. Answers that had never been good enough were suddenly and clearly understood. The surprise turned into a wry smile.

Coddy went into detail about Fox and the secret army of enforcers. He described how and when they were used, how they were financed. He coloured in the grey areas of the past, secret wars that had been fought to gain control of racketeering, gaming and prostitution, opposition that had been taken out or brought under control. Dave heard it all, how it started, how it grew. He heard about the Chinese wars and the South Coast wars. He was given a history lesson about things that happened during his own childhood, time that he'd spent in complete ignorance, before he knew about any of it. And even though he knew a great deal about the present business most of what Coddy told him was new. Suddenly his father was no longer that dependable fatherly figure, that intimate friend who had grown older as Dave had grown older, but something more than that. They spoke for most of the afternoon and again after dinner.

It was approaching midnight when Coddy's wife, Mavis, interrupted them. They could see immediately that something was seriously wrong.

She spoke quickly, "There's been trouble. It's dreadful. There's been a newsflash!"

Coddy levered himself from the chair, his rigid expression draining of colour.

Dave remained silent.

"People are dead," she said, breaking into a sob. There was something else. They could see it in her swelling eyes.

"Come on, old girl," Coddy said gently. "What is it?"

Her voice grew fainter. "It's Ted," she said.

A muscle in Dave's jaw began to throb. His eyes narrowed fractionally and that veil of anger drew across them like an inner lid.

Chapter 24

Hearing about her brother's torment left Theca emotionally exhausted. After leaving him that evening she had no idea where to go.

Without consciously deciding to see her friend she rang the ornate brass bell on Margaret's door. She felt wretched. Drink on an empty stomach hadn't helped but she knew that tiredness and despair were the main cause.

In plum-coloured cropped pyjamas and without make-up, strands of her long black hair damp from a recent bath, Margaret Caveille was beautiful but in a completely different way from Theca. In the dimmed light her olive skin and long-lashed hazel eyes were darker and faintly exotic. She was in her mid-thirties, of part Spanish descent. Ten years previously they had used the same maternity ward and slept in adjacent rooms.

"I didn't know where else to go," Theca said.

Margaret recognized Theca's distress at once. She put her arm around her and led her into the sitting room. There was an unfinished painting of a nude woman on the easel and a palette of skin colours next to it.

"Come on, sit down. Jack's in Paris, the kids are in bed, so we've got the room to ourselves."

"I couldn't face my mother again," Theca explained, "Going over it all again and again. I couldn't face Ted. I can't stand the deceit anymore. Not now. I don't want to have to worry about every word I say."

Theca looked about, as though seeing the room for the first time. Margaret's paintings, including some of Theca, were on every wall.

Margaret had coffee splashing from top to bottom in the Kenwood. She poured another cup and set it down in front of Theca.

"There, I've made it strong," she said.

Theca tried a smile but failed as her face fell to pieces.

"Now, come on, tell me all about it. I've seen the news, but there weren't any details. Is it bad news?"

Theca nodded. She lifted her drink. The tiny cup rattled on its saucer.

"My father's dying. They say a month but I think that was for Mum's benefit. He looks terrible."

Margaret hid her surprise.

"Have you seen Lewis? Does he know?"

She had known about Theca's affair from day one. There was little they didn't share.

"I saw him earlier. I couldn't go back. I'd never wrench myself away and Mum's waiting up."

"What are you going to do?"

"I don't know." Theca's voice was just a whisper.

"What do you want to do?"

She threw her friend a wide-eyed, despairing look and said weakly, "I want to be with him."

Margaret waited.

"But I can't, not now."

"Why don't you take one step at a time. You don't have to make decisions. They'll still be there next week or even next month. You don't have to rush anything. In any case, you're not in any state to decide anything right now. Best wait a while."

"I'm sorry," Theca said. "I shouldn't burden you with all this."

Margaret smiled softly. "Of course you should. I'd be hurt if you hadn't come to me."

"What can I do? I feel so weak. I can't think for myself anymore."

"The most important thing right now is to get some sleep. Can you stay here?"

"No. Mum is expecting me back."

"I'll ring her."

"No," Theca shook her head. "She needs me. That's the point, everyone needs me, but I need someone too."

"You have me," Margaret said gently. "And I'm here any time you want me. I can come back with you if you like. The neighbours will look after the kids. I can listen. They can talk to me. It doesn't matter who listens, does it? 'Cos all we're really doing is talking to ourselves."

Theca glanced up and flicked a stray smile. "That's a bit profound for this time of night."

"It's no trouble for me to stay with you for a few days. I'd like to help."

"No. Suddenly I feel better. Just talking to you has helped. I'll be all right now. Maybe that's what I needed, to talk instead of listen."

Sensing her friend's resolve and fearful of it, Margaret said suddenly, "Theca, what are you going to do?"

"I'm going home to see Ted."

"You're going to tell him?"

"Yes."

"I don't know that it's wise at the moment. Can't you wait? Emotions make things so unclear."

"I am clear," Theca said. "I need to be honest with him. I can't handle my father's death while I have to watch every word I say. It all needs to be out in the open, I can take it from there. It's best to get it over with."

"What of the children?" Margaret asked. "What if they find out? Losing your dad is going to be bad enough. If they thought that you and Ted were splitting that would destroy them."

"I'll keep them out of it."

"Can you be sure that Ted will?"

"Yes," Theca said. "I honestly don't think he cares!"

It was nearly midnight when Ted parked the car in his drive. With a couple of foot soldiers in tow he'd been over to King's Cross to lean on a club owner who'd been late with his monthly payments. The owner in question was known for his dealings in hardware, particularly handguns that could be traced to Manchester, so the armed guard had been necessary. He hated the place. It was a shithouse. Argyle Street was littered with raving skagheads, the urine-soaked doorways were filled with beggars lying under threadbare blankets and newspapers, the stairwells filled with junkies scoring for Glasgow Rangers, and the dealers with their mouth's full of cellophane wraps made their money as openly as the shivering toms who waved at the passing punters. There wasn't any way down from the Cross. It was rock bottom.

Ted was surprised to see Theca's red Mini for she'd arranged to stay with Sally. Perhaps one of the kids had been ill. The house was dark and he guessed that she was in bed. He hoped that she was awake to explain the change of plan.

Quietly he closed the front door and headed for the kitchen. Her voice came in from the drawing room.

"I'm in here, Ted," she called.

He turned on the light, narrowed his eyes to dull the sudden brightness, and saw her in the leather armchair, legs drawn up, drink in hand, and still not changed for bed. She'd been crying. Her eyes were swollen and hurt.

"I need to talk to you," she said.

He sat down opposite expecting that a sympathetic ear was required, that whatever it was had to do with Tom.

Theca drew a deep breath, hardening her purpose, and spoke quietly, "I'm in love with someone else."

Suspecting something was nothing like the certain knowledge and Ted was stunned. He knew how serious it was from the sudden tears in Theca's eyes. She sobbed into her hands. He stared at the floor, fixed expression, while the implications drove into him from all directions. Love, she had said. Not affair. Not slept with. Love. There was a difference.

"Who is it?" he asked eventually.

Not moving her hands from her face she shook her head. "It doesn't matter," she said. "Does it matter?"

"I suppose not." He nodded. "How long has it been going on?"

"Six months." She looked up. Beneath her cold brow her wide eyes looked frightened and uncertain.

"What do you want to do?" he asked gently. His voice seemed incredibly controlled. She'd expected some show of anger.

"I don't know."

"Are you leaving me? What about the kids?"

Again she shook her head. The things she wanted to say were blocked in her throat.

"Sweetheart, you certainly pick your moments. You're going to break their hearts."

Her Smith's eyes flashed. "It's not me you're worried about, then? It's the kids!"

"I didn't say that. I guessed there was something going on. I didn't want to believe it. I've been waiting for you to tell me. Every time we've sat down and talked these last few weeks I thought you would tell me about it. I've already got used to the idea."

"Do you want me to go?"

"No," he said quietly. "I don't want you to go. I know I haven't shown it of late, but I love you. I always have."

She wiped her eyes. "I've got to get back to Mum. She'll be worrying."

"So what are you going to do?"

"Let's have dinner tomorrow. We need to talk."

"We talk every day. Talking isn't the problem."

Her lips trembled again.

"OK," he relented. "It sounds good. But it will have to be lunch. I've got a meet with the caterers in the morning and I'm with the Merseyside crowd tomorrow night."

She nodded.

Ted thought that sleep that night would be difficult but it came with surprising ease. The following morning he looked in on the children before he left. They were still asleep. Jean arrived at eight and he gave her some cash and told her that he'd be back late. Theca would come home early. Jean was happy to be able to help at such a time. She'd been working for them for a number of years. He wondered whether Theca had spoken to her about the situation or whether she could sense the oppression and made more of it than Tom's illness.

"Don't worry," she told him. "I'll stay until Theca comes, and if she needs to go to the hospital or get back to her mum, then I'll stay over in one of the spare rooms."

As he motored across to Soho he listened to the end of the first act of La Bohème. He parked outside the Kowloon House and for a few moments he sat and watched Chinatown wake up and spit until the last notes faded.

Lo Fok was known as both the Charley Man and the H King. He'd spent the sixties in Kowloon when the British troops were there and had spent the evenings of his youth in the Princess cinema just up from the Dairy Farm on Nathan Road. He resembled Christopher Lee, albeit a foot shorter, but he walked the pigeon-toed walk of John Wayne in *Rio Bravo* and had cultivated the voice of the Chinese interpretation of Peter Ustinov, but not very well for he used Wayne's inflection and paused before he finished every sentence. "You want fried…rice?"

When he first set up in England he imported his dope – in those days it came exclusively from the golden triangle – through the merchant shipping lines, mostly hidden in the boxes of servicemen returning from a posting. It was common knowledge that few army boxes were ever inspected and with the continuous movement of troops it had been a ready-made supply line. When that supply line eventually broke down he switched his imports to the Scottish islands and Ireland from where it could easily be transported to the UK mainland. It made more sense for the crescent was now competing with Latin America as cocaine grew in popularity.

Lo Fok's restaurant was in the city's secretive triangle, just off Gerrard Street, an odorous little place where the Georgian terraces had been converted into rows of restaurants and cinema clubs and oriental supermarkets. Rubbish filled the gutters and the narrow side alleys. At night, after the punters had gone and the mah-jong bricks rang out, some appetites satisfied by fried rice and beef and vegetables in oyster sauce, others satisfied by the performance of naked women, and sometimes men, or the still commonplace smoking of opium, especially by the older men, the rats came out to satisfy themselves on the piles of rotting vegetables and discarded takeaways and the occasional pool of vomit. All the tourists had heard of Soho and were marked by a little excitement at the prospect, but the area had been cleaned up beyond recognition. The punters came to be titillated and thrilled and maybe a little shocked but they never found any of that. Only the locals knew where those places had been relocated.

Once before, perhaps, the area had been a refuge filled with surprises, little courts and alleys full of curiosities, sinister maybe, but then, eroticism always had been, but it was a place that pulsated with family businesses and loyalties and it was real. The girls that paraded and earned the place its reputation had been up front and human. And now...Wolfenden had a lot to answer for. The humanity had been replaced by a pretence, sex shop windows and simulated orgasms as superficial as the facades that replaced the Georgian fronts, and the streets had been filled with drunken louts full of violence at being ripped off on Ribena and water, and Schloss Boozenberg, a fizzy drink they called Champagne, ripped off at live sex shows where the only things likely to move were the cockroaches. The Raymond Revuebar in Rupert Street was the glittering centrepiece but even that was stale: ice-cold beaver, air-dried split figs without the cream. Any local football club offered more on their stag nights, and a lot cheaper. And with half-a-dozen exceptions, once these places had been shut and the police force of the capital returned to basic wages, then the heart of Soho had been ripped out. It had become a memory. The paint was already beginning to peel from the junk dragons and pagodas.

Ted watched a Chinese chef working behind his steamy window in a little glass-fronted booth under flattened duck carcasses and strips of pork hanging from a line of hooks. It was a cheap parlour, frequented more by the local Chinese community than the tourists.

He left the car and sniffed at the sticky soy-sauce air and crossed to the worn stone steps of the restaurant. He acknowledged the musical greeting from the chef in the window, busily chopping his cold meats, and climbed the stairs two at a time, heading for the second and third floors and the dim staleness of the scuffed red-flock wallpaper. The top of the building was in three sections. The largest area contained Lo Fok's sideline, a couple of quack acupuncturists. Since the quacks were his wife and mother-in-law he had little option even though it would have been more profitable to extend the restaurant. The third room contained his office.

"Ah, my very good…friend. I have waited for…you." His thin hands made waves in the joss-smoked air. "You want…breakfast?"

Ted shook his head. He lit a cigarette while Lo Fok removed his apron.

"How is your father-in-law's…illness?" he asked. Eyes became slits over shining black pearls of curiosity.

"He's poorly but not as bad as we first thought."

Lo Fok's bony hand twirled one side of his weak moustache. His eyes never left Ted's face.

"I hear about the…hit. Everyone hears it. Too much worry. Tommy…?"

"He's all right. They missed!"

Lo wrinkled his nose, "Amateurs then."

"That's what we figured."

Satisfied, Lo turned to the business. "I have what you…want. Six altogether."

"You had them checked out?"

Lo put on an exaggerated expression of hurt. He muttered in Cantonese then said, "Of course. No AIDS. No clap. No nothing. All very…beautiful."

Ted waved Lo's show aside. "The youngster?" he asked.

"Yes, yes, all that you ask for; a virgin, never before, and with her mother. What time you want? Need sedating, of…course."

"Seven. No earlier. We'll leave the docks at seven. I don't want them hanging around. What about the others?"

"They'll arrive whenever you…require. Earlier, maybe, eh? Number seventy I will hold with…thirteen." Number seventy was listed under the beverage section on the menu: Coke.

Ted noticed the table next to the desk, the scales and test tubes, the wad of cellophane envelopes and the tissues to keep off the dabs. He sniffed the air for the ammonia the joss couldn't hide.

"It washes back at over ninety percent," Lo Fok said nervously, "Only the...best."

"Don't give me that shit!" Ted snorted. "Where do you think I was born? I don't give a monkey's fuck how much menatol you use so long as the punters are happy. If they're not, you'll be on your own fucking menu!"

Lo nodded apprehensively. He moved back on to safer ground. "You want to see the pictures? I have...pictures."

He took an envelope from the top of a battered green four-drawer and drew out some snapshots. Ted took out a handkerchief to handle them. Photographs could photograph your fingerprints. He leafed through them. They were poor quality Polaroids. Even so, he saw that the women were handsome, a combination of hair colours, all pretty, all slim, all in their late teens or early twenties. A Chinese girl was particularly eye-catching. Lo noticed Ted's interest.

"You like her...yourself? I arrange."

Ted grunted. The Scousers would not complain. The youngster was pictured with her mother. She was a skinny girl with wisps of hair, slight breasts, prominent pubis, legs held apart; she had the body of a ten-year-old but her face was older. There was a striking likeness between mother and daughter but about twenty years difference. He studied the mother for a moment. She was in good nick herself. Naked, her arm outstretched, one hand parting her daughter's legs. Ted felt nothing, neither compassion nor disgust. He didn't wonder how a mother could do such a thing. It was money. It was that simple. Perhaps it was to pay for coke or crack but more likely it was heroin. He searched for the tracks but if they were there they were well hidden. A between-the-toe job, he guessed. He felt nothing. He'd seen dozens of them and not one had ever interested him. Ted knew that it was only recently that the Chinese had used European girls. Before that, youngsters from the age of six were rounded up in the Far East and sent to visit non-existent relatives in the UK. They came for two or three months at a time and were installed in one of a number of houses across London. It was known as the Bird's Nest Run and had been a hugely profitable arm of the Chinese underworld.

He handed back the photographs. "Don't put her to sleep. That happened last year."

"Leave everything to...me!"

Ted nodded. He turned to leave but sensed that Lo Fok had something else to say. "What is it?"

Lo lifted his hands. "It is nothing. Only..."

Ted crossed his arms.

"It is the overheads."

Ted grinned but Lo took a step backwards; behind the laughing monkey...

Another babble of Cantonese then: "It was such short notice. No time..."

Ted waited. His grin was still there but his eyes weren't sharing it.

Lo Fok had lived with the Smiths for too long not to be wary. He turned away, not wanting to look at the threat. "I don't know what I can do. I will lose...money." He turned back. The grin had disappeared and Lo cowered.

"Lo, spell it out. Tell me what you want?"

"If I can use the young one again..." He shrugged. "Last time it was...impossible. Too much dick! Liverpool! They are animals!" He began to stammer.

"OK," Ted nodded and his features relaxed. "You'll get a slice of it. I'll have a word with the accounts department."

The blood came seeping back to Lo's face. He hurried around to open the door. "Good. Good. Nothing will go wrong. I'll make personally... sure. Everything will be as last...time. Thank you. Thank...you!"

Ted next visited the restaurant that was preparing the buffet and confirmed that everything was on schedule. He wanted the chef and waiters off the boat before she sailed. His own people together with the crew would do the necessary. From there he went directly to The Barge.

Chapter 25

The Barge glinted like a jewel against the greys of concrete and water. She was a 136-foot converted minesweeper bought from the family of a well-known American film star who had died a few years previously. In her build she was old-fashioned, carvel built of teak and oak and remodelled to Tom's instructions by Trough Brothers. She had been converted to a pleasure cruiser in 1961 and the actor had made huge alterations. Tom, in turn, had taken out the American ostentation and produced a British Queen. In addition to the pilothouse on the top deck, it had a master stateroom and a guest stateroom each with its own bathroom, a sixty-foot after-deck for relaxing and a dining room that seated ten in comfort. On the main deck were two further staterooms, some lesser bedrooms and a large salon. In the murky daylight, under the canopy of grey drizzle, she looked a picture, but when the night fell and the lights reflected on her polish she became something exotic. Berthed next to the warships and run-down pleasure steamers she was the one that immediately caught the eye. She was a symbol and Tom was immensely proud of her. He had personally supervised the workmanship and the involvement in design and décor had been, if not an obsession, then a delight. The Barge was not opened as a nightclub. The family used it, of course, but more importantly, it was used to entertain the people whose business dealings were of interest to the family. Politicians and councillors and architects used it. And the police used it more than most. And for six months of the year, Tom chartered it, together with its crew.

The captain, Gavin Weerasirie, wore a nautical peaked cap and dark blue jacket and had a crew of four including an engineer, a cook and a steward. Weerasirie, the three men and one woman, were all loyal to Tom. Two of them were always on board to look after the stateroom with its leather and Persians and original paintings.

Ted recognized Jimmy Jones' car as he went up the gangplank and found him in the office.

"Hello Ted," Jimmy said, trying to judge Ted's mood. Every meeting held a question mark. Had Ted discovered the Star's affair? Since one of his jobs was to keep an eye on the family, Jimmy had known about it from the start.

"All right, Jimmy."

Jimmy decided that the Star's secret was still safe. "Yeah, things will go like clockwork."

"Have you heard from Dave?"

"Not yet."

Ted sighed, "You don't suppose it's possible that the old man knows about the youngster?"

Jimmy Jones raised his dark eyebrows. "Tom? No chance. That's why he asked Tommy to help out. Slags are one thing but kids are another. You know the boss and kids. He adores them. Nothing makes him angrier than to see kids hurt. He'd go fucking apeshit if he ever found out." Jimmy grunted. "Things aren't black and white anymore. Would the Scousers come down here unless Vic brought them? And he only comes for one reason. No questions asked. No chance of his old lady finding out and all the mess taken care of. He calls it his once-a-year treat!"

"What about Tommy?"

"Dave said to tell him there's been a chance of plan. Get him back to The Tower before we sail. Tell him to keep an eye on his mother."

Ted nodded but Jimmy could see that he was unhappy.

"It's not getting to you, is it?"

"Fuck no. It's business. But things are getting out of hand. I don't like keeping things from the old man, or from Tommy either."

Jimmy's eyes hardened slightly. There was a hidden, unintentional threat in Ted's concern. Dave had been right. Before long Theca's affair was going to blow and how Ted would take that was anybody's guess. And if the old man learned about the extras put on for the Scousers, then Dave was going to be embarrassed to say the least. The possibility was out of the question. And Tommy was too young, too naïve, to understand. He still needed shielding. When Dave got back from seeing Coddy he would have to sort out Theca and Ted and he would have to do it quickly. Jimmy knew that Ted would be devastated by Theca's admission and devastated men act out of character. They get pissed up and start mouthing off. The business could not afford to have Ted hurt. Not now.

"Leave things as they are for now. Talk to Dave when he gets back."

Ted agreed but his nod did not convince Jimmy. He had a gut feeling that things could go terribly wrong. If only Dave's sister could guess at the consequences of her fling.

"I'll get Tommy off The Barge before we sail," Ted confirmed. "You can use Pete Hough to keep the beer flowing on the top deck."

Jimmy nodded and walked from the office, leaving Ted staring thoughtfully into space.

Tommy arrived and they inspected The Barge together. The band was setting up slowly and methodically, as bands do, whistling through their microphones, finding the note on the keyboard or drum. The family owned them and played them as a second string in the various clubs. They were middle-of-the-road and not too noisy, and if he overlooked their self-importance Ted could just about put up with the noise they produced.

"Dickheads," he muttered. "Would they know if their instruments were out of tune?"

Tommy gave him a quizzical look and wondered what had annoyed his brother-in-law.

"Well...fuck it!"

"At least the weather's fine," he said as he peered through a porthole. "Remember last year when we had a Force Four?"

Ted grunted. What the Scousers had in mind took place downstairs anyway. It was only their followers and bit players that did the dancing and they knew nothing of what really went on. They brought their own entertainment anyway, secretaries and girlfriends, and boyfriends, anyone they wanted to impress. The Barge and the surroundings generally did that.

They checked the salon and the various bars then found Jimmy Jones and Peter Hough.

"Don't forget to take down the oil paints," Ted told Jimmy. "Put up the rubbish."

"Even the copies cost a fortune," Tommy muttered through the smoke of his cigarette.

"On my list," Jimmy confirmed.

Tommy accepted that he wouldn't be sailing without comment. If he was disappointed it didn't show. He guessed that Dave was concerned about his mother and wanted one of them close at hand, just in case.

"I'm having lunch with the Star," Ted told him. "Then she's going to the hospital with Sally. I'll be back here about six. You can take off then. Is that OK?"

Tommy agreed.

"Scousers will start turning up then, in any case. They'll want to brush-up and change."

"And the rest," Tommy grinned as he searched for an ashtray.

"Will you give Pete a lift into town?" Jimmy said.

Ted nodded and glanced at Hough, "Problems?"

"Nothing I can't handle," Hough said. "Bit of a barney with Denise before I left. She's not happy with me for coming back. You know what the girls are like."

Ted shrugged and said, "Fucking women! They're all the fucking same!"

Jimmy Jones threw him a thoughtful look.

In the car Ted tried to lift Peter Hough's despondency, even though his own was hitting rock bottom.

"Don't worry about it. Things will work out." He grunted at the irony. "It's good to have you back on the job."

"I'm glad to be back. I didn't think Dave would have it. He ain't normally into second bites, is he?"

"Dave's all right. How did it start? You leaving, I mean?"

"Fuck knows. It was my fault. You know how it is? You can't help yourself."

"Go on?"

"I saw some extra cash and went for it."

"But you got nicked? If you had cash problems you should have come to us. We don't like free enterprise."

"I know. I was grassed up. No one's to blame. Still, it won't happen again. I learned my lesson."

Ted nodded.

He dropped Peter Hough and motored across to Covent Garden. He parked under a giant hoarding advertising a performance of *Tosca* and made a note of the time, hoping to catch it.

He anticipated a heavy discussion full of recrimination and was surprised that it developed into something else. It was almost make-believe, a light-headed time. They purposely steered the conversation away from all things important and threatening. They knew fully well that the subjects would have to be addressed but this was not the time. The lunch was boozy and enjoyable; the moment, suddenly free from reality, was a necessary respite.

"Look at this! They've turned it into a Cockney Kindergarten," he said.

The garden, that little surprise that had shone through the surrounding brick since the 1600s, had gone, moved west, stolen by the town planners.

"It's all coloured brick and cobbles! The garden was a landmark, an institution. Look at it now. It's just a pile of junk to rip off the tourist!"

Theca flashed him a look of amusement. It had been a long time since she had seen him passionate about anything.

"What?"

"You, you're showing emotion. I'm not used to it."

"Sweetheart, these people need a little slap."

"I was thinking this morning," she said, "As you do."

He nodded, "Me too."

"I remember you asking Dad for his permission to marry and him saying, 'I'll think about it'." She sighed. "It seems such a long time ago."

"It was a long time ago. Things change. We've changed. For fuck's sake, just look at how Covent Garden's changed!"

With lunch finished, in his heart there remained a glimmer of hope for the family and his future with Theca, but in his head there was still anger and a mild, fleeting thought about the authorities that had the power to damage the city.

Soon after Tommy left The Barge, just before seven, the Scousers began to pull up in their shining cars. Ted watched them swagger aboard.

"Why those bastards walk so tall I'll never know," he said to Jimmy Jones.

"It's the city, the football, the Beatles, even Cilla."

"It's a shithouse, my son. It always was. It's looked over by a couple of birds that should have been shot years ago."

They staggered up the gangway, wide alcoholic grins on flushed faces, hands groping the hard girls who held them up.

Ted turned to Jimmy Jones. "Where were you anyway? I've been waiting an hour. And where's Houghie?"

"Fuck knows," Jimmy grunted. "His missus has done a bunk, or something and left the kid. He's trying to sort it."

Ted frowned. He didn't like sudden changes of plan.

"Denise pissed off? Left the kid?"

"Yeah, that's what he said."

"That doesn't seem very likely. Not from what I remember about Denise. She dotes on that kid."

"We'll sort it out later," Jimmy said.

Ted nodded, but a sense of unease still clawed at his gut.

Vic Hannington's face was red and bloated, his open-pored skin flared by booze. He removed his steel-rimmed bins and scanned the length of the Barge before placing a heavy foot on to the gangway. His expensive grey suit was too slack for his stocky build, bunched at his thickened waist; even the jacket fell forward as if each pocket was loaded with a big win from a slot machine. But he was happy. And as he stepped unsteadily on to the deck there was a confidence about him, or perhaps it was that booze-induced sense of invincibility.

The family knew all about him. There was far more than the loud-mouthed piss-artist picture he tried to paint. Controlling the Scousers needed a firm hand. Thirty years ago, when Hannington was twenty, a police dog had growled at him outside Anfield. He'd returned ten minutes later with a 12-bore and, in front of a white-faced copper, had blown off the dog's head. That was the story. It had made the papers so there was an element of truth in it. Hannington was still a mad bastard, but the madness was now controlled. Perhaps it was down to age or his marriage to a Liverpool girl. His arms spread to embrace Ted in a false show of affection. There was nothing between them that wasn't business.

"Vic," Ted said, fixing his smile on the give-away black bits of his eyes. The hug continued.

"Teddy, sunshine, it's good to be here," he said loudly, and to save his brain from exploding he replaced his dark glasses. He'd snorted his way down from Merseyside and the light was destroying his brain cells. Hannington let Ted go and stood aside while his entourage piled on to the deck. He patted the behind of a woman who wriggled by on neck-breaking silver heels.

"Dirty cow's been gobbling me all the way down here," he chuckled. "She's got a mouth on her that could Hoover up the whole of fucking Stonehenge. I'll tell you, Teddy boy, the MOD should employ her as a secret weapon!"

The women's fashions were out of the seventies and their make-up even older. They were already smashed; the party had started in the back seats of the cars. The drivers, smart men in dark suits, Ian Rush clones, watched from the wharf where they'd parked the cars in a neat row.

Pawing their women, eager to get on with it, the couples headed for their allotted cabins. The single men struggled to the bar below. The evening was a ritual. And it would go like clockwork.

Ted moved back to the side of Jimmy Jones. "We've got half an hour," he muttered. "It'll take them that long to change."

He saw Lo Fok's van pull up. His girls had arrived earlier and were tarting themselves up in one of the forward cabins.

"Here's Fok," he said absently, momentarily checking the wharf for any strange vehicles: post-office vans, council workers, that sort of thing.

"That's my bag," Jimmy Jones said and started toward the gangway. Ted checked his watch, spent a few minutes with Weerasirie then went to the office and the adjoining quarters. It was all in hand now. He would, from time to time throughout the evening, make the odd appearance but, come the dawn, the Scousers wouldn't remember whether they'd seen him or not.

Traitor's Gate slipped by as Jimmy Jones checked out the salon. The party was underway. Lo Fok's girls, all of them quite beautiful, were kept busy. Apart from short transparent aprons they were naked. One was already on her back, circled by guests. A white Merseyside arse moved between her legs. The onlookers applauded. Liverpool had scored.

Jimmy Jones moved into the office and glanced through the open door to the private quarters where Ted rested on the sofa. His legs were drawn up on to a glass-topped coffee table. A bottle of malt lay in his lap, the golden liquid swinging gently from one end to the other, picking up a sparkle from the wall lights set in the oak panelling. In his repose Ted's mouth hung open and his breath rattled. Jimmy Jones smiled gently and his craggy features softened. He moved the bottle and set it quietly on the coffee table then turned down the lighting to barely a glow. In the office he opened the horizontal slats of a long blind that concealed a two-way to the master stateroom and leant closer for a better view.

Mother and daughter were in there. Fok had laid out his instructions to the letter. The daughter was doped, drooping, a slight, fragile figure in the centre of the master bed. Her wrists were tied by loose ribbon that looped over each corner of the bed. She had some freedom but no escape. The older woman sat by her, stroking her hair, reassuring. She was undressed down to her briefs. Her daughter was naked. There was no sign of Hannington.

Jimmy Jones saw nothing but the girl and he felt anger tighten his chest. He saw the white soles of two small feet, bony knees held almost together, long thin legs, a raised pubis barely touched with hair, a flat trembling belly, the outline of ribs and the protuberance of small breasts with the soft tips hardly defined. She lay motionless on the wide bed, her neck and shoulders propped up on a high pillow. Her mother, kneeling beside her, used one hand to rub oil between the youngster's legs; her other was hidden by the girl's curls as she stroked and caressed.

Jimmy Jones had already decided that after the event he would look up the mother and cause her some terrible grief, but for now he said, "There ain't no way that slag is her mother!" overlooking the remarkable likeness.

"That is her mother," Ted said from just behind him. Jimmy hadn't heard his approach and was visible shaken. Ted swallowed half his drink and leant forward over Jimmy's shoulder. "What's happening?"

Vic Hannington marched into the room. He wore an open bathrobe and his semi-erect penis dangled out like a kozzer's truncheon.

"Get the state of that bastard!" Jimmy whispered as though he might be overheard. "Look at his minces. He must have used up half Fok's supply already!"

Hannington was barking orders, slapping a small bamboo cane he carried into the palm of his hand. The youngster was oblivious to it all, just stared out of wide slipping eyes, but the mother jumped. Hannington looked enormous beside the two of them, the fat on his sagging chest and belly concealed by a mat of greying hair. The older woman half stood to meet him but he lashed out with his fist, splitting her jaw, and even as she fell back on to the bed her blood splattered the cream cover. Hannington held her face down while he grabbed at her flimsy underwear. For a moment her behind was lifted up until the material gave and she fell back over the end of the bed. Her knees barely touched the floor. He used the cane, drawing a welt with every swipe. And like an old-fashioned pump, each swish of the cane jacked up his penis. He left the older woman crying. They couldn't see her face, pressed as it was into the bed, but they saw her entire body shaking as her knees sagged to the floor. Hannington crawled on to the bed, between the girl's skinny legs. He moved his hands beneath her to lift her like a rag doll.

Jimmy Jones turned away and said, "I can't stand any more of this shit! That bastard needs putting down."

Ted closed the blinds and shrugged weakly. He waited until Jimmy had gone then returned to the other room. He poured himself another drink and flipped the play on the stack. The advertisement in Covent Garden came to mind and he selected a disc. *Tosca* filled the room. He turned up the volume and lay back on sofa finding his earlier position. The music washed over him. His expression was fixed, tired, almost resigned. He might have been considering the state of his marriage, or puzzling over the accounts; he might have been thinking about the youngster next door and the cries he thought he could hear above the intoxicating music.

Chapter 26

The explosions lifted The Barge almost clear of the water and punched a forty-foot long gash into her belly. One man, throwing up over the gunwale, somersaulted off. There were three explosions, remote controlled, instantaneous and, even as she settled back, she was rolling. They were not deafening explosions, more of a loud roar that seemed to rush down the corridors and companionways. Observers from the bank would certainly have heard them and seen the bow lift and roll slightly and glimpsed the gaping hole that settled back below the water line. The black gash would have been visible in the dark because of the red glow and the lances of orange flame that hissed up above the water. On the after-deck the crowd began to panic and shout and scream. The roll had caused the deck to dip and people slipped as they fought to reach the raised starboard. Bow and port were down. The black water crept over the portside railings. A few people jumped and began to swim towards the bank.

Ted thought that thunder was clapping around his ears. He was pitched off the sofa and thrown against the cabin wall. Even as he regained his feet and felt the angle of the floor he knew that The Barge was going under. He reached the door as the cabin rolled. He hauled himself through even as the cabin slipped farther. Smoke poured out of the corridor and the stairwell. Above the increasing roar he heard the screams and shouts from the salon below. He peered down the well through the smoke that hissed upward as if it were a chimney and saw the teak deck planks bowing and lifting. The boat shuddered. A surge of water rushed through the corridor and the well became a cauldron. Ted made for the pilothouse door and was all but carried through it by the rushing water. He clung to the railings, waist deep, legs carried almost horizontally by the current. The Barge turned slowly on to her side. Most of the people from the upper deck were in the water, clinging to the wreckage and splashing to the banks. On the banks a crowd had mustered. People waded in to help others to the shore. Small dinghies and rowboats moved out to the sinking hull. Jimmy Jones surfaced clinging to Vic Hannington.

"Where is she, you bastard?"

Hannington's naked shoulders caught the light and looked white in the swirling waters. The rubbery mouth was not smiling but there was a grin about it. Under the water Jimmy Jones used his switchblade. He tugged upward into Hannington's gut. The fat man's grin turned to a grimace. He growled and rose out of the water. For a moment he was suspended above Jimmy, hands on his shoulders. Jimmy laughed. His hands were still on the knife, above the water now, slicing into Hannington's ribcage. Hannington embraced him and his weight carried them both under.

The Barge rolled farther and began to slide. Her stern cleared the water, and the topside of her massive rudder and propeller appeared. From the hawsehole a jet of steam shot into the air as the bulkhead fractured. For the first time Ted was aware of the cold water. His hands were numb around the rail. He felt as though he was being controlled by another force, that he had no choice of his own. He let go of the railing and slipped back toward the pilothouse door. As the water rose he forced a deep breath and ducked under. The first thing he noticed was the silence, silence except for the clanking of the hull. He kicked forward from the doorframe and swam down to the stateroom, using the fixed partition of the wall for purchase. Incredibly the lights still shone and threw a ghostly green illumination into the water. The water itself was like a soup, full of specks that caught the dim glow. His visibility was down to about two yards but it was sufficient. He dived almost vertically through the narrow width of the master stateroom. The pressure on his ears was almost unbearable. The light became brighter.

The girl was suspended on the loose ribbons, her body half turned toward him, her hair like a sea anemone curling about her face. The bed was fixed to the floor and was therefore at an angle. It framed the girl like a giant picture. As he approached he heard the music. *Tosca* was etched into his head, perhaps into this tomb.

His breath was running out. Even as he struggled to unfasten the girl's wrists he thought of his children and he saw them in the dead face and spindle limbs of the youngster. His body was numb, giving up, his lungs at bursting point. He pulled the girl through the stateroom. The lights began to dim and he wondered fleetingly whether it was his consciousness. The opera had played out its last tragic note.

Above, the stern swung farther up before sliding and disappearing. A life raft, still tied to the hull, bobbed on the surface for a moment before being swallowed like a fisherman's float. Floating wreckage was all that was left; a few people still thrashed the water; a group of small boats marked the spot. On the banks the police-cars and ambulances and fire engines wailed and flashed blue and orange and searchlights came on one by one. The lights shone on the wreckage and on the dirty smear of grey smoke against the midnight sky.

Chapter 27

The Chinatown wars resulted from the scramble to fill the vacuum left when two of the major London gangs, one from each side of the river, were locked up in the late-sixties.

With only minor interruptions, the Chinese community in Britain had been quietly going about their business, paying their local dues certainly, but filtering larger payments through Gerrard Street to their masters in Hong Kong. Fuelled by suggestions from these masters to fill the gap left by the gangs and expand their interests, particularly in heroin and prostitution, the Chinese gangs in London tried for complete independence. Naturally the smaller London villains were opposed to losing their rake-off from the eating-houses and they sent in some unsophisticated muscle to deal with the problem. The masters sent in skilled assassins to counter the threat and two local figures, Reynolds from the Wet End and Hipkiss from the south, were hacked to death on their own doorsteps. Cleverly the Chinese played off one local gang against another, spreading the rumour that each gang was making separate deals. More killings followed with the small gangs having a go at each other. Public houses were wrecked by gunfire. Before long it became apparent that the Chinese had got themselves a leader and, from the loyalty and fear that the man generated, it was accepted that he was a master sent from the Far East to take charge. The way that the Chinese fought, their victims mutilated by knives and machete, sent panic across the capital.

The smaller gangs were losing the war, their strengths depleted more by desertion than casualty, their financial reserves exhausted and, more importantly, left empty because the various collection points had broken down with the collectors themselves too frightened to venture into the open.

Tom Smith had kept a low profile. His non-involvement in the war had mostly to do with his lack of interest in Gerrard Street and the fact that he felt no great allegiance to the other gangs. He was dismayed at the way in which the twin's organization had turned on them and his time was now spent in confirming the loyalty of his own people. At this stage, though, the gangs approached Tom Smith and asked him to try to negotiate a peace with the Chinese.

At a meeting held at The Tower, Tom listened to the five gang leaders complaining bitterly at the Chinese tactics. They explained how they had never wanted the war, that they had always been willing to negotiate even though it meant giving up huge areas of profit. The Chinese had been unwilling to talk. They described the present situation where their families were afraid to walk the streets of London, where even their friends were afraid to be seen with them. They told how their arsenals and their finances had all but been wiped out and they pleaded with Tom to intervene. His forces were intact; the Chinese would listen to him. In return they offered him a cut of their future business. In effect, they were asking him to lead them.

"I'll think about it," he told them. "But I'll tell you this much. I'm not all that keen on seeing the streets of London run from the other side of the world. I make no promises, but you all know me. I'll see what can be done."

The five men left The Tower reasonably confident in their new ally. Any reservations were put aside in a situation that left them few options.

Against the advice of the few men that Tom Smith held dear he had stuck to his guns and distanced himself and his organization from the warring gangs. He'd gone out of his way to make it known that he wasn't interested and had no plans to expand. Others, including his son Dave, had argued that if the Chinese were allowed to win the war they would be in a strong position to threaten the Smith's own interests. But Tom was adamant and ordered his people to keep away from the trouble.

At the same time, quietly, unobtrusively, he increased his own muscle. His payments for information and influence were more than doubled. Long before the meeting with the gang leaders he already had a shrewd estimate of the strengths and weaknesses of the various participants. Although the Chinese leader's identity remained a mystery, Tom Smith was not unduly worried. He knew enough about their set-up to have already identified some of the key figures.

Dave was young and eager to make his mark. He was not yet ready to lead his own men and, although there were a few that worked for him, their loyalty was first and foremost to his father. This was a source of frustration for Dave. Patience had never been his strong suit. He'd sat listening intently throughout the meeting but once the others had gone he turned to his father.

"Pop, let me handle this one," he said earnestly, almost pleading.

"And do what?" His father smiled. "The other day I heard a Chinese proverb, about golf. Even if you hit your ball three hundred yards and straight down the middle it won't improve your game if you're aiming at the wrong flag!"

"What's that supposed to mean?"

"It means that before you go in you've got to know where you're going. What are you going to do, eh? Take out every slant-eyed geezer in London?" He regarded his son with affection. "Don't worry, my son, things will work out."

Dave was surprised by his father's casual attitude.

His father smiled and told him, "Something could happen that would make our further involvement unnecessary. Always remember that when you're thinking of rushing in. And one other thing to remember is that when you've got a point to make, make it with such a noise that no one will ever forget it! Brutality is a lethal weapon but it's got to be used sparingly and selectively. It must never be wasted. Brutality for its own sake is mere indulgence. And indulgence has got no place in business."

Few people knew when it was that Sek Hoi first arrived; he had been seen in most of the restaurants in Soho long before his credentials swept like a cold wind through the Chinese community. He was an unassuming seventy-year-old man. His back was bent and his short legs carried him with the typical Chinese gait. His face was criss-crossed with lines and strands of white hair fell on either side of his mouth, a mouth that would open to reveal a line of gold teeth. Each morning at seven-thirty he arrived from Leicester Square underground station and made his slow way around to Gerrard Street. He would stop and talk to a few colleagues standing on the narrow pavements before their grocery shops and restaurants; he might stand to scrutinize the posters advertising the latest crop of films that came out of Hong Kong that were showing in the local clubs and then, promptly at eight, he would enter his son's restaurant that was situated in one of the small alleys just off Gerrard Street.

His son, his son's wife and his nephew were his only family in the cold wet country and each morning he looked forward to seeing them again. He didn't sleep well and the nights were long. They, particularly his son's pretty little wife who came from Peking and spoke only Mandarin, made an absolute fuss of him and made him wish that he was forty years younger. They were his only comfort in the months he had been here. He had left behind two other sons and their families and was impatient to get back to them.

On this particular morning his son wasn't at the door to greet him and he entered the silent restaurant feeling slightly offended. His nephew had started to hang the cold meats. The flattened ducks and strips of pork hung from hooks in the front window. In the dimness of the restaurant he saw the ivory mah-jong bricks scattered between the tables and chairs across the threadbare carpet and he wondered what had happened. He was considering what degree of anger he should show toward his son and nephew as he made his way to the back of the restaurant. As he neared the kitchen the air grew heavy and held in it the sweet aroma of cooking meat.

He had taken three paces into the kitchen before his old eyes grew accustomed to the bright lights and then he was stopped in his tracks, his mind stunned by the scene before him. First he saw his nephew hanging on a meat hook. Blood dripped from his flip-flops and splashed into a pool beneath him. Hardly daring to look further, his neck rigid, the old man's gaze shifted to the torso on the work surface. It might have been his son but since the head was missing it was at that moment just a guess. The deep fat fryer contained the body of his son's wife. She was sitting in it, waist deep, naked except for the batter that she'd been rolled in. Her legs dangled over the side. The overheated fat bubbled and smoked. The batter had crisped and given her a golden corset and her small breasts projected over it.

His cry was not a scream but more of a long moan as though it was his very life that was being sucked out of him. The scream came from outside the restaurant. It came to him with such piercing clarity that it pulled him back from the horror, back through the restaurant, stumbling over the chairs, spewing a trail of vomit across the threadbare carpet. At the door he saw that three people had gathered at the window. A woman was screaming, being held up by the two men. One of the men saw Sek Hoi at the door and used his free hand to point to the window. The old man came out into the street and peered through the misty glass at the ranks of hanging meat, at the flattened duck carcasses, at the strips of pork loin and at his son's head. And then his scream was real and no longer the prolonged moan. He screamed and screamed and people ran out from the nearby buildings to see the old man slipping into madness. From that day until the end of his life some said that Sek Hoi never spoke another word of sense.

No one ever found out who was responsible for the murders but a lot of people thought they knew. The only witness described four men gathered by the restaurant in the early hours. He remembered one in particular because of the scar on his head, he said, and because of his size. But since the witness was a wino using the doorway opposite for comfort not many people gave much credit to his description.

Twelve days after the meeting in The Tower the war was over. The local community had threatened to withdraw their payments to the masters in Honk Kong because they were too distant to guarantee their safety from such a merciless enemy. The masters had no alternative but to sue for peace and they agreed to a set of higher percentage payments to the various gangs. In turn, they also stated a peculiar allegiance to the Smiths. There was no such thing as status quo.

Tom Smith entered into an agreement with the Chinese that remained good to this day. The smaller gangs had few options, since their forces were totally depleted, and since Tom had given them richer pickings from the Chinese trade they elected him their unofficial leader. There had been a vacancy. It had been filled.

Chapter 28

A chair scraped the floor as Tom Smith's youngest son drew it towards Ted's hospital bed. He sat on the hard green plastic and leant forward.

"The filth's outside with questions harder than *Mastermind*, know what I mean? There are two nurses and a doctor holding them on leashes but they'll be here in a minute. Are you all right?"

"Am I all right? I was blown out of my fucking office, swallowed half the Thames, got myself a dislocated shoulder, and you ask if I'm all right! What are you, a fucking comedian?" Ted shook his head and relented, "That's as close as I'm ever going to come. I started hearing *Songs of Praise* back there, and it wasn't Sunday."

"It could have been worse. You were lucky."

"Worse? How could it have been worse? Waking up and finding it wasn't a fucking nightmare is worse. I wasn't lucky. I was stupid. I put it on the line trying to keep the family out of it."

"You're part of the family," Tommy said seriously. "Weerasirie told me what happened. The girl hasn't turned up."

Surprised that the captain had told Tommy about the girl he said, "There was a bastard tide. She'll turn up sooner or later but they'll have a job proving anything." He paused and rubbed his shoulder before asking, "So what's the final score?"

"Nineteen bodies: twelve Scousers and seven women. They would have stood more chance if they hadn't been totally legless. Some of them started swimming up river! Jimmy's dead. Vic's dead. That one's a bit dodgy on account of a knife sticking out of his chest and his guts feeding the fish between here and Southend. I don't think the filth will buy a drowning. Liverpool is totally wiped out. There's still four missing."

"Who was it? Do we know yet?"

"Everyone is saying Mad Mick but it doesn't make much sense. Why should he want to take out the Scousers? That sort of stunt is guaranteed to have them line up with us. As it happened they've been wiped out but Mick couldn't have guessed that. If anything they were going to side with Mick."

Ted agreed. "You're right. It doesn't make sense. But who else could it be?"

"I'll see Pop first thing. Maybe he'll have some ideas. He'll go off the wall about The Barge."

"No point in telling him about the girl," Ted said hesitantly.

"I suppose not," Tommy said. The veil was in and out of his eyes. "They found the mother's body. Fok has already been on the blower, wanting to bill us. I'd like to know what it's all about."

"You can ask your brother."

"I will, Ted. I'll ask you both."

"Fuck off, Tommy. I've swallowed enough crap for one night. I don't need any of it from you."

Tommy nodded slowly but the steel glint in his eye indicated that the subject wasn't finished with, not by a long shot. "I'm off then, before the filth arrives in force. They've got Weetasirie and the others but they'll sit tight. The captain was telling them it was the IRA thinking we had a police convention on board."

Ted grinned. "Is Peach with them?"

"Yeah, he's heading it up at the moment but the top brass will get involved without a doubt. The anti-terrorist mob as well. There's no way he'll keep it under wraps. It sounded like the Argies were having a go with Exocets again!"

"Well it's about time Detective Inspector Peach earned his keep. The least he can do is keep some of the heat off us for a while."

"We'd need a fucking Commissioner to do that."

Tommy stood up to go.

"One other thing, Tommy," Ted said. "Find out what happened to Peter Hough. He didn't show. Something about Denise going missing but it rang all sorts of bells. And for Christ's sake watch your back. If it's not Mad Mick then there's another mad bastard knocking on our door who knows his way around explosives – and The Barge! How can someone get on The Barge without being seen? Get a message to your sister for me. Tell her… Tell her they're keeping me in overnight. Don't bother coming because I'll be with the filth anyway. I'll see her in the morning."

"OK, I'll do that," Tommy said thoughtfully. "By the way, whatever the girl's about, you did us all a favour."

Ted grunted and waved a dismissive hand.

Another grey day dawned; the sky wept for the dead. It had rained heavily during the night. The roads and pavements glistened, the gutters dripped. It was after nine when Tommy arrived at the hospital and it cost him to get in to see his father and then only for a short time and in a starkly lit bathroom, not in the ward. Slumped in a wheelchair his father looked tired and fragile, the disconnected end to a drip feed still plastered to his arm but the nose tube had been removed. Below his dressing gown his pale, bony ankles bridged blue pyjamas and slippers. His pyjama collar was rumpled over his dressing gown. A white film of stubble matted his chin.

"Blimey, boy, what's been happening out there?"

"Pop, it's good to see you," Tommy began.

Tom nodded and affection clouded his eyes. He smiled. "Calm down, my son. Come and give your old man the full SP. I'm hearing some diabolical things."

Tommy perched on a wall radiator and apart from the details about the girl he told his father everything he knew. Tom took it all in. His eyes narrowed in disbelief. At the end of it he remained silent, thoughtful, nodding to himself. A tiny muscle in his jaw throbbed and an inner lid matted his eyes. Eventually he said, "It's a diabolical liberty, that's what it is. I saw the BBC and couldn't believe what I was seeing. It looked like a bleedin' war zone down there." He nodded some more. "I'd like to call Dave back but that's out of the question. The boy's got things to do. Anyway, my son, you can handle it. Backs against the wall, Stanley Baker and Michael Caine, know what I mean? Let Ted handle the law and the financial angle. This is going to cost us a pretty penny. I want you to get over and see Mike Mountford. If he isn't there you find him. Don't come home till you do. Get him to put the feelers out. I want to know who's done this to us. I want to know if it's Mick. I'm going to drop a fucking atom bomb on somebody. Maybe Glasgow, maybe not, but someone's going to pay for this. Every last one of them, right down to their last conker, is going to be wiped off this earth."

Tommy couldn't remember seeing his father so angry. But he knew that part of it was down to him not being able to lead from the front.

"See Mike Mountford," his father repeated. "He'll know who turned my boat into another *Belgrano*." He sank back into the wheelchair. "Barry Theroux is going to have to take Jimmy's place for the time being. You can trust him. Get him to see Jimmy's family. Make sure they're all right. They won't be, of course, but get him to do what he can. If you've got the time, then look into Houghie's business. Don't do anything yourself. Just check it out quietly. I want Dave to deal with that personally, when he gets back." Tom sighed. "There might be nothing to it but let's make certain. One last thing, boy, this is going to upset your mother. Look after her. Play things down. No need to worry her more than necessary."

Tommy nodded. "There is something else Pop, but it's not important."

"What's that, my son?"

"It's Jane. The old girl has gone to pieces. There's no fobbing her off, she's too wise for that, knows you too well. Although we haven't said anything she's put two and two together and come up with how serious your condition is. I've caught her in the office twice now, crying like there was no tomorrow. She made little of it but I know it's more than that. She's making herself ill. I'm thinking of sending her home but she won't have it."

Tom's eyes glazed. "Don't do that, boy, not unless she wants to go." He smiled wistfully. "You can do something for me, on the QT. I want you to make sure she gets a proper slot at the funeral and that she's taken care of. Bring James Jessel out of retirement and give him the job. He's an old geezer, but he's got the old days behind him. He'll know how to handle her. I want her escorted all the way, there and back. She's treated like royalty, boy, make sure of that. And afterwards, she wants for nothing. Understand? There's nothing more to say on the subject. Not now, not ever." His father's lips tightened and Tommy knew that was the end of it.

Tommy bent low and whispered, "I can't handle this. I'm dying inside."

Tom's eyes sparked into life. "Yes, you can, my son. I never thought I'd die in a hospital bed, from something as common as a fucked-up chicken-Madras, but there you go. The gods have a sense of humour. Take care of your mother, Tommy. Apart from Mike Mountford she is your only concern."

Tommy hugged his father before leaving. It was more than a gesture of affection, more even than a need for comfort and reassurance. It was the cold embrace of a warrior about to go to war.

"Go on then," Tom told his youngest son. "You've got things to do."

Tommy was angry about being kept out of the business and shielded, now more than ever, but more than that, for even ignoring his sense of outrage at the abuse and death of the child, he felt that keeping the details from his father was a betrayal. He could barely believe that his bothers were involved in such violation, but in hindsight he shouldn't have been surprised. Nothing about Dave would surprise him any more. He remembered a girl named Isobel Ferreira. She was a fellow student in the sixth form, a seventeen-year-old brunette whose natural good looks could melt a man's heart, and certainly melted his. She liked to sing and dance and was involved in the college dramatic society. They'd dated a few times but that's as far as it had got and he was still working on breaking down her resistance. On what was to be their final date she had asked him to get her an audition at one of the nightclubs.

When he approached Dave he was a bit taken aback by his bother's attitude. He looked at the snapshots she'd supplied and said, "I've seen dozens of girls like her. She's just using you to get a job on the stage."

"It's not like that, Dave. I've seen her dance at the college and she's really talented. You could at least give her a chance. You've got the clout, haven't you?"

Dave laughed at him. "Why don't you just fuck her and get it over with?"

Tommy felt embarrassed and knew his colour was rising.

"All right," Dave relented. "Get her to come in and I'll ask Leigh to take a look at her. No promises." Leigh Fraser was in charge of the club entertainment.

When Tommy met her after the audition he was totally blanked. "Your brother is a total shit," was all that she would tell him.

Dave told him, "She got the job, what's the problem?"

She left the college that same day and Tommy rarely saw her again and it wasn't until a year later that he saw her in the club but still she ignored him. Up until that time Tommy was not allowed in the clubs, his father's rule. He was eighteen before the directive was relaxed and even then he was kept out of the casino. It was Jimmy Jones who confided that Isobel's job involved private dancing and porn films and a whole lot more in the penthouse suites.

He never asked Dave for a favour again.

The earth at the back of Mike Mountford's garage was sterile and black. There wasn't even a weed to be seen. It crossed Tommy's mind as he made his way between a line of second-hand cars that, in a thousand years time, when the garage had gone and assuming that oil was still just about the most important thing to the Western World, some prospector was going to drill a hole here and think he'd hit the jackpot.

The garage was dark and dirty, every surface littered with spare parts and tools and grease. A bench was piled high with invoices and MOTs, tea-makings and dirty cups and full ashtrays. A Jaguar stood over the well. To the right of that, in mint condition, a red Stag stood with its bonnet up. Light flickered beneath it. A spanner dropped on the concrete floor and a woman cussed. Tommy walked across to the legs he could see protruding from beneath the car. Black leather soles stuck over the end of a duckboard. He touched one of them with his own foot. The overall clad legs stiffened, then, "Is that you, Mike?"

Tommy said, "I'm looking for Mike."

The duckboard eased out. Flat on her back on the board, holding a spanner across her chest, she looked up at him. A smudge of grease blacked her forehead and cheek. She looked about seventeen, without a hint of make-up, short brown hair cropped, her body enveloped in a massive boiler suit. She'd left the light beneath the car and in the gloom the shadows caught her features. Her dark brown eyes were deep set above prominent cheekbones.

"Who wants him?" The question was cold and clipped.

She saw a man in his early twenties, short curly black hair, steely blue eyes, brown leather jacket, loose white shirt, jeans and expensive shoes. Too stylish for a copper, and the shoes were way too expensive for your average MOT inspector, so he was probably a villain. He stood against the garage door with the light behind him and her squint was to increase the detail. He thought the frown and the narrowed eyes were a look of disapproval.

"My name's Tommy Smith. Mike's a friend."

"He never mentioned you," she said. She struggled up from the duckboard and began to wipe her hands on a rag. She was taller than he first thought, around five eight or nine.

"Does he tell you about all his friends?"

She glanced up at him and again he noticed the calculation in her eyes. When she spoke he noticed her lips and his gaze was drawn to them. They were wide and full and the little V on the top was prominent and covered with a film of fair hair.

"Yes," she said. "He tells me about all his friends, and his enemies." The eyes glinted now, full of mischief. Perhaps she'd noticed his nervousness or perhaps he'd become less of a threat.

"He must have forgotten to mention me."

"I don't think so. The Tommy Smith he talks about is older, and he's in hospital. It's not you." She held the heavy spanner by her side, not letting it go even while she wiped her hands. She moved across to the bench and plugged in a kettle.

"That's my old man," Tommy said.

She turned to face him. "So that makes you Tommy junior?"

Tommy decided that she was too confident to be seventeen.

"There's a law about employing minors. Does Mike know about it? How old are you anyway?"

Her lips pursed. "That's none of your business, Junior."

He laughed out loud. "You're right. Do you think you could tell me where Mike is? I've been to the house but there's no answer."

"Do you want a cuppa?"

"I want a word with Mike," he insisted.

"He's not here."

"You're not the easiest person to talk to, you know that? Any idea where he is?"

She shook her head, smiling now.

"What time is he due back?"

She sighed and said, "Pass on that as well. It's not your day, is it? He never came home last night. I haven't seen him since he packed up here yesterday lunchtime. Some guy called for him. It's no big deal. He's done it before. Crawled home two or three days later with his tail between his legs and a hangover between his ears. He's like that. He does things on impulse. Probably met up with a friend and gone on a bender. It's happened before, more than once, and it'll happen again."

With these few short words and in these few short moments Tommy was aware of his gut fluttering and he knew that it wasn't just another pretty face that had done it. He needed to get out, breathe some air and shake her image out of his head. He knew it wouldn't be easy.

"Who called for him?"

"What is this? He didn't tell me. A face is a face, right? He was a big untidy guy, not up to much. Will that do?"

"What's that mean, not up to much?"

"Well, he was driving a Lada for a start. Now, cars I do know."

"Dark blue?"

"So what? Nine out of ten of them are." She put down the spanner. The threat had ceased to exist. "What's going on?" For the first time there was concern in her voice. "Pop's all right, isn't he?"

"You're family. That figures." Tommy smiled and nodded. "I'm sure Mike's OK."

"Why are you looking for him?"

"It isn't about an MOT."

"He can't help you then."

"Someone's been playing battleships with our boat. We were hoping Mike could help us."

Her eyes widened fractionally. "That was your boat on the news?"

"Yes, was is right."

"Pop can't help you. This is a garage not a boatyard."

Tommy grunted. "It needs more than a dry dock. A scrap yard maybe."

"What happened?" Without asking she stirred sugar into the strong tea and pushed a mug towards him.

"Somebody put a bomb on board."

"I heard that much on the news. I meant who was it? Why should the IRA have a go at your boat?"

"Who said the Micks were involved?"

She shrugged. "They're the only ones throwing bombs about."

He shook his head. "No, Sweetheart, I doubt if it was them. They've got no argument with us."

"Don't call me sweetheart, my name's Jill. You still haven't said what Pop's got to do with it?"

"He's got nothing to do with it. He knows a lot of people, that's all. He might have come across a whisper."

"He didn't."

"What's that supposed to mean?"

"Well, if Pop heard anything about something like that he would have been on to your dad straight away. That's what friends are for or didn't you know?"

"I didn't mean before it happened. If something was going down with explosives your old man could probably point a finger. He knows more about that scene than anyone in the Smoke. They don't call him the fireman for nothing."

She studied him for a moment and a frown touched her brow. "That might have been the case once, but not now. Why do you suppose he spends half his day knee-deep in engine oil?"

"Just because he's retired doesn't make him less of an expert. And he's all we've got."

"You haven't got much then. In any case why should he help you? He's finished with all that."

"That's what friends are for, or didn't you know?"

Tommy didn't tell her that when Mike Mountford was first released from Parkhurst it was his father who set him up in the garage business.

"What are you doing now?" she asked. "I mean, I haven't got a clue where he is."

"I'll try again later.

"Well, you could buy me lunch while you waited. A girl's got to eat."

Tommy smiled. He knew he should have got out before.

"I'll be back in ten minutes," she said. "There's a shower in the back. It's the one thing I insisted on when he asked me to help run this place."

"I'll wait in the car."

She regarded the Rover through the open double doors.

"Not bad," she said. "I'll drive."

She changed into a white V-necked sweater, jeans and white sneakers. She'd added a touch of lipstick and her short hair was still damp.

"Ready?" she said and he handed over the keys.

She drove expertly across to Westminster Bridge. He showed her where to park in the Trading Company's private spaces and she said, "You'll be clamped or towed," and seemed surprised by his response.

He smiled and shook his head and murmured, "I don't think so."

But she understood, or at least she thought she did. She had heard of the family. Most people in the Smoke knew the name. It was whispered in every boozer north of the river. Her father had often spoken about them, and always enthusiastically, but just lately the newspapers had depicted them in less than favourable terms. They'd painted a frightening picture of the underworld where gangsters and hoodlums ruled. But there was something about Tommy that she found curious. He was nothing like the characters the papers were describing, the hard vulgar men that lacked all feeling and morality. If it were possible he seemed to be too natural, and at odds with his apparent self-assurance was a shyness she found both appealing and puzzling.

He turned to her. "What I'd like to do, if you've got the time, is to take the boat trip. It'll take us 'round the Dogs and I can get to see what's left of The Barge. How about it? We'll be back in an hour and then we can eat at Arpino's. That's the best little Italian in town. Do you like spaghetti?"

"I'll settle for that."

"That's good. We can get a drink on the boat. You are old enough to drink?"

She smiled easily and said "I told you before, junior, that's none of your business. You didn't set this up just to find out how old I am, did you?"

"Would I do that? Just didn't want any more trouble with the law. We've got enough of that already."

"You're safe," she said.

A semicircle of Sally Anns played to the tourists. Across from them a seafood and pie-and-mash stall was set up. A few of the more intrepid sightseers were trying jellied eels and pulling faces. A group of Japanese and American tourists weighed down with cameras and foot-long lenses paid for their *War Cries* before clambering aboard.

Tommy barely had time to order drinks before the pleasure steamer set off. They sat in the prow along with the tourists. Jill studied her plastic beaker containing dark rum and martini.

"They didn't give me a cherry," she said.

"They're right out of cherries. I'll get you one another time."

She glanced up and smiled at the shielded invitation. "You're being a bit presumptuous, aren't you?"

"Well, I hope there'll be another time."

"I heard you Smiths were a bit predatory."

"Not all of us."

"Huh!"

He tasted the plastic and pulled a face. "It's not very sophisticated, is it? Do they serve drinks in plastic cups in the rest of the world? I've been all over and this is the only place I've found them."

"I doubt it. But you're right. This place is not very anything nowadays. Do you think it ever was?"

Amplifiers crackled and a taped Cockney voice said, "The stone on the bridge is self-cleansing…"

The tourists swung their heads from left to right.

"That small yellow building is the former residence of Christopher himself and from there he could look over the river and see the brickies at work. We're approaching the site of the Old Globe where my old mate Bill Shakespeare used to sell ice creams. What's to say about the famous Billingsgate except that the local councillors did something that Hitler's bombers never managed? And here's Traitor's Gate where those bleedin' councillor's heads should be hanging. Look at the ravens, the Bloody Tower, the torture chambers! Gor-blimey, you're seeing it all today!"

The steamer passed under the final bridge and chugged on around the slow bend. The Barge lay on her side, secured as close to the wall as possible. In the low tide she was only half-submerged. Dozens of people crawled over her. Small boats including two gleaming police launches were tied to her hull. Up above, between the series of cranes that had been drawn up, the area had been completely cordoned off and the long mobile incident rooms were already in place. Out of the gloom the flashing lights from the vehicles sparkled like blue and gold gems and were reflected on the low water.

Tommy's look turned dark. She saw the distress in his eyes as the extent of the catastrophe suddenly hit home. The news reports on the television showed nothing of the scale; somehow it had been miniaturized. The tourists babbled excitedly, pointing toward the wreckage and clicking off dozens of snapshots.

"As great rivers go it's a poor bastard river," Tommy said quietly. "It's got no rapids or waterfalls. And just lately even the fish have pissed off."

Unaware that she had done so, Jill had placed her hand on top of his. He turned to look at her and for the first time she saw fear and uncertainty.

Softly she said to him, "I'm so sorry."

Arpino's Pizzeria stood on the corner opposite Westminster Bridge. It was a small, bustling glass-fronted parlour that held a dozen white and red tables. It had a continental feel and was spotlessly clean. Frank Arpino and his brother Marc, distant cousins of Pinchera, ran it and owned fifty percent of the place. The Smiths owned the rest. They were regular customers and had the utmost respect and confidence in the Arpinos. The partnership had developed into something more and the brothers were considered part of the family. Frank and Marc and their wives who helped out made a great fuss of the grandchildren. If there was ever a problem it came when the bill was settled. The Arpinos wouldn't hear of it but Tom Smith made it clear that the bills were to be paid. The Arpinos gave in to this and would present the bill but only when their father made one of his infrequent visits. He would bring the grandchildren during their school holidays and on the weekend of the boat race and he would make a great fuss of counting out the exact money. No tip.

Jill was mildly surprised by the attention and guessed that it was special even before it was confirmed. The Arpinos wanted to know about his father and about The Barge, showing genuine concern. She waited until they were served before she said, "All right, junior, I'm impressed."

He toyed with his long glass of lager before looking up.

"That wasn't the intention."

"Oh no?" She held his gaze for a moment longer than necessary then said quietly, "You're not what I expected at all."

"What did you expect?"

"Something else. Something dangerous and definitely something to stay a mile away from."

"You read too much. You shouldn't believe everything in the papers."

"I don't. But I hear people talk about the Smiths. I bet they used to talk about the Krays and the Richardsons in the same way, in whispers and in fear, glancing behind them before they spoke the name."

"You can't blame us for what other people say or think."

"Where there's smoke there's usually fire. People aren't frightened without cause."

"Who's frightened? We help out loads of people. They come to us. I'll tell you something. For every hundred favours we dish out we get, maybe, one in return. I'd say that had more to do with giving than taking."

She said abruptly, "You're into protection, everyone knows that."

Tommy flashed a quizzical look, "Protection? If that's true nobody told me about it. If everybody knows, like you say, then why isn't the Old Bill interested? When you get a name you have to be cleaner than clean. That makes sense. Listen, if there was anything dodgy about our affairs the Old Bill would be all over us. We've got the clubs, the hotel and casino, so why on earth would we want to be involved in something like that?"

"You don't have a very high regard for the police?"

He grunted contemptuously. "Not a lot. They don't actually fill you with confidence, do they? Don't get me wrong. Not all of them are bent. And I actually know a couple of them who know their dads."

She grinned.

"But since the characters have retired or died, Fabian, Capstick, Nipper, the geezers who played by the rules, the force is filled with little grey men and they play as dirty as the villains."

Her grin settled into curiosity.

"Anyway, what do you know about protection?"

"I know it's a dirty word. You're going to tell me differently?"

For a moment he paused to watch a thread of spaghetti disappear between her lips.

"I'll tell you that the owners of the clubs and shops and restaurants got together and actually approached people like the twins and my father. They wanted a guarantee of safety from the small gangs and from the villains that hid behind the fifth's uniform. And remember, there were fringe benefits as well. Some of these merchants were always in trouble; they'd be losing their licences every other week."

"Go on," she said.

"Well, think about it. If you pay someone who has influence it means that you're free from bother from other villains, from hooligans, from people trying to rip you off. The local filth won't bother you. And nor will all these departments of snoopers the council sets up. Or at least, if you are going to get raided you know about it in advance. That sort of guarantee has got to be worth something."

She shrugged and murmured, "Health and Safety inspectors, Department of Health, checks to make certain we're not eating condemned food – they're all doing their jobs to look after us."

"You think so? There's more condemned meat out there than there's ever been. But you can guarantee it's not being served in any of our places, or in any of our friend's places. If the filth did their jobs properly and made the streets safe then you wouldn't have to employ anybody else, would you? Listen, you've got to help yourself. If you're in trouble you can't rely on the police or the authorities. They don't give a monkey's. If you're burgled they won't even come and see you. If you're robbed and fight back you're more likely to be arrested than the robber. Do you blame the people who ask us to protect them? They've got no one else on their side. Anyway, it's all beside the point, we aren't into protection or dodgy goods or anything else. Obviously we help our friends out if they ask, but we don't tout for business. We never have done. You've been listening to the wrong people."

She was not convinced but her expression indicated that she was not too concerned either. He should have guessed as much. The garage business was as wise as they come. You learned to drive before you could walk, and you learned to con before you could drive. Half of London's villains had something to do with the second-hand motor trade or scrap metal, which invariably meant the same thing.

"So, tell me how it started?"

His blue eyes narrowed fractionally. He dared her. "You really want to know?"

"I asked you, didn't I?" She held his gaze.

"The Smoke was about little gangs until a guy named Rafferty came into it. He wanted a cut off everything in sight and he had the muscle to back him up. Before the war my father got to know a guy named Bryant who ran the docks in Folkestone and Dover. He was down there visiting the Hursts. They were my mum's cousins. Anway, Bryant was into protection, labour, that sort of thing. When Rafferty began to get nasty, Pop contacted Bryant. He was doing bird at the time but that made no difference. He controlled the channel ports from inside. Bryant sent some muscle to help Pop tidy up Rafferty but only on the understanding that Pop took over this end and paid a divvy. For a while things went well. Then the percentages went up and up. Eventually people had to pay more than they'd been paying Rafferty. By then Bryant was out and running things from Folkestone. With the help of some friends, Pop moved in on Bryant's people.

"What happened?"

"The story goes that in one night they rounded the lot up, Bryant included, forced them on board a trawler in the Folkestone Harbour, then took them out to a sandbank and made them get off."

Jill frowned. Her fork remained suspended below her lips.

"What happened then?"

"The sea came in."

"He left them there?" Her voice was deep, incredulous.

"That's the story."

She shook her head in disbelief.

"All that happened before I was born."

"What then?"

"Most of the cash went into property. He put together some major deals out of the war damage and turned more and more to his clubs."

"That it?"

"That's it. That's how it started."

She was silent for a moment, lost in thought. Eventually she looked up again and said seriously, "They used to say, in these parts, that the Richardsons hurt people for business and the Krays because they liked it."

"You're forgetting the Foremans. They hurt people for money!"

She nodded. "I heard that too. But what do they say about your family?"

"You're going to tell me?"

"They say the Smiths hurt people out of revenge."

He shrugged. "Yeah, I've heard that too, but most of it is crap."

"Dad knew Reggie before he went down. They met up again inside."

"What about you?" Tommy asked. "What happened to your mum? I know Mike isn't with her."

"She left him when he was inside. I don't blame her for that. He got unlucky but he knew what he was doing and he knew the risks. He put his family at risk and that included me. Anyway, Mum left. She's got a flat in Stepney. She never did meet anyone else. It wasn't like that. They still see each other from time to time and maybe they'll go out to a show or have a meal. But that's all."

"What made you stay with the old man?"

"I didn't. Not at first. But he couldn't look after himself. He was a mess. He couldn't cook an egg without instructions. And it suited me. In some ways I've always been closer to him."

"What about brothers and sisters?"

"One of each. My brother's still at school – lives with Mum. My sister married a fireman from up north, Stevenage, do you know it?" She smiled. "Nothing like keeping it in the family, is there?" She paused before glancing up. "Tell me about your family?"

"I thought you knew it all. My old man's dying. He's got stomach cancer and there's nothing they can do. Not that he'd let them. He's got a few days, maybe weeks. Everyone is devastated and walking around in a trance. It came right out of the blue. He was having trouble with his leg again. He'd been getting pains in his leg. We thought it was gout or something. This has knocked us all for six."

"What about the other trouble, The Barge?"

Tommy spoke slowly, searching for a reasonable path between the truth and a lie. "There's a guy up north who wants a piece of clubland and he's trying to get it the old-fashioned way. People won't want to come to our clubs if they think there might be trouble."

"What are you doing about it?"

"At the moment we're trying to talk to the guy. Hopefully we'll come to some kind of agreement. These things happen from time to time and then they die down."

"The conversations are punctuated with bombs, are they?"

"Eh?"

"The Barge. I take it this northern guy had something to do with it? Nineteen people are lying at the bottom of the river and you're sitting here telling me you're going to have a cosy chat and that it's all to do with an old-fashioned takeover. For God's sake, what happens when war breaks out?"

Tommy raised his hands in mock surrender. "I can't say with any certainty that Mick, that's the Jock we're talking about, had anything to do with the bomb. For one thing it's not his style. We often let The Barge out to MPs. Local councillors hire it from time to time. The police hire it for their special parties. Last night we held a party to entertain some businessmen from Liverpool. It could have been the Micks, like you said before, or the Arabs, or anyone with a grouse against any of these people. Who knows? It might not have anything to do with us at all."

"But you think it has?"

"Yes, maybe. The Irish wouldn't go out of their way to upset us. We do business and they've got too much to lose. And the Arabs are staying low profile at the moment. I think it is personal, but I'm not so sure it's Mick."

"Who then?"

"There are a few old gangs knocking about that might be on a vengeance trip or something. Some of the Costa mob might have paid somebody. There's the Caribbean mob from Brixton and the Irish in Tottenham – not the IRA. Then you've got the South London remnants that have started dealing in dope again. There's the Yardies from Kingston, but they're small-time even if they do have big ideas. Take their shooters away and they'd be back punching tickets on the Underground! But any of these geezers might have decided to move into the bright lights. Who knows? That's why I wanted to talk to your old man. He might have picked up a whisper that now makes sense."

"Right then," she said suddenly. "Let's get back and see if he's turned up."

There was still no sign of Mike Mountford. Tommy told Jill, "Don't worry. I'll put out the word to find him and I'll send him home to face you. Blimey, I don't envy him that."

"Thanks for lunch," she said. "I hope things aren't as bad as they seem for your pop."

"I'll bell you later."

"Don't forget the cherries."

"No," he grinned. "I never will."

Chapter 29

On his way over to The Tower Tommy Smith felt a heady combination of grief and excitement; there remained the heavy weight of sadness that pressed down on his chest and seemed to block his throat but there was a flutter there also and he felt guilty that his thoughts steered towards the girl instead of dwelling on his father's predicament. But she was there, forcing her way in; the things she said, the little grin, the rueful smile, her sparkling eyes. And while all this happened his heart was racing faster and other thoughts were pushed aside.

Ted was in the office talking to Barry Theroux. Tommy closed the door and without the usual preliminaries he asked, "Has Houghie turned up?"

"He came in this morning," Barry said. He looked pale, his usual immaculate suit slightly creased. Managing The Tower didn't leave him much time in the sunshine and the added problems of security were telling. He couldn't remember the last time he'd taken more than a few hours off. "I had a go at him. He knows he let us down."

"Denise turned up yet?"

"No, she hasn't. He's got one of the neighbours looking after the nipper. Is there a problem?"

"Yeah, maybe," Tommy said. "But I don't want it mentioned outside this room. Pop wants Dave to deal with it personally. I didn't ask why."

Ted knew why without asking. Dave's affair with Denise before she married Pete Hough was common knowledge.

"What happened?" Ted asked.

"He paid a call to Mike Mountford yesterday. The fireman hasn't surfaced since. I've got a bad feeling about this. I don't know why Denise has done a bunk. When I talked to her a couple of days ago everything seemed fine. I know she wouldn't leave the kid without good reason. We'll keep a discreet eye on Pete, know what I mean?" He turned to Barry Theroux. "Sorry about this, Barry, but the old man wants you to pick up Jimmy's responsibilities, at least for the time being. We'll give you all the help you need. Try and offload some of the running of this place, maybe the casino. Pull in some people from the Castle if you need them." He glanced at Ted. "How did you get on?"

"It's too early for much but Peach gave me the first reports. It looks pretty sophisticated. The lab sheets won't be available until the end of the week, perhaps the weekend, but the prelims indicate very upmarket. The equivalent of a thousand pounds, remote controlled, three separate units. If one of them failed the other two were enough to sink her. Buttoned from the bank, even a passing car. There's been similar stuff used in Ireland and the Middle East. Most of it comes out of Czechoslovakia. The only thing he's certain of is that whoever's behind it is very well connected. We're not talking small time."

Tommy nodded thoughtfully. His expression hardened. Barry Theroux had heard the news a few moments earlier. Hearing it a second time didn't make it better.

"They've found the other bodies," Ted continued. "The girl turned up by the Old Albert. The filth don't know what they're in to yet so they're only asking around the edges. They're certainly not convinced that the girl's a separate issue but with the water being so cold they'll never pinpoint exact time of death. Even so, there are two things that worry Peach about her. The first is to do with this genetic business. If they somehow tie Vic in with her and decide to run these tests they'll have proof that she was on board. Let's hope he didn't have time to finish before the bombs went off. The other thing is the dope. If they find that half the bodies were doped with the same shit used on the girl then there's going to be some very awkward questions. That's without Vic's gut feeding the fish between here and Tilbury. Fok's confirmed that his shit was loose. He better be right. If it was still in cellophane then we're in deep water and that isn't a pun. It's way over Peach's head. The top brass are watching his every move. They see it as a golden opportunity to nail us. Now is the time to pull in every favour that we're owed."

"What about the labs? Have we got anyone in there?"

"No, unfortunately, but they're being as cagey as hell. Peach can't even find out who's dealing with it. He's working on it."

"He better had. He's paid enough." Tommy sighed.

"Well somebody better come up with something," Barry said. "I'm getting pissed off with all this. Looking over your shoulder, frightened of the shadows, it's not natural."

Tommy's smile was humourless. "I know what you mean. We're in a corner, trapped. Sooner or later we've got to go on the offensive, win or lose." He shook his head. "We can't just stand back and take it or we'll never recover."

The others looked on, surprised. He was beginning to sound like Dave.

Tommy and Ted turned up at the hospital to find the women already there.

"Hello, darlings," Tom said. His eyes sparkled as the women fussed around him. "Gawd, I should come in here more often!" Theca squeezed his speckled hand. "I've been thinking about the grandchildren," he said, addressing Sally but telling them all. "I don't want them here. I don't want them seeing me like this. They'll only be upsetting themselves. Make sure they understand."

"Of course," Sally said.

"Now, listen, all of you, there's something important I want to say. The grandchildren must be taken care of. It's all down to you now. Times have changed. It's necessary today for them to have an education. They've never wanted for nothing and that worries me a bit. I don't want them growing up thinking they don't have to achieve nothing. Know what I mean? When you struggle for something and get it, then it's something to be proud of. Now, I don't talk to you about the business but this is different. There might be trouble and because of it we've got to keep a special watch on the kids. Understand, my Star?" He patted his daughter's hand before continuing. "When they go to school or to play then someone's got to watch over them. I know you don't like it but it's important and necessary. The same goes for you girls. If you go to the shops or go to get your hair done or, what is it?" He looked at Theca. "What is it, Star, what is it you do with the wax? Well, that as well. If you go to get the wax treatment or anywhere else, wherever you go, then someone's got to go with you. That's all of you. The same goes for Jessica when she gets back. No exceptions. Dave is taking care of it but he must have your support."

When Sally, Theca and Pat went out for coffee the boys gave him the news. When he was satisfied that they'd covered everything he said, "Dave will be back in a couple of days. By then things will have cooled down."

Tommy held on to his mother's hand as the five of them made their way toward the exit along a wide noisy corridor, barely noticing the faces in the crowd, the other people carrying flowers and brown paper bags filled with apples and grapes, other faces straining under the threat of illness and death.

"OK Mum?" Tommy asked reassuringly.

"I'm all right, Tommy," Sally said.

"You're a lady."

"And you're a gentleman, my son."

At lunch, the day before, Theca had told Ted that she didn't know what she was going to do, that if he agreed, she wouldn't make a decision about their future until after her father's – she didn't say death but that's what she meant. She used the words, 'Until the results come through and we know what's happening'. But she meant death.

"Are you going to carry on seeing…?" he'd asked.

"I'll talk to him, that's all. I'll tell him what I've told you."

Ted was already resigned to the situation. He would have agreed to anything. His only concern was that the children be kept out of it for the time being.

Since then The Barge had been sunk and the Star had found herself totally confused about her own feelings. She'd spent the night worrying about Ted's injuries. Tommy had explained what had happened and without giving her details of the youngster and the reason Ted went back, he told her that Ted was hurt trying to rescue some others. On the way out of the hospital he caught her glance and recognized an appreciation. It was something he hadn't seen for a long time. They sat in the car for a while.

"Dad needed the loo," she said to him. "I helped him back. His dressing gown wasn't tied properly and I saw this...tube, sticking out of his penis. He saw that I'd noticed and I felt so embarrassed for him. I feel so protective." The tears welled up. "I love him so much. He was such a...big man!" The last words were uttered in a whisper.

Ted held her hand. He couldn't say anything. There was nothing to say.

Chapter 30

Coddy Hughes laid on an impressive show of armed strength. From the moment his visitors cleared the main gate and were out of sight of the road his men were very evident. So were the weapons they brandished. It worked two ways, for Coddy had guaranteed the safety of the men attending the meeting. There would be no trouble, and negotiation was not even called for, simply a statement of position. Wars were costly. They resulted in police clampdowns and interruptions to business. Even the parties not directly involved were concerned. And local wars had a nasty habit of spreading.

On the gravel drive before the house the shining cars parked in a semicircle. The drivers and the minders stayed with them. They watched Coddy's men and saw the dogs straining on their leashes. It was sometime before they relaxed.

As each car drew to a halt Coddy and Dave were outside to meet their guests. Valenti was the first of the wops to get out of their car and he turned immediately to help the old man, O'Connell, supporting him by the arm. O'Connell's spine was curved, his thick, black overcoat reached down to his ankles. His small cloudy eyes fastened on Coddy. He reached out to shake Coddy's outstretched hand. Standing beside O'Connell, Valenti glared at Dave. His eyes were on fire. This meeting between the two of them had been a long time coming.

"Welcome to Lincolnshire," Coddy said.

O'Connell's gaze moved toward Dave then back to Coddy again.

"I'm glad to be here. It's very pretty country. Very green." The man shuffled across to Dave and offered his quivering hand. Dave noticed the long discoloured fingernails. They dug into his palm as they shook hands. "David Smith," O'Connell rasped. His breathing was heavy, drawn between every word. "I've heard about you." He glanced at Valenti at his side. Valenti's expression remained rigid. He shook Coddy's hand quickly then walked past Dave to lead O'Connell to the house. Coddy exchanged the briefest of smiles with Dave as he recognized the snub and then followed after them. Dave turned to see O'Connell's driver.

"It's been a long time, kid," Herman Tartt said.

Dave hid his surprise and nodded. He glanced down at the stick Tartt leaned on.

"You haven't changed that much," Dave said.

Tartt frowned. "What's that supposed to mean?" His pale blue eyes were still as dead as ever.

"You've still got shit on your nose!" He nodded towards Valenti's back. "Is it his, or O'Connell's?"

"Regular comedian, ain't you? Let me tell you something." He waved a hand. "All this doesn't mean a damn. You screwed up once, a long time ago maybe, but your reprieve was only temporary."

"Does O'Connell know you're mouthing off like this? Or Clough? Or Valenti, come to that?"

"Are you going to tell them?"

"No. I wouldn't want you to be sent home before the fireworks begin. I wouldn't want to have to come all that way to find you."

"As I recall, it was you lying in a heap of steaming pig shit."

"Yeah, but it was you that ended up with an old man's walking stick. It suits you. You're a typical fucking Yank, Tartt! The only people you're likely to damage are those on your own side!"

Tartt scowled. "There'll be another time, and it's closer than you think."

"No, I don't think so," Dave said and smiled. "Time is something you guys have run out of."

He left the man glaring after him and made his way to the wide steps of Coddy's manor.

It was ironical that the chief protagonist was missing and had sent a deputy in his place. Mick's grandmother was celebrating her ninetieth birthday and that was a good enough reason. It was a snub, of course, and compounding it his apology was not received until earlier that day and too late to delay the meeting.

Mick's mouthpiece, Don McLachlan was the last to arrive. He was a calm, refined man of fifty, more suited to an executive office that to a meeting of the country's underworld. Immaculately dressed in a dark suit and tie, the short, neat figure acknowledged the cautious greetings from those he knew and that meant the majority of men in the room. His voice was mild and friendly and it filled the small moments of greeting with warmth that was not there. His ruddy northern complexion beneath severely short white hair lent an edge to his wide no-nonsense features. He took his place at the polished mahogany table and carefully placed his slim black briefcase before him. He looked up at the twelve faces around the table. With the obvious exception of the men from Liverpool almost all the major centres were represented. The Coons from Stoke on Trent were missing but their allegiance to Coddy meant that he would speak on their behalf. There was no head to the table. It was round for that reason.

Twelve of the fourteen men at the table had carved up various parts of the country into defined territories. The boundaries were not guarded but in every other sense they were as clear and as respected as borders on a world map. Interests sometimes overlapped, some of these men co-existed in the same area, some business was conducted on a nationwide scale, but in all cases agreements had been reached. But just as there was conflict between nations, sometimes to do with territorial rights and border disputes, sometimes to do with business and greed, so it was with these manors. There was aggression, appeasement, war, winners and losers. It was the nature of things.

Coddy Hughes was the host. His area covered most of Lincolnshire and a large part of the East Midlands including the ripe City of Derby and the riper town of Nottingham. In the old days he controlled the Potteries, Birmingham and Manchester, but when his health began to deteriorate he handed over those areas to Lewis Rayatt and his gang known as the Coons. But things had not gone well. The Coons didn't have Coddy's natural flair to control, nor did they have the respect that he had earned, and the major cities that they'd taken over had become lawless with smaller gangs out of control. Cheetham and Moss Side, the coconut jungles, Rusholme, the turban ghetto, were examples. Territorial battles had made Manchester one of the most volatile places in Britain.

With Tom Smith and Mad Mick McGovern absent, Coddy Hughes was the most respected man at the table. And respected for reasons other than power; he was trusted by the others. Coddy Hughes was essentially a businessman and his interest lay almost solely in the building industry. The Midlands, in their heyday, had made him a fortune. He was also an old-fashioned man totally opposed to the drug scene, to porn and to prostitution. The inexorable traffic in hard drugs was, apart from his health, the other factor in him handing over – in those days – the slum cities. He remained a force to be reckoned with and no one would take him on lightly. His army was small by any standards but it was his friendship – his family ties – with the Smiths and, to a lesser extent, his pact with the Coons that gave him the edge.

Richard Hurst had died in a car accident on the Dover Road and his brother Ian was serving a life stretch for manslaughter and conspiracy to commit murder. Ian's thirty-year-old son, Roger Hurst, had taken over on the Kent coast. There were problems down there but they were for the future. The old Hurst gang had broken up completely and there were now so many independents operating it would take someone much stronger than Roger to pull it together. Before long someone would emerge or move in; the lucrative pickings from the channel ports demanded it. Roger Hurst's hold, perhaps even his life, was on a tenuous thread and if the Smiths lost this war he would be gone in an instant.

Lewis Hicks from Carlisle and Ray Turner from Blackpool were in each other's pockets. They might have been family for all the difference it made. In their territory they were into everything and controlled with a vicious, unforgiving style. They were the undisputed slot-machine kings. They were into protection, drugs, prostitution and pornography. Their area was a walled city and they believed in isolationism; they seemed not to have the slightest interest in anyone else. They were an unknown quantity and just how strong they were no one really knew. While their strength was questionable, Stafford Carr's, the man from Hull, was most definitely weak. He was a tall, queasy-looking man, fastidious and easily upset, never comfortable, always fussing with his lighter or cigarettes, always flicking non-existent dust from his clothes. It was common knowledge that he suffered from some kind of persecution complex and for that reason the others viewed him with more than a little circumspection. This exacerbated his condition. The decline in Hull in the industrial sense had reduced Carr's influence even further. He was now considered second or even third rate, of little consequence. He'd recently lost his most valuable contract, the importation of heroin from Holland, and now he was effectively finished.

Tony Valenti sat next to him. Then O'Connell. Next to him sat McLachlan, and then John Bracey from South London.

In the old days Bracey ran one of the scrap metal companies owned by the Richardsons. He now ran his own gang, operating drug smuggling out of Gatwick and Heathrow. Baggage handlers were recruited to intercept marked bags from South America and the Far East. They contained cocaine or heroine. It was the start of the rip on/rip off scams that involved teams of handlers at both ends. Before being checked at customs the bags would be forwarded directly on to internal flights to places such as Manchester or Edinburgh, with all traces of their origin removed and replaced with domestic flight stickers. Bracey also had financial interests in restaurants, hotels and pubs and it was heavily rumoured that he was setting up a film company. While the background suited most of the others in the room, he liked the glamour and the high life and had even graced the television talk shows. He'd grown up with the likes of Billy Hill who ruled the gambling dens in the fifties and the razor king Freddie Andrews. He served two and a half years at the Scrubs for his involvement in the Royal Victoria Docks robbery and now, when most men thought of retiring, he was expanding. He was financed from the Costa Mob, the South London remnants, and a good deal of his profit went back in that direction. He was an old man, his gang was not an army and, given the present situation, he posed no real threat. He could cut off supplies, he could provide financial help, but that was all.

John Arnold from Southampton had taken hold of Jaffa Smith's (no relation to Tom Smith) old business, tied it together with the vacuum left by Chris Holloway and Tommy Hughes and become the leading distributor of porn. The video business and the requirement for moving pictures on every street corner had boosted his turnover. Because his stock was bulky he had a huge force but most of his men were unreliable. The filth industry was notorious for employing objectionable characters and, although most of the men in the room dealt with Arnold, it was through business alone. It would never be friendship.

The other faces in the room belonged to Terry Ives from Leeds, Peter Bonja from Ipswich and Adrian Styles from Bristol. Styles' interests covered the whole of South Wales. Similar in strength, they were not big enough to threaten anyone alone, but if they joined forces with one of the larger gangs then they had to be considered.

There was some restless shuffling and clearing of throats; watchful, expectant glances went from McLachlan to Dave and back again.

"I apologize for keeping you gentlemen waiting," McLachlan said through Coddy Hughes.

Barely moving his head Coddy angled it slightly on the pink neck brace and looked sideways at Dave who sat beside him. He faced the front again and tapped the silver head of his cane against the mahogany.

"We all know why we're here," he said slowly. "So let's not beat about the bush. I want some blunt speaking today so we all know where we sit. One thing is for sure: this uncertainty is shit and can't go on! Today we become friends again or else a lot of us are not going to need our retirement plans!"

There was general agreement; it took the form of grunts and nods of approval.

"Everyone is going to have an opportunity to share his views," he continued. "But first I want to hear from Don and from Dave."

McLachlan began immediately. "Dave, everyone, do you mind if I start?"

Dave nodded and gave a tiny gesture with his open hand.

"Mick gave me a personal message this morning and I want to give it to you before this meeting gets properly underway."

All eyes turned toward him and most showed a little surprise.

"Mick's sorry he can't be here to say this himself. We all heard about the Barge and he wants you to know that it was nothing to do with him. His hand is on the Bible when he tells you that. He wants to express his sympathy for all the innocent people hurt, especially the women, both from your place and from Liverpool. Hitting innocent people has never been his style and he knows it's never been yours. Mick wants you to know that unless it's been in bed he's never personally hurt a woman in his life." There was a murmur of laughter before he continued. "It's a code. And he hopes that you'll believe him. Also, to the point as Coddy requested, we know that your father, Tommy Smith, a man we all respect, is fighting for his life, and losing. This terrible illness is the only thing that was ever going to knock over a man like him. Not the rest of us and not the filth. It had to be something like this. Mick is going to miss him hugely, like we all will, and he wants your family to know that. Out of respect for your old man, as Mick puts it, and out of respect for the innocent victims of the Barge, Mick gives you his word here and now that he'll start nothing until after the funeral. That is, if it has to start at all. He hopes, sincerely, that it won't have to!"

The room fell silent and expressions were grave, waiting for a response.

Eventually Dave said quietly, "He started it already by using my kid brother as target practice."

All eyes swivelled back to Don McLachlan.

"We heard about that. This much I can tell you, Dave, and I think your old man will bear me out. If Mick tells you he won't start anything, then you can believe him. Anyone who knows Mick knows just how much his word means to him. It's the only Commandment he's ever kept. As long as you don't include the kozzers in this, he's never given false evidence in his life. His father was a leading member of The Kirk and it's a family trait. Of course, his father disowned him for other things, but never for breaking his word."

Dave fixed his gaze. "Let me get this straight, Don. Are you telling me that turning Mill Hill into a shooting gallery had nothing to do with Mick?"

McLachlan said genuinely, "If Mick says that he won't start anything until after the funeral you can take it that he hasn't started anything yet. What else can I tell you, Dave? In any case, from what I hear, Mill Hill was a failure. We don't make mistakes like that."

Dave's thoughts raced. Coddy's expression hardened. This admission created a whole new ballgame and everyone around the table knew it. Surprise had dropped a few mouths and widened a few eyes and some of the men shook their heads as they wondered what was going on. It had been taken for granted that Mick had used shotguns on Tommy. But why had he waited until now to deny it? Why had he risked the possible reprisals? Unless...

Slowly Dave turned to face the man opposite him. Small dark eyes stared out of the expressionless sallow features of Tony Valenti. The surgery on his big nose had never been totally successful and the flattened scar tissue on the left side gave an uneven balance to his sharp face. A was a small, thin man and the years had not been kind; he looked a good deal older than sixty-two. He held a cigarette close to his mouth so that he looked through a continuous flow of smoke. A thick gold bracelet hung loosely from his wrist. His unblinking eyes never moved from Dave and he made no attempt to conceal his contempt. It was there for all to see. Dave pushed thoughts of Sharon and a moment's ludicrous jealousy from his mind.

Dave said, "Thank Mick for his sympathies. I'll pass them on. I believe what you're saying to me, Don. Now I'm going to say something to all of you."

He held Valenti's gaze just long enough for the American to get the message. Sitting beside Valenti, O'Connell seemed utterly oblivious to what was going on.

357

Dave said: "Somebody in this room is responsible for sending the Barge to the bottom of the Thames. Someone here is responsible for sending one of Vic's bollocks to Southend and the other to Huddesfield. Now, that person hasn't got the bottle to speak out. He's letting Mick take the blame. It might be the case that Mick knows all about it and knows who is behind it and is happy to let him carry on, or it might be that he has no idea and is pretty pissed off at being set up. I don't know. What I do know is that if anybody around this table knows who's causing this grief then I'll remember this silence. And sooner or later fucking doomsday is coming. That is something you can all guarantee!"

Apart from O'Connell and Valenti, both of whom stared straight ahead, there were some uncomfortable glances passing around the room. The peace was a long way off.

Coddy turned to the Americans.

"What is your position, Mr O'Connell?"

The old man's eyes slid slowly across to Coddy. "You better call me Augustus," he said. He spoke breathlessly, in almost a whisper. The others leaned closer to listen. "We're all friends here, aren't we? First-name terms, eh? If that doesn't offend your English reserve."

A few faces softened in relief and a few chuckles spread around the table. Dave guessed that the old man was sharper than he looked. He shouldn't have been surprised. The Americans were never going to let a bonehead run their European affairs. Valenti blinked and glanced at his boss.

O'Connell cleared his throat and said, "Our position? We have no position. This is a local problem and since Nam we've learned not to get involved in local problems. Isn't that so, Tony?"

Valenti's smile was thin and forced. Stafford Carr laughed quietly and a few others joined in.

The old man continued: "We'd prefer to deal with one face but that's always been the case. We have no preference as to whose face that is." He shook his head. "You've got major problems here, that much is clear. But from where I sit it seems to me you've got to resolve it amongst yourselves and then come back to me." He lifted his hand in a throwaway gesture. "Hell, Coddy, the problem isn't in your area at all. You've always made it clear that you're not dealing. It's your decision and I respect it. I think everyone here respects it. If someone takes an option on your territory with regard to that one item and can come to an arrangement with you I can't see a problem."

O'Connell had laid it on the table. Coddy's refusal to allow organized dealing had led to the present situation. Without his agreement, in principle anyway, then war was a certainty. Mick would move south and Dave north and somewhere in Coddy's manor they would meet. The Americans would deal with the people left standing. But it would be Coddy's fault.

Surprisingly, O'Connell spoke again and pulled Coddy off the hook. "The problem is the Smith's deal with the Chinese."

Only Dave recognized Coddy's relief. He was also aware that in bringing up the Smith's agreement with Garrard Street, O'Connell had shifted the goal posts. Suddenly it was beginning to make sense. The Americans were trying to make capital out of the trouble. Tom Smith's arrival and his subsequent deal with the Chinese had signalled a huge boost in the Smith's influence. It could just be that his departure presaged the end.

"We want to deal with one face, but we want to deal nationwide. Understand? That means the Chinks are history!"

The attention turned back to Dave. His response was measured. He said, "Any dialogue with us will have to take the Chinese into consideration."

That was it. They waited for more but the pause became a full stop.

O'Connell waved at the air again, this time in resignation. Beside him Valenti's lips curled downward into an ugly smile.

"I don't know why we're wasting our time here," Valenti said to O'Connell. "These people don't want to negotiate!" He turned to the others around the table. His voice became louder and even more hostile. "There's your problem!" He pointed at Dave. "These people aren't reasonable. They've got no taste for the cake themselves and because of it they don't want any of you tasting it either. You want to solve this problem then you've got to sort these people out! What the fuck are you all waiting for? What the fuck's Mick waiting for? You can tell him from me that Christmas is a fucking long way off!"

O'Connell reached out a hand and patted Valenti's arm.

Valenti's outburst left a long silence, broken eventually by Ian Hurst's son Roger. His freckled face and red hair gave him the image of his father. "Whatever happens the south coast will line up with Dave."

McLachlan smiled. "I don't think you had to say that, Roger. If it comes to it then you, the Smiths and Coddy here will be isolated. I'm hoping that we can reach an agreement but you must know that the situation has been discussed with everyone here and the rest are against you. Some, like Lewis and Ray, want to sit it out, stay neutral, but they'll want it over as soon as possible if it starts interrupting their business and it will. And at the end of the day, they'll be against you as well. The rest of the gentlemen here, with the exception of…" He paused and smiled. "…Augustus and Tony, who have made their position quite clear, will line up with Mick. This is not a threat. It is a statement. If you want confirmation then you can ask them now. Dave doesn't need it, nor does Coddy. They already understand the situation. We don't want a war – like Coddy said before, it's bad for business, but if it comes then you're going to be hit from six different sides. Roger, your people in Kent have been riding on the backs of the Smiths ever since your dad went down. You couldn't get an overdraft together, never mind an army. The fact is you'd be more of a disadvantage to the Smiths because they'd have to look after you and spread their forces accordingly."

Roger Hurst was young. He had spoken out of turn and now he wished he hadn't. His freckles seemed to fade as his face coloured.

Dave scratched his forehead. "Talk to me, Don. That's what you're doing, isn't it?"

McLachlan smiled. "Maybe it is, Dave."

Valenti grinned belligerently. Dave met the American's gaze again and felt the hatred pouring through. He watched as Valenti pushed O'Connell's hand aside and half rose out of his seat.

"I can't believe what I'm hearing here," he said. "You people are letting this guy walk all over you." He lifted his hand and pointed at

Dave. A heavy gold ring glinted and his bracelet swung. "Let me tell you something you son of a bitch!" He began to shake. "Without your old man you're nothing. Hear me? Nothing! We shouldn't even be talking to you. Who the fuck do you think you are? What the fuck do you think this is: a walk around Buckingham Palace, eating cucumber sandwiches?" He turned to McLachlan. "You fucking limeys are all the same. You tell Mick from me..." His wagging finger turned to McLachlan. "...You tell him to take care of this fucker, or I will!"

O'Connell reached out again and caught hold of Valenti's arm. It seemed impossible that the old man had the strength in him to force Valenti back into his seat, but he did. He leant across and whispered into Tony Valenti's ear.

For a few moments Valenti remained motionless, then he pushed back his chair and stood up. He glared once more at Dave then turned abruptly and walked from the room. The double doors closed behind him.

Dave took a deep breath and settled back in his chair.

O'Connell cleared his throat. "You'll forgive Tony for that little outburst," he said. "He's been under a lot of pressure lately. Personalities should never come into business. Isn't that right?"

Around the table sighs of relief replaced the shock.

Coddy tapped his cane. "Does anyone else want a say? Anyone disagree with anything said? Now is a good time to speak up."

He was hoping that some of the others were not as keen to back Mick as McLachlan had indicated but their silence gave him an answer.

Lewis Hicks from the northwest, surprisingly neutral since he was on Mick's doorstep, said, "I've got no axe to grind with any of you. I don't like to see old friends falling out. We've had peace for sixteen years. Things have been good. There's been no aggro. Some of you I've known all my life. I don't want to see you getting hurt. If it comes to war there won't be any winners. We'll all lose. I'd like to make a suggestion. Mick has said that he won't start anything until after the funeral. Now, that might be sooner or later. Who knows? Only God knows, right? But I propose that before anything is started by anyone here, we meet again. Same venue if Coddy agrees on account it's central to all of us. We meet again in a last-ditch attempt to try and solve all this." He waved the air. "We can all go back and cool down and maybe rethink our positions." He turned directly to Dave. "I've known your father since the war, Dave. He was never one for getting himself into a corner. Maybe he can deal with the Chinese. I'm sure we'd all be willing to come up with the ante."

Dave threw him a stray smile. Lewis Hicks was as neutral as hell. He'd been primed without a doubt. That was the longest speech he'd made in his life. When his daughter got married two years previously his dinner speech hadn't been that long.

"I'll give my old man your regards," Dave said.

"Anybody else?" Coddy asked hopefully.

Don McLachlan spoke again. "What happened to the Barge was a disgrace. No one should be able to get that close." There was a veiled criticism of the Smiths here. "Liverpool has been wiped out. What we're going to get very quickly and without any doubt is anarchy. Twenty percent of our goods come through the Reds and there's no way we're going to let a bunch of amateurs take over. We've had no time to think this through but as we see it at the moment there are two alternatives. In order to safeguard our interests we're going to move some forces in. Quickly. Today. They are there to maintain law and order. As soon as the Scousers sort themselves out and are able to function again we'll pull back. If this doesn't sit well at the table we're willing to be a part of a multinational force."

Stafford Carr, the tall chain-smoking representative from Hull waved his cigarette and said, "Another alternative is to redirect your imports to us."

McLachlan exchanged knowing looks with Dave before he said, "Staff, with respect, you haven't even got your own authorities under control. You're losing more goods than are getting through. It's common knowledge that you lost the Dutch contract."

O'Connell coughed loudly.

Carr grimaced and sucked on his cigarette.

Coddy asked, "What's your feeling, Dave?"

"I've got no objection to Mick's people policing Merseyside on a temporary basis. I think it's a good idea." He turned to McLachlan.

"With Vic dead I think you'll have some major problems. Since you'll be looking after all our interests we'll help out with the overheads."

McLachlan looked pleased. He allowed himself the faintest smile of satisfaction. Dave was happy for other reasons. The more he could tie up Mick's forces the less of a threat they became. He knew very well that once Mick obtained a foothold it was going to be difficult to shift him, but that was a future problem. His main concern was surviving the present. He had to tread the narrow path between appeasement and practicability.

It was some time later after the last of the guests had left that Dave sat in the leather armchair resting his elbows on his knees, leaning forward toward Coddy.

"Things are becoming clearer."

Curiosity narrowed Coddy's eyes. He was keen to hear what Dave thought. Tom's eldest son had made his mark during the meeting and impressed a lot of people there with his maturity. He swallowed some brandy. The flames that flickered over the logs in the massive fireplace reflected in the crystal.

"Work out the why," Coddy said, "and more often than not it will get you the who. Tell me what's on your mind?"

Dave's voice was edged with annoyance as he said, "After all this time Valenti hasn't forgotten. This has got sod all to do with Mick. He's just a tool, willing perhaps, but that's all he is. This is a vendetta, Coddy, a fucking personal vendetta between Valenti and me. And it's happened now because for the first time, the wop is in a position of power. He's moved up in the ranks and now he's big enough to override business. He's taken over from Clough as O'Connell's number two. Why else would he have been here and Cloughie not? This has got nothing to do with dope and distribution. It's personal. And he's backing Mick. He's never forgotten!"

Coddy finished his drink and carefully set his glass on the side tray.

"Every morning when he shaves he sees that mess in the middle of his face," Coddy said. "Would you forget? Every time he looks at his wife he's going to remember that you crawled all over her. Would you forget? When he looks out of the window at the grey skies he's going to think of the Florida sun and he's going to blame you for making him lose face, for his exile. Do you think these things go away? If anything, the years make things worse. Hatred grows. Age clears a path, intensifies the need for vengeance. And hearing your name over the years, and lately as you've taken on a lot of your old man's workload he's heard it more and more, this feeling has sharpened. It's no longer about the sense of injustice, a leg-over with his wife, the beating he took, or his exile, for the reasons no longer matter. Of course he hates you. He's dreamt of nothing else but getting you for the last ten years. He's just been waiting for his chance!"

"So what do I do? Sit back and wait for them to take me apart?"

Coddy cut in quickly: "You do what your father told you. Nothing! You trust that he's got it all in hand."

"For him to have it in hand means he knew about it all along."

Coddy nodded and said grimly, "That goes without saying." He tapped the side of his nose. "Remember the scratch on the shoulder, Dave. Go home and take care of the family."

Dave swallowed a large measure and felt the glow spread out in his chest. Eventually he nodded. The old guys were still in charge.

Chapter 31

The dawn wept across Coddy Hughes' manor; its tears glistened on the early summer grass and whitened the cobweb hammocks hanging heavily on the hedgerows. The trees threw their swelling fingers into the dull sky.

Dave found his mother-in-law, Mavis, in the massive kitchen. She looked pensive. Early mornings had never been the best time of her day. He kissed her cheek while she poured some tea.

"Mavis," he muttered.

"David," she began and paused.

"What is it?"

"Be careful, boy," she said. She knew the signs. Looking at her son-in-law brought back memories of her husband and the number of times he'd come home with problems that had kept him awake. And then much later she would read or hear about a happening in the twilight world of gangs and villains – the underworld. Of course she put two and two together. She had never questioned him; that would never do. But she knew of his involvement. And now her son-in-law had that same dark look of concern and foreboding.

"There's nothing for you to worry over, Mavis."

She had heard that, too, more times than she could remember.

"I'm worried about Coddy," she said suddenly. "The doctors are worried about his breathing, the strain on his heart."

"Maybe you could talk to the doctor. He's due in today."

"Maybe I will," she said, brightening at the prospect. "Yes, if I get the chance."

"I'll phone you."

Mavis nodded reflectively; her expression held a vague look of hopelessness.

Dave's car rocketed south through the early mist, swinging about the country bends and along the raised narrow roads, a black streak on the dripping landscape.

During the drive home from his father-in-law's manor Dave felt both anger and embarrassment; the realization that the present troubles were down to him weighed heavily. A vendetta! A personal feud had got in the way of business and threatened to bring down his entire family. An affair that as far as Valenti knew was a one-off that happened ten years ago had festered all this time and would lead, in all likelihood, to a major war.

Dave tried, unsuccessfully, to force indifference into his mind, but his thoughts kept veering back to the meeting, to Coddy Hughes who had guessed all along, to his father who also knew about it, and to his wife. Coddy's home had been full of photographs of the girl he had married, her smile only half concealing her crooked front tooth, her bright eyes beneath the spectacles, the adoration in her look when they were pictured together at the wedding, the little things about her that he had forgotten. This throbbing mix of emotion was so intense that it blocked out the road ahead. She had never been a fearless person; her greatest daring had been during their first encounter, and he thought of her as fragile, a gentle, dignified and private woman. The ideas and images, the memories, came at him from all directions. The children were everything to Pat; she'd turned them into a passion, their upbringing into an art form. When their eldest daughter had got married and gone off on honeymoon at the weekend he had found her in the dark, in tears, suddenly a stranger in her own house. Her house. When he came home in the late evening she would be waiting for him in the quiet while the children slept. There was warmth there, orderliness, everything in its place, secure. It mattered. Her hand had become tender and gentle. He remembered their first meeting, the intensity of it, his first explosion inside her, the bond... And even though time had taken away that razor edge he still craved her. In the end it all came down to that, the physical coupling, the fusion that was both symbolic and necessary, and as he thundered through the capital, her legs shifted against him, the touch of her thighs felt cool and charged, the snatch of dark hair parted and the heat consumed him. He was filled with that mixture of desire and guilt.

He drove directly home and passed the minders on the drive. The schools were shut for the late-May holiday and the children were playing in the far reaches of the garden. From the car he watched them for a while but they remained unaware of his presence. He considered his children and the notion that he'd seen too little of them. He could blame the business, the hours, but he knew that was just an excuse. His children were growing up without his involvement. Somehow he hoped that they realized that he was a part of Patricia and that when their mother hugged them, or listened, or spent time with them, that his spirit was there also. But he knew the nonsense of it. Their ties would always be to her; he would remain alienated, an observer, not a part of it. Dave tried to show an interest; he listened intently while Patricia gave him the news, updated him on their schooling and clubs, described the moments in their short lives that he'd missed, but it was all second-hand and she had dealt with it. His business was war and violence and the safety of the family. The two were not compatible.

No one but the minders saw him as he went into the house. He guessed that Pat was in the pool, or the sauna. He made a quick call to Tommy at The Tower and to his mother at home. She was going to lunch with Ted and Theca and their children. He showered and cleaned his teeth to get rid of the journey then wrapped in a towel lay back on the bed.

When Pat walked in he remained silent and she didn't see him. His guess had been correct. Her green bikini bottom was wet. He watched her from the bed. His gaze was not critical as much as reflective. Her breasts had flattened slightly, her belly rounded; gravity and time were tugging southward. Her rigorous exercise and the heat of the sauna had kept her tight and fat had been steamed away, but it was there nevertheless, age creeping up, and her belly was notched with the triumph of her five babies. In the dim window light her tan was even darker. Unaware that he was watching she leant across the dresser seat to use a moisturizer and her briefs stretched across her behind, taking away the slack. Hairline tributaries, one of two faintly varicose, reached up the backs of her legs toward the elastic. In all the time he'd known her, over ten years now, she had worn her briefs to bed. Even after they had made love she would put them on again. Without them she felt vulnerable and couldn't sleep.

She saw him in the mirror and turned to face him. "Sweetheart, how did it go? How's Daddy?"

"Hush," he said.

She recalled their first encounter. It had become something of a joke between them.

"That's my line," she said thickly. "Tell me how he is?" She looked at him knowingly. Without her spectacles she had that faraway look of short sightedness.

"He's fine."

She nodded. "Well?"

"Take your knickers off and come over here."

Moments later she was beside him, guiding his fingers to that exact, familiar place, quite satisfied to lie there indefinitely under the warm wrap of pleasure. But at the same time she knew that their lovemaking was affectionate now, dutiful rather than instinctive, and she missed the passion. She no longer lay there, afterwards, feeling that a double-decker had driven right through her. It wasn't just age that had slowed it up, it was more than that. In the beginning she'd been covered in love bites without realizing that he'd bitten her, he'd turned her inside out, his desire all embracing and inexhaustible. She missed the intensity, the simple lust. Love had got in the way, perhaps, or that shadowy idea of availability.

She went to him willingly as she always did, and wrapped her legs around his waist. She wondered at his gentleness and heard his whisper, "I love you."

In the calm aftermath, as she lay on his arm and before she got up to put on her briefs, she said, "I never ask you about the business. The last few years have been quiet in any case. But something's happened. I know it has. And I don't mean just the Barge. You're looking worried and earlier Tom warned us to take special care. Tell me what to expect."

Dave's breathing was flat, controlled. He broke a rule.

"Some people are trying to muscle in on your father. Because of our relationship they're having a go at us."

She turned to face him and watched his expression grow stony.

"Don't worry. I've got people looking after the family, the kids, everyone. And your parents are safe."

She curled up against him feeling the security of his strong arm as it wrapped around her.

The bedroom door was rapped and startled them. Jackie, their second eldest, called out, "Telephone!"

Dave switched it through to the bedside table. Even as he lifted the receiver his gut was knotting and there was an incredible certainty in his mind that it was the hospital.

"You had better gather the family and come in," they said. "He has had such a bad night. His condition has deteriorated," they said gently.

In lieu of Jessica, still on her honeymoon, Dave and Pat left Jackie in charge of the young ones. Dave called Tommy at The Tower and then drove carefully across to his mother's house.

Sally, Theca and Ted had just arrived back from lunch. Sally still wore her raincoat. When she saw Dave and then Pat at the back door, perhaps it was his expression that he tried to soften, or more likely it was Pat's, but Sally's hand flew instinctively to her lips.

"What's happened?"

"It's OK, Mum," he said quickly. "It's just that he's had a bad night and they want us to go in."

He knew that the explanation was inadequate. It was always going to be. Sally turned into the dining room, away from them, weeping into her hands, a tiny figure, at once inconsolable.

They heard her silent words: "Oh no! Oh please no!"

Dave followed her in and put his arm around her.

"We don't know, Mum. Let's get over there and find out."

"I shouldn't have gone to lunch," she whispered.

She wiped her raw eyes and tried for some composure before going back to face the others.

Dave asked Theca, "What about the kids?"

"They're with Nan. It's OK."

Len Mannings, Sally's father, had died shortly after Sally and Tom were married but their grandmother, Joyce, battled on, and now in her nineties was still sprightly and she was housed in a small bungalow close to their house. Her babysitting duties were the highlight of her week.

Dave knew they would be safe. There were enough minders watching the family homes to guard the Royal Family. He nodded. "Right, let's not waste any time. Ready?"

They trooped out to their cars. Their escorts were ready, their motors idling, their weapons loaded. The sun shone. Tufts of cloud scudded across a bright sky. The lawns were fresh. The flowers along the borders were exploding with colour. Things at once seemed different.

In the car Sally said, "He looked so well last night, didn't he Star?"

Theca nodded, wise enough to know that it should have been a sign.

"He looked much better than the afternoon. He had a glow to him and he was relaxed. Joking even..." Sally said.

By now they knew the hospital corridor well, the flower stall and the newsagents and the bank, but in their haste they barely saw it. Their footfalls echoed louder. The ward sister was waiting for them. Her experienced eyes had a curious hardness about them and yet they were filled with sympathy and touched with failure. Her gaze was, nevertheless, steady and searching. She looked from Sally to Theca and then to Dave: twin pools of cold compassion that stated the bleak conclusion. She had seen it so many times before.

"He's had such a bad night," she said. Her voice was breathless yet gentle. "We thought it best you come in. We've had to give him an injection to ease him a little, and it's made him a bit... Well, don't take any notice of what he says. It will wear off in a little while. There's a bit of a smell in the room but don't worry about that." She offered a little reassuring smile and went on, "He's comfortable. That's all that matters, isn't it? We've moved him into a single room so you can all go in. There's a private waiting-room through here and you can use that." She paused, getting eye contact with each in turn. "Don't worry about visiting times. In a little while I'll get someone to make you some tea."

The sight of him upset the others but Sally didn't seem to notice. The difference that a few hours had made was incredible. His head seemed to have increased in size, or his body shrivelled. His swollen face seemed flushed and yet at the same time grey. His eyes, great bulging angry circles, kept slipping, pulling back, intense and yet uncontrollable. It looked like madness. His words hit them hard, drug-induced delirium, a seething mass of ideas spitting from his sore lips.

"Hello darlings. Come in. Nothing's fair. Fucking not, you know. For a start some people are born ugly, and that isn't fucking fair, is it? Ted, it isn't, is it? Dave boy, how are you? What happened? Coddy? Hello, Darling, my little Star. How are the kids? Pat, is he treating you all right? You're looking peaky, girl. Beef stew, that's what you need. Cunts! Fucking cunts they all are! Hello, darling, you hold my hand like you used to."

Sally fussed around. If she had noticed the change she had instantly dismissed it. She sat by him, unloading her bag, holding his hand, leaning over to kiss his cheek. She was safe.

The others were visibly shaken. Theca sat on the other side of the bed but was hesitant. She gripped his hand willing him back to sense. Dave placed a chair for Pat on Theca's side of the bed and she sat there stony-faced and fearful.

Tommy was horrified. He leant against the wall to steady himself. Beads of sweat gathered on his forehead. Ted edged back to the door. He kept his gaze on Tom and off the drainage bag. The few moments had been enough. A terrible stink held in the air. He made his way back to the private waiting room and lit a cigarette. A short while later Dave and Tommy joined him. Tommy took one of Ted's cigarettes. The smoke stayed low and clung to him. For a moment it seemed that his clothes were on fire.

"I didn't expect that," Tommy said quietly. "I don't know what I expected, but not that. I don't think I can handle it." As he lifted the cigarette his hand trembled. His eyes stung. Suddenly the room was too hot.

Dave felt strangely detached. "I hope he goes quickly," he said. "It's about dignity now." He glanced at Tommy, "You all right?"

"Yeah," Tommy said and expelled a jet of smoke. "No, I'm not. I want to break something. I want to kill something."

A while later Pat joined them. She hugged Dave before sitting down. "He's tired," she told them. "He keeps dropping off for a few seconds."

"Is he still delirious?" Dave asked.

"Not so bad. Sally's concerned that they've taken him off the drip. She says his lips are sore because he's not getting any liquid. She's using a flannel to dampen them. The nurses want to go in to straighten him up and change the...bag."

As Sally and Theca arrived to make way for the nurses, the tiny Chinese nurse carried in a tray of tea.

"Here you are," she said. "Have your tea. We won't be long. We'll just make him more comfortable then you can go back in."

The afternoon dragged on. The nerves, taut earlier, became jaded; the adrenalin had wasted and left a feeling of nausea; eyes and throats became sore. The heat in the hospital increased the discomfort. The walls of the tiny waiting room seemed to move in.

Sally and Theca sat by the bed, holding his hands, sobbing quietly, willing him to glance their way. By mid-afternoon his fitful sleeps fell to unconsciousness, and the last thing he said to the girls was: "I feel so drowsy. It's the drugs. I think I'll have a little sleep." Earlier, when that horrible delirium had worn off, he had said other things: "You're all here, that's good," and to Theca, "My Star of the Veldt, you've turned out so beautiful," and to Sally, "I love you, girl. I always did."

Now he was unconscious. His breathing was laboured. It rattled and rasped. They watched his still face. They held his hands. Moments of silence when his breathing stopped had them momentarily alert, holding their own breaths, gripping his hands until his breathing started and they relaxed again.

In the waiting room Tommy said to Dave and Ted: "The sister asked if we wanted a priest or something. I don't know what you think, but I reckon there's enough religion in that room already."

In the ward the periods of his breathing became shorter and those silent moments became longer and the rattle, when another gasp was taken, was louder.

Dave came out and told Tommy and Ted, "It won't be long." He glanced at his watch as if to make a point.

Pat appeared a moment later to say, "The Star's breaking down in there. I think she's upsetting Sally."

Ted moved to the door.

"I'll get her out for a while. She needs a break anyway. She's been in there for hours."

Dave nodded and said, "Good idea."

"C'mon, Sweetheart," Ted said to Theca and pulled her gently from the bedside. "This is doing you no good and it's upsetting your mother."

For a moment the Star hesitated, pulled her arm from his grip, but then she stood and allowed him to escort her from the room. Her eyes were swollen. She wiped them on a wasted tissue.

"Let's take a walk," he said. "Come on, you need some air."

She nodded and followed him weakly from the ward. He led her to the lift and down the main corridor. He put his arm around her.

"I'm not handling this very well," she said. "I thought Mum could lean on me but it's me that's gone to pieces."

"Perhaps that's not a bad thing. Looking after you is keeping her occupied."

They walked through the entrance and hit the damp evening air. A few flashbulbs went off but a couple of uniforms kept the press well away from them.

"I don't think I'm ever going to get over this," she said seriously.

They remained outside for five minutes. He smoked a cigarette and Theca regained some composure. Eventually, when she began to shiver, they made their way back.

They saw Pat and then Dave behind her. Pat's expression was enough.

"No!" Theca cried.

Dave tried to catch her as she rushed by.

"It was just this minute, Sis. It was only a moment ago!"

It was no use. She turned back to them, to Ted, and through clenched teeth said, "I wanted to be there. You! You!"

She hit him in the chest and on the shoulders, again and again. Ted was too stunned to react. He stood immobile gazing across at the helpless, almost fearful looks from Dave and Pat.

"I needed to be there," she whispered. "I'll never forgive you!"

The blows weakened and she dropped her arms. She turned and hurried into the private room.

Dave moved across to Ted and touched his shoulder.

"Don't worry," he said. "She'll be all right." But Dave was not at all sure. At that moment he wondered whether Theca and Ted would ever be right again.

The three of them followed Theca.

Moments earlier, after Ted had taken Theca from the room, Dave, Pat and Tommy had returned to make certain that the Star's distress had not upset Sally. She was composed, sitting there beside the bed, waiting, clutching Tom's hand in hers. There seemed little change in Tom. Slowly, slowly his breath was expelled, a harsh whistle, and then a pause, a still, silent pause, a heart-stopping moment, until once again with a quiet rattle, slowly, so slowly, his breath was drawn in.

There was nothing holy about death: it was a little thing. There was no atmosphere of sanctity: it was a wasteful thing. There was nothing immortal, no sign of the freeing of the spirit: it was an unimpressive thing. There was not the slightest hint of an ongoing process, hardly even an end; breathing did not cease, more, the next breath did not begin. This death was an easy thing; the thread of life was broken but so thin it was that the difference was subtle. But the silence, when the next breath did not come and people around held their breaths to listen, was absolute. Silently they watched as Sally leant closer, confirming, and then threw her arms around his neck and sank her head on to his still chest and then the silence was broken by her shriek. It was a lament, all the saddest sounds ever made in one mournful note, the saddest sound that they had ever heard.

Dave watched her and, still curiously detached, a feeling that he wasn't really there, noticed that his mother's hair was still dark and thick. It had never thinned or peppered grey, she had never aged like the rest of them.

It was over. They stood shattered, motionless, fixed expressions gazing at Sally rocking on her husband's chest, dropping stinging tears on to his blue pyjama top.

Dave suddenly moved. He had to find Theca.

And now they were all there.

Eventually the stillness was moved. Dave glanced across at Theca to see how she was coping. Her gaze was fixed on her father's face. The wet patches beneath her eyes and on her cheeks glistened in the stark light. Her features slowly softened, as if the end had been for her a terrible relief. He glanced at his wife to find her coping in a different way. Like Ted, a relative-in-law, there was a deep sadness of course, but there was not a snuffing out of one's own cells, there was no amputation of a part of life itself. The hurt they felt most of all was for the others. Pat sensed Dave's glance and looked back out of wide eyes and from under her spectacles she threw him her heart. He looked at Tommy. His younger brother was still, leaning backwards against the walled partition. A single tear trickled over his cheek.

It was over.

It was approaching eleven when they left the hospital. Sally carried her shopping bag. It contained those important things that she'd insisted on collecting together: Tom's shaving gear, watch and slippers and a half-used bottle of orange squash. She walked erect and independent.

Barry Theroux ran out of the cafeteria entrance as they passed.

"It's all over," Dave told him.

"I heard. Listen, half of Fleet Street is out there. The hospital's sent someone out to make a statement, but you don't need it."

Dave agreed.

"Come this way. We can get out here." He led the way and Dave ushered the others toward a side entrance. Barry hung back and whispered to Ted, "Peach has been trying to get you."

Dave overheard. "What's that about?"

"Detective Inspector Peach; he's been trying to get in touch."

It was nothing, Ted discovered later. There was no further news of the investigation. Peach simply wanted to be the first to extend his sympathies. He was filth, albeit bent filth, so his sympathies were meaningless and Ted didn't bother to pass them on.

They went out to the waiting cars. The night was darker. The stars glinted cruelly, coldly, polished by the terrible feeling of loss.

Chapter 32

The family motored from the hospital to the Lodge in Briar's Court. A few reporters had gathered by the gate and were pressing for statements. Half-a-dozen minders held them back. Once inside Sally had a long list of relatives and friends to call and she was on the telephone for the best part of an hour while the others sat quietly to marshal their thoughts.

While he listened to his mother's calls, Dave scanned the photographs lined up on the dresser, scenes from their childhood, of Theca, Tommy and him, pictures of the grandchildren, of Theca's wedding, of his wedding, and one in particular caught his eye – a black-and-white group photograph of his parent's wedding. Familiarity had hidden it. He'd never really studied it before. His mother, in white, quite beautiful and so young and fresh, clearly pregnant and yet looking oddly chaste, and his father, a wide boy if ever he saw one, surrounded by their friends and families. His grandmother, Rose, was there, a little woman standing next to the imposing figure of Peter Woodhead with his bowler pulled down to his ears, a badge of royalty. His mother's parents, Len and Joyce Mannings were there, Len looking quite ill and broken, with Reginald and Elizabeth Hurst next to them. Their sons, Ian and Richard, were in Maidstone prison at the time. Dave had heard the stories, the legends that had grown from the family history. Next to them was Coddy Hughes, his father-in-law, with Mavis, a slip of a girl, at his side. How young and eager they all looked, as if their last breaths of life would never be taken. He gazed impassively at some of his father's old army buddies, James Jessel and Pinchera and Norman Dileva leaning on his stick. And standing at their side, fragile and oddly forsaken, was the bespectacled young woman that was Jane. He barely recognized her. He'd not noticed her in the photograph before.

Eventually, in the small hours, they wound it up and went their separate ways. Theca would return later to spend the night with her mother but first she had to collect the children. She and Ted drove a few hundred yards to Nan's house. In the car they spoke of breaking the news gently but once inside she rushed to find her children and blurted: "Your granddad's dead and we're never going to see him again!" Her arms wrapped around them while Ted stood watching helplessly.

As they motored home he said, "He waited until you were out of the room before he decided to call it a day. He was ready to die but he clung on until you left."

Theca turned to him and said honestly, "That's the only thought that's stopping me from hating you. I keep telling myself that that is so and maybe one day I'll believe it."

"What are you going to do, Sweetheart? Have you decided yet?"

"I don't want to leave," she said quietly, ready with her answer. "I want to be with my family."

After a late breakfast Theca left Sally and went across to The Tower and found Dave in his office.

"Hello, Sis. How's Mum?"

Theca shrugged.

"I must get over there," he said.

"That's not why I'm here, Dave. I've decided to stay with Ted."

She saw the relief in his eyes.

"I'm pleased, Star, really pleased. I hope you can work it out. Does he know?"

"I told him last night."

Dave nodded. "What about…?"

"I'll tell him later."

"That's not going to be easy."

"Nothing ever is."

"These things happen," Dave said reflectively. "It's for the best."

"We'll see."

It was just on twelve when she met Margaret for lunch.

"I saw it on the news," Margaret said. "I haven't stopped crying. I tried to call."

"I was at Mum's."

"Yes, Jean told me. I thought it best not to ring there."

"I've decided to stay with Ted."

"But you don't love him."

"That's not important. Not anymore. I love my family and he's a part of that."

"Well, I think you're making a mistake. I think it's all a dreadful waste. Why on earth did you tell him in the first place?"

"I don't know. That's the silly part. I've hurt him for no reason and yet we'd reached the stage when something had to happen."

"How can you think of living the rest of your life with someone you don't love? I know. You want to be some kind of martyr. You need to hurt and feel pain. I'm right. But Theca, what happens when you can live with the pain you feel now? And you will, one day. Oh, I know that at the moment you think you'll never get over it. But you will. What happens then? When you've got to get on with your own life again? When suddenly you find that what you had before, and that was never good enough, is all you've got again. What happens then? I don't think that you can give Lewis up that easily. People like us can't do without passion! It's what keeps us alive."

Theca smiled weakly. She knew why Margaret was her best friend. The past and the future barely seemed to matter to her. She lived for the moment. Her exuberance excited the air about her and other people breathed it in. It was only a few days earlier that she had been doing her level best to talk her out of leaving Ted in the first place, or at least of telling him about her affair.

"I know. I know," Theca said. "But the family has suffered enough. I seem to have left a trail of bodies all over the place."

"Well, I think you should wait a while. I told you before that this isn't the time to make decisions. Why don't you wait a week or two? Get the funeral out of the way. You must give yourself time. You're talking about the rest of your life. Put things on hold. Why rush into it?"

"I have to. I can't explain it but there's a voice screaming at me to put things right. I can't ignore it. I have to tell Lewis that it's over and then I have to pick up the pieces and get some sanity back into life."

Margaret sighed. "Oh dear, life is so complicated. Why couldn't you just settle for a comfortable little affair like the rest of us? Passion on Wednesday night three weeks out of four and any other time you could fit it in?"

"Because I wanted more," Theca said sadly.

"And now you're not even going to have that."

After lunch Theca drove down to Victoria. Her route was uncomplicated and she didn't bother checking in her mirror. A tail now would be for her safety and for no other reason. The Barge weighed heavily and security had been tightened accordingly. As well as that, her father's death could well have been the signal for further attacks. Two cars and three men had followed her every move since leaving her mother's house.

She left the Mini in the enclosed square and trod carefully across the cobblestones to the back entrance of the mews. Lewis led her into the sitting room.

She said bluntly, "I'm not going to live with you. I'm staying with Ted. I'm sorry."

His nod was a meek acceptance. Ted had said the right things; her father had died at the wrong time and thrown family loyalties to the fore. Lewis was disappointed and angry but hid it well. There was nothing else to do. He had to keep open even the remote possibility that at some stage in the future, when things had settled down, Theca might change her mind. He was angry, but he was not to know that Theca's decision had saved his life.

That ethereal time between a death and a funeral is governed more by a timetable of necessary actions than by desire. For them everything was hurried. There was little time for reflection. And yet even that little time was too long. The nights were endless, restless wakeful moments full of guilt and regret. Those dreadful feelings in the throat and chest refused to go away. Sally would lie there in the dark, waiting for him, her hand on his cold pillow, listening to a silent melody as the smoke swirled around Ella Fitzgerald and she would mouth the words of *I'll Never Forget You*. And the living outside of those necessary actions was in the past. The recollections of the past poured out at every meeting; the same memories were described over and over again. Lucia came back from France early and that was a godsend. Sally was able to share the old days with someone new, someone who hadn't heard her stories a dozen times – a thousand times – before, and it took some of the pressure off the others.

And so it went on, an ungodly time, surrounded by sympathy cards from the rich and famous, from the studios and castles, from the Costa and from Brazil, and they discussed the choice of coffin and flowers and cars. One day fed into the next without the necessary pause for unbroken sleep.

The soft light threw a waxen image on to his features so that he was no longer real and yet in another sense he looked alive and simply sleeping. They went in alone. Dave was the last to arrive. Ted and Theca were in reception, waiting for him. All day a steady flow of people had paid their respects. Sally had been the first, along with Tommy, and now Dave was the last.

"Hello, Sis," Dave said thickly.

The Star's dark eyes betrayed her. She nodded quickly. Her lips were tight. Ted's arm was an unlikely shield around her shoulders. His nod to Dave said it all.

Dave felt flat; the things to do had left him mentally exhausted and in the taking care of the others, particularly Sally, his own feelings had been pushed aside, postponed. He felt cold.

He was led into the parlour and the door closed quietly behind him.

He stood just inside, not wanting to look. The air-conditioning increased his sense of chill. At the same time it was oppressive, lacking air, as if there was something else living there. He felt a breath and it made him shiver. He looked up and approached.

His father was immaculate in his double-breasted suit and tie. His shoes, spit-polished, reflected the room like a pair of black mirrors. He noticed the hands and fingernails, scrubbed and polished. He was drawn to the face, the amazing relaxation, the lack of expression, and yet it was his father, ludicrously content. So real, he expected a breath, a sign, and yet so unreal it gleamed like a wax model. Suddenly it was a peaceful place; and in the stillness a life stirred in rebirth; and in the silence his father simply slept, dreaming a peaceful dream.

"I had a dream too," Dave heard his own voice, quiet, detached. "I saw you last night, in the bedroom, and I had the most wonderful feeling that everything was all right. That you were still here, somewhere."

But when the night was done and the pale dawn was creeping at the windows he was gone and the comfort of the dream faded quickly.

He leant over the glistening wood and felt his father's cold kiss.

"Goodbye, Pop," he said softly.

He heard a faint knock on the door and Ted was there.

"You all right, Dave? You've been in here half an hour."

Dave looked up, astonished that time had been suspended, and Ted smiled compassionately as he saw Dave's bloodshot eyes.

He said gently, "Come on, Dave. Always come back again, can't you?"

Dave sighed. He wouldn't be coming back. This was it. All over, the final stamp on the exit papers.

Ted put his arm across Dave's shoulders and led him out. The embrace was accepted and in that instant Ted thought that Dave had changed, that a streak of humanity was trying to shine in.

And so it went on: days that never ended somehow disappeared without being lived, punctuated with grief and memory and guilt. During that week the police showed an apparent lack of interest in the Smiths. Their investigations seemed to have slowed down while records and evidence went unaccountably missing. No one was hauled in for questioning, not a word about the drugged bodies, nothing about the girl. As far as Peach was concerned, he told them with a knowing wink, the top brass were waiting to see what happened. The word on the street was war. The police could afford to bide their time, not that they had much left to go on, but at the end of it they could pin the blame on who was left.

Jessica and John returned from their honeymoon. It had been pointless trying to keep the news from them for the papers, albeit received by them a day late, carried stories of Tom's death. Some of the tabloids quoted police sources and suggested that a battle for the control of the underworld was about to begin. Old Villains from the past, pictured against a backdrop of sun-bleached beaches, filled the captions with their memories, mostly exaggerated if not completed invented, of the old days when they had rubbed shoulders with Tom.

In the office, some time during that week, a morning because in the casino training sessions were in progress and, in the club, girls from the cabaret were being put through their paces, John was privy to his first management meeting.

"Could it be the Chinese?" Theroux asked. "Perhaps they got worried that Tom would deal them out and let the Yanks in."

"Pop's word was everything," Tommy cut in. "You should know that, Barry. The Chinks, even more than most, respected his word."

"Well, someone else from the past, the Jamaicans or the Maltese," Theroux said. "Or the fucking Cypriot lunatics."

"I've wondered about that," Tommy said, "Someone out there jumping on the bandwagon, deciding to have a go while we're down. It might even be funded by the Costa. They're into dope again."

A puzzled look from John prompted Tommy to explain.

"They are remnants of the old Krays and Richardsons. We never crossed any of them; kept an eye on their interests but that was all."

Dave chuckled and said confidently, "You're way off the mark. They are old geezers now, well out of it, living on reputations. They talk big but mostly about the old days. How fucking great it was and all that! They were never that big, anyway, and the only reason they make the headlines today is because the press have made them Robin Hood figures. They were villains, sure, but by today's standards they wouldn't have made the small ad's column. They're down there in Marbella getting suntans and pissing it up on Watney's. If they're into anything it's small time, African shit and hash oil, maybe a snort or two, but that's all. They're all running out of funds, that's why they're writing their biographies and doing spots on South-East at Six!"

"Are you telling me the twins were nothing?" John asked, not convinced.

"They covered a patch of the Smoke, right? Even the local villains today cover entire cities. Take Mick. That bastard has the whole of Scotland under control. The only thing that made the twins big was their sentences. Nowadays you could top the Queen Mum and not go down for that long! The big villains today, Christ! They're government backed. They talk in billions."

John shook his head. "Why is this distribution deal so important?"

Dave spoke matter-of-factly. "The authorities are closing in on the Mafia's Las Vegas business. The Yanks had to make up for it and out of sheer panic they bought a mountain of white dust from Colombia but they could end up snorting it all themselves. We'll deal with the Yanks – we always said we would – but not exclusively. Not to the exclusion of the Chinese. There's something about eggs in one basket here, and that isn't for us. It's not good for business. Once they have the monopoly they'll be in control. That's what they really want. It's that simple. They want to deal with one face and they want to be the only dealer."

"So what will happen now?"

"We've got our problems with Mick, but the Yanks are up shit creek too. They've got to start moving the stuff in a big way or they'll go fucking bankrupt. They'll put pressure on us by making out they're backing Mick, but they're running out of time."

"Are you sure they're only making out?" Tommy asked.

"I hope they are," Dave said but he didn't sound confident.

He kept his thoughts regarding Valenti to himself. Only Coddy Hughes shared his fears. And since the guinea bosses didn't know that it was their own Tony Valenti causing all the grief, they probably thought it was Mick, and that everything was going to plan. But it wasn't Mick.

Dave was almost certain of that. And that was his one good card. It would give him some time.

"Why did your old man want you to deal with Houghie personally?" Theroux asked. It was a fair question. "We normally take care of business."

Although he hadn't asked it the question also puzzled Tommy. His old man couldn't have known about Denise's kid. Or could he?

"Probably because I took him on in the first place," Dave muttered.

It was the obvious conclusion but it was the wrong one and it was going to be a few days yet before Dave understood the reasoning behind his father's instruction.

Chapter 33

The town planners had castrated his city. The squalid streets were lined with fast-food chains and launderettes, bingo halls and video shops. What the hell had happened, he wondered, that it had become a city of neglect? Had he really slept through it all? Driving through it he glanced up at the tower blocks and considered the thousands of little people behind the squares of glass, going about their business completely unaware that a major war was being fought; unaware that in the safe streets of the city there was another world, a dangerous place, where the stake was life itself. Unaware also, that he now had the power of life and death over every one of them.

He cut a line through the intersection where the ugly block fortress of the Bank angled across to the columns of Mansion House. The past silently echoed from the ancient façades as their solid reflections slid across his windshield. He stepped angrily on the accelerator and the car leapt through a set of reds and belted down Queen Victoria Street and left to the river. He pulled up on the Embankment just beyond Blackfriars where he could look over the steely grey warships at Southwark and the National. The river was high; gulls wheeled and dipped over the swell, squawking soullessly into a warm southerly breeze that carried the scent of the sea. The reflections of fluffy clouds raced across the surface like ghosts from the age of sail.

Dave thought about his grandfather sinking slowly under the heavy metallic water and his father who had lived through it all and he was stung by nostalgia for those times he never knew. In that moment his mask slipped; the hardness melted away and he felt the downturn of his lips as they began to quiver. In that moment he could have wept. He shrugged off the sentiment as though it was something repugnant, a mark of weakness, and his face tightened in anger at his own feelings. Back came the hooded eyes and the contempt with which he held all but a few.

"Fuck you!" he said to the river and reached down to start the car again.

His father had insisted: "Do nothing until after the funeral." The words, spoken in a calm knowing way came back to him. "Just hold the fort and keep things ticking over." The humour in the eyes, the certainty that things would work out, that everything was under control, was just as evident now as when the words were spoken. Somehow his father had planned for the future, was – even in death – in control. But Dave was less than confident. It just didn't seem possible that his father could have known about Valenti or, indeed, that Mick was just a mouthpiece? He sighed. For the next few days he would hold his peace and play a waiting game. But once the earth had been scattered on the polished mahogany, then Valenti and all who ran with him, including Mick, were going to pay for causing the Smiths additional grief at such a time. He didn't know how he was going to achieve it with the Mafia and half the other gangs lined up against him but, to his mind, there was nothing more certain.

One thing at a time, he kept telling himself as he took a right into the Strand and let the traffic carry him along Fleet Street. He turned back into Queen Victoria and headed up Bishopsgate toward Spitalfields.

His father had wanted him to deal with Peter Hough personally. That was another surprise. Was it the old man's way of telling him that he knew all about his affair with Denise? Dealing with Houghie and with Denise would bury another of the family skeletons. Dave nodded grimly. Perhaps his father had enjoyed the irony.

He turned south into Commercial Street. A few moments later he turned again through a pebble-dashed archway set in a terraced row into a small courtyard surrounded by two-storey warehouses. Just inside the entrance two men leant across a car engine. They were close enough to block the way to any unwelcome face. They recognized Dave and one of them acknowledged him with a slight nod. Dave parked next to another black Rover. Barry Theroux walked slowly towards him while the two men closed the high double gates.

"All right?" Barry said as Dave climbed out of the car.

"Yeah. I'm not all that on these early morning calls though."

Barry yawned. "I know what you mean."

Dave turned to look at the crumbling buildings. "What have we got here?"

"It used to be a milk depot," Barry said, "till the supermarkets fucked up the trade. They tell me that way before our time it used to belong to the family."

Barry Theroux turned to his own car and opened the boot. Carefully, using both hands, he lifted out an axe and held it towards Dave. The curled handle was three feet long.

Dave took it one-handed, felt the weight then ran his finger along the sharp edge.

"Nice one," he muttered. He rested it on his shoulder. "Where is he?"

"This way," Barry pointed toward a steel door in a red-bricked building, "Cold storage. We turned the fridge back on to keep him cool. He's stark bollock naked, probably got frostbite by now."

"Has he said anything?"

"Not a word. He's taking it very personal."

"Let's get on with it."

Together they walked up a slight incline toward the building. At the large sliding door they were met by another man carrying a sawn-off 12-bore. Barry nodded and the man drew back the heavy steel door. The cold air hit them immediately. It came out in a dense cloud.

Dave turned to Barry, "You coming in?"

Barry shrugged. His sad eyes were resigned. He followed Dave into the cold bare room.

Peter Hough was at the far end. He was hugging himself and stamping his feet. His face was ashen, his body tinged with blue. Hough saw Dave and moved forward. He saw the axe and stopped abruptly. Fear widened his eyes.

"Houghie, boy, you know what we're famous for, don't you?"

"Dave, what…?"

"Revenge, Pete, that's what people say, isn't it? It's time. Let's not waste any more time."

"What are you talking about?"

"If you don't know, Pete, then you can't talk me out of it, can you?" Dave swung the heavy axe from his shoulder and held it out with both hands. The head glinted cruelly in the stark strip light.

Peter Hough had seen Dave in action many times and knew what a heartless bastard he was. In his time, especially that spent in the Scrubs, he'd mixed with the real evil villains but Dave was in a different league. He wasn't human. There wasn't the slightest hint of compassion in his make-up.

As Dave advanced waving the axe from side to side Peter Hough stood as if mesmerized, defenceless. His barely raised his hands.

"Have a heart, Dave. I done you some good turns in the past. I think they've got Denise. I couldn't take the chance."

"Denise was still at your gaff when you had a go at Tommy."

"I swear that wasn't me, Dave. Tommy came to me. I even tried to get hold of you."

"Don't fucking lie to me you little toerag. Don't you insult my fucking intelligence! My phone wasn't engaged at five in the morning. You were letting Valenti know that he'd fucked up. That's why you came back to us the next day. He wanted you on the inside, telling him all our moves!"

"Tell me what to do, Dave. Is there anything I can do?"

"Not a lot, Pete. You didn't really think you could fuck with me, did you?"

"Come on, Dave, for old times' sake. I've been with you a lot of years."

"That's the shame of it."

"I know you ain't religious, but your old man was. Can't you give me another chance on his memory?"

"You're right. I'm not a religious man. I don't believe in forgiveness and I'm not all that on second chances. And nor was my father."

Abruptness crept into Hough's voice. "You're finished, Dave. Can't you see that? Valenti's backing the whole country against you, so what's the point in having me now? He's got it sewn up. Next week it'll all be over. You're going to need some friends. Why don't you just back off and disappear to the Costa or something? He'll let you do that."

"Why the fireman, Pete? We know you ferried him out."

"Honest, I never knew they were going to top him. They told me they wanted him out of the way for while, not permanently. It made sense."

"Why?"

"He was the only one who could have fingered Valenti. He knew too many people in the game. Even after all this time he's pretty well tuned in. He would've picked up a whisper. They all like to mouth off, and you've got to admit The Barge was a pretty tasty job. You've got to admit that. But I swear to you that topping him was never an option." He shook his head regretfully. "My hands were tied. I don't know what's happened to Denise. She wouldn't have left the kid."

"Yes she would. If she thought her life was on the line she'd do anything, same as you would. She's done a runner. You should have followed her. She knew me. She knew what I'd do when I found out!"

Dave swung the axe. Hough tried to dodge but he'd left it too late. The blade hit him just above the ankle. He heard the crunch of bone and felt a terrible pain explode in his leg. He stumbled forward and tried to grab Dave's neck but his strength had gone and instead he sank to his knees. He looked back. His foot was a yard away, on its side. He could see the flesh and bone protruding from it and the blood gathering in a steaming pool.

He looked up. Even through the pain his face was a mask of disbelief. He began to cry. Tears streamed down his face and dotted the dark concrete floor.

"You didn't need to do that," he gasped.

"Dry your tears you fucking big girl." Dave stood over him. "Let's go back ten years," he said calmly. "About the time Valenti lost his fucking nose."

Hough's sobbing stopped with a sudden intake of breath. His eyes widened as he stared up at Dave.

"It was you, wasn't it?"

Hough swallowed hard. His face twisted as another wave of pain swept up from his leg.

"Please, Dave, I'm bleeding to death. I'll tell you everything but don't-"

"Tell me about it."

Hough broke down again.

"If there's one thing I hate it's seeing a man cry. How did you know where to find me, Pete?"

"I knew how long it took the car to get back." Hough's voice quivered. His breath came in short bursts. "It had to be the Hursts in Folkestone or Coddy up north. Once your driver said you were knee-deep in pig-shit, it had to be the farm. It had to be Coddy's manor."

"All this fucking time," Dave shook his head in disgust. "How much did Valenti pay you?"

"Please Dave –"

"Whatever it was, it wasn't enough!"

Hough screamed as he saw the axe come down again. He snatched his hand away but part of it remained on the cold dusty concrete. For an instant his fingers continued to claw at the floor. As he lifted his arm blood spurted over his face and covered his chest. Through a red mist he watched Dave's approach and heard his voice, calm and deep: "Cheers, Pete. Say hello to a few dead people for me. I don't want you thinking this isn't personal. It fucking well is!"

Hough's scream bounced off the icy walls. Dave stood back and steadied himself before swinging again. The blow landed on Hough's neck. For a moment his head hung at a ridiculous angle, swinging on skin and sinew, until the body collapsed and it hit the floor. Blood turned black in the dust.

Dave dropped the axe to his side and bent low over Hough's head. The face was turned toward him, the eyes still open, the mouth wide in a silent scream.

"Now, don't you fucking well do it again," Dave said.

Barry Theroux walked across to stand at his side. "Feel better?" he asked.

Dave nodded. "Yeah," he said breathlessly. "There isn't anything to compare with it."

Barry grunted and switched his gaze from the body to the head. The air was filled with the sweet sickly odour of blood. He said, "Bit of a fucking mess, though."

"Keep the head frozen. Once Denise shows up I want it dropped off at Traitor's Gate. I want some headlines in the *Standard*."

Barry nodded grimly. "We've got to tighten up, Dave," he said stonily. "Make sure this sort of thing can never get out of hand again."

"It's not over yet," Dave muttered.

Barry went on as though he hadn't heard. "The only way to do it is to make people so scared shitless they wouldn't dare take us on. Like Leeds United in the seventies!"

A smile tugged Dave's features. He turned to Barry. "That severe, eh?" he said. "Fuck me, you'll have them calling me Norman Hunter next!"

Dave caught Tommy at The Tower and told him that the fireman was dead. He was surprised at Tommy's sudden concern for a man he barely knew. He explained that Hough had been working for Valenti and that it was Valentu himself who had ordered the destruction of The Barge. He told him about Sharon so that Tommy understood the nature of Valenti's hatred for the Smiths and for Dave in particular.

"It's not the wiseguys we're fighting," Dave said. "It's Valenti himself moonlighting. The Mafia didn't sanction the hit on The Barge. Sure, they're trying to put us under pressure but that's all. It's Valenti. He's not playing the game. It's his personal war. And he's played it perfectly. His bosses think that it's Mick causing all the grief."

"So what do we do?"

"We wait until after the funeral. Pop was working on something, so we'll wait and see. After all, that's what you wanted and that's what he asked us to do."

Tommy looked at his brother and shook his head. He knew very well that Dave had not been sitting back. Quietly, unobtrusively, he'd been getting ready to go to war. Safe houses had been set up, men had been armed, trusted reinforcements had been recruited, police connections had been primed to clamp down on Mick's business and make his movements difficult, informers were paid for the SP on Mick's strengths and weaknesses, men had been shifted from Kent to strengthen Coddy Hughes. The Hurst's old empire was defenceless so there was little point in keeping even a token force there. And while this was going on so was the talking. To secure the backing of other gangs promises were made and deals struck. Financially the situation was crippling. The consolation was that Mick was running up the same costs.

Tommy hadn't yet come to terms with the discovery that his brothers had been involved in the procurement of minors. For the first time in his life he felt a sense of hostility toward them and the business. Only slightly satisfying was the certain knowledge that his father had played no part in it. On his way across to see Jill Mountford he wondered what other dreadful secrets he would uncover. His outrage compounded the anger he felt at the loss of his father. He felt like running but had no idea where to run.

The sadness was there, overriding all else, but something even more than that, a detachment, an illusive sense of isolation, a sense that he no longer had the chance to earn his father's respect and approval. He felt, as all children must, that he'd been cheated of the right to prove himself, that he would never recognize that important mark of pride in his father's eyes. His ambitions had been downgraded because of it, his possible achievements had become necessarily less important. For this selfish reason the bitterness was more acute and the anger burned that much deeper.

He went to the garage first but found it closed. He found her at the house. She'd heard him drive up and met him on the path. She wore a pair of tight cords and the white sweater he'd seen before. She led him into the sitting room.

"I heard about your dad," she said. "It was on the news. I'm so sorry."

"Yeah, well, it happens, I suppose. It doesn't make it any easier, though."

"Mike still hasn't surfaced." She met his steady gaze and added, "I was going to call you and let you know. I've been thinking about you."

"I've been trying not to think about you."

"Were you successful?"

He shook his head and said, "It was the cherries that did it. Bowls full of them."

She laughed.

"What?" he said.

"It doesn't matter."

He led her to the sofa. She caught something in his expression and turned hesitant. "What is it?"

"Jill, sit down. I've got to talk to you."

She frowned. "What is it?" she repeated, cautiously.

"You're not going to see him again, Sweetheart."

"How do you know? What's happened?"

"Listen to me. I know. I do know."

Her lips trembled. "I don't believe you."

Tommy gazed at her. His eyes were dark and concerned, his lips tight, and she recognized an honesty that she couldn't ignore.

"What happened?" Her voice shook.

"I don't know what happened. The Yanks had him taken out. That's all I know."

She stared at the carpet, her expression grave and hard. Slowly her face filled with accusation and her eyes flicked up to meet his. "It's to do with your father and all this trouble!"

Tommy nodded. "I'm sorry, but I had to tell you. I found out just an hour ago. He had nothing to do with us. The Yanks thought he would finger them for the bombing."

"Damn your family."

"It's been damned a long time."

"I'm shaking like a leaf. I don't know what to do."

"Let me help you."

"What can you do?"

"I can do anything that you let me, everything or nothing. I want to help you. I want to be with you. You haven't been out of my mind since I first saw you. I wish I could do something to put things right, but I can't."

"Hold me, Tommy. Please hold me."

He reached forward and embraced her. Her face buried into his chest and he felt the wetness of her tears through his shirt.

"Will I ever know what happened?"

"I don't know. Maybe we'll hear something, get a whisper, but I doubt it. He's just never going to come home."

"Oh, how can I carry this?"

There was no answer. He held her closer.

"I loved the old sod so much."

"I know."

"It's so unfair. Why him? He was harmless."

He held her for what seemed like hours and listened to her intermittent sobbing, not wanting to move, and finding his own solace in her touch. The light from the window began to fade, sucking the colours from the room. She had calmed, perhaps even dozed. Eventually she made a move and freed herself from his arms. She caught hold of his hand and led him silently into the hall. He thought she was leading him to the door and was disheartened. She did blame him after all. He tried a weak smile. He couldn't blame her for feeling the way she did. If it hadn't been for his family none of it would have happened.

When she paused at the bottom of the stairs he was caught unawares and the relief left him light-headed. Very deliberately she tugged at his hand and with slow steps led him up the stairs and into the back room, her bedroom, and to her bed.

"Make love to me, Tommy," she said firmly. "Let's forget everything else for a little while." She pulled off her white sweater and coyly uncovered her breasts. The chill in the room touched her and she shivered. Goosebumps ran up her arms, and under his admiring gaze her breasts quivered slightly and her dark nipples firmed up. She struggled out of her tight cords. There was a determined, unemotional look about her that Tommy found curiously unnerving. A wedge of pubic hair showed through her pale briefs. Shyly she threw up her hands to shield herself from his look.

It was a sad embrace and there was something innocent in the conclusion. She held on to him and refused to let him withdraw and in that moment she whispered, "Oh, darling!"

They lay together, not out of urgency or compassion but out of life itself. And later, entwined under the cover of darkness, with Venus a trembling spark on the glistening window, she said, "Darling, I'd like to come to the funeral," and he stroked her cheek and said, "I'd like you to come and be with me."

Chapter 34

Tosca filled the air. It was being performed in Milan and the BBC was broadcasting it live. It began at 11.30 a.m., UK time. So did the funeral.

There were early summer flowers everywhere, wreaths and sprays, bouquets and hearts. They spread either side of a narrow concrete path running through the cemetery and up a slight incline to a mound of freshly dug earth and the hole beside it. They circled the trunk of a young birch that threw its shadow across the hole.

Stillness descended and time stopped and the ranks of gravestones that fanned out down the hill sucked out the warmth of the late morning sunshine.

Once the coffin was lowered and the earth was scattered to end the obsequies and the old soldiers had made their salutes, it was over. There was something so final, so absolute, that it left nothing of the past. It was the cold beginning of something else. They left that rise straight-backed and determined.

Tosca played on, quietly now, out of the back veranda doors and the open windows of the detached houses backing on to the cemetery. On the way down the hill, with his arm around his mother's shoulders, Dave said to her, "You're a lady, d'you know that?"

She tried a quick smile. "And you're a gentleman, David," she said, then added, "I'm all right, really. I'm all right now."

Lingering at the grave, not joining the crowd of people who made their way down the slight hill and not at all perturbed by the workmen who had quickly moved in to finish their job, three people stood in isolation, fenced in by an invisible barrier. Jane stood between James Jessel and Pinchera, raw-eyed and weeping, looking over the hole but not seeing, remembering another time when everything was possible and they would all live forever. Her memories were misty now, the images faded like an old photograph. She was seeing the faces from the past: Simon Carter, the fool, killed in 1952 when his Norton took off from the Isle of Man mountain road. How he had loved his bikes and cars and what a fitting way for him to go! Had he been a quicker man he would have been her first. She smiled through her tears and her green eyes sparkled again. Norman Deliva followed him two years later, felled in Brick Lane by two members of a South London gang. Richard Hurst went in the early sixties in a head-on collision on the Dover Road. Not for them a desolate hospital bed and an undignified end. And now Tom Smith had followed them. It was too much for her to bear and she buckled between the arms of the two men.

"Come on, old girl," Pinchera said. His curling Italian accent had grown stronger as he'd grown older. "It's time to go. It's time to put away the old days. Let's catch up with the others."

She nodded, sniffing back her tears and slowly, so slowly, gave her arm to Pinchera and they moved off down the hill. The wop walked with a strange limp, but those who didn't know him would not have noticed.

Suddenly she stopped and pulled back on his arm,

"What is it?" he asked, at once concerned.

"I don't want to go back to the Lodge. I'd be looking for Tom in every corner. I don't want to hear all the eulogies from people who never knew him."

"What then?"

"I'd like to go down and walk by the river, perhaps buy an ice cream. I'd like to breathe in the past, just for a little while longer. And then I'll let it go."

Pinchera smiled and shared a knowing glance with James Jessel. He said, "Of course you can, Jane. We're both of us at your service."

She nodded and they began again and followed the line of wreaths and cut flowers down the deserted path.

He was a tall man, this old man, pockmarked and bent. His movements were stiffened by age and yet there was something dangerous about him, perhaps his soulless grey eyes or the ugly scar that ran across the side of his head. It was not an easy thing he had to do but he relished the prospect. It began with a girl, an ex-stripper, an ex-whore, and she was the key that would make all things possible. It was odd how the past stacked up and repeated itself. Scratch Fox had heard the stories. The firm had taken shape on the back of a young woman's charms. By all accounts Nathalie – he remembered her name – had led her suitor a merry dance as she whispered French nothings into his ear. And now they needed the charms of another girl to keep the firm afloat.

"The family needs your help," he'd told her and she'd understood. She'd always known that sooner or later the business would call her back. It had been, almost, her destiny. She left a note for her husband telling him that the Smiths had a job for her and she placed her child in her neighbour's care. Before he left the house, of course, the pockmarked man took the note and slipped it into his coat pocket next to the old army-issue Webley pistol that he always carried.

There were things to do, specific paths to follow. They filled his mind until the headaches came back. They were written in blue on a blackboard in his headquarters on Mount Pleasant. Only three other men were privy to this information and they worked exclusively for him.

They needed layout drawings of Runnymede and they needed to log the movements of the wiseguys living there.

They needed to establish a safe house within walking distance of the river. They needed to install hardware, some of it hot from Glasgow, and that was not going to be easy. Most weapons that had been used and therefore identified ended up at the bottom of the Clyde.

They needed a caretaker to look after the safe house and the soldiers who would live there and then to arrange the clean up afterwards.

Washing services that guaranteed the removal of every dab and flake of dust needed booking well in advance.

They needed supplies for the army – food, booze, trusted girls, videos and comics. They could be there for up to a month. Death was rarely punctual.

They needed four fast cars with false number-plates.

They needed a make-up artist and a soldier who resembled Vinny Grey, one of Mad Mick's key men.

All that and that was just the London end.

In Glasgow they needed to install Denise.

They needed a safe house in Glasgow in which to install Vinny Grey.

They needed to log his movements.

He began the meeting with his three senior men.

He regarded each in turn and said, "It might be a week, or it might be two, but we've got to be ready." Making plans was never going to be easy when the timing had to tie in with a funeral. "We've worked together before so there will be no surprises. You were all with me in Chinatown. As it was then it is now: a statement, something that will be talked about for the next twenty years. No one in business today will ever forget it. We've got one more job to do and then it's retirement. We're getting too old for all this shit anyway. But this is the big one. It's bigger even that Chinatown. Anyone we use has got to be one hundred percent. Even the slightest question mark and we don't use him."

So it began.

Vinny Grey was known as the Snake. It had to do with a strange tattoo of a cobra on his left forearm. Where Don McLachlan looked after Mick's financial interests, Grey was the undisputed leader of his forces. He was in charge of Mick's army and had been with him ever since Mick had first made his mark on the Scottish scene. Over the years his leadership qualities had been established and he ran the army with rigid control. He had one weakness that few people knew about. He was partial to the pretty, darkly tanned face.

Denise had been learning her trade for a number of years and she was the perfect bait to use on Vinny Grey. At fourteen she'd arrived penniless on Charing Cross Station to be snapped up by the first ponce in the queue. She'd looked older than her age and he'd introduced her to the sex-show circuit. She took off her clothes in various clubs and pubs, making her way through the London streets to six or seven different venues on a single night. The pimp used a heavy hand to control her; he hit her in places that didn't bruise and stuck heroin into her veins. He held her down while his friends raped her, and had the event filmed on two super-eight cameras. He sold hundreds of copies of the film. Stripping led to prostitution and live sex acts on darkened stages with men she didn't know. Three at a time, two from the audience, became her speciality. When Dave Smith found her she'd been close to death; her pimp had unpaid bills hanging over him and Dave worked him over to within an inch of his life. Rehabilitated, she began to work for the Smiths and became one of the highest-regarded toms in London. It stayed that way until Dave himself took an interest in her. When he eventually lost interest she was pregnant and for whatever reason, decided to have the baby. Peter Hough replaced Dave and she married him and let him believe that the baby was his. Now she had a chance to repay the Smiths for saving her life and she threw herself into it with little regard for her own security.

Once installed in one of the clubs frequented by Grey, Denise used her old routine. Subtly, but leaving in his mind no doubts whatsoever, she made herself available. For him there was no escape. Denise was special. She toyed with him. It became a game. It took her moments to be noticed and less than an hour to get him drooling. She flashed her eyes wickedly and she used her body, baiting him with glimpses, sitting on his expanding lap and gently shifting her weight, playing every card that she held. He never stood a chance. And she kept him that way for a week, until she was given the word. And so eventually, the day before the funeral, she gave in, but on her terms. Because of the secrecy she demanded, they would meet in a motel and he would arrive alone. He'd finished once and had started again, forcing an anal entry, when two men burst into the room and dragged him down and covered his mouth with a rag full of chloroform. No one he knew saw him again for forty-eight hours. By then it was all over. It was too late. And no one that mattered believed him.

It was surprising how safe the Americans felt in Britain. Their confidence was built around the fear of reprisal and the fact that they were mere onlookers, albeit instigators, of the present situation. Where, in the States, the families employed an army of bodyguards, those that headed the British end made do with two or three. This complacency and their involvement in the local problems led to their destruction.

The three leaders went to Tom Smith's funeral and remained in a small group at the bottom end of the cemetery. Their presence was not unnoticed but neither did it cause concern. It was the Smith's loss of control that had the Americans putting distance between themselves and the family gathered around the plot. That they were there at all was respect enough and if the Smiths were to regain their position then relationships could easily resume. The old man, O'Connell, dressed in black, held at the elbow by his driver Herman Tartt, bowed his head and clutched his personal bible with thin, bony fingers. His weak eyes could barely make out the crowd on the hill but he could hear the mournful notes of *Tosca* filtering from the windows. The younger men, Valenti and Clough, dressed in similar black suits and overcoats, stood beside him, ready to move quickly to their vehicle as soon as the service was finished, before the crowd came back down the hill. They had made an appearance. That was enough.

The drive back to Runnymede was interrupted by early lunchtime traffic and it took them almost an hour to reach the detached group of houses on the bank. There was no sign of the kids playing in the gardens and that was surprising. Tartt let the three men out of the car before driving to the garage and using his remote control on the door. He parked inside, switched off the ignition and opened the car door. His last thoughts as he noticed the garage doors closing, was that he'd touched the remote control button on the handset by mistake. In the dim light a lick of flame flared and, from an explosion, slugs tore into Tartt's face and blew the back of his head into the passenger seat.

The last act of the opera blared from the open doors of the patio.

A canopy of willows produced a dappled pattern on the shimmering water. The boats moored at the water's edge breathed sluggishly. The gardens that ran down to the footpath were splashed in early summer colour; the first blooms of glistening honeysuckle on the arches reflected in the still ornamental pools where carp moved languidly between the lily pads. A whisper of breeze stirred the lilac and the camellia leaves. Under a brilliant red rhododendron lay a dead child, a boy of about eight, and from a gaping wound in his neck blood trickled into the pond and coloured the water pink and the carp began to dart quickly producing occasional flashes of silver light on the surface.

On the perfectly rolled lawn, on a tartan blanket, a baby girl babbled happily and played with colourful toys while a couple of red admirals fluttered around her; a couple of flies buzzed around the corpse and made preparatory landings on the open neck. The pool water thrashed with activity.

The dining room's huge French windows mirrored the scene. Crimson skids on the glass began to dribble. Behind them, O'Connell had taken two bullets in the chest; a third had smashed through his teeth and lodged somewhere in the back of his head. His slide down the thick, toughened glass of the French windows left him lying next to his wife who had died moments earlier. Clough saw the bodies of his children before a single bullet caught him in the forehead. His wife lay bleeding to death in the kitchen while on the AGA the spaghetti she'd prepared for lunch was boiling dry. Tony Valenti had no children and had no idea that his wife Sharon was upstairs. Twin barrels from a sawn-off shotgun took away his face. Out of three families, twelve people, only two remained alive. The baby girl on the lawn still played with her toys and in Valenti's front bedroom, his wife Sharon, on her hands and knees, groped about for the telephone. While they waited to complete the final executions some of the men had dragged her upstairs. She was pinned to the bed by two men while another man, a man with a strange snake tattoo on his forearm, had raised her skirt and ripped off her underwear and blasted through her anus. Grey had always preferred it that way.

And when he'd finished he whispered in her ear in a broad Glaswegian accent that he'd always wanted to put one up America's arse. For good measure he asked for her autograph. Before he left he smeared semen containing the odd pubic hair on to the bedclothes. Both had been collected from the commander of Mad Mick McGovern's armed forces.

The final tragic notes rang out. The silence that followed the applause and the shuffling of the audience was absolute, uncomfortable, a mark of the drama that had gone before. Into the early summer gardens, away from the baby, the birds flew back to chatter and flit and a warm breeze whispered through the shooting foliage and where there was none, suddenly there was promise.

He was a tall man, this old man, and he had a vague memory of Dover cliffs; through a red haze the cliffs had turned pink; Tom was holding him in his arms; the boat was rocking; he was so cold, shivering, and the blood kept seeping into his eyes from the bandages covering his head. What was it they used to say? God save the King – Queen nowadays, of course, but how did it go? *Let's talk about a soldier; teach him to march and dig ditches; play him God Save the Queen; and turn him into a killing machine!*

There were numerous caves in the cliffs, most of them filled up at high tide. He wore his old army jacket and before him he placed his old army pistol. It was dark in the cave and it stunk of seaweed. Through the entrance he could see the solid grey-green swell and the gulls swooping and crying plaintively at the rising tide. He swallowed his pills and his scotch and felt quite easy about it all. He laughed out loud. Who'd have thought it would end this way? As the faces of the dead moved about the dark shadows of his cave he laughed at life. The little Chinese girl was there somewhere, screaming at him. He chuckled. He would never forget her look of horror, and the way she clung to him as he picked her up, her waist slippery and covered in batter, her legs clamping to his sides as he carried her over to the smoking vat, her fists beating helplessly against his chest. He would have killed Denise too, but Tom Smith had been adamant that she was to be returned home safely. It had crossed his mind that she would remain a weak link, that out of everyone involved she was the one who could tie the Smiths in with Glasgow and possibly even Runnymede. Still, he knew that the old man would have his reasons. Tom Smith always had his reasons. Even so, he would have enjoyed killing her. She was the right age and the right shape. He supposed that she would have been like the rest – and there had been plenty of others. It wasn't a sexual thing – he was far too old for that in any case – and it wasn't even about revenge. It had more to do with the destruction of beauty so that only ugliness was left, ugliness and desolation. But he would've enjoyed seeing Denise dangling in front of him with her limbs jerking like a puppet, the fear in her face, her naked body shrinking from his touch, those smooth fucking contours beaten and ripped and destroyed. Yes, he would have liked that, marking her soft skin with his gnarled hands. The idea glazed his eyes and tugged his cracked lips into a faint soulless smile. His eyelids were suddenly heavy, his vision slipping. Christ! These pills didn't hang around. The screaming faded; the ghosts faded; he was left alone. He shivered as the weeping walls sucked out the last heat from his body. It was best this way. It was the only way. When there was nothing else to live for it was quite easy to die. Sergeant Adam Fox, Scratch to his few friends, fell asleep and the sea came in.

They pulled Denise out and dropped her off on the Mill Hill Broadway.

She entered the house the back way, as was her custom, struggling with her case along the alley and across the small square of back garden to her door. She set the case down in the hall and closed the door. Before taking off her jacket she filled the kettle and plugged it in next to the cooker. She slipped out of her jacket and carried it to the hall cupboard.

A slight noise behind her had her turning and for a moment her heart stopped. Even as she turned Dave's arm snaked around her neck and she was jerked back on to his shoulder. She gasped and let out an involuntary cry. She gripped his arm to loosen the constricting hold. He dragged her into the sitting room.

"Why are you doing this?" The calm sound of her voice surprised her.

"Where have you been, Denise?" Dave's familiar voice whispered into her ear. She felt his hot breath and recognized the expensive cologne.

"North," she said. "Where d'you think?"

"Tell Mick all about us, did you?"

"I've been helping your family, for God's sake!"

"Yeah, like Pete helped us?"

"What's that supposed to mean?"

"You know what it means, Denise. But it doesn't matter anymore, does it? It's all over."

"Where's Pete? Where's the kid?"

"Pete's dead and I've got the kid."

She was silent for a moment before she said thickly, "You're his bleedin' father."

"You kept it quiet, didn't you? As soon as I saw him I thought I might be. Pete must have seen it too. That sort of thing can play on a man's mind, especially if he's the jealous kind. You should have told me about him, girl."

"Even a cruel bastard like you can't kill the mother of his own kid!"

Her thoughts raced. Tell him about the set-up, about the old guy with the scar, that she had been busy keeping Vinny Grey out of the way. Make him believe! She mouthed the words but they emerged as strangled noises as she began to choke. His weight forced her down. She kicked out. Her flared skirt rose. She heard his voice.

"Close your eyes, Denise. Think of the good times. There were a few."

She saw the glinting blade snap from his hand. She stopped struggling and he eased the pressure on her neck.

"Relax Sweetheart," she heard. "And don't worry. I'll take good care of the kid."

Out of dark eyes she watched the blade sweep towards her side. Her hot breath expelled in a long gentle sigh.

From the kitchen the boiling kettle began to scream.

"Oh, Dave."

It burned, red hot. She watched her blood spread out on her shirt and seep down the handle over his hand. He released the grip on her neck.

"Hold me," she said. "I feel so cold." She took his hand and held it tightly. "Oh God, it hurts so much."

He felt her legs twist away and her body relax so that she became heavy. Her hand fell away from his. Slowly he moved his hand under her skirt. Moments earlier her bladder had relaxed. She was wet. The heat was still there. He smiled faintly at the novelty. He laid her gently on the carpet and wrenched her skirt away. He peeled off her underwear and stood between her legs and with his foot he drew them apart.

The room was gloomy and heavy, the lack of air almost intoxicating. He caught sight of himself in the wall mirror. What he saw surprised him. Blood was everywhere. It smeared across his cheek and over his lips. It stained his white shirt. But it was his eyes that really shocked him, fiery and shot through, reptilian. In that moment he was overwhelmed by a combination of pain and exquisite pleasure, of utter violation and destruction. He used her damp underwear to wipe the blood from his cheek and sniffed the scent of urine. When he looked in the mirror again he saw his own rage. His eyes were hooded, deadly, filled with hatred, but there was something else there also, something beneath the fury. It was the brutal acceptance of his evilness. Beyond his reflection, over his shoulder, he could see the girl. She looked quite beautiful. Her eyes were open, her features as soft as he had ever seen them. The pool of blood had spread out and left a black stain on the green carpet. Her mouth was open, just as he had kissed it. Her legs were apart, just as he had left them.

Chapter 35

"It's all over. It's a matter of picking up the pieces. You're big enough to do that by yourself." Coddy's voice was marked both by relief and fatigue.

Dave knew that his father-in-law was a late riser and would have left his bed in order to take Dave's call in the study. It was six-thirty. An early sun tumbled through fluttering young leaves and flooded Dave's front windows. He heard the chink of bottles and saw the milkman walking back down his drive. A minder watched the milkman from his black Rover parked beneath the oak then got back to his Mirror.

"Your old man had it all in hand. You should never have doubted it, Dave."

Dave nodded into the phone.

"Monopolies dictate supplies and prices. Never forget that. There was no way Tom would allow such a thing. You think your old man was a Tory, for Christ sakes?" Coddy chuckled. "That's a thought." His voice levelled again. "He knew that by throwing you and Valenti together at the meeting the wop would lose control and be seen pressing Mick into a corner. The idea that anyone could lean on him, never mind a bunch of Yanks, would send Mick into orbit. That's what everyone thinks anyway."

Dave said: "Will you come down for the service? They're having one here before flying the coffins home."

"Of course; I wouldn't want to miss that. There might be another one farther north before long."

"I know what you mean. Every flight from New York brings in more of their armed forces, and it's all asking the way to Hadrian's Wall."

"Mick is going to need a good hiding place. Maybe I could rent him that old thatched cottage on my estate, what do you think?"

Dave chuckled. "That belongs to me and your daughter. It holds a special place in our hearts. Don't even think of letting someone else have it."

"I'll bring Mavis," Coddy went on. "She can spend some time with Pat. Now it's safe again maybe they can do some shopping. They didn't really have time to get together at Tom's funeral. She'd like that."

"Yeah," Dave said flatly. The thought that it was all over was somehow depressing. His feelings seemed to travel down the line.

"You know, Dave, some people like to think that they rule: the politicians, the councillors, the civil servants, even some members of the bench and the armed forces, and definitely some of the police. But they only think it. They're false pretenders, every one of them. They're alive today because they don't interfere. Understand?" Coddy paused and then said quietly, "You're holding a heavy responsibility now, boy. You go and make your father proud of you." That was it. The conversation ended and Dave hung up.

He made his way to the bathroom, stripped off his towelling robe and stood under the shower. He turned the temperature to hot until it hurt and the steaming water cleared his head.

Coddy had been right. The burden was now his. In the beginning the murder of two villains had given a man respect; and there was a time also when a single act of violence in a dingy Chinese restaurant in the middle of Soho had elevated a man and his family to a position of power in the capital; now another act of violence had raised that family to a similar position, but nationwide.

Dave was still under the hot water when Pat called into the bathroom.

"Peter Hough's been on the television, on the news. His body's been found."

"Oh? Are there any other details?"

"It's horrible. His head was found by Traitor's Gate."

"That is horrible. I wondered where he'd got to."

When he walked into the bedroom moments later Pat said, "He worked for you, didn't he? Peter Hough?"

"Yes." Dave shook his head. "But he wasn't all that. Know what I mean? He was an unreliable sort. Always was."

His mother was staying with them for a few days, until the press lost interest and left her alone.

Over breakfast she glanced at the child who sat at the end of the long oak table. His new school satchel lay next to his cereal dish.

"You can't keep the child," Sally said to Dave.

Patricia watched them from the kitchen. She looked at the boy and saw again the remarkable likeness and knew that her mother-in-law was wrong. They would keep him. There was no doubt about that. Curiously the thought was not upsetting.

"The authorities will have something to say about it," Sally persisted. "You can't just bring someone's child home. It's not that easy, David."

Dave smiled at his mother's apparent innocence. "Mother, we can do anything we want to do," he said.

Sally gave him a fearful look. He grinned at her.

"You're a lady," he said.

She didn't respond.

The will was read sometime later and in it Tom Smith had written: 'To each of my grandchildren…including David Hough'.

The sun was a watery ghost above the wet tiles; the paving slabs of the footpath had darkened with the rain. The rain had stopped but the air was close and held the smell of rain. Across the glistening road a milkman was finishing his round, his float filled with empties, glass on glass, rattling; a hawk-faced man with protruding cheekbones and chin and dark, button eyes sunk into sleepless holes.

The youngster hesitated to watch the milkman stack another empty crate and pulled back on Dave's hand until he slowed his pace. Dave glanced across at the milkman and muttered, "Some people are pretty and some are ugly but by Christ some are pretty ugly!" He looked down at the boy and grinned. "You don't understand a thing I'm saying, do you?"

The youngster looked up, at once attentive but frowning in an exaggerated fashion as youngsters do. He shook his head and gave Dave a broad grin and flashed his small pointed milk teeth.

"Listen to me carefully," Dave said to him. "This is important." They walked on. Holding hands seemed natural. Father and son; there was nothing more natural in the world. The boy didn't look up. He barely heard his father's voice; his thoughts were still with the milkman. "This is a fine country, my son," Dave said. "Don't let anyone tell you any different. Here, you can do anything you want. You can have anything you want. All you got to do is know what you want; the rest is easy. You name me another place in the world that's as fair as that?"

The boy didn't look up but Dave heard the tiny whisper. "I'm goin' t' be a milkman."

Dave chuckled, "Why not, my son? That sounds like a good job to me!"

Hand-in-hand they walked on toward the nursery school and crossed the road at the zebra crossing just beyond where, in the beginning, the empire had begun in the darkened, smoke-filled rooms of the Eagle; father and son moving through the streets of the capital, cherishing the moment and considering their opportunities in this country fair and fine.

AUTHOR'S NOTE

Thanks to the usual cops and robbers for the insight (they know who they are) and to James J Shimmin for his invaluable help on this book, particularly the passages relating to money laundering. Thanks also to Sid the Bookie for the various scams. A special thanks to Maria Smith at MP Publishing who worked on through the darkening skies. I'd also like to pay tribute to John Morris and Arthur James, Dunkirk Vets, for sharing their memories of that ghastly affair.

REVIEWS
COPS AND OTHER ROBBERS (1998)

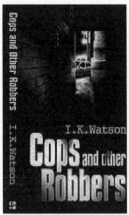

The same crime shelves that gave me Paul Johnston's books also gave me Cops and other Robbers by I. K. Watson. It's a nasty book about a nasty subject. A paedophile has killed one of his victims. Another child is missing.Can the police find him before this one too is murdered? This is a raw and nasty story and the writer pulls no punches. No details are omitted, no veil is drawn over the brutality. It is no secret that I like gory, gruesome books; but this one was a bit too much even for me.

- Alan Robson (Coprolithicus)

I picked this one up with apprehension - are we tired of police procedurals? Not if they have the energy and idiosyncratic detail that Watson specialises in. Even the now overexposed plot devices (including a hunt for a paedophile) are handled with a commanding freshness, and it's axiomatic that writers as talented as Watson can shuffle warmed-over ingredients to produce something rich and strange. Watson is also good at dealing with the disillusionment involved in the day to day life of a copper, and DI Rick Cole is a trenchant hero, even if his drinking is another one of those over-familiar touches. The plotting is bracingly original, and this deserves to do every bit as well as Watson's earlier books.

-Barry Forshaw (Crime Time)

This is not a very nice book. It's peopled by a cast of rank low-lifes and strungout cops and the villain of the piece is a killer paedophile. You can almost smell the sweat and stale nicotine in the police canteen, and the panic, fear and hopelessness on the mean streets you have to walk in Watson's new novel. There is a numbing mundaneness to the way the characters talk, reflecting the fact that the horrors they face, horrors that should turn their stomachs, don't any more. Much as you might want to find out exactly why DI Cole had to leave Scotland Yard for Sheerham, and what happens when the paedophile kidnaps DS Baxter's daughter, it won't be a pleasant journey. This isn't so much a work of noir fiction as grise fiction, bleak, soulless and so hardbitten it's got no nails left. Dark entertainment, if that's your fancy.

- Publishing News

Serial killers, drug dealers, prostitutes, cat burglars and corrupt coppers abound in this above-average La Plante-esque crime thriller about a detective inspector's daughter who goes missing — last seen getting into a car with a policeman.
- **Focus**

Another sensational novel from Watson. A furiously paced story line leads the reader from scene to scene whilst the in-depth knowledge of police procedures lends an air of realism to what at times is an almost frighteningly gruesome read. The reader is dragged from one horrific scene to the next torn between the compelling story and the need to escape from the darkest side of human nature. The cold descriptions add a new depth to the shocking scenes of child abuse and the reader has no difficulty empathising with the hardened policemen as they reel from shock at the sights they are forced to endure. An exceptional new novel from the country's leading crime writer marrying an almost gothic horror with an in depth guide to police procedures. This book is simply too good to miss.
- **Seamus Kelly, Amazon**

GRITTY, GRIMY, FURIOUSLY exciting police procedural in which the squad at Sheerham nick postpone their own sexual misdemeanours (adultery, occasional harassment) to pull out the stops which will identify and nail a paedophile whose crimes culminate in ritual murder. Action counter-pointed with violent doings of local drug lords. A deeply disenchanted (hence, realistic) view of our boys in blue who, despite their flaws ranging from graft to ultra-horniness get the job done, Unlikely to make you sleep more soundly, but well worth reading if you're lying there, awake and worrying.
- **Philip Oakes, Literary Review**

Det Insp Rick Cole has an exceptionally dirty case of paedophilia to solve when it starts to look as if victims are being picked up from school in a police car. The language and action are uncompromising. Only for strong stomachs.
- **Oxford Mail**

This twin-themed novel part police procedural hunt for child killer, part gangster turf war — is an uneasy mix in places, but gripping, and packed with gruesomely authentic detail.
- **Mike Ripley, Daily Telegraph**

REVIEWS
WOLVES AREN'T WHITE (1995)

"You're alive today because you do not interfere."

Not since Ted Lewis's Get Carter has there been such a tough, uncompromising novel about the realities of life in the British underworld.
- **Peter Day**

If you like your crime writing on the tough uncompromising side, then IK Watson is the man for you.

His second novel, Wolves Aren't White tells the story of tough guy villain Paddy Delaney, who is back in town. He likes to hurt people, especially men who make a pass at his little sister Julie. Not surprisingly, he gets the hump when Lennie Webb, singer with the Wolves Aren't White jazz band, gets fresh - but Julie wants Lennie, that's the trouble.

In fact, Lennie finds himself in trouble not only from Paddy, but from Julie's nasty habit of lighting matches in the middle of the night. Caught in a situation from which he can't escape, Lennie is forced to unravel a web of deception and murder that has made Julie's life a nightmare.
- **Sandra Feekins (Burton Mail)**

Hard boiled crime in the tradition of the late Ted Lewis.

REVIEWS
MANOR (1994)

The Smiths are London's leading crime barons, but Dave Smith's old man is close to death and the family empire, suffering from its past refusal to enter the drug trade, is under siege. The Liverpool mob is in town for a spot of whoring on an up-market Thames barge. The Scots contingent, led by Mad Mick McGovern, is getting out of hand, and the pushy Americans, who want some of the U.K. drug trade, include Tony Valenti, who once caught Dave servicing his centerfold wife and isn't about to forget it. The book, which recalls Barrie Keeffe's The Long Good Friday... Features several scenes of nasty brutality...
- **Publishers Weekly**

It was "like the marriage of two royal families" when Tom Smith's son wed Coddy Hughes's daughter, a union that joined two of England's most powerful crime dynasties. But even the best families fall out, and in his sleek first novel, Manor, I. K. Watson gives a cool account of the savage mob wars that erupt when business alliances are compromised by nasty domestic quarrels. Ten years after that royal wedding, Tom Smith is dying, Coddy Hughes is fading fast, and the younger generation may not be ruthless enough to turn back the barbarians. "The end of an era was drawing in," says Dave Smith, to whom his father's empire has fallen. "The men, the legends, were dying out." Without softening these hard men or adulterating the cruelty of their crimes, Mr. Watson has us rooting for the royal scum.
- **Marilyn Stasio (New York Times)**

I.K. Watson, a British writer, tells a great story in his debut novel, Manor, of the Smith family. They're the modern inheritors of the crime kingdom of the Krays and Richardsons who now find themselves under siege in this hard-boiled crime novel that I feel is destined to become a classic.
- **Gary Lovisi, The Hard Boiled Way**

A good, old-fashioned gangster story of revenge and factions warring over who controls what, where and for how much...
- **Liverpool Daily Post**